Just Politics
An Alaska Cold Case Mystery

by **Nancy Buell**
With **Bill Buell**

Just Politics
An Alaska Cold Case Mystery
Copyright 2021© by Nancy Buell. All rights reserved.

Library of Congress Cataloging-in-Publication Data

Names: Buell, Nancy, Author
with Bill Buell
Title: Just Politics/Nancy Buell
Description: Mystery
Identifiers:
e-book ISBN 978-1-7375579-4-4
Paperback ISBN 978-1-7375579-5-1

Just Politics

Prologue

The Budget Strategy meeting was over by 5:45, but it was October in Juneau, already pitch dark. And wet. He could see nothing through the window by the elevator on the Governor's floor but rain patterns and a few residence lights reflecting in the collecting water of the building's back parking lot. It hadn't taken a genius to know it was going to be raining when he came out; it had been raining when he went in. He didn't like the rain running down his neck, but he didn't like hats either. He shrugged the collar of his overcoat up around his ears.

No one else got into the elevator on the way down. There was no guard at the station on the street level. He could hear the guard around the corner, laughing with someone. Probably filling a coffee cup from the machines in the stairwell; he

1

heard the thunk of a soda can hitting the bin and smelled the bitter scent of machine coffee. These guys didn't have enough to do if they could stand around and chat. Anyone could get into the elevator and ride on up to the Governor's Office. If anyone could ride up there, what was the point of a guard? If the guy worked for him, he'd bring him in, shut the door, and scare the shit out of him. Make him think it was just a reprimand, then fire him anyway.

Or not. Let one get away now and then. It made people sloppy.

He was tired, but he had that buzz that came from engineering someone else's loss upstairs. Commissioner Pearl Pureheart Prentiss, of the moral high horse, hadn't even known what hit her. A few carefully placed questions, one legislative poker game marker drawn in, and one meeting where he told everyone in public what she'd helped him to understand in private: there wasn't going to be any big payoff for the extra budget increment she'd kissed up to the Governor for last term.

There was always one cabinet position for that type of big fucking flagship initiative in the first term. Campaign promises. But when the second term was assured, the memory of any promises was dim. He'd been friendly with Prentiss for a year or so when they were both appointed. Long enough to know that she was on a mission from God. Everybody had bought into her showcase programs in the first go-round, but they were just that, show. This year her department would take the big hit. And a couple of key legislators on the budget committees would finish the job.

She was probably still up there gasping like a fish on the bank, all hurt looks and righteous indignation. And that would, literally, teach her to fuck with him, he thought with a small cold smile.

He hunched more deeply into his collar and crossed the street to the loading dock at the back of the State Office Building, which squatted over three floors of parking garage like a hen on a concrete nest. The hill was so steep here that the loading dock, ground level on the Capitol Building side, was the actual seventh floor of this building, whose public entrance was on the next street below, a block to the west. In the space dug into the hillside under the back half of the structure, the parking garage was off limits to employees of the building, used exclusively by those going to the legislature, legislative offices, or the Governor's offices. Parking on the street was that scarce. The commissioners and other dignitaries had their own parking floor, with their spots labeled. He liked having his spot labeled, he had to admit.

He never looked up at the brightly lit glass-walled sky bridge above his head. He knew people stood there and watched comings and goings from the Capitol, had coffee at the espresso cart at the bridge's end by the State Library. A cat could look at a king, he thought, but the king doesn't look back. And that made him smile again. He felt good. He might pick up a pizza on the way home, surprise the children. No, the kids and their mom were over in Sitka, at a basketball tournament.

He might pick up a pizza anyway, eat it all himself, watching Monday Night Football. He paused on the loading dock to turn down his collar, brush the rain from his shoulders and run a hand through his long, damp hair. He went in. The door slammed behind him with a dull clunk. The hallway was dimmed to the night lighting system. Entering the seventh floor to go across to the elevators that went down to the parking levels was like going into the catacombs. Still, as he walked past the mail distribution offices to the elevators at the far end of the hall, he hadn't quit smiling.

God he hated these stupid meetings. Everyone came in with their whine list, and their holdback list, and their behind-the-scenes done deals. When it came to whose budget got stuck, and whose job got axed because of it, however, the meetings got really interesting. People cried, for chrissake. They nattered on about jobs lost, the quality of children's lives, and whether there was a ranger on Grizbite Creek. Who the fuck cared? To him, it was a poker game being played with other people's money. The winner might bluff, he might rig the deck, he might have an ace hidden away. It wasn't luck. There wasn't any such thing; that was a concept that he thought was probably invented by a fucking woman.

He'd spent a year watching and pretending to be a team kind of guy before he had enough trust and information from the career employees and the lower-level appointments to make his move. After that, it had been easy. Everyone wants the new Commissioner to understand, and they are pathetically ready to tell him what he needs to know to pull all the right strings. He had discovered who was immune because of some legislator's pet program and who was in a position that had no protection at all. It was his favorite thing: get information through commiseration, and then deep-six the dumb bastard messenger. Fucking career government employees, they were a joke all over the state.

It wasn't even a matter of money, he mused, shaking his head, as he punched the elevator button. Alaska had so much money it could pay off the national debt. Or buy some small country, for that matter. Hell, he mused, it *was* a country, and not so small at that. But everyone seemed to be elected to cut this, and cut that. And if you could show that you'd cut before, tightened the bureaucratic belt, there was a reward on up the political line.

The elevator groaned to a stop and the doors opened. He stepped in, punched the parking level reserved for commissioners and legislators, and faced forward. He looked up at the numbers as the doors closed. The car jolted into motion, going down, down to the parking levels. It grumbled to a stop at the third level and the doors opened to a big, overweight janitor with Buddy Holly glasses, an ill-fitting uniform, a ball cap, a surgical mask and yellow "loving hands" kitchen gloves, who had managed to position his damned cart just outside the elevator. *A surgical mask.* Another paranoid asshole getting ready to make an OSHA complaint like the ones in the Goldbelt building who kept smelling mold. The Commissioner frowned and stepped out of the elevator; the janitor pushed the trash cart right in front of the opening. He stepped around it and fixed the janitor with a "you idiot" stare.

He heard the doors shut behind him, and the elevator started back down. Briefly, suddenly, he and the janitor were face to face, and made eye contact. "You!" he said, and that instant in which he froze, trying to reconcile something was out of place, was all the time required for something to jolt his chest and wipe anything else from his mind. In desperate fear he spun as though to run, and jerked, made an awkward grab at the spot that hurt, hurt. A strong arm caught him around the head and shoulders. Somewhere in the dregs of his consciousness, he felt the point of something go into his neck. There was a hazy awareness of great danger, but for some reason, he couldn't wrest the arm off, though he tried, bringing his other hand up over his shoulder in an attempt at the leverage he had learned in lifeguarding years ago. He tried to marshal his strength.

His assailant was implacable, and his ability to coordinate a struggle was curiously ineffective. Briefly, he felt a great sense that something was wrong in his chest. He could not mount a defense. His mind went in one direction, his arms in another; his legs collapsed. Involuntary throat and facial muscles tried to suck in a gasp of air, and he forgot his purpose, his mouth open and his eyes wide with surprise. That was all he knew: surprise at the end of a day of brutal certainty.

The Janitor did not let him fall, but caught him under the arms and held him until he hung like a sack of sand. Then dragged him two steps to behind the half-wall of concrete that bordered the elevator's little lobby. And reflected that it had seemed to take no time at all. A quick look each way revealed no one, nothing. No dome lights on in cars, no shocked faces, no echoing footsteps running for help. The Janitor put the Commissioner's limp weight over the edge of the canvas trash cart, pulled a black bag over it, and rolled the cart toward the Commissioner's parking spot.

It was that easy, then, wasn't it. Easier than the planning would have led one to believe. The planning had included half a dozen fail-safe points—would he come out of the Capitol Building alone? Would he use the seventh floor to the elevator? Would he come down alone? Would anyone else be waiting for the elevator at the third-level garage? Would anyone else be going to or from a car? And in each case, there had been nothing, no one, not the slightest hitch. But that was what planning was for, wasn't it? Up until the last moment it could have been aborted, with no one the wiser. The Janitor breathed deeply once, twice, to calm the raging adrenaline. This part was done.

The Janitor wheeled the cart down the unlit walkway between the fronts of parked cars and the wall, to the third spot labeled "Commissioner Fish and Game," and stopped beside the passenger door. The truck keys were in the limp Commissioner's right coat pocket. The passenger door of the truck opened to reveal nothing on the seat and floor but dog hair. Lots of dog hair. Not a good place. It would be too difficult to put the heavy body into the seat, and push it onto its side, divesting it of its coat at the same time. Shielded by the open door, the Janitor reached into the trash cart and relieved the Commissioner of his long coat.

From its hiding place between the parking space guide block and the front tire of the Commissioner's truck, the Janitor took a nylon duffel, unzipped it quickly, and traded the mask and glasses for a curly wig. In short order, the "Commissioner" stood up, straightened his wig as though he were merely pushing back his wet hair, and pulled the coat up around his ears. He closed the truck door and walked around to the back. The canopy was not locked. The Janitor looked both ways, opened the back of the truck, positioned the trash cart and laid a garbage bag on the tailgate. Then heaved the body onto this slick surface, and pushed it quickly into the back of the truck. Closed the tailgate and the canopy top. The trash cart went quickly back to the passenger door, between the cars. Once again, the janitor cast a furtive look both ways, and saw nothing. Nothing.

But the person who stood up beside the truck and adjusted the collar of the coat would have aroused no alarm, even from someone knowing the vehicle and its driver. The size was about right, the hair about right, the coat definitely right. Illusion trumped observation. No one appeared to have seen the Commissioner putting garbage into his truck. Again, a look around; again, no one. If there had been someone watching, they would only have seen the Commissioner push a janitorial cart halfway to the elevator and give it a shove. It came to a rest in the little, lighted space where people could wait for the cars to come. Anyone there would see only that the Commissioner walked casually back to the driver's door of his truck and got in.

The truck started up and moved carefully out of the parking garage. Now anyone watching would see the Commissioner take his normal route to his office. Right onto Willoughby, past the Fiddlehead Restaurant, the bowling alley, the grocery store, the deli. Over the river spillway. Past the Federal Building, and the Goldbelt Building. Left at the light at Egan Drive. Right into the parking lot beside the Labor and Fish and Game Buildings. The normal path this truck would take, this time of night. Including going behind the Fish and Game building, next to the Channel, where it nosed in beside the dumpsters and stopped.

With all of the truck lights off, it was inky dark behind the building. The Janitor looked up, saw no one at the upper floor windows, though some were still lit at this time of night. But that would be normal. Still, it would be best to work rapidly. The Janitor turned off the switch that triggered the interior lights to come on and got out. It took only a moment to come around the truck, open the canopy, lower the tailgate and jump up to the platform it made, conveniently even with the edge of the dumpster. Drag out the heavy but pliable body and heave it into the bin. There was no movement, no groaning, no gasping breaths. The tailgate made the transfer to the dumpster easier than anticipated. A moment to get it upright, arms over the dumpster rim, and then one, two, three, boost it into the dumpster, where it fell with a satisfactory *squoosh*.

The Janitor *cum* murderer got down, closed up the tailgate and canopy, and looked over the edge of the dumpster. Stared down at the body. It was right where it belonged, face down in the garbage. A brief review of the alley showed no one, and no one stood in the windows overhead, their hand over their mouth in shock. There were, again, no people in sight, from any direction. There was only one thing left, and that was to obliterate the mark the syringe had left. The nylon duffel yielded a plastic, pint orange juice bottle: a perfect silencer for the little .25 automatic which had been hidden in a shoulder holster. One shot in the neck over the injection site. The orange juice bottle worked well; there was barely a pop. The bottle and the gun went into the coat pocket.

The next step was harder, somehow. The janitor took out the new fillet knife, and pushed it hard into the Commissioner's back, between the spine and the ribs. The knife came out more easily than it had gone in. Blood came out, but not much. The Commissioner's body lay still. Careful to avoid touching the blade, the Janitor put the knife inside of the coat, with the gun and the used syringe. There was nothing left to do but rearrange a few sacks of garbage over the body, close the dumpster lid, get back into the truck and drive on around to the Commissioner's regular parking spot. Anyone watching by this time would simply have seen a familiar man throwing garbage into the dumpster and getting back into his truck.

Still so far, so good. Look once more in all directions, but casually. No hurry now. The Murderer picked up the nylon duffel, scanned the seat and floorboards. Satisfied that nothing had been left, got out, locked the truck and canopy, and put the keys in the coat pocket from whence they had come. The secluded alcove behind the Labor Building could not be viewed from anywhere but the Channel, and the Murderer walked there, casually, swinging the duffel as though just going to take a look out back before going up to the Office. Once in Labor's shadowed and private picnic area, screened by bushes and a small tree, the murderer transformed. The gun, taser, knife and syringe were removed from the coat and set aside. The nylon duffel yielded up a rain slicker and athletic shoes, and accepted the wig, glasses, hat, coveralls, overcoat, rubber boots, and finally, the empty orange juice container. Nothing to be remarked upon by any type of scanner. A piece of souvenir ore from the tailings of the old Juneau mine was a weight of opportunity, and made the duffel a little heavy, and full.

Redressed, still gloved and carrying the duffel, the murderer took the little footpath which lead up to the main sidewalk along Egan Drive, stopping to look back through the now heavy rain. Still no one, still nothing. It was hard to believe how easy it had been. Harder to believe that it was over.

Nothing remarkable about another person walking down the sidewalk in the rain. The last cruise ship was still in town, and its lights, as it took on its passengers for tonight's departure, were as glittering and festive as they could be in the persistent downpour. A few tourists were still downtown in their cruise-issue ponchos and umbrellas. They were joined by people walking home from work, walking to work, leaving the athletic club, going to dinner at the Prospector Restaurant.

And if this one, unremarkable person walked out onto the wharf that led around the shops and the Hanger restaurant and stood for a moment looking out over the Channel, no one remarked that, either. In the comparative dark of a walkway next to the old warehouse building, the gun was a dark splotch through the gloom, entering the water with no splash distinguishable from the chop of the incoming tide. In another moment, the knife followed, and a little farther along, the syringe in a weighted plastic sandwich bag. Then the unremarkable person was just another tourist, walking around the boardwalk, emptying pockets into the trash cans before turning toward the main cruise docks.

Chapter One

Monday, October 7, 1998 - 8:30 p.m.

The Scandinavian Princess, the last big cruise ship of the season, left Juneau's harbor at 8:30 p.m. The high tide dictated her comings and goings from these small ports. A sea-going tug escorted her into the deep channel, and followed solicitously until she was well underway. With deck lights and running lights ablaze, she looked like the floating carnival travel brochures touted. *The cruise of a lifetime, through the Inland Passage to Juneau, with stops at historic Wrangell and Ketchikan.* Even the rain paused momentarily, as though to watch her go, representative as she was of Alaska's greatest source of revenue.

The cruise of a lifetime. Despite the wet chill of the moving air, the woman stood at the railing of the fourth cabin deck, watching, marking each increment of the passage as the mainland slid by. The huge ship moved out of the Gastineau Channel into the wider, white-capped waters of Taku Inlet, a glacier-fed fjord. The rain resumed its business, a gray curtain all around the ship, ruffling with the wind, but the woman remained at the rail.

She would never come to Alaska again. There would be no point in it. There was too much she had now buried here, too much that would rise up to mock her, and disturb her rest. She needed the rest, or at least peace. It had been years since she had slept deeply, and years since she had not been afraid to lay awake in the dark. The dark seemed to strip away everything she used to blot out the memories, and everything which had happened to her, here, marched solemnly to shake its fist in her face in the middle of the night. Faces. Words. Humiliation. Alienation. Perhaps now, these would leave her be.

There was an observation deck at each end of the ship, where passengers could sit in padded recliners and look out, in inclement weather, through glass windows. Her parents had gone to sit there after dinner to watch the progress down the Channel, but she had told them she wanted to unpack and put away a few things. In truth, she did not want to watch this from inside. It was as though she needed this transitional challenge, needed to use up some of the residue of adrenalin still causing her arms to shiver and the muscles in her thighs to tense. The powerful surging of the ship was soothing, the necessity of holding onto the rail a relief. The deeper water of Taku Inlet was black and pulsing with small waves and the indecision of the high tide. Like a proper tourist, she leaned over the railing and tossed the offering into the sea. The wind carried it far out, past the area lighted by the ship into the darkness, and then it disappeared.

There, it was done. Let them find it now, she thought. Let them find *her*. That which had mocked her all of her youth and adult life, that which had found its most cruel mockery here in the Last Frontier, was her cloak, her disguise at this extremity. She turned her face into the wind of the ship's passing, into the now slanting rain, and let it wash over her. A kind of peace, to be less than the elements. A kind of peace, to feel small and unnoticed. Clean.

"Sir? Do you know where the door is to the observation deck?"

She turned her head sharply and looked at the dripping teenager, who immediately blushed at his error.

"Excuse me, *ma'am*. Do you know how I get to the observation deck?"

"Sure," she said with a slight smile. "I'll be glad to show you."

Chapter Two

Wednesday, October 9, 1998 - 9 a.m.

Clyde "Burner" Bunsen had a drinking problem. He knew he did, and too many other people knew it, too. But he had been able to keep his job as a janitor in the Alaska Office Building up to now. Burner knew better than to drink at work, though he had come a little tooted at times, in the early days, before he found out that not only did state employees work all kinds of odd hours, but there were janitors on some of the floors of the building who minded everybody's business.

So Burner only did a little weed at work, and they were no way the same, weed and hooch, no matter what they said at AA. Maybe a little upper now and then, or if he could afford it, a little coke. With just a little of that, he was a wastebasket-emptyin' fool. He could follow that vacuum around the floor like Mario Andretti. He was hell on toilets. He could clean stoned.

'Clean stoned' sounded pretty good right now. Burner licked dry lips and looked around. The fancy-ass secretary in the desk outside of Deputy Director Allison Cunningham's office wasn't lookin' at him, wasn't even lookin' up though he knew he was a handsome dude. He liked that she wasn't obviously starin' at him. Made him nervous when women came on to him. He covered his mouth with his hand, and snickered, his eyes crinkling with pleasure at the picture of this fine lookin' woman shinin' up on him and…He stopped and blinked, once, twice, and shook his head.

There it was again. That little 'ding dong' like he was knockin' at some door he was at before. He knew he had to stop bringin' it to work. Good thing no one seen him night before last. When he had waked up in the john yesterday morning, propped up against the wall behind the trash can, he didn't even remember how he got there. He didn't know where his trash truck was. He waked up because there was some dude come in early to take a leak. Gave him such a look, so he knew it was daylight. Those types only came out in the daylight.

Took him some time to find his trash truck. Had to think hard about where he could have left it. Finally rode the elevator down, see if he could just remember everything he did after he parked his POS Ford Fairlane in visitor's spot 4 on level 1. Elevator doors opened for some status dude on the third floor garage, and there it was, sittin' against the wall. He must have gotten really good stuff to leave it there. Just got it into the Janitor's Closet, too, before anyone saw him. Changed out of his blue coveralls and went home to sleep some more, then his phone rang. *Come in tomorrow morning to Admin Services and see Ms. Cunningham.* That was no good. Full daylight hurt his eyes, nearly as much as Ms. Cunningham. Anyway, here he was, so the jerk in the shirt and tie must have turned him in.

The door beside him opened. "Mr. Bunsen, please come in," said the severe looking woman in a blue pantsuit who Burner thought of as either his boss or his mother, *dependin' on how bad a dream.* "I've taken the precaution of having Fred Vetching join us, Mr. Bunsen. Please be seated here."

That was no good. Fred Vetching was the shop steward. Burner Bunson sat and looked anxiously from Fred, who smiled encouragingly, to Deputy Director Cunningham, who did not. She cleared her throat. "Mr. Bunsen...Clyde, I've spoken to you before about our concerns over your performance, and you assured me that you understood our concerns were serious."

"Yes, ma'am. Did I miss something cleaning last night? I don't recall missing anything." That was certainly true. "But if I did, I can come in early tonight and..." Burner looked at the shop steward, who was slowly shaking his head. He stopped. "I shouldn't say that?" He asked.

Fred Vetching winced. "Now Burner, I'm only an observer, to make certain that your rights as an employee under the bargaining agreement are preserved. Ms. Cunningham, is there documentation in Burner's file that he was warned about his performance in the past?"

"It was put there by two previous supervisors, as you know, Mr. Vetching, as well as documentation of a verbal warning last month." Allison Cunningham sighed and turned again to Bunsen. "You were observed sleeping in the rest room yesterday morning, Clyde," she said, taking a more sympathetic posture. "Were you ill?"

"No ma'am. I'm never ill; I don't know what happened," Burner said, a sincere look of surprise corroborating his words. "Guess I must have finished early, and was overcome with weariness." He looked at the two people staring at him and knew it wasn't his best selling job. "I lost my trash truck," he muttered, looking down. Then he looked up, brightening. "Found it, though, nothin' missin'."

"Be that as it may, Clyde," Allison Cunningham said carefully, as though she were reading, "after your sleeping in the lavatory was reported to me on my return from Anchorage yesterday, I asked each unit secretary to determine the cleanliness of carpets, whether wastebaskets had been emptied. They had not. The room which houses the copy machine contained two overflowing barrels, and my own secretary determined that the paper products in the women's restroom had not been replaced. Do you have an explanation?"

Bunsen looked at Fred Vetching, who was examining his cuticles. He thought about what he had done that night. He remembered gearing up to take off with the vacuum cleaner, and he smiled a little. He looked at the clock on the wall. Fancy clock, with the hands twitching over a gold map of the state. He was sure tired, being that he had worked extra hard last night to catch up.

"Clyde?"

"How could you find out all of that in one afternoon?" Burner asked.

Now both Fred Vetching and Allison Cunningham sighed. Cunningham straightened, made a few notes on the pad in front of her, and said, "Clyde, I have increasing concerns about your job performance. I intend to do a little more fact finding about the past week's cleaning. If it shows last night was anything but an isolated incident, I will prepare a formal, written warning that if any more incidents occur, you will be dismissed. Do you understand?" She waited as he nodded, and the shop steward nodded. "Now, I suggest that you go home, and that you take tonight off. We're calling in a substitute from the agency that cleans the Goldbelt Building. Tomorrow, I'd like you to come in to see me and I'll have a written record of our meeting. Will you be able to come in at 4:30?"

"Yes, ma'am." Burner could hardly wait to get home and tell his girlfriend that they had the night to party. He got up, and left, closing the door behind him.

"This has to stop, Fred," Allison Cunningham said. "The Union doesn't gain credibility by supporting this type of non-performer."

"No, Allison, it doesn't. But the last two supervisors have waffled: he has several 'satisfactory' ratings."

"That's the story of my life around here," Allison said sharply. "I not only have to do my job; I also have to finish the unfinished jobs of those before me. Thanks for coming in on short notice." Fred Vetching left. Allison Cunningham sat for a moment, looking out the window her status in state government afforded her. Rain. There was a view of the harbor and down the Channel, which looked strangely empty. It always took awhile to get used to the cruise ships being gone for the season. The legislature didn't come back until January, and the two scarce commodities in Juneau—a parking place and a seat in a restaurant at lunch—were briefly available. And things went on sale, with no tourists to inflate the prices.

Which reminded her, she'd promised to keep an eye out for the Galligaskins sale so she could send the two Alaska sweatshirts to her friend Sue. They'd looked at them during the days Sue stayed with her, waiting for her parents' cruise ship to arrive. Too expensive to buy then, because everything went up by a factor of six when the tourists were in town.

The sweatshirts would probably be cheaper this week, maybe even on sale. Sue had left some money with her. Sue was a good friend, though Allison seldom saw her these days. They had met in Fairbanks, where Allison had gone from Colorado during last of the Pipeline days, when you could still make $60,000 as a waitress. She had met Sue in a bar, actually, when Sue was between leaving the military and looking for a job in her chosen field. They had both gone into government, and ultimately Allison had moved to Juneau. Sue had stayed in the interior with the majority of the animals to which she was so devoted. In the intervening years, they had kept in touch. By the time Allison received her appointment to a higher-level position in Juneau, both of them had gone through some pretty horrific life changes, with Allison's husband having died of cancer and Sue--what had happened to Sue she had never asked, although she had cobbled bits and pieces together. Something about work.

It had been good to see Sue again. Allison had few friends in Juneau, and her job didn't leave her much time to make more. She and Sue had had a good time together last weekend before Allison had left for her meetings in Anchorage. Sue had left a nice note, the cat had been fed, the bed changed, and the condo was spotless. A really good friend. Too bad Allison hadn't been here to see her off. She wished Sue the best for her new job in Idaho. Someone was going to escape the rain. Allison wrote a reminder to check on the sweatshirts, in her daytimer, next to tomorrow's appointment with the irritating-and-soon-to-be-someone-else's-problem Clyde Bunsen.

Chapter Three

Sunday, October 13, 1998 - 10:20 p.m.

Annie Brewster hated it there was a crime against a Power Person.   Get on an airplane, go somewhere, stay there for a long time. None of the big ones to which she was assigned seemed to happen in Anchorage, which was downright ironic, since it was the only large city in Alaska. No, Power People had to be assaulted in Angoon, kidnapped in Klawok, or drowned in Dillingham. And the worst, jumped in Juneau.

Traveling to the scene of the crime had long ago lost all shreds of allure. Maybe 44 wasn't old, but she had come to appreciate the creature comforts of a more sedentary life, and to miss the warmth and security she had finally attained at home. She would surely miss Fred and Bones. She would miss having someone to shower with, having her back washed, and touching Fred in the middle of the night to remind herself of the miracle which kept him there when she was no damn fun to live with. She would probably even miss the three TV shows they watched together every week and chances were Fred wouldn't remember how to record them. He and the VCR had a running feud. This time of year, she would miss reading in front of the fire, with Fred watching some sports thing and Bones on his dog pillow.

She started off most of these cases cranky, not just because she had to be away from home, but also because when a Power Person was killed, there was a good deal of attention paid to the crime, and that messed up the evidence and made it more difficult to solve, which made it take longer. Cranky, and in this case bleary-eyed with fatigue and anti-anxiety meds, in the baggage claim area here in the Juneau airport, because this was where the Power Person had been, allegedly, murdered. Not in the airport, but in Juneau. Murdered, because at least it was pretty certain he hadn't committed suicide in the Juneau Dump by shooting himself in the head and then stabbing himself in the back.

Seniority dictated that Special Investigator Annie Brewster, of the Alaska Investigation Bureau, was the most likely one of the four holding this title to be at the top of the list for an air drop in any high-profile case. This didn't necessarily result in any attitude from local police because Alaska, for all of its huge size, was tiny when viewed through the numbers of people in any given profession. Law enforcement personnel were so scarce that detectives and investigators knew one another by name, sight and reputation. There was no pretense of "we could handle this here without you," because most local departments didn't even have detectives. Of course, Juneau did, being the capital and a town bulging with tourists, legislators, lobbyists and journalists for about half of the year. That generally slowed down by October, but with something this big unsolved for several days, a Special Investigator was going to be called in sooner rather than later.

Annie had watched the news related to the crime, and two days after the discovery of the body she had heard the magic phrases: *Juneau Police Detectives say there are no leads at this time*, and *Governor Skope has expressed outrage that a public servant...* She had packed and called the airline, nearly a full day in advance of the assignment. This didn't mean she was psychic. There was a protocol associated with a capital crime, and in the Capitol, capital crime meant the big microscope of the otherwise hibernating state media, daily outrage from the Governor's office when it wasn't immediately solved, and the more the merrier to try to get it done.

Annie was feeling anything but merrier at the moment. She was waiting in the baggage claim area for her luggage, for Lt. John Sullivan of the Juneau PD to come and get her, safely, in her present condition, to her bed. There, she could sleep off her flight medication without the cab ride resulting in her having an inappropriate conversation about the case with some stranger. She always flew at night if she could, because though the turbulence was likely to be worst, she wouldn't have to go to work when she got off the plane. Coming into Juneau this time of year, the words "worst" and "turbulence" were an inevitable pair. Annie watched the bags and people moving toward one another, humming *all shook up.*

For reasons that currently escaped her, the baggage claim was a popular place tonight. She stood off to the side of the room, slightly away from the crowd of people who took the late plane from Anchorage, who were mingling with the crowd of people from the last nonstop from Seattle, all of whom were watching the carousel go around and around with the baggage of passengers who came in on the milk run from Yakutat and Cordova 20 minutes ago. This caused her to ponder why airports could sit idle for hours at a time, and then three planes came in within 45 minutes of one another.

No one noticed her. Even though strangers were beacons in an Alaskan airport, she apparently attracted no one. This was a good thing, she thought. In middle age, of medium height, with neat, short hair blonde going white at the side-brushed bangs and temples, and lacking any flamboyancy other than her vocabulary, she blended into crowds. Especially now, in her long, lined beige raincoat, worn jeans and muddy running shoes. She did nothing to call attention to herself, especially when drugged. Ha ha. She never flew in her business costume, which was invariably something simple, tailored and monochrome. Her normally serious, intent and busy eyes were hazy with medication, she knew, and at this point, she was focusing them on her carryon briefcase so that she would know if someone ripped it off. Not likely she could do anything about it at this stage, but it would be nice to know.

She just wanted to crawl into her own bed. A facsimile of which she happened to have here, in a room over the garage of a little rental she and Fred had bought several years ago. Her mind was going like a hamster in a wheel, and picking up speed. It wasn't that there wouldn't be anywhere to stay in Juneau. The lodging choices in the capital were, relatively speaking, dramatically less than in Seattle, or even Anchorage, but they were dramatically greater than Bethel, Nome or even Glennallen. On the state per diem rate, Juneau was classified as a relatively inexpensive place to stay. Relatively. In matter of fact, if you weren't sharing the expenses of a room and cab from the airport with someone, you would eat the per diem by lunchtime just having the senior specials.

On the road, she didn't have any other office regardless of what they gave her at the police station. She had to spread out, and pace around. And she didn't want anyone in her room. She thought best when nibbling. The floral bag had been going around for an hour, hadn't it? You were supposed to check because bags looked alike, but there couldn't be two of those. Of course there were motels—even choices among motels. In Juneau and Fairbanks, she could stay at the Motel Six, where they left the light on, perhaps out of loyalty to Tom Bodette, the only Alaskan voice on national television. Or the Best Western. Or the Super 8. Who gave them these names? But a motel put even less trustworthy clientele in her room rummaging through things, or using any tidbit of gossip about what she was doing there as legal tender

An increased activity in the crowd before her, and a blast of cold, wet air from the automatic door leading outside to the ground transportation drew Annie from her lodging reverie. She shouldered the strap of her carryon and moved forward into an empty space. Her battered green wheeled suitcase appeared, either by magic or because it had already gone by several times. She dragged it off the belt and wheeled it out the door, into the chill, rain, wind and momentarily refreshing night.

She had no trouble finding John Sullivan, whose unmarked police vehicle was in front of the cabs, where buses parked in the summer when the tourists poured off the planes and collected there to be taken sightseeing. He was standing beside the car, talking to the airport rentacop.

"Annie?" he called, popping the trunk. "Everything go okay? How was the flight?"

"John. It was up in the air, John, and you know what that means."

Lt. Sullivan smiled, and opened the passenger door for her. "Let's get you to the barn," he said.

John Sullivan was approaching his fifties. He was one of those fortunate men who couldn't seem to lose his youthful physique, no matter what he ate and no matter how infrequently he exercised. Annie liked him anyway, because he was all business and no melodrama. She had worked through cases with him twice.

The ride into town along Egan Drive was long, and dark, the rain and lights of oncoming automobiles mesmerizing through the incessant windshield wipers. She would go to sleep if she didn't talk. "Any progress since we spoke yesterday?" Annie asked, stifling a yawn behind her hand.

"None. Less than none. We had a good line on where he was up to a point, and then he disappears and ends up where he was found. Nothing in the middle, yet. No real evidence, no suspects. A list of people we've talked with. We've impounded his truck. The usual. First thing in the morning, I'll meet you at the Dump and we can talk to the guy who found him, although I don't know what that will gain us. We're searching the garbage in the general vicinity, but no murder weapons. Until we hear back from the Medical Examiner's office, we don't have a cause of death ..."

"Whoa. That's new. I thought he was shot...and stabbed." Annie shook her head to clear it a little.

"He was. The undertaker who prepared the body for transport couldn't say which came first. He was wet, in a puddle, actually, and there wasn't much blood. Clothing was soaked. Blood, if there was blood from the stabbing, could have just washed away."

"So what does that mean," Annie wondered out loud. "Already dead when stabbed? Was the bullet in his head?"

"Bullet? No, in the upper neck, right side. Small caliber, by the holes, through and through. Since we don't know where he was killed, we don't know where to look for bullets. Could be several places."

"No gun, no knife? Killed and dumped, or dumped and killed?"

John shrugged, and turned off Egan onto Tenth, and then threaded up through the little houses and cars squeezed on both sides of the tiny street to a small, yellow frame cottage that looked like it grew out of the steep hillside. "We'll see what the Medical Examiner says. Body's already in Anchorage. We sent it up yesterday." The only real destination for a murder victim was in Anchorage, and the funeral home which doubled as the city morgue was only a temporary stop for complex homicides such as this one was shaping up to be. Like many states, Alaska was rushing to catch up with the exploding field of forensics, and forensic pathology.

They sat briefly in the driveway. "The undertaker is a pretty careful guy. Hopefully the ME will tell us something by later in the week."

Annie could tell that John wasn't all that hopeful, but that was about all she could deal with tonight. "Okay. What time at the Dump?" she asked.

"Eight-thirty. Shall I send a car for you?"

"I'll get myself there, thanks."

Mindful of the time of night, they got out quietly and carried Annie's luggage up the narrow stairs to the garage apartment. Annie set down her things and shook John's hand. "See you at 8:30…at the Dump," she said. "Thanks for the ride and the update."

She listened to John's footsteps descending the stairs. She took off her coat and hung it on the peg by the door, set the alarm and even put the tiny coffee pot on its timer, filling the basket with grounds she kept in the freezer of the small refrigerator.

Shot in the head, stabbed in the back, dumped in the rain. Murder by cliché, was her last thought as she crawled into bed.

Chapter Four

Annie slept off her medication by 6:30, and woke in the little studio apartment over the garage of her rental when the tenant started a car beneath her bed. Or someone did. The tenant was a single mother with two children, and she worked at the Post Office in the Federal Building, which meant she could walk there. Annie shook her head, reminding herself that the woman, who was a good and stable renter, was entitled to whatever company and hours she wanted to keep, and entitled to start her car whenever. She stretched out her arms, listening to her shoulder joints protest, missing Fred. She hoped that the car heralded a lover, sneaking out. She began to hum *Sundown,* and shifted immediately into *Early Morning Rain.* Apparently this was going to be one of those folk rock days.

She punched the button to disarm the alarm, which had not yet gone off. She only set the alarm to remind her to call Fred, as if he wasn't the first thing she thought of when she woke up. She generally turned alarms off before they rang, so it was anyone's guess why she set them at all. To remind her to call Fred and make sure he was up, which she did, using the ancient "Princess" phone they kept in the apartment.

"How was the flight?" he asked sleepily.

"Great, hon, just great. I'm thinking of doing it again this evening for kicks."

"You coming home?"

He obviously wasn't awake enough to detect sarcasm.

"No, dear," Annie sighed, "no. But it was okay, and I'm here, off and running to the Dump this morning. Are you awake now?"

"Yeah. I'm up. Bones is up, anyway, aren't cha, boy. Why the Dump?"

"That's where they found the body, remember? We saw it on the television?"

"The Dump. Yeah. I'm with ya now. Okay, Bones, okay. Bones has to go out. Thanks for calling and getting me going. I'm up. I smell coffee. I'm tracking. Good hunting today. Be safe."

"Love you. I'll call you tonight."

"Do that. Love you too."

He sounded warm and sleepy and friendly, and she almost got cranky again, holding the phone to her chest. Almost. Instead, she got up and turned on the public radio station, which was in the midst of an interview with a composer who played the jazz kazoo. At least that was what it sounded like. The murmur in the background was what she was after, the sound of people talking about something interesting, even if she didn't get to participate.

She showered, opened up her suitcase to find underwear and ended up putting all of her traveling clothes away in the little closet. A bad sign, putting clothes in the closet. In her undergarments, she sipped coffee with a spoonful of instant breakfast powder and a dollop of evaporated milk, and switched on the tiny TV for the 7:30 news. She combed her hair, put on eye liner and mascara—there being no point in lipstick because she chewed it off—and dressed in a toffee-colored pants suit with a dark brown turtleneck. During these habitual, comforting activities she thought about nothing of any consequence, letting the various news broadcasts take her mind from here to there, humming "*Devil with the blue dress…*" when the weather girl appeared, an impossible twit who was laughing about rain and overcast this early in the morning. Where were all of the mature women? The weather was a serious topic in this state. Annie was tired of Anchorage television being the junior high of broadcasting.

She didn't know enough to think about the crime yet. She could feel the energy building, but that might go up and down over the next week, or maybe even longer, while she was gathering information. She didn't yet know what was relevant, which meant casting a wide net. She didn't have any immediate hunches or visions, and she wasn't on a clock. Here, true crime departed from the media version.

Annie's personal belief was the biggest lie in all types of crime shows, even those that paid lip service to how long it took to solve the "real" crime, was a rapid, and generally satisfying, solution. Crimes were translated into a half hour, an hour, a two-hour movie. Twenty minutes before the end of a movie, ten minutes before the end of a television show, everything came together. Life's underbelly had no such commitment to a time schedule. Actual police work could be boring, most days. Lots of dead time, waiting and carrying out tasks on other crimes. Annie got occasionally frustrated with the slow pace of investigations, but she was also zealously thorough. She had cut her investigative teeth on Sherlock Holmes. "Nothing is small" in a crime scene. The "obvious may be deceptive."

"Notice everything." And Annie's own codicil, "Don't be in any kind of hurry."

She called a cab at 8:00, and armed herself with all manner of rain gear and a waterproof document envelope that held note pad, pen, tape recorder. By the time she got down to the street, the yellow cab was turning onto her block. The cabbie looked at her briefly in the mirror when she announced her destination.

John Sullivan was waiting, in the same unmarked car, at the Dump entrance. It was still raining, and Annie saw him through the intermittent slap of his windshield wipers, gesturing her to come and get in. She did. Sullivan, predictably, was business from the onset.

"Annie, I'm glad you're here early on this one. It's going to be a circus."

"Yeah? With a fence around the crime scene?" Annie wasn't good at small talk, but she knew John well enough that it wasn't necessary.

"This isn't the crime scene. This is the drop-off point."

Annie logged that away and let it pass for the moment. "No witnesses?"

"Witnesses, no. Crime scene, no. Weapons, no. Murderer, no. Rain, yes."

They both chuckled shortly. Rain could rapidly undo a lot of information. Sullivan sighed.

"Transport vehicle we do have, and beyond that, go figure. How do you get into the Dump? In a truck. How do you get into the truck?"

"Someone puts you there, or you're in a dumpster."

"Yeah, but which one? "

"Truck, or dumpster?"

"Hell, either. No one even reported him missing until the next day. A new round of garbage had been picked up by that time, so forget any evidence on the garbage truck itself, if we can figure out which one it was."

There might be something on the truck, but Annie let that, too, pass. Don't come in and immediately begin criticizing or grandstanding. "Let's go look at what you do have," she said by way of reassurance, because for John, he was pretty hyper, and she didn't like hyper when she started a new case. It clouded the mind. "Show me where they found him."

Since AIB wasn't called in unless no red arrow pointed to the perpetrator, Annie's consistent way of picking up the case was to start any investigation at the beginning. The casual observer might think she was ignoring what had been found so far, and perhaps at some level she was, if she could. She began by assuming that nothing made sense. She resisted seeing any patterns in information. She let facts, evidence, hunches come straight in and mix it up in her subconscious. She didn't pass over something someone else thought unimportant, what had led someone else to a dead end. She pretended that she had been "there" from the beginning.

Of course, there was no undoing what had happened, or the investigation to this point, so "beginning" was a relative term. But Annie had learned to avoid a predetermined scenario. She trod a fine line between respect for the work that had already been accomplished, and awareness that if it were that simple, she wouldn't be here.

John drove down a well-maintained gravel road, past a mountain range of garbage, to the spot where the body was found, now cordoned off with yellow police tape. "Here we are," he said when she raised her eyebrows.

"Looks like big pile of wet garbage."

Of course the victim was no longer there, and in between then and now, six days of 'mostly rainy.' If this were the crime scene, there would probably be little of use here.

"He was found by…?"

"The senior garbage cruiser."

Annie gave John her "give me a break" look. "How does he rate a title like that and we don't? And you have a statement from him?"

"Yeah, but it doesn't give us much to go on. I have you set up to talk to him as soon as you see what you want to see here." John picked up a waterspotted steno pad, and flipped back a few pages. "Bud Smith. He found the body at 10:30 a.m. Thursday, *because the birds were causing such a fuss*."

He used a deep, *good ole boy* voice Annie suspected was meant to sound like Bud's. She listened with half an ear as he went over his notes; then they got out and walked around. Industrial garbage bags, mostly opaque green, full of paper. Lots of rain-filled footsteps. "Did you pick up all of the surrounding bags?" she asked.

"Yeah. We moved them out of the rain. Haven't found anything yet. Are we going to get forensics help, assuming we find something that looks promising?"

There just wasn't forensic expertise in small towns—that was for the lower 48. Even the Crime Lab in Anchorage sent anything complex out of state.

"Sure," Annie said. "For right now, whatever we can isolate we'll send up to Anchorage." Annie hoped something, anything, could actually be isolated. She guessed that something was here, if it could be found. She would bet any amount of money that the crime scene was somewhere else. Still, something had been transported here, in the dumpster's contents, with the deceased. "Let's go talk with Bud Smith," she said.

"Fine," John replied, "Get ready. This guy was born here."

Annie smiled, because John couldn't resist reminding her that local color, in Alaska, was more colorful than in most places. But she expected that she'd learn something important. She always did.

Smith turned out to be an interesting and observant man, in a labyrinthine sort of way. Annie never assumed anything about an Alaskan. He may have been born in Alaska, but he had been out. Way out. He had Vietnam Vet on his hat and Boston College on his sweatshirt. His speech held a hint of West Texas. He was a big man, rough complected, bearded, and muscular, not fat. When John Sullivan introduced them, he extended his hand to engulf Annie's, and opened with, "the birds found him," which was basically what was in John's notebook.

It sounded reasonable to her. A secret little known to outsiders was that the best place to see the national bird is at a dump. There were many other birds, and if there was something to find that was meat, they found it. Annie nodded politely, returning the Senior Garbage Cruiser's intent stare, which caused him to smile a bit, nod back, and begin his story.

"I was in my bobcat with the plexiglass window shields up, checking the perimeter."

"It was raining?"

"When isn't it?" He shook his head. "Yeah, raining. And I'm watching the birds, lots of birds, lots of eagles, circling and talking it up. That was my first clue something was where it shouldn't be."

What Bud thought was unusual and 'where it shouldn't be,' was what Annie wanted to hear, because birds fighting over garbage wasn't unusual in her experience. "And that was..." she prompted, but Bud was not to be straight-lined to anything.

"It isn't pretty to see the Bald Eagle fighting over garbage," he said, "tour buses would have had a real view of it last Wednesday. They bring 'em by here, to check out the birds. The last cruise ship was gone by Tuesday, Monday night really, so there weren't any tour buses. But it they'd been in town, Wednesday is about the time the downtown garbage percolates enough to bring in the birds for the mature garbage. So in that way, it wasn't unusual to have the birds, but it was where they were that got my attention."

Annie took some mental notes about Bud, especially that he used words like "percolate," and "mature" to talk about garbage. She jotted down physical pieces relating to the timing—the departure of the last cruise ship, the last of the tourist garbage, the last time the restaurants would be full until the legislature came into session in January. Sullivan was beginning to sigh a little, but Annie was patient about these wandering stories from witnesses. "Where they were..." She began, and Bud nodded again and continued.

With, apropos to nothing, "Winter's coming on and the fish runs are over, so all the birds come here to eat, but the eagles are the biggest, and they'll actually eat your other birds. Not the national symbol for nothing."

Well, apropos to Bud's politics: Juneauesque with a pithy liberal overlay.

"Eagles make the other birds nervous and noisy, but they don't want to give up. Actually, eagles are fairly lazy, willing to watch and see what the other birds uncover and then steal it." They all looked up as an eagle circled overhead, and screamed that eerie cry.

"Yes," Annie said, still watching the sky, "you saw an unusual number of them in a place where they aren't normally..." He was painstaking, but Annie needed detail, if for no other reason than to eliminate the unimportant. He told Annie what she already knew: in the normal order, gulls found something, crows tried to take it away, ravens drove everyone off, and eagles came to see what there was to steal.

"The eagles are always the last to come," he said. Annie regarded him silently, and he went on,

"The point is that Thursday morning, the birds were fighting over something special, the eagles were circling, ready to clear everyone out and take it over. Lots of birds, lots of eagles. But not in the restaurant garbage; in the government waste."

Annie almost laughed out loud. She translated it into a cough.

Smith's eyes were actually twinkling. "That's your paper waste," he went on. "Shouldn't be any meat. This is a good dump, as dumps go. Compact, not much odor. Everything we get is either burned, buried or sent back south, like your scrap metal we bale and barge out, and the concrete, asphalt and rocks that are hauled off for fill. We've got four guys who work the garbage, two on bulldozers, one on the incinerator and the cruiser. That's me, and I supervise the public, those who come in to dump. Pretty good business coming and going—pay to dump, pay for anything that you take away. Clients use the outer loop road.

"I'm cruising at about 10:30, because even at that hour, someone is dumping something, like a washing machine, and if you don't watch them, they'll put something from the pile in their truck. It's part of the Alaskan recycling experience. If you have to pay to have it shipped in, you can get creative," Bud warned Annie, who nodded in agreement. She was beginning to feel like one of those bobblehead dolls.

There hadn't been any problem with the 'pay to dump' piles that morning. Just one guy who couldn't get rid of his washer/dryer combo fast enough and get back out of the rain. "I cruised next to the big section near the incinerator earmarked for burnables such as paper, because that's where the birds were. Damn government offices generate enough paper to bury the Mendenhall Glacier."

Annie got the point. Birds shouldn't be attracted to paper. That's why they were where they shouldn't be and triggered Bud's attention. If it had been in the household-restaurant-fish waste pile, Bud wouldn't have remarked it at all. But the activity was in paper.

"Thought, a dead dog, maybe," Bud said. "Not supposed to put them in the trash, but people do. Closer look, I think it's a dead bear. At the time, I hoped not, because then Fish and Game is over here having a hissy fit. Bear paws and human hands look similar, under the skin," he told them seriously.

"I wanted to be sure what it was, because once I called the police over a Halloween costume and they gave me no end of shit about it." He cast a look at John, and looked quickly away. He wasn't wrong this time, and nobody was making fun of him. "It was a hand, all right, pointing up out of the trash in a way that a hand looks when it's attached to something dead. I saw that in 'Nam enough that I'll never forget it."

Bud didn't tell Annie that at this point he lost his breakfast; John had told her that before they left the car. John had laughed; she hadn't. Bud Smith might well see that partial hand--all he said he saw until he went in for a closer look--for the rest of his life. Annie wasn't so blasé about crime scenes that she was callous to the long-term effects of the tiniest details of the indignity of death. Not that John Sullivan was...he was probably laughing in the kind of relief that it wasn't him. It wasn't a good thing to come upon a body unawares.

Bud, recalling, became rather abruptly specific, saying rapidly, "I lifted the plastic bags off to see if it was another dummy, from some office party. They were those bags that came from the government buildings, so I didn't have much trouble lifting them. And there was a body under them, a good-sized man by the look of it. Face had been in a puddle of water, and that made him look like he'd drowned." Bud stopped and swallowed. Annie thought about a drowning victim she'd seen once, the ghoulish, puffy, dead-fish whiteness that was enough to cause anyone to throw up.

At that point, he said, he stepped back and called the police. Annie thanked him and said she would perhaps contact him again later, that he had been helpful. He raised his eyebrows, shook her hand and went back into the little trailer.

John and Annie walked over to the government waste, accumulating mud, but not much, because the road was well graveled. Annie measured the distance from the pile to the fence. About two car lengths. John said, "Either someone heaved him over the fence in the middle of the night, dragged him out here and picked this particular pile to bury him under, or he came in the dumpster load. We checked the fence. No tire tracks on the other side, no evidence of anyone lifting that big a man over."

"I vote for the dumpster," Annie agreed. "So you're probably right about the transport vehicle being a garbage truck. What about any unbagged garbage in the same vicinity?" When John didn't respond Annie didn't look at him, she just thought out loud. "Everything that was bagged around him is a hint at what dumpster he was in, and everything that wasn't bagged could have been thrown in the dumpster with him by the killer. Was there a bullet in the skull? Wait. I asked that last night. Sorry. Bullet in upper right neck, through and through."

"Yeah."

"So, the bullet or bullets could have been in the dumpster?"

John shifted, stared at the mountain of garbage. They both thought about hunting for a bullet in that. "God, I hope not," he said. "We do hope to find the knife. The ME may give us some help on that, you know, by telling us what we're looking for. The way the wound in his back looked, the dumpster…the truck…We haven't found the knife yet."

John Sullivan was squeamish, apparently, about describing the impact of a garbage truck's digestive processes on a corpse. Even with a cushion of paper, as it must have had.

Annie said, "Government waste." Follow the paper trail, she thought. No piece of information is unimportant.

They were both quiet for a moment more, and then John offered, "I'll take you over to where we've got the surrounding garbage. The truck crushes it up pretty thoroughly, but people here know almost to the cubic foot what a truck holds, so we took that much and put it out of the rain in their equipment shed. Mostly gone through now."

"What building does it seem to come from?"

"Actually, three different places. Could just be what the truck picked up, or how it picked it up. There appear to be several bags of household garbage mixed in, so we suppose maybe they picked up in a neighborhood. We've got the drivers' logs, matching up the runs with the garbage. Everything appears to point to one of four government buildings."

"And those would be?"

"Labor, Fish and Game, the Copy Center over on Willoughby, and the Federal Building. Odds are it was the Fish and Game dumpster, or Labor, since Grossman's truck was in its parking place."

Annie nodded, thought it would be a good move for a murderer to put him in a dumpster other than "his own," and take the truck to its normal spot, to throw off the investigation. John had no doubt thought of this, and there was time to say it. "And has anything turned up around those dumpsters?"

John Sullivan looked at her blankly. "Everything from the dumpsters is here."

"Someone went around all of the dumpster sites?"

"Yeah. You want to see them anyway?"

"I'd like to do that, if we don't have a positive on the Fish and Game, or Labor, dumpsters."

"Sure. We did, but go ahead. I'm going to need to drop you at the station. Do you want a car?"

"I'll take one of the unmarked and go ahead, look around a little. And talk to the last-seens on your list. I know," she said apologetically, intuiting that there would be that frustrated feeling from JPD that they had already covered this ground, "I know you've done it, but I need to get myself in the zone."

Sullivan said, "I knew that. I have three appointments for you. See what you think of what we've got so far. I had my notes typed up for you. Let's go back to the office. I'll give you my list, check out a car, and you can get to it."

Chapter Five

Monday, October 14, 1998 - 10:00 a.m.

Annie wasn't holding out hope, though logic said maybe, that there was anything of value in the collected garbage. She had driven back to have a look at what had been salvaged from around Grossman's body.

When someone died violently, the violence itself left important information, often more important to solving the crime than what had been done to the victim. While obvious examples such as shell casings, footprints and fingerprints received a lot of attention, the unintentional damage that might occur through the violence or its aftermath left other, less noticeable or obvious clues. Murderers were, in this day of forensic sophistication, careful of fingerprints, footprints, semen and blood. They were less careful of doorknobs, window casings, locks, screens, furniture legs, or, in this case, trash receptacles. If

Annie could put the body back into the milieu of the crime, and look around, she knew even at this late and soggy date, she might find clues that were important, revealing, meaningful.

Disposing of a body among garbage could be clever. One could mix evidence among artifacts of so many people that it would take months to find. One would be aided by some of the most effective of evidence-destroying machines: the trash compactor. Between the munching of garbage trucks, and the mess in most dumpsters, Annie didn't expect to find anything on the body. More accurately, the body would be covered with all manner of things, from which it would be impossible to determine anything of use. If they were lucky, fibers, maybe a hair.

Anything they found could be from last week's trash, which skillful lawyers ate for lunch. It was always more difficult when the body had been moved, but into the rain, and the leavings of everyone's office waste, this was not good. People sat at their desks and pared their fingernails, cleaned out their hairbrushes, and emptied out drawers used by others over the years, who had pared *their* fingernails and cleaned out *their* hairbrushes. Employees dumped their lunch, read their personal mail, weeded files, cleaned the glacial moraine out of the treads of their sneakers. So, waste was pretty literal.

That said, garbage generally told a tale of its own. Annie believed it would get them back to the scene of the crime.

Commissioner Grossman was in Anchorage being examined for evidence, and confirmation of the cause of death. The ME had promised to have a report for Annie by Thursday. That left her walking up and down the space under the roof of a pole barn-like structure, where the equipment used in the Dump was normally parked, looking through the bags from the "neighborhood" of the crime. Bagged garbage--much of which had been flattened, ripped, mangled and soaked--was spread out on a number of makeshift plywood tables. She hoped for the murderer's gloves, but she already felt this wasn't likely. There were probably gloves, all right. Everybody had 'em these days. But they were somewhere far away; she just had that feeling.

A metal detector had isolated, among the paper trash, aluminum pop cans, a section of weather stripping from the bottom of a door, a stapler, two steel rulers, hundreds of paper clips, staples and a Nissan thermos. If the offices were actually complying with the government recycling guidelines and archival guidelines for retired files, the resulting equation of paper consumption was somewhat beyond Annie's high school Algebra II. Metal bits, aside from the staples and paper clips, had been grouped, and the paper trash separated into the piles that had helped the Juneau detectives identify antecedent buildings.

There was also miscellany, the type of thing Annie might have put in her own garbage, give or take a season. Annie looked at the three shoes, lined up in a neat row. She had put on her surgical gloves, but the shoes weren't threatening. Two, unmatched, would have fit a five-year-old with a big right foot. The third was a man's shoe, a baseball cleat which had seen much better summers, no doubt. It was worn around the outer edges, and the little toe area was gone. *Piggy went.* Leon and the Busboys danced into Annie's ear, *goin' downtown* for some new shoes. The shoes didn't fit with the government paper garbage, but then neither did the package of breakfast cereal, the dog food sack, or the odoriferous batch of used diapers. Wads of paper towel covered with oil. Coffee grounds, egg shells, an empty bacon package, three brown banana peels and something nasty in aluminum foil. A flattened, half-gallon white plastic milk jug. A mangled plastic orange juice container. An unopened box or toaster tarts. *Take out the papers and the trash,"* Annie hummed. Then, frowning, called Bud in to look at what had been picked up from around the body. "Is this mixture normal for that area?"

"Normal, I would say," Bud answered, looking up and down the tables. "There's always some household stuff. People bring their garbage to work, maybe, to put in the dumpster, or it gets there some other way. Special pickup at someone's house, lunch meeting at the office." He smiled. "Won't want to speculate about the diapers."

"Thanks."

"No problem."

"Bud, what access would people dumping trash from private homes have to the site where you found the body?"

"They could come at the pile from the back, I suppose. If no one saw them, they could get a vehicle around to that area, push something out, maybe pull something over it before we saw them, especially if they came in when it was busy." Bud looked thoughtful, as though the idea of someone sneaking into a forbidden area of the Dump to leave something had not occurred to him.

"So, it is possible," Annie said, just to make sure.

"Possible," Bud said abruptly. "Not likely." His eyes glinted and his chin firmed as his jaw set. Annie caught herself about to apologize for the inference, but he was not looking at her, he was looking at a light blue late-model pickup that was driving off the scales, heading into the public dumping area.

"Do you mind if I drive around and look at the area from the back side?"

"Stay on the gravel, is all. Be my guest. Trucks start comin' in about an hour. Best be out of the way by then," he said, turning away, watching the pickup.

"Thanks," Annie repeated, logging away Bud's scrutiny of the pickup.

Bud went over to his bobcat. Annie walked around the tables again. She had the distinct feeling there wasn't going to be a needle in this haystack, that any important clues commonly found in proximity to the body just wouldn't be here. Good move, she silently told the *killer*.

She hadn't used that word to herself as yet. But there was a killer. In these piles might be a link to someone using a dumpster to accessorize a crime. She asked the uni on guard whether there had been any personally identifying materials in the household portion. He said not that they had found, yet. She said, "I'll be back to look at this again," and left to do her drive around to the spot where the body had been found.

The loaner car, a sedan with damp seats and a foggy windshield, had a cranky defroster. Annie found a kleenex and wiped a little hole in the fog while she waited for the defroster to heat up. She watched a miniature fork lift cross the road in front of her, and then eased out onto the gravel road which circled the mounds of garbage. She passed heaps of concrete and asphalt, yard waste and deceased appliances. She drove around the farthest piles. When she was totally hidden behind the mounds, she stopped, and looked in all directions. Saw no one. Then she drove forward until she connected with the road which ran back to the pile where the body was found.

Well this wasn't a logistically friendly place to try to deposit a body in the government waste. If you came in during the day, there was a record of it. The Dump wasn't open at night. And John had said no tire tracks leading up to the fence. Big fence, like in a prison yard. As she sat, another pickup passed at the end of the road, and a dump truck came up the way she had come. It was, as Bud had said, possible to dump something unobserved. Not likely.

Annie sighed. She wasn't sure that circling the Dump was the best place to spend her first day here. John had made appointments for her with the last people who had talked with Commissioner Grossman, and she was running up on the time it would take to get herself there, find a parking place—always a delightful experience in Juneau—and warm up a bit so that she could talk without shivering. Shivering made a bad impression.

Chapter Six

The last people to see Grossman on the evening of his death were all in the same meeting. John had suggested Annie might want to talk to the Budget Director, and one of the Commissioners, the last person who had actually talked to Grossman. Maybe someone had seen an anomaly in the eyes of someone leaving the room. It was a stretch, since this murder didn't have the feel of fiscal revenge, but at these levels of organization, Annie knew the infighting wasn't done with fists.

The Budget Director's name was Frieda Schwartz, which was appropriate in a time of reductions and belt tightening, but all Annie could think of when she met her was *Frieda Pain.* Obscure mental connections to 60's pop singers-- Annie couldn't seem to stop making them. *All that's left is a mound of gold*...no, *band of gold.*

The woman was small and pale with close-cropped red hair, light blue-gray eyes, no make-up, a pinched face and jackboots. No. Laced-up, sensible shoes, simple blouse buttoned to the top, light gray tailored suit. No color. No nonsense.

Annie corralled her vivid imagination and focused on the woman who stood in the office doorway. Took in the unmistakable signs of nervousness. Ms. Pain (stop that, she said crossly to herself) put out a hand, then half took it back, clutched it with her other hand, and then stuck it out again. It was white, white, with calluses on the index fingers and bitten nails.

"Detective? Or should I say..."

Among the bureaucratic but nevertheless politically vulnerable, not knowing someone's title was the worst possible faux pas. Annie rescued her. "Annie Brewster. Special Investigator, Alaska Bureau of Investigation. Ms. Schwartz, I know that you've answered some questions for Lt. Sullivan, but at the point at which I'm brought in on these cases, I reconduct some interviews to make sure we have all of the information possible to help with the investigation. I understand this is a busy day for you; I won't take long."

Schwartz nodded. "Please come in," she said, and led the way, bypassing her desk to sit at a small, round table by the window. Half of the table, and all of the desk, was piled two feet deep in paper, computer runs, stacks of clipped copies, folders with various papers sticking out the edges, and ledger sheets, which Annie didn't know were even used any longer. She looked at all of this, and Frieda Schwartz seemed not to notice. "What would you like to ask me?" she said tidily, her demeanor strengthening in her domain, among her projections, facts, figures.

"You understand that we are interested in exactly what transpired in the hours before Commissioner Grossman was killed."

"Yes, of course."

"And, reviewing here, Commissioner Grossman came to the meeting around 4:30, and left about 6:00 or so?"

"He came at 4:20, and he left at 6:03, yes, so your estimates would be approximately correct."

Whew. "And you noted these times…?"

"On my meeting notes. I showed them to Lt. Sullivan. I can't, of course, give you my notes, but he made copies of those pages. I can't think that the notes themselves would be of any value to you."

"No?" Annie said, "You never know. I wonder if you could tell me, to the best of your recollection, what occurred in the meeting and how Commissioner Grossman behaved."

"Behaved? I don't understand." Ms. Schwartz's response was slow but not hostile, and she looked at Annie quizzically. As though what she was being asked made no sense, or was in another language.

Maybe, thought Annie, to her it was. Too bad we can't do this by the numbers, she thought. "Did he seem relaxed, did he seem agitated, was he nervous or angry when he left, like that," she asked patiently.

"Why would you want my impressions of that?" the Budget Director asked, seeming genuinely interested.

"If I understand correctly, this was a meeting to make preliminary decisions about the Governor's next budget. Those who came would have some stake in the outcome. Some people will get what they want and some won't. And that might mean that some people were upset, some elated, some irritated, and so forth."

"I see where you're going." Ms. Schwartz looked at the wall behind Annie for a moment, and then her eyes swung up to the right of her forehead and she said, "He sat to my left, down the table, at a place where I couldn't see him without bending forward and looking around Commissioner Prentiss. He sat between Commissioner Backson and Commissioner Doyle and across from Deputy Commissioner

Rearson and Attorney General Greese. He sat back from the table a little, which was normal. I could actually hardly see him. When I did, he was watching everyone who spoke, intently. He said little, but that's normal. Except once, during the meeting..." she stopped and seemed to search a minute for words. Her eyes darted to Annie, and then away.

Annie had to brace herself to keep from leaning forward expectantly.

"Sometimes he gets agitated, especially on certain topics. There was a discussion of the gradual phase in--for which the next fiscal year budget would include an increment--of a new e-mail server, which I recollect is a topic about which he feels a great ownership. During these meetings, everyone is somewhat nervous, except people who know in advance that their budget is safe, or have been told that they will actually be dealing with an increase. We don't cut Public Safety, for example, and last term we didn't cut H & SS, because those were the flagship programs. Which isn't to say that the finance committees will agree." She paused again and looked at Annie carefully, as if to see if she was following.

When Annie nodded, she went on, "He became agitated, and then, it seemed, quite agitated, and then conducted what I would have to say was a louder than normal exchange with

Deputy Commissioner Rearson." She was quiet for a few seconds, and the she said bluntly, "Rearson asked whether the existing e-mail server couldn't just be upgraded and Commissioner Grossman called him a 'knuckle dragger,' I believe."

Annie made notes, Doyle, Rearson, agitation, anger, e-mail servers, 'knuckle dragger.' Frieda Schwartz sat somewhat stiffly, waiting. Then, apparently uncomfortable with what she had said, she offered, "It's just an opinion, and often the discussions among cabinet members do become quite lively."

"He gets agitated, he raises his voice, on the one hand. And on the other, he says little," Annie said, as though that was what she had written. Ms. Schwartz nodded. "And on that afternoon, he did all of these." She nodded again. "And the subject of this meeting, again, was?"

"We were just going over the parameters the Governor and his staff have identified for the next budget. This gives an opportunity for everyone to see the projected bottom line, to hear the priorities, to clarify what will be the areas and percentages to be cut and why. That way, everyone can go back to their staffs and prepare information on the impact of projected cuts for the upcoming budget retreat where the final decisions will be made."

"And was Fish and Game to absorb a cut?"

"No, as a matter of fact. They were cut last year, and the feeling was that other departments have had the benefit of additional funding during the first four years of this administration—is this important?" she asked somewhat suspiciously, as though the budgets of the various departments, and who was to be cut or not cut, was a state secret.

Like her meeting notes, no doubt, Annie thought. Perhaps, in this town, that was true. "Not really," she offered conciliatorily, "except in so far as it might shed some information about his state of mind when he left the meeting. So, he hadn't gotten any bad news. And what was his demeanor just before and at the actual time he left the meeting?"

"Well," Ms. Schwartz said carefully, watching Annie as though she couldn't quite bring her into focus, "he was having an increasingly loud discussion with Commissioner Doyle, at least *he* was loud, and then he just stopped, after Commissioner Doyle didn't say any more."

"And how was he behaving when he left?

"Commissioner Doyle?"

"No, Commissioner Grossman."

"It's really not appropriate for me to say. I don't think...no, I'm sure my personal impression has no bearing on this investigation."

"Oh, but it might. Please, go on. I'm only writing impressions; there's no tape recorder and you won't be quoted anywhere at this point. But believe me, his state of mind upon leaving the meeting can be extremely important," Annie said firmly. Then, seeing that Frieda Schwartz was not buying that, she explained. "He left the meeting and went out into the night, presumably on the way to his car. Was he paying attention to things around him, or was he angry, and perhaps still thinking about the meeting? Was he feeling triumphant? Was he brooding? Was he distracted enough to go to the wrong floor, the wrong car, down the wrong street? Was it possible that he was angry, and insulted someone on the street, a driver who swerved unexpectedly in the dark and the rain, and that this driver then is the person we're looking for? Or did he happily hail a friend and they walked together to where he parked.

"At this stage, with no real leads, we have to take into account what he might have done to contribute to the ultimately perilous situation which precipitated his murder, because his contributions are all we have. One thing we do know, you're just about the last person to see him alive. So how you saw him, even from your perspective, is important." She stopped. That was a lot of explanation for this quiet, reserved woman. She could see nothing in the woman's demeanor, other than that her complexion had paled further to almost gray. She was probably the right temperament for a budget director, in that she seemed to have no emotions, and no agenda of her own. But beneath the business, this murder frightened and affected her.

And she was clearly an intelligent woman. "I see," she said, and drew an unsteady breath. "Then I'll try to recall everything. He was, as I said, agitated. His behavior was consistent with several past meetings I have observed. By this I mean he's quiet for a time, apparently attentive, watching and listening. He doesn't take notes. He doesn't often smile. Then, and it's somewhat unpredictable, he says something, never a general comment, always about a specific thing. Depending upon the issue and the reactions of others, he can stop there, or he can become more and more agitated until he seems actually angry, especially if someone disagrees with him. He gets…excited. Louder. He seems to be able to pick just the right words to refute everyone else's objections or arguments, and he goes on, and on. It can be intimidating to some, and embarrassing to others. The more agitated he becomes, and the louder he talks, the more people begin to look away, or look down. And then when everyone else is looking down, or away, he just stops, abruptly, and makes some little joke, and yet there's this tone to his voice, as though he…" She stopped, and shifted a little in her chair.

"Yes?"

"As though challenging anyone to say anything else, I suppose."

"Why does it seem that everyone looks down." Annie was suddenly thinking of animals, assuming a submissive posture, ducking their heads, showing no threat.

Simultaneously, Ms. Schwartz confirmed her image by saying, "Because it feels like if you make eye contact with him, he'll do something in retaliation." She thought about that for a moment, and said, "If you don't say anything, he will probably just sit back and say nothing further."

"And what happened after he had the exchange with Commissioner Doyle, and shut down Deputy Commissioner Rearson with the 'knuckle dragger' comment? I presume it did shut down Deputy Commissioner Rearson?"

"Yes, of course. He was only there for Commissioner Flores," Ms. Schwartz said as though that was supposed to make sense.

Actually, it did.

"Yes," she went on, "he sat back, and was quiet. And then we finished with the general parameters the budget will take, and Grossman left."

"Did he leave ahead of others?"

"Yes, he left ahead of everyone."

"Why was that?"

"I honestly don't know. Everyone else was putting together papers, and talking about the upcoming budget retreat out at the Sheffield House, and so forth, and I saw him put on his overcoat and go out the door. I believe he went out to make a phone call, and then he did not return."

Annie made more notes. "You've been helpful," she said. "Can I call you again if I run across any inconsistencies in the recollections of others?"

Frieda Pain was back. "Don't say anything to anyone else about what I told you," she said anxiously. "I was...you said it was important. But it was just my observation, and I would..." She straightened herself in her chair and her voice changed slightly, the tone becoming more businesslike. "...I would hate to have misunderstood, and have it cause problems for...anyone who was there."

Or, more likely, have it heard by anyone there that Ms. Schwartz was an observant woman, and not as narrowly focused on numbers as some might think. Far be it from Annie Brewster to blow anyone's protective cover, especially a woman who sat in such a position of simultaneous power and peril. "Not a word, I assure you," she said kindly. "Not a word."

Annie walked out of the Alaska Office Building and into cool sunshine, a brief hiatus in the rain. There was a thick, wet fog on Mt. Juneau, behind the Capital Building, but the sun was glancing off the tramlines going up Mt. Roberts, off the harbor and off the Channel. Douglas Island, what she could see of it, was a gray blur behind what looked to be clouds blowing slowly down that side of the Channel. You had to be not only in the right place, but at the right time and facing the correct direction, she knew, to see the famous Juneau scenery. It was there, behind the fog. The Bureau secretary in Anchorage had lived here once, and said it was the only place he had ever lived where mildew thrived in the trunk of his car. Annie's feet felt damp, and her right shoulder was murmuring resentfully. Best not to listen to any of it.

She walked over to the Capitol Building, and stood for a moment in the foyer, which was crowded with furniture: dark wood occasional tables, display cases, and old fashioned phone booths with wooden seats. In the back of the foyer, hallways went left and right to the legislative chambers and offices. and a stairwell opened over the marbled tile. A security guard sat making notes in a ledger. He was dressed in a white shirt with military epaulettes and a navy blue tie; the tips of highly shined black shoes peeked out from under his desk. It was a tiny desk, Annie noted, about half the normal size, and completely wood. On the modesty panel, in relatively small print, a sign warned of various conditions and ordinances that could be invoked to remove visitors from the building.

Annie watched as the elevator doors opened. Three people came out, coats on, briefcases at the ready, all silent. None of the three looked at the guard, and he did not look at them. She supposed eye contact could be dangerous, to say nothing of giving the impression of courtesy. Did Commissioner Grossman make eye contact with the security guard when he left? Did the security guard know who Commissioner Grossman was? Political appointments changed, in this town, with relative frequency, and, ironically, the higher up the appointee, the fewer people among those who lived and worked in the capitol might recognize a transient face.

More to the point, no one was signing in or out, though there was a lectern-like structure behind the desk with a book, something like a guest book, open, with white lined pages. What was that for? She stepped to the side of the door and watched as people entering from the street walked to the elevators, talked as they waited, got on, disappeared. The security guard may have looked at them in the brief interval during which their bodies were between Annie and his desk, but they did not appear to have taken any notice of him, and they did not sign the book on the lectern.

Annie already knew the name of the security guard who had been on duty the night Commissioner Grossman had left his last meeting. She and everyone else assumed that the Commissioner did not walk down seven floors of stairs. She and everyone else assumed that he took the elevator. The security guard who had been on duty had been shown a picture of the Commissioner, but he did not remember having seen him. But this was not a checkpoint, and the security guard wasn't guarding anything that Annie could see.

She crossed the foyer to the elevator doors. Little elevators, the kind old buildings had, narrow, tall opening doors in a wall of dark paneling. She waited for a short time, during which she turned and smiled at the security guard, who smiled back but said nothing. Different name on the tag, so more than one guard. The elevator came grouching down the shaft, and stopped on a floor above, and then came down to the lobby.

Three young women, each carrying a stack of papers, came out.

"Hi Wilton," one woman sang out. "Caught any terrorists today?"

"Yeah, six before lunch," the security guard responded in the same cheerful tone. "Off to the bindery again?"

"Yup. This year, we'll be ready for 'em when they get here," she laughed, and the three rounded the corner and disappeared.

Annie stepped into the elevator, pressed the button for the seventh floor, and noted the absence of security. She rode up to alone. The door opened to plush carpet, rich wallpaper and a polished sideboard holding a fragrant bouquet of what must be, at Juneau prices, $100 worth of flowers. Windows to the left, a graceful walnut and fabric couch with eagle claw feet to the right. Pictures of the governor and lieutenant governor hung over the couch, with the seal of the state between them. The teak reception counter, glowing in the muted light, supported another vase of flowers, a gold pen rising from an ivory stand, and a telephone which reminded Annie of a Rolls Royce without wheels. A gold plaque read, "Jean Beaudreau" and "Receptionist."

Behind the receptionist's counter was, presumably, Jean Beaudreau. He was a handsome young man with a good deal of dark hair, a smile like an airline steward, and the same white shirt and navy tie that she had seen below. No epaulettes. "May I help you?" he asked in that perfectly friendly, modulated voice reserved for the receptionists to the powerful.

Annie introduced herself. She already knew that the receptionist had gone home by the time Commissioner Grossman had left the meeting in the Governor's conference room. She knew that this was normal, that after 5:30 this station was unattended and the doors into the Governor's suite, at this time of year, were locked. Annie asked whether there was another exit from this floor, knowing that there must be stairs. Two sets, it turned out, one down the hall and another, the emergency escape out the back of the Governor's suite, which went to the parking lot. A blind alley, explored and set aside.

Best to assume that Grossman had left the conference room, called the elevator, ridden down and gone outside without drawing anyone's attention. Annie had an appointment at Natural Resources, down the street, and a 3:00 at Fish and Game. As it seemed that there was nothing particular to be gained here, she took the public stairs down. On her way out after leaving the stairwell, she passed the security guard getting a cup of coffee in the stairwell. She made eye contact and smiled. He nodded, but he did not appear to recognize her. Huh.

She stepped out onto the street and looked across at the State Office Building, where she knew the parking garages were. She made a note to herself to see if anyone had verified that Commissioner Grossman had driven himself to the meeting. If someone had dropped him off, it would be important to know, especially if they were going to try to retrace his path back to one of the dumpsters. Parking garages were a good place for the boogeyman. Annie made note to ask John if someone had collected whatever might be in his parking place here.

On to Commissioner Doyle, the last person to speak to Grossman.

Chapter Seven

Monday, October 14, 1998 - noon

Commissioner Ralph Doyle, head of Natural Resources, was an Alaska Native man of impressive stature and distinguished aspect. His office walls held plaques and an engraved gold pan testifying to his long service to corporate boards such as the Cook Inlet Native Corporation and the Alyeska Pipeline Service Company. He apologized for only having the noon hour to meet with Annie. He, too, avoided his desk, and sat with her at a conference table before a window with panoramic views of the harbor and the Channel.

"How can I assist you in your investigation, Inspector?" he asked, his Athabaskan heritage apparent in tone and cadence. "I believe that I have told the police everything I remember."

"Yes, sir, I'm certain that you have. I'm coming in a week later, because, as you must know, we don't have the case solved yet. I am reconducting some interviews. I'll be brief." Annie flipped open her notebook, to the notes from Frieda Schwartz's interview. "I understand that you were at the meeting which was, apparently, the last place where Commissioner Grossman was seen alive."

"Lamentably, that appears to be correct. We were all—the Commissioners—except Flores— at a Budget Strategy meeting." He waited, leaning back comfortably in his chair, hands resting casually in his lap. No signs of nervousness, no mannerisms of discomfort of any kind.

"Yes, I understand the nature of the meeting. I want to ask about the exchange which was witnessed between Commissioner Grossman and yourself, something about email servers?"

"We had a difference of opinion on that, but I don't see how that's germane." His eyebrows raised a little, but his voice changed not one whit.

"Apparently the exchange was somewhat strongly worded."

"Not that I recall." Commissioner Doyle sighed. "He was a man who occasionally voiced strong opinions. We disagreed, that was it."

"So neither of you was upset by the conversation?"

"Upset? No, I was not upset. For Grossman, who knows? He could be strong on some topics, yes. But I don't know that he seemed upset either. Grossman and I have some contact, but outside of the fact that there is some overlap between our departments…Fish and Game are among the natural resources of the state…I really don't know him that well. Don't have that much reason to talk with him outside of Cabinet meetings." Commissioner Doyle looked at his watch.

"Did you see Commissioner Grossman leave the meeting?"

"Yes. He left before I did. I stayed to talk with Pierson—the Governor's public relations aide—and Commissioner Prentiss."

"Did he leave alone?"

"Yes, I think so. I don't remember anyone else around him when he went to the door, but I wasn't paying too much attention."

"And so you left at what time?"

"About 6:30, I think, though I don't look at the clock much."

"And when you came out, were you alone?"

"No, there were three of us. Prentiss, Jepsen and I. And I think someone else, but I don't remember. The elevator is small. About four coming down at a time is enough. Why?"

"I'm interested in whether you, or anyone else who came down with you, saw Commissioner Grossman on the street."

"No. It was dark, though, and raining pretty hard. I don't think I looked around. Anyone who has to get to the parking garage from the Capitol Building in the rain would probably move pretty fast."

"Do you know that he was headed for the parking garage?"

"Just a guess, but he would have been hard pressed to find a parking place for that truck around the building. Pretty much everyone who can parks in the garage."

"Okay. Commissioner Grossman left, and when you came down, a few minutes later, you didn't see him. Where did you go then?"

Commissioner Doyle had not gotten to this status in the halls of white power by being in any way a slow thinker. "Hmmm. Did I follow Grossman and kill him, do you mean? Wouldn't likely tell you that if I did, would I?" He smiled as he leaned forward, but the smile was easy, sociable. "I was picked up at the curb by my son, who was waiting. We went to a birthday dinner for my cousin, who lives out on Thane Road. We were there all evening. Then my family and I went home together. I have no reason to want Grossman dead, or to kill him if I did."

Interested in the Commissioner's choice of words, Annie smiled back. "Nothing personal, sir, just a set of questions we have to ask. Do you know of anyone who had, as you put it, 'reason to want Grossman dead?'"

"There were people who didn't like him. Commissioners make enemies. Some people make more than others. I'm sure you've found that out already. But government officials…why kill them? More seem to sprout in their place, as far as I can see." He laughed quietly, as though he was enjoying himself.

"One more question, if you will, and then I'll let you go to your luncheon. Did you witness an exchange between Commissioner Grossman and Deputy Commissioner Rearson during which Grossman called Rearson a 'knuckle dragger?'"

"Yes, I think I remember that. Why?"

"How did Rearson appear to take that?"

"I don't know. He may have blushed, and then looked down, I think. Then I asked a question, and that was when, as you identified, Grossman and I had a 'difficult' exchange. I wasn't watching Rearson."

Annie made a note, and when she looked up, Doyle was looking out the window. "You know," he said, "Rearson shouldn't have spoken up."

"Because?"

"Because it wasn't his place."

"I understood he was there in the stead of Commissioner Flores."

"It wasn't his place."

"And do you remember Rearson leaving the meeting?"

"I don't. Does that about do it?"

Annie felt skillfully dismissed. Interested in the perception that Rearson, in the pecking order of government appointees, could come to the meeting but shouldn't have spoken. Interested that Doyle, apparently, didn't believe that Grossman's putdown of Rearson was unjustified.

"Yes, I think so, for now. Thank you for your time."

"Anytime, glad to be of assistance." Commissioner Doyle rose, the fluid movement of tall, powerful men, which made it seem that they did not merely rise, but the chair fell away. He showed her to the door of his office, shook her hand, and began immediately to put on his coat.

If there was something here, Annie couldn't see it. It sounded like an exchange at a meeting, perhaps an unpleasant exchange, especially for Rearson, but it didn't sound like something that led to a homicide.

Lunch was what sounded good. Her next appointment wasn't until 3:00, plenty of time to make notes, think a little, drive the path Grossman would have taken from where he was last seen to where his truck was found. She went across the street to her car, which was in a visitor space at the bank. She went into the bank and used the

ATM machine. It was a police car, it wasn't going to get a ticket, but Annie was fastidious about some things. She hummed "Rainy Night in Georgia" and drove down to The Hanger, a restaurant on the wharf, which always had good salad.

Once there, in a tiny booth for one, she looked over her notes, thought about the connections which wanted to be made. It was too early to make them. Could someone have been so angry with Grossman after the meeting that they followed him and killed him? That was possible, but unlikely, as Doyle had so succinctly put it. They were all potential enemies, really, in such a meeting. There were other people at the meeting, Prentiss for example, whose budgets had been targeted to lose big, but was any of this the motive for murder?

Who knew. Motive was a dicey topic. It was early. She didn't know the Plot. She was at the stage where the Plot was a squiggly thing, shape shifting with each new piece of information. Only the murderer knew the Plot, and she needed to cross his trail, already growing dim. What if the murderer had left town? There were a dozen ways out of Juneau, landlocked though it was, and to get out quickly. She made a note to have her research assistant "count the ways."

They could go three directions looking for someone with a motive. There might be someone so close there was daily contact, who had snapped from some aspect of the proximity. Abused spouses and friends who had been used. Like that.

Or there might be someone who was from the victim's past, someone who had been singed, burned or, more likely, ordered to self-immolate. Sometimes fired because it was expedient. Sometimes a close confederate, sometimes just a person who was casually eliminated, a bug too small to note, but who was badly hurt by some action of the Powerful Person. You might also find *these* people by interviewing, if you knew where the hell to look. Generally, you didn't. Because the people in this latter category sometimes took years to plot careful revenge.

Annie broke open a roll and buttered it absently, then set it down and looked around her. Chances are, someone in this restaurant--say, the big guy over there in overalls and a soiled cap-- was thinking about killing someone else. The bar music was Jim Croce, singing the one about the little guy who had his revenge on "Big Jim." Appropriate, she mused. Most murders were about revenge.

But these first two categories of motive were actually the norm. Most victims are murdered by someone they knew. Between these two categories--friends and family vs. co-workers, there were always similarities. Someone close to him might want to kill him for the same reason that someone who was distant by proximity or time would also want him dead You might find, for example, by interviewing those currently closest to the deceased that he had a problem keeping his hands to himself. And you would find that that problem extended far back in time to someone who had been out of the picture for years but was still angry or hurt.

Though it was popular on television and in books, most murders weren't conducted by strangers, or serial killers. There was little to do at this stage if the murderer was not a close friend, associate, family member, but rather was a chance acquaintance, or a stranger, which Annie always mentally called the Sniper. If you had a Sniper, you were lucky if you stumbled across the casings and traced them to the gun, so to speak. It was a metaphor, but an apt one. Some killers were so distant that you never saw them after the actual deed. You had to start by eliminating those close enough to have a daily opportunity, and who were angry enough, at some level, to cross into the irrational zone of killing.

No detective wanted the murderer to be a stranger, because it complicated everything. Smiling to herself, Annie thought of the number of stranger killers who had eventually provided the only clue that enabled them to be caught. Sometimes they became bored and taunted the police. Sometimes they simply killed the one person who had been their target, and slid quietly into the fog.

Some murders, many murders, went unsolved. A smart, careful murderer, who made and worked a plan, who knew about fingerprints and trace evidence, and who let the links between himself and the victim go cold and indistinct, was what Annie most feared. Right off, some aspects of this crime were pointing to that type of suspect. But she would start close, because at least she could eliminate some people as suspects, and she had found she learned a good deal doing that.

Running down both productive and unproductive leads was the basis of solving murders. But real life investigation was a lot closer to "Unsolved Mysteries" than it was to "CSI." Right now, the most important question was what happened to Commissioner Grossman between the time he left the Capitol Building and the time he turned up at the Dump. Somehow, he had gotten into a dumpster, most probably the dumpster right outside his office. His truck had been found there, impounded, and gone over carefully. Nothing found.

Nothing found. There was something in that, but it escaped her. She went back over it. Coming from a meeting, he should've been carrying something. Maybe he'd taken it back up to his office. And then what? Sullivan's notes said there was a cleaning crew there, all over the floor, and no one saw him come back into the office. Detectives hadn't found any evidence of struggle, any evidence of anything, in or around his office, the door of which was locked, the suite to which was locked. Annie felt the need to jump ahead and go see the space in which he'd worked, the place where his truck had been parked, even knowing that it hadn't told the local detectives anything.

Did he have a briefcase? She'd have to remember to ask that when she talked to his secretary this afternoon. Surely he wouldn't have gone to a meeting at the Governor's office without any notes, any materials, any portfolio to protect papers from the rain. Her chopped chicken salad with soy ginger dressing came, and she picked at it thoughtfully. If he was carrying important papers, perhaps that was a motive. She needed to ask about what was found on him, with him. *Some people make more than others. I'm sure you've found that out already.* Enemies. What did Doyle expect that she'd found out already? That Commissioner Grossman had more enemies than most people?

Annie thought about that, and the garbage, and the dumpster, and Frieda Pain's reaction that Grossman was "dangerous" juxtaposed against Doyle's casual response to their argument. Nothing fit yet. Pieces shouldn't be cut to fit; they should just lay on the table until their place emerged. She finished her salad and reread Sullivan's printed notes. No one had interviewed Rearson. She would do that, just to see what that might add, but she didn't, based on these interviews, think the murder was over the meeting.

She paid her bill, negotiated her car out of the parking lot onto Egan Drive, and then turned onto Willoughby. She had some time to kill, and decided to look at the dumpsters along the way. Due to lighting, fencing, and other obstructing vehicles, she eliminated those behind the Federal Building. Those behind the Post Office had their own security. She found out a sign that said those gates were locked to non-employees at 5:00.

She went back out on Willoughby and drove down to the Copy Center, which was a warehouse-style metal building enclosed in chain-link fencing, dumpsters around behind, and a tiny parking lot on the street in front. There was a sign beside the building which read, "Not a public thoroughfare." And another which read, "Fire Lane, keep open." The dumpster was in plain view of the street. No, Annie thought this one could be safely eliminated too.

Chapter Eight

Monday, October 14, 1998 - 3:00 p.m.

Humming *tell me how long can this rain last*, Annie pulled her loaner car into a space in the parking lot in front of Fish and Game and Labor. Her appointments here were with the Commissioner's staff, who had already been interviewed, and from whom there had been no particularly useful information. She went through the unprepossessing foyer of Fish and Game, past one unhealthy live plant and one healthy fake one, and took the stairs up to the Commissioner's office on the second floor.

It took all of 30 seconds on the second floor of the Fish and Game building before everyone knew who she was. Everyone was courteous and quiet, and no few were looking away and pretending to be incredibly busy. Annie's appointment was with Deputy Commissioner

Harlan Roberts, a lifer in the state political system and long-time Juneau resident.

The Commissioners came and went with the Governor, but the Deputies ran the day-to-day operations of the various departments. If the Governor was of the same party as the last, the Deputy might stay through several commissioners and become a power him or herself. If the Governor was of a different party, the Deputy would probably move to some other position, lying low in a nonpolitical area like Administration, or become a legislative aide, and later resurface when the party of original appointment regained the governor's chair. All of which seemed pretty silly to Annie, because, as far as she could tell, the Deputies had no allegiance except to politics. Being in the arena, regardless of the uniform, was their party.

Deputy Commissioner Roberts was a slender redhead, or partial redhead. Graying around the ears, gone on top. He seemed deceptively mild behind dark-framed glasses, but he was alert and focused entirely on Annie, not looking around, not reacting to the phone ringing, not even twitching. This made her think of a lizard. She expected his tongue to show any minute, but it didn't show, even when he talked.

"Mr. Roberts, I understand that you may have already answered some of these questions for Detective Swearts. Because I've been called in on this case, however, I need to ask them again."

"Fine," Roberts responded. "Fine. Anything I can do to help." He didn't smile, but he wasn't nervous, at least not that Annie could tell.

"When was the last time you saw Mr. Grossman?" Annie begin, setting up the frame which would, hopefully, become smaller and smaller until it pinpointed time and place of death

"The Co and I spoke before he went to the budget session, and that would have been about 3:00 last Monday."

"And how would you characterize that discussion?"

"Excuse me?" He looked intently at Annie, as though she were not speaking English.

Strangely, it made her feel a little as though she wasn't. Oooo, she thought. It's *The Voice.* She raised her shields, metaphorical and professional. Roberts had a bookshelf, somewhere with Winning by Intimidation." And sitting right next to it, a worn copy of Dune from college days. She bumped the question up a notch. Actually, *The Voice* was a thing, and Annie used it herself.

"Please describe the nature of your last verbal interaction with the deceased?" This seemed less comprehensible to Annie, not more, but then, she believed he understood the original question. She stared at him, and he nodded as though he approved of the rephrasing, and briskly answered.

"I see. I would describe it as brief, direct, neutral in tone. I had gathered some information for his meeting. I went over it with him briefly. He was prepared to defend the parameters we set up for support of key initiatives, and he left in a positive frame of mind."

"Positive?"

"Yes. He both said he was confident in the meeting's outcome, and seemed relaxed and even looking forward to the meeting."

"And you would know this because?" Annie was interested, in spite of herself, in his clinical analysis of such a 'neutral, brief, and direct' interaction.

"When he is…was…confident, he would smile, and his eyes would be alight, like he was looking forward to something. And he had few questions."

"And you didn't go with him, because…" Annie waited. She already knew from her interview with the Budget Director that there were deputy commissioners at the Budget meeting. Not at the conference table, but in their stanchions behind each commissioner. She watched Mr. Roberts for some sign of irritation that he had been excluded, but there was none. Instead, there was a small smile.

"The Co liked to maintain a minimal presence at these meetings."

The "Co." Annie had heard that slang before. An abbreviation which morphed into an oxymoron. She put Roberts' *minimal* together with the Budget Director's description of a man who sat quietly and then lacerated his opponents with words, intimidated others with the underlying willingness to follow his words physically. It didn't want to mesh.

"That was the last time you saw him?"

"Yes."

"What was he carrying, if you saw him leave? Did he have a phone?"

"Nothing. He didn't carry things to meetings, even here. He hated phones. He didn't have a briefcase. He sometimes put notes in his pocket, especially if he needed figures at his disposal. He didn't take notes, and he didn't like it when anyone else did. Often wanted to know what they had written. I quite admired the command he had in extemporaneous meeting situations. Perhaps he rehearsed."

Annie was seeing the "I quite admired" writ large. Here was someone who appeared to have liked Grossman's style, or perhaps was envious of his persona.

She didn't expect that a man who didn't want notes of any kind would carry one of the slightly clunky phones that were issued to administrators. He might have had his own, however. "And did you hear from him, otherwise?" she asked.

This time there was a slight hesitation, and then Roberts shook his head.

"Yes? Was there anything unusual in your not hearing from him?"

"Not necessarily. However, when it was a late meeting, he often called from the Governor's Office, and before he went home. He required the legislative liaison, his secretary and I to stay while such meetings were in progress, in the event that he wanted information, and he would call to tell us to go home. He didn't call."

"So, how did you know when you could go home?" Annie saw from where the hesitation came. Roberts made a decision to have people leave, and Commissioner Grossman hadn't called to say that was okay. She added to her emerging picture of Grossman that he could make subordinates nervous from the grave. Morgue. She waited while Roberts constructed an answer.

"I called the Governor's scheduler, and he told me the Co had left. I assumed that that meant..." Roberts paused, then shrugged, as if finally remembering that it hardly mattered any longer if he assumed something. "I told the women to go home, and I tried his mobile phone but he didn't answer, which is what happens when he's talking to someone or has turned it off. Or left it in his desk. (That's where it was, by the way. The JPD detective took it.)" Roberts looked about for a moment, shook his head and restarted his narrative. "I tried again 15 minutes later, and five minutes after that, and then I went home. If he had been coming back here, he'd have been here by then."

That was quite a number of things to digest. Annie nodded and made a few notes, then translated it back to him for verification. "You and other key staff were asked to be here by the phone during such meetings, and you were here because of that. You expected him to call. He didn't call. You tried calling him and determined that he had left the meeting. What time was that?"

"A little after 6:00. Probably closer to 6:10. I already had my coat on and was actually out in the hall the last time I called. And they said he had left."

He didn't check any notes. He didn't look away to think about it. He had rehearsed his answer to that one, perhaps with Detectives Sullivan or Swearts. He sat quietly until she prompted him to say something else. Not only *The Voice*, but he used time well.

"And you left at…"

"I left at 6:15."

"And when you went to the parking lot, where I noticed your car is next to the Commissioner's slot, did you see anything unusual?"

"No. His truck was gone, but then he had taken that when he went up to the Hill." Roberts stopped for a moment, eyes scanning memory, clicking up and down rows mechanically. "No," he said finally and rather quickly, "nothing."

"Were there other cars in the lot?" Annie didn't need this particularly, but she wanted to see what he did with his eyes in response to the question. It was her own personal lie detector test. Identify what the eyes do when being truthful, recalling, and anything else was...invented?

Same scan. "Yes, I think so. There are always some staff cars in the lot. At the far end, I think. I don't recall any that I would recognize, but then that would not be unusual. Why?" His eyes narrowed a little, and he seemed to become a bit larger in his chair.

Annie was beginning to see how he dealt with staff. Deceptively mild to deceptively dangerous in one tiny move. He was probably neither, except that he certainly had the power to hire and fire, and give and take away money, which was not to be ignored in this line of business. Paranoia and politics were closely related.

"No particular reason. At this stage of the investigation we're looking for anything that anyone close to the deceased might notice as out of the ordinary."

"So you have no suspects?" Those lizard eyes again.

"Did I say that?" Annie looked at her notes, as though she was checking, but disinterested in the answer. "In your recollection, did Commissioner Grossman ever vary from the behavior of calling when he left the Hill on any previous occasion?"

Roberts thought about this one. He tilted back in his chair for a bit, and he took his eyes off her for the longest time since she had been talking with him. He stared at a point on the wall over Annie's shoulder, with such intensity that she really wanted to see what he was looking at. Probably just a picture of a fish, she thought. She expected that he was back, in his mind, to whether he should have gone home or not. It was possible that he felt somehow guilty, that if he hadn't left, he could have helped his boss in some way to avoid the murder. But it was also possible that he was only interested in framing his response in a way which made him look like he was a zealous, committed public employee. Innocent of any wrongdoing, just working his brain to the bone.

"I don't recall specifics, but there have been times. And I can tell you..." He stopped, as though hauling himself up short. "That's of no matter. Did you have other questions of me?" He was all brisk business, all of a sudden.

Finally, the smallest hint at something which was behind the careful responses. "Mr. Roberts, what were you about to say?" Annie asked in her least threatening voice.

He sighed, sat forward as though suddenly tired. "I suppose it doesn't matter now, does it. If I hadn't thought it likely that he would have had no further need of us, I'd have been here all night." He didn't look at Annie now. He knew, because he had apparently well developed interpersonal radar, that Annie was going to ask him what he was talking about, and it gave her, again, the feeling that this part of the conversation was rehearsed, staged. But she decided to play it out, though it might only tell her more about Roberts and his desire to be in control of the interaction.

"Was that frequent?"

"He expected staff to be on call, yes. If they were in town." He gave that slight smile again. "He expected them to be in town."

"Was he a difficult person to work for?" Annie knew it was pressing her luck, but what the heck.

He still rested on his elbows on the desk, but he stiffened. "I don't think my personal opinion is of any importance on that topic. 'Difficult' is highly subjective and individual." Roberts was all business and distance, but the lizard man was gone. Steel man, busy man, organization man, all were kicking in. "Those of us who are lifetime employees of state government have learned to adjust to the styles of a variety of Commissioners. The Co described himself as a highly competent steward of the state's wildlife resources. If his management style was brusk, which you will no doubt hear, it was also businesslike and professional."

Annie knew that you didn't get much out of organizationspeak, that it was designed to be offputting. But she understood that even Roberts thought the dead Commissioner was a sonofabitch to work for. That would be about as much as she was likely to get from him. Investigate the calls, how long it took Roberts to get home, tie up any loose ends there, but Annie didn't expect the liontamer, here, had killed the lion. They needed each other. She wanted Roberts to help her identify gazelles with an agenda, personal or familial, because that's where her sense of this crime told her to go next.

"I'd like to ask you some questions about Department employees who might have a reason to dislike the Commissioner." Deputy Commissioner Roberts was prepared for this shift, which, since "going postal" had become common in American English, was probably what he had expected Annie to ask about in the first place. He announced his preparation by, sliding the paper on his desk toward her, and sitting back, with his hands relaxed, but folded, in front of him.

"This is a list of the employees who have been terminated, or who have resigned, during the Commissioner's tenure. Detective Sullivan called to say that you'd like to have it. Of course, we aren't prepared to open any personnel records without a subpoena, but these are a matter of public record."

Annie had been expecting him to say, "I don't think this is a productive line of investigation," or something like that, but he did not. No telling why, she mused. She asked the thing that was on her mind and her agenda, "Do you know of any person on this list, or any other 'list,' who at anytime threatened the Commissioner's life?"

"No." He smiled that little smile. "Mine has been threatened a time or two over the years."

"By anyone on this list?" Annie's turn to smile a little smile.

"As a matter of fact, yes. The third person down. I filed a complaint with the AG's office against her and her husband, because he stood to benefit from a contract issued while she was on staff here."

"And under what circumstances was a threat issued?"

"The usual—in tears and on the way out the door. 'If I had a gun I'd shoot him.' No one took it seriously."

"You never know. I see that this person left two years ago, just after Commissioner Grossman was appointed. Is that a coincidence?"

"No. Actually, her husband left the state, and she was just waiting for their house to sell. It sold, and she left. I'm sure she would otherwise still be here."

"So, other than that, this list represents anyone who…"

"Has resigned, been terminated for cause—there's only one of those—or whose position has been eliminated due to budget cuts or reorganization."

"Did anyone on this list have a reason to hold Grossman responsible for the loss of employment?"

For a moment Annie thought Mr. Roberts was actually going to break out into a full smile, but he caught himself. "It would be easier for me to identify for you those who would not. There are four we tried to convince to stay. I'll check them for you here. Ethyl Rubens, retired and moved to Tucson. Mae Thipsin, whose restaurant finally paid all of the bills so she didn't need to get up in the morning. Burton Wertz, who moved over to the University where the work year is considerably shorter and the benefits the same. Carole Bluever, who married a man who had a big sailboat, and went off into the sunset."

"So the rest had some reason to dislike or harbor a grudge against the Commissioner?"

"You can talk to them and see what you can find out. I have a staff meeting coming up in a few minutes. Is there anything else I can help you with?" He was through, and Annie had asked the questions on her list, all but one.

"I'd like to know if there is anyone currently on your staff who has reason to want the Commissioner dead."

He just looked through her, his eyes hooded as though someone had drawn the shades. "Not that I know of," he said. He rose, and walked her to the door of his office. He stepped outside and walked over to a counter, where a small woman with grey hair was busily typing at a computer.

"Ms. Burke? This is Inspector Brewster. She would like to speak with you for a few moments. You may use the Commissioner's conference room. I'll be downstairs in Habitat Restoration."

Annie played with that image for a moment, and he was gone. "After you, Ms. Burke," she said, and they went into the room off the counter's end, and shut the door.

Nadine Burke was a woman of middle age, below-average height, with a layer of pasty plumpness. Her pale blue eyes were large behind old-fashioned bifocal glasses attached to a silver chain around her neck. Her graying blonde hair was curled tightly, in the manner of someone who has lived in the bush where the water is scarce and felt curled hair looked cleaner for longer periods of time. It reminded Annie unaccountably of her mother, for whom the only good permanent was a tight one. Burke wore a gray suit over subdued polka-dotted blouse and a vague perfume. Her only spot of color was her red rain boots, for which she immediately apologized.

"I had to run over to the bank on my break," she said, looking down at her boots--which she had apparently been about to exchange for her shoes left at work--as though in surprise. "How can I help? We're all upset by what has happened. Would you like some coffee?"

"No, thank you," Annie said firmly, to put the woman out of her subservient misery. "I'd just like to ask you a few questions about the last day that you saw the Commissioner."

The woman actually winced. Her eyes darted to the left, down, encountered her errant boots and flipped back up to Annie's face. "All right," she said hesitantly, "but I'm not sure what I could know that would be of any help."

"Sometimes we know things which we don't recognize as helpful, but they turn out to be," Annie said. "First, can you tell me what your relationship was to the Commissioner?"

"I was his secretary," she said, "but I've only been here two weeks."

"And before that you were...?"

"I was the secretary to the previous Commissioner of Education. For the past few months I've been the secretary to the State Board of Education, and I've been assisting the new secretary there in the transition."

"Two weeks. During that time, you have had how many actual days where you worked closely with the Commissioner?"

"Let's see. About five, actually. He was out of town the first week I was here. He hated to travel." She stopped, clearly embarrassed again. "That is, I don't know that really. Caroline Hayes told me, before she left. She was his secretary before me."

She seemed to run out of words, and sat looking at Annie, with her mouth opening and closing in a way that made Annie want to swallow for her. What was making this woman so nervous? *Nadine? Honey, is that you?* "And on the last day you saw him, on Monday afternoon, did you observe anything which was out of the ordinary?"

"I'm not that sure what was ordinary. But Mr. Roberts said he was behaving normally when he left here. I didn't see any suspicious people following his truck…"

Annie watched as Nadine Burke's eyebrows disappeared into her bangs. "You observed him getting into his truck?"

"Yes, because I went to his window to see if he had forgotten his umbrella."

"Okay. Had he?"

"He had his raincoat. He doesn't use an umbrella." When Annie didn't say anything or write anything down, she added, "Mr. Roberts told me. Or a briefcase. I was worried about his papers getting wet, but Mr. Roberts said that wasn't the type of assistance the Commissioner wanted from me." Then she clasped her hands together and waited for further direction.

"On the night in question," Annie said slowly, "Commissioner Grossman left for the meeting, and that was the last contact you had with him?

"Yes, but the last contact I had with him was earlier in the day. He spoke with Mr. Roberts before he left."

"But you were here?"

"Yes, I saw him leave."

"And you didn't hear from him after that?"

"No, but that wouldn't have been unusual. He didn't call me yet."

"And so your last contact was earlier?"

"Yes, after lunch, when we went over his schedule for the week and he gave me several things to schedule, reschedule or cancel."

"And did you notice anything unusual in his demeanor at that time?"

"No."

Nothing by way of expansion, just no. Annie was getting the distinct impression that Burke was not a source of information about anything related to the Commissioner yet, and that was in some ways understandable. One week was short to identify anyone's habits. "So, he talked with Roberts, picked up his coat, and left, without an umbrella or briefcase. You saw no one approach him when he got into his truck. Is that about it?"

"Yes. I'm sorry I can't be of more help."

On an impulse which fed out of Nadine Burke's discomfort with talking about the Commissioner's habits, Annie asked, "You said that Caroline Hayes was his last secretary?"

"Yes, for two months."

"Two months. And before Caroline Hayes?"

"Let me see. I think someone told me Jennifer Fouts. Or Barbara Smalley. I forget the order." The woman was now looking at her hands, but she no longer seemed nervous. "Mr. Roberts has been here for several years."

Annie understood. "Thank you, Ms. Burke."

Walking down the stairwell, Annie thought about what she knew now. Several secretaries in the past year. Roberts the only survivor of an inner office which turned over frequently. Maybe it was nothing. She was still carrying the list of potentially disgruntled employees. She stopped and added Caroline Hayes, Jennifer Fouts and Barbara Smalley to the bottom.

Two important pieces of information--maybe three. Yes, there should be an overcoat, and there was not. Yes, everyone here, with the possible exception of the "Deputy Co" was afraid, still, of their boss. And Grossman avoided technological evidence. Strange, that.

Chapter Nine

Monday, October 14, 1998 - 4:00 p.m.

Fortunately, Juneau was really a small town, no matter how many school children in the nation could recite its name. In fact, it was just about the smallest, if not the smallest capitol, and the only one no other city in the state could reach by car. Annie thought about it. What an airline bonanza. And what a way to hide the political infighting.

Still, for a small town, there were a lot of dumpsters. Annie wanted to revisit them and look at their surrounding areas in the dark. She was pretty sure that most of the dumpster reconnaissance had been related to the contents of the pile in which the Commissioner was embedded, so to speak, and not to the dumpster itself as a potential crime scene. It was getting dark. Actually, full dusk. That was good. Annie had a list of the dumpster sites, and sat in her car eliminating those in an area other than the government buildings. She began, one by one, visiting the dumpsters, taking special note of those which were secluded enough for someone to dump their own garbage, and then dump a Commissioner.

She had already eliminated the bins behind the federal building and Copy Center. She cruised the bins behind the Capitol itself and eliminated them for their openness to windows and people leaving for home. Several bins between the state office building and the human services building were possibilities, though, again, there were streets on both ends, and they were not what you would call secluded.

The building which was shared by Education and the Permanent Fund Dividend Corporation had dumpsters right on the street, and next to the Fire Department. Again, not a good place. Community and Regional Affairs had a little alley behind it, so that was one to ponder, and look at from several angles. If he had followed Rearson back to CRA, and they had gotten into it? She needed to talk to Rearson.

When she got to the dumpsters behind the Department of Fish and Game, she found herself wanting to stop looking, which was dangerous at this stage. But here were dumpsters a block off the big, multi-lane main street, facing away from people and out onto the Gastineau Channel. Further, between it and Egan Drive was the Department of Labor, which effectively blocked anyone from seeing the dumpsters from all of the areas of traffic except the public parking lot, already emptying this early.

One could see down to the dumpsters from the bridge over to Douglas Island, but in the dark, and rain, one wouldn't be able to see clearly enough to distinguish someone putting a body into the dumpsters there. Annie used the chunky phone John had loaned her to call him from the car. She told him she was sitting in front of Fish and Game and had a couple of questions before she came up to see him.

"What do you know about these dumpsters?" she asked.

"Well," he said, somewhat distracted by something, "people come there, even at night, to run their dogs along the edge. It's one of the few places close to town where there aren't cars. Also, that shop over there is maintenance for the borough, and the police cars come in here to gas up."

"That's not good. Would it be common for a police car to check on anyone who was parked here?"

"Nope, I don't think so. I can ask them."

"Let's do that. This place has the kind of seclusion it would take for someone to heft a big guy into the bin, and it also has the kind of seclusion necessary for John Q. Citizen to dump his lawn clippings and fruitloop boxes. See you in a bit; I'm through with my day's interviews."

"Good enough. I'll be in the back desk by my office. My computer won't work."

Annie drove back out to the valley on Egan Drive, which already had what passed for heavy traffic. People in Juneau, she recalled, referred to it as "the rush minute." At 4:30, it was dusk, with low clouds, rain and early automobile lights vying for dominance. *I love a rainy night,* she hummed. There were lots of songs about rain. Like the Del Shannon one, ostensibly about runaway girlfriends, but what did he keep talking about? Rain. She bet she could name 20 rain songs. She was to eight when she saw the new police station. It was on the K-Mart exit, though the K-Mart itself was closed, and Annie turned onto the loop road, adding "Listen to the Rhythm of the Falling Rain," to the list at number nine, and relaxing her mind by free associating. What had happened to the K-Mart? Had the building itself been a blue-light special? Had she ever bought a blue-light special? Two blue shirts--local slang for state troopers—were stationed in Juneau. She needed to read their report. So much for relaxation. She must be into the case, now. "Yes, K-Mart shoppers," she said quietly, "crime *is* down in Alaska. But over on aisle three, we have a special in homicides, where you'll find everything you need to bump off...your boss." That sounded right, after this afternoon's interviews.

The police station, when it appeared, was...blue. A bargain. She drove around to the back, past the new jail compound, and parked in the lot with the other nondescript four-doors in shades of brown. She could see the compound with the 20 prison cells, and looked reflexively back against the cleft of the mountain that held the state prison.

This might be the last frontier, she thought as she walked up the back steps to the employee entrance, but there was plenty of conventional crime. Three to one, most murder victims were men. And the number one motive was revenge. Most victims died at home, but this was followed hard upon by those who died while working. Annie didn't think this was random. And she was beginning to think this wasn't a nice man who was dead, and the list of people who might have wanted him gone was potentially long, and most of those had worked for him.

Lt. Sullivan's office was down a hallway, past the chief's office, the receptionist, and the dispatcher. Annie could see the squad room of desks, and a pile of boxes still being unpacked, the building was that new. Two uniforms were talking beside one of the desks, and another was doing paperwork at a computer. Sullivan was at a desk in front of an office which he apparently shared with Swearts. He was alone, also staring intently at a computer screen. Whatever he was doing involved swearing.

Annie reflected how offices had changed once computers and the nascent cell phones came on the scene. These days, you could walk through a room of employees, all doing the same thing, and no one would look up at you, it was that compelling to stare into the box. Me too, Annie thought wryly. I even carry mine with me.

"Annie," Sullivan said, quickly closing the screen on the form he was completing. He gestured behind him vaguely: "come in." He gestured again to a chair under the window "Well?"

"Did anyone like this guy?"

"Not that we talked to. Of course, everyone was 'shocked,' and 'saddened.' But no one cried. I take that back, no one he worked with cried."

Family. Annie filed that away for the moment. "That was what I was afraid of, and I've only talked to four people. I need to see the family and the dumpsters."

Sullivan raised his eyebrows. He'd worked with Annie before, and he knew that she had several tracks running in her head at the same time, but he had been trying all afternoon to simultaneously unpack, get the computer system from the old office morphed into the new one, and pick up the calls and pieces of cases which had emerged in the past week but had been put on the back burner. It must have showed in his expression.

"Sorry," Annie said. "Okay. I talked, as you suggested, to the budget gal, and the Commissioner of Natural Resources, the Deputy at Fish and Game, and one terrified new secretary. You know," she mused, "the whole political-speak thing down here is like every conversation is in code."

"Yup. If you aren't careful, you start understanding it. Anything?"

"I think we wouldn't have to look too far for motive, depending upon what the ME's report says. Let me ask you, John, did you have any sense when you looked at the body that the wound in the back was possibly caused by something in the garbage that he, uh, that the truck, you know, forced into his body as part of the compacting process?"

"No. Clean, thin blade, obviously a knife. I think the ME is going to tell us it wasn't the killing wound, either."

Annie nodded. "Why shoot and stab. Unless it's symbolic. I'm thinking this is revenge. Somebody who knew him, maybe got "backstabbed" by him. So, the interviews with people who were fired by him since he got here could be pretty important. I get the impression he was exceptionally callous in letting people go."

"It's pretty common for new commissioners to clean house wherever they can, especially when the governor was a different party than the last one. Anyone who can be associated too closely with the previous administration is on the block, but the state budget has been cut a lot in the last two administrations. Not too many surplus people in most departments. And a strong union, as you know. So, that's where you're going next? Recent fires?"

"Depends on what the ME says. Too early to have a strategy like that, but I want to talk to anyone who had direct access to him that night, before their recollections become some kind of party line."

"I hear you on that."

"Appreciate the interviews you did, John. I need to talk to his wife next, I think, and then try to figure out, if we can, where the body entered the, uh, garbage system."

"Yeah. I'm glad you're here, because that got us nowhere fast. Want coffee?"

Something in Sullivan's tone reminded Annie that this case had been investigated, hard, for a week. "No, thanks. You guys haven't been in here long, have you." Annie changed the subject. There were no jurisdictional issues, really, but that didn't mean John Sullivan, or his partner, needed to have their face put into the lack of progress.

"Two weeks. We have a brand new building, but with the budget restrictions, we're just barely able to set up shop again—no money to buy chairs, for example. The damn computer system is going to be great, but we're in line to have everything hooked up, and no one has had training yet in using the new stuff so we've got the old stuff, in some cases, sitting right next to it."

"See that. Hope I can help. You know…whoever did this could be long gone or a block away." Annie broached the subject which was lurking under all of the methodical investigations open in the state.

"Right. We're a sieve. Easy to get in, easy to get out. The night he was killed, there were six bush flights to six different villages; two ferries, one to Sitka, one to Haines; four Alaska Airlines flights, two to Seattle, two to Anchorage; and the last cruise ship left. That doesn't speak to private boats and planes. So, still basically the same. Most of those have some passenger manifest, but no real identification requirement yet, except on the jets."

"I'll keep doing the legwork. I'll see the widow tomorrow. I assume that she's still in town?"

"Yeah. She didn't go to Anchorage. They had two boys and a girl. She's here with them."

"Right. I'll need some names there, and contact numbers, if you have them. And I'd like to keep the car another day. I need to see the dumpster areas. And I want to go out to the Dump again," she paused to look out the window, which showed that the Dump wasn't that far away.

"The widow is Carolyn. She's an elementary teacher. There are two boys, Shannon and Jesse, and a girl, Penny. Mom and boys were in Sitka at some athletic event when Grossman was killed. They came back on the ferry the next day. Daughter was with a friend."

"You have the phone number in your notes? I'll call her and ask if I can come and see her in the morning. I don't think I need to talk to the boys yet. I'll play that by ear. What was your take when you talked to her? Did she have any ideas?"

Sullivan flipped through a note pad, wrote the number on a piece of paper and gave it to Annie. "No, she was in shock. Ditto the boys. To hear them tell it, this was the nicest man in the world, with no enemies except those which might naturally come to a man who was 'the boss.' They were clueless. Looked to be clueless. I don't think it was in any way an act, but you see what you think." Sullivan looked at Annie, who was staring off out the window.

"You never know, do you," she said. "You never know. Still, that's not that unusual, people being one person at home and another at work. Or maybe we'll find that he's different with women. Most of the little comments, most of the affect, came from or about interactions with men. So maybe that's it."

They both mused on that a moment. "Okay, off to the dumpsters, I guess," Annie said, "before the rain starts."

They both laughed at that. It wasn't really funny.

"Where do you have his truck?" Annie asked.

"It's in the first bay beside the three black and whites. We had a forensic guy go through it, and packaged up samplings of hair--this was a hairy guy, and a curly, and the headrest of the truck is covered in that and dog hair. Possibly the dirtiest front seat for a guy who goes to work in a suit and tie that I've ever seen."

The Detective sat back, his eyes bouncing about until they lit upper right on his forehead. His chair slapped forward. "Where was his overcoat? What kind of person goes anywhere in Juneau without a coat? Goddammit, Annie, that's embarrassing. When you go see the wife tomorrow, see if you can get a description of how he left the house the last time she remembers, and any details you can get on a coat."

John was fairly agitated with embarrassment, but Annie just smiled. "Yeah, the Budget Director specifically saw him put on a coat. So, where's the coat, and why wasn't it on him. What if the killer took it off so the knife would be more effective? What if it came off when he was being hoisted into the dumpster and is somewhere in the garbage? What if someone saw it on the edge of the dumpster and just took it? Or, of course, what if the killer took it and still has it? What if it's in a trash can in the airport? John, it's early. We'll look for it now. It may actually be somewhere in the garbage heaps, you know. Move on. So he was found with no coat. What about a suit jacket?"

"Yeah, suit jacket, tie, white shirt. Made it easy to see the stab wound. The Coroner packed everything in plastic and sent it up to Anchorage. Do you want to go look at the truck?"

"Can't hurt."

They walked through the building to a loading area of sorts, and across to the garage. The truck was in a bay that had big lights and four yellow posts with crime scene tape wound around them, presumably to remind everyone to stay away from it.

Annie put gloves on and opened the driver's door. There was hair everywhere, and dried mud, and some old cassette tapes crammed into the center console. She looked at the seat, way back like a big guy would have left it, and the tilt of the steering wheel, likewise. She walked around to the passenger door, and that seat was mostly dog hair, woven into the seat cover. She looked down at the floor of the passenger side.

"Did they take out the floor mat?" She asked casually. "Was there anything on it?"

"More hair. Long and short. You might see if you can get some dog hair from the house, when you see the wife. We bagged all of the samples that were loose, but we don't know how many dogs they have. Some of the hairs were pretty long." John was interested in what Annie was looking at, bent over with her little pocket flashlight and her nose about six inches from the filthy carpet on the passenger side. He looked over her shoulder.

"What's that?" he asked, almost disinterested. Forensics had looked at the car, but no one knew if it was in any way associated with the murder, and how would they ever?

Annie carefully pulled a long, curly hair loose from the base of the shift lever on the hump between the two floor areas. She said, "humor me here. Do you have an evidence bag on you?"

"Happens I do. Is that another hair?"

"It's among many, but this one is probably one of his, because dog hair is all over the seat, and it's short and thick, like a Shepard. So why was one of his hairs wedged under the shift lever casing? Huh." Annie put the hair in the baggie and left it with John, but something was poking at her. She walked around to the headrest on the driver's side, and looked at the hairs there. Some looked the same, some didn't.

"I think," she said, "that this vehicle has a secret. I don't know why I think that, but I do. Probably just a red herring, because he probably shed as much as the dogs. I know I do. Thousands of hairs a day. Have your tech try to get me a sample of every type of hair she found in the front seat, including those on the headrest, and I'll get you some dog hair--don't think that will be hard. I'll probably have it all over me by noon tomorrow."

Chapter Ten

Monday, October 14, 1998 - 6:30 p.m.

At 6:30 that evening, Annie drove into the big public parking lot across from the Department of Labor and the Department of Fish and Game. These buildings were before her. A little access road completely encircled Fish and Game, going down the Gastineau Channel in a horseshoe shape around the building. She drove down the channelside drive, following a "one way" sign, and found herself in full dark off the southwest corner of the Fish and Game building, at the edge of the rock bric a brac, overlooking the water. Across the Channel, narrow at this point, the lights on Douglas Island were just visible through huge trees.

She put the car in park, leaving the motor running and the lights on so someone didn't come around the little drive and rear end her. She got out and walked to the edge of the Channel. Below her some thirty yards, the tide was out. Huge chunks of granite reinforced the Channel's edge in both directions. She turned slowly, following rock shapes to the west and north with her eyes, past the Borough maintenance sheds and under the bridge to Douglas Island. Then with equal, methodical care, she looked to the east and south, taking it into her memory. The boulders ran on to the southeast around the little cove, defining the curve of Egan Drive, and under the Coast Guard buildings, the first on the wharf that skirted downtown. Standin' *on the dock of the bay*, hopefully not *wastin' time*.

Because it was low tide, the rocks stretched down an exposed spit and away to the dark water, wet surfaces reflecting city lights, harbor lights, automobile lights, street lights, giving the impression of illumination where there really was little. It was quite dark. Over a block away and trending around to the downtown area, the brightly illuminated walk on the Channel edge of Egan Drive glistened as though newly varnished, but neither this nor the safety lights from the parking lot behind her reached the spot where she stood. She could barely see her feet.

She turned back toward the buildings. The Department of Labor, nicknamed "the plywood box" for its simple construction and T1-11 siding, was to her right, closer to the main road. What a seriously boring, if not actually ugly, building. Some lights on. Three floors. Probably a janitor on the top floor. She watched the lighted windows for a moment, but she saw no one moving.

The Department of Fish and Game, before her, was shaped like a "T", with the top bar abutting the Channel right before her, and the longer part of the letter stretching toward the big, public parking lot. Beyond the parking lot, the rise of the bridge. Beyond that, she knew, was a shallower harbor full of small boats, any view of which was blocked from here by the bridge.

The configuration of Fish and Game created an alcove for a fancy public entrance on the big parking lot to the north, and a second alcove, which was apparently meant to be a staff entrance, in the back. Tucked into the crossbar of the Tee, on the Channel's edge, were a few secluded parking spots. So no one would try to go down the tiny alley between the buildings to park in the VIP spots, apparently. Everything here was political. It was a one-way drive so no one would enter from between the two buildings, on the single-lane drive. The parking places back here angled toward the Channel. To get into them properly, you had to obey the signs and come in around the Fish and Game building.

There wasn't much space back here. You could easily throw a rock from the Fish and Game building into the Channel. The narrow drive left only a thin strip of gravel along the outer edge, and a thinner strip of vegetation, on which were perched three picnic tables. Presumably, in nicer weather, employees came out to have lunch overlooking the water. In the dark, even with the reflecting lights, the wet tables looked precipitously close to the edge. Annie stood next to one, looking down the Channel, then back toward town, and finally behind her at the two-story office building.

The place where Annie stood was secluded on the north and west and open to the Channel on the south and east. But to see her standing there, especially at night, one would need a spotting scope from Douglas Island, or to be walking along Egan Drive in the one brief stretch before bushes between Labor and Egan Drive would obscure any vision from that direction. And you would have to know what you were looking for, because the night and shadows would distort shapes. Secluded. And dark. Annie walked back to car, and moved it to the VIP slots at the building's staff entrance. Slick. You came around the building and were perfectly positioned to head into the Commissioner's parking place. Two small floods and the doorway lights provided illumination for the parking spaces, prominently labeled "Commissioner Fish and Game," "Deputy Commissioner Fish and Game," "Director Commercial Fisheries," "Director Habitat and Restoration," "Director Subsistence." It also provided these august persons, presumably, with simultaneous convenience and reassurance of the order of things. What wasn't political here?

She looked around carefully before she got out. There was quite a bit of light, suddenly, especially in comparison with where she had been. The other side of Fish and Game was dark. No lights back there at all. But here...? How would a potential murderer ambush Commissioner Grossman in such an open place? Could have been someone he knew, and they could have approached the truck smiling, or in a businesslike way that meant they had something to tell him. Did he then get out of the truck, as though he was ready to greet or shake hands with someone, and...what? How was he subdued? Could you approach a truck such as his surreptitiously, and when he got out, hit him from behind? Would the ME find head or neck trauma? She would have to wait on that, but this was a possible scenario. She didn't like the light, but the secluded lot was worth thinking about.

Was the truck locked when they found it? Was there a finger print on the key fob other than

Grossman's? Did they have a key fob? She took out her tape recorder, recorded her impression and recorded the questions. She stopped and made more notes, ticking through more questions that had come to her since she had gotten here. Parking lot questions. Access questions. Opportunity questions. Forensic artifacts of the murder...where were they?

Along the back of the Labor building to her right, as she looked toward the big parking lot down the little drive, was a small chain link enclosure housing what looked like heating and cooling units. And next to that, against the wall, was a single dumpster. She walked over to the dumpster, and stood in front of it. As she looked about, a police car suddenly passed not 20 yards from her, going toward the maintenance sheds and gasoline pumps that were the western border of the parking lot, next to the Channel. The passing took two seconds, during which the officer did not look toward the dumpster or her.

Annie walked back past her car, around the Channel end of the Fish and Game on a little sidewalk, to the end of the building where she could see back toward the big parking lot, and see where the police car had gone. She could see two mounds of sanding material, the flood lights in front of the maintenance facilities, and the roofs and backs of the buildings themselves. And arching over and behind, the bridge, with its constant traffic. She did her distance reckoning methodically, because she wasn't good at it, and counted football fields. Two hundred yards to the bridge.

She retraced her path down along the backside of Fish and Game, this time on foot, immediately aware of the dark again. She stopped in front of the two big dumpsters she had passed coming in. She looked over at the maintenance sheds. The tail lights of the police car, apparently fueling at the pumps on the far side, was now just visible. She turned to face the dumpsters, back to the Channel. She looked left and right, pondering the hidden feeling of this place. No source of exterior light, beyond a dim bulb over a maintenance door behind the dumpsters. Could someone have been waiting in there?

Public vehicles fueled at all hours from the self-service pump in the Maintenance compound; to reach the pump, they had to come through the public parking lot. It should be an open, public place, and maybe in the daylight it was. But at the moment, these dumpsters on the back side of the building were in nearly total darkness. There were no exterior floods on this side, and little light from the office windows directly above--from which it would be difficult to see straight down in any case.

The police car, apparently finished fueling, made a loop around the Maintenance buildings and started out of the compound. Reflexively, Annie stepped back behind one of the dumpsters, and the car drove past the end of the building toward Egan Drive. The officer couldn't have seen her unless he had been looking for her, she was sure of that.

Annie walked again back toward the spot where she had looked out over the Channel, and on around to a small area of lawn and five parking spots. Standing there, humming *saw Aunt Mary comin' and he jumped back in the Alley,* she was fully hidden from the maintenance sheds and only possibly (and dimly) visible by anyone driving along Egan Drive on the other side of Labor. She looked at the smaller dumpster, the Commissioner's parking place, the continuation of the narrow drive up between the buildings to the big parking lot.

It was a toss up which dumpster was more likely. She liked the dark, hidden option, but the Commissioner's truck had been here, in its normal spot. If the Commissioner had gotten out of his truck here, and someone had taken him here, this nearest dumpster made the most sense. But it was, because of the lights by the alley and those at the back of the building, also the most open. The Commissioner was a big man. To have dragged him from his truck, and over to the dumpster, and then to get him into it, required several minutes of bright (relatively speaking) vulnerability. But, possible.

The dark around the two Fish and Game dumpsters was broken by the wavy glitter of lights off water and wet pavement, but it was still dark. She liked the secretive positioning, and she wasn't bothered that Grossman's truck had been parked in his normal place. These more hidden dumpsters were calling her.

As if on cue, she saw lights reflecting down the little drive that came past the dumpsters to where she stood. Headlights staring out onto the Channel, at first moving and then still. Someone had started towards where she stood, and stopped. She walked back along the narrow sidewalk and peered around the building's edge. A blue, or black, Toyota pickup was stopped next to the dumpsters. A dark-haired man in a rain jacket opened the back of the truck's shell and took out a black bag, which he threw into the dumpster. He didn't even look up at the building. Annie calculated the odds that he wasn't a janitor, especially at this early hour—and that he wasn't an employee, who might have dumping rights from a number of angles. She squinted and made out the front license plate. CKJ 785. She took a small pad of paper from her pocket and jotted it down. She stood next to the wall of the building as the man got back in his truck and drove past her, between the two buildings, and out. He, too, did not look in her direction.

Interesting. Since the dumpsters had prominent labels warning against illegal dumping, one had to conclude that even this early in the evening, with a chance driveby from a city police car a random possibility, at least one person thought it was safe to pitch his garbage in anyway. It was Alaska, after all. A dumpster was probably considered an attractive public nuisance, placed to lure the unsuspecting.

Such a dumpster, perhaps this dumpster, lured an otherwise apparently careful murderer. So if this was the dumpster, then how did the Commissioner come around to these dumpsters? In his truck? He stopped to throw something in? His meeting notes? His household garbage? Or did he go to his parking place, and was there subdued and dragged around the end of the building? Suppose someone waited here, by the more shadowed dumpsters? But if someone waited there, what if he hadn't stopped? Arlo Guthrie, asking, in "The Pause of Mr. Claus," how the FBI thought of all of these questions in such a short time, made its niggling way into Annie's conscious. She shook it off. It wasn't even a song, for heaven's sake.

Annie walked on out to the public parking lot, across the front of the building, and back down the alley to her car, but nothing additional caught her attention. So, if the Commissioner stopped there, at the back dumpsters, someone had moved the truck around to the spot where it was found. Which might mean there was evidence in the truck. Or not. This part was hazy, in comparison to her growing conviction that the Fish and Game dumpsters were The Spot.

She got in her car, made a few notes on the pad she had left on the seat so it wouldn't get wet, and was just getting ready to leave when two Labs, one dark and one golden, came sprinting around the Channel edge. Annie watched them run almost frantically to and fro along the rocks, pause to prodigiously relieve themselves, and then bound toward a young man with a beard who came from behind the building.

Then they all disappeared again. Annie started up and decided to follow them in that direction. As she drove around the corner, the owner was standing against the open back end of a pickup, watching the dogs as they snuffled along under the picnic tables. He continued to watch the dogs as she went by, slowly passing between him and the dumpsters, moving toward the parking lot.

This was interesting. People came here after work to run their dogs. To dump their garbage. To fuel their official cars. Nobody seemed to look around, no one seemed to be furtive or stealthy, even when breaking the law. Apparently it was not at all unusual for cars to come and go here in the evening. There were still lights on in top story offices, but there was no evidence that there was still anyone on that floor other than the night janitors. Even if there were, who would look out at, or take particular notice of, traffic here by the dumpsters, of the dumping itself—dogs or humans--if it was a such a common occurrence?

On the other hand, she saw more clearly now, if someone had been waiting to ambush the Commissioner at his parking spot between the buildings, it was too open, too light, with a high probability of someone going by at this time on a rainy night. She didn't know whether the Commissioner would have stopped, even if someone had hailed him, so it made sense that he had driven here.

Or the murderer had followed him from the State Office Building's parking garage, bumped into him here so he would stop. She didn't remember a dent in the bumper of the big truck. She made a note. Stagger Lee, lurking in the shadows, Labs running every which way and local dumpster felons heaving ho. But that didn't feel right, even though it was logical. What murderer would want a big, irritated target coming toward him, already on the defensive?

Didn't make sense. It felt like the possibilities were mutating and populating, rather than falling away to illuminate the truth. Perhaps she was getting ahead of herself, but at least she now knew how some personal garbage might have gotten into the pile holding the Commissioner's body. And that, all by itself, might point them to this spot.

There was a scattering of cars in the public lot, some in the shadows, some under the lights. Annie made note of the license plates on a separate sheet of her notepad that she could tear off and give to Sullivan. Someone working late might have been working late that night as well. Might have seen someone, or something. At this point, any possibility had to be pursued. But the type of call a uniform could make.

She drove from the parking lot out onto Egan Drive, and then turned onto the side street which led to the grocery store. The A & P (which here, unlike in the lower 48, stood for "Alaskan and Proud") was brightly lit, the lot full of cars and the store full of people. Annie went up and down the aisles, filling her cart with enough staples for a week's stay, but which could be frozen if she left earlier. She got a ready-baked chicken from the deli, and a generous tray of green salad, checked out with her purchases, and headed for the apartment, scenes of the two remote dumpsters playing and replaying in her mind.

Chapter Eleven

Tuesday, October 15, 1998 - 9:00 a.m.

Annie stood outside of the Capitol Building, humming *raindrops keep fallin' on my head* and looking at the panorama of Juneau's "commercial" district, the Channel, the Cruise Ship docks, the Alaskan Cultural Center, the picturesque houses glued to the edges of the mountain that had Juneau's back. It was raining lightly. She didn't put up her little umbrella, because light rain wasn't rain, exactly, but being in the fog.

She was meeting John, who was going to take her on Grossman's route: across the street from the Capitol Building to the loading bay behind the State Office Building, through the door on the loading dock, down the hall to the elevators, down to the third floor parking garage.

This was the path the Commissioner must have taken after leaving the meeting.

It was just about the only way he could take to get to his truck. To get to the parking garage without using this route, you could have to go a block up, around the State Office Building, down two blocks to driveway openings to the parking levels. All of which, linguistically, helped Annie to understand why everyone went through the State Office Building. How would you explain this to someone standing in front of the strange, hybrid shape that was, literally, built around a hill? That it was two buildings and a number of levels of parking, but you couldn't see it from here, you had to start somewhere else...

When Annie had asked for the "retrace his steps" tour, John had just shrugged. They agreed that neither had learned a great deal from this tactic, but often enough there was some missed clue that was right there, in the mind of a witness, on the tiles, on the wall, in the elevator. Grossman may have walked right past a janitor, or a government employee trying to finish a report, as it was budget season. It was also remotely possible that he was killed here, in the restroom or elevator, wasn't it? Just not likely. Too open, too many other people coming to their cars and trucks from similar, or the same, meetings.

Perhaps it was a waste of time. She just couldn't afford not to do everything that might have produced some positive result in a previous investigation. She tried to get her head into it. You came out the door of the Capitol Building, though no one remembered seeing you. You put your collar up, because, everyone said, "he doesn't wear a hat, and he laughs at umbrellas." So, in the coat, but no hat...where was the coat? Annie took out her little pocket recorder, which made more sense than drying the pages of her notepad with a hairdryer every night. Find the coat.

She abandoned thinking about the coat with some difficulty, wrenching her mind around to the dark in which he must have been walking, given the time they said he left the meeting. With his collar up, looking at the street because of the wind and rain, and walking briskly about a block to the loading dock behind the State Office Building. The hill was so steep that the loading dock came out on the sixth floor of the building. The parking garage was only accessible by a special bank of elevators that originated on this floor. The elevators on the public entrance went down to the loading dock floor, but then you had to cross to the other elevators to go down any further, or vice versa to go up to the State Library. If you looked up from where Annie stood, you could see the loading dock, and above it, the glass sky bridge where people this early were walking to or waiting at the latte cart, or standing about in the atrium where the meeting rooms and the Department of Transportation were.

A police car pulled up and John got out. "Can you give me a ride back," he called, and when she nodded, bent and said something to the officer, who waved and drove off. "Got it solved, yet?" he asked, jocular in the morning as he was taciturn in the afternoon. Morning brought possibilities, she supposed.

"Nearly," she said wryly. "I've been thinking that the crime scene could begin here, somehow."

John said nothing. He looked across at the loading dock. "Dark, rain and wind, coat up over his head, maybe, or at least pulled up like horse blinders. Yeah, we talked about that. He was a pretty big man. How would they wrestle him back to the Fish and Game building?"

"What if they didn't?" Annie said, thinking.

"But his truck..."

"What if the killer drove his truck."

John looked at Annie sharply.

"What if the hair fiber on floor was his. His head might have been on the floor."

"Oh geez, Annie, that truck was full of hair."

"Including one on the head rest, I heard. Did you have that analyzed?"

"No root, no DNA, but the lab person who's doing it said it didn't look like a hair."

"John, what if it was a wig hair?" Annie said casually.

"Huh. A wig?"

"Go with me here. Someone in a wig zaps him, drags him to his car, puts him on the floor. Drives to the dumpster, badda bing."

"Huh."

"Let's go look at his parking place again. Do you have gear? I have gloves and a baggie, no camera."

John sighed and looked across to the loading dock. "If we see something, I guess we call back for trace to come photograph it. First we talk to the Admin Deputy."

The Department of Administration had offices on the loading dock floor. They climbed the steps and went in. The door closed behind them with an audible and institutional thunk. Ahead of them, the corridor to the elevators was basically just a lighted tunnel. They walked to the first set of office doors. To the left, a door with half glass announced "Administrative Services," and one to the right, "Mail Room." They went into Administrative Services, and threaded their way among the cubicles to a secretary who fronted the big corner office of Deputy Commissioner A. Cunningham. Though new if you compared her to

Roberts, this woman was reputed to be on a normal path to last, having started in Borough government in a comparable position and having come with the current governor. Time would tell.

John stepped forward and smiled reassuringly at the slightly alarmed-looking secretary. "Is Ms. Cunningham ready to see the cops?" he asked in a warm and friendly voice.

Yes, she was. They were shown in, they all introduced themselves, and Allison Cunningham did the government thing: "I have a meeting in 25 minutes, but until then, I'm all yours! How can I help. Isn't this terrible? I don't know what I can tell you. No one from my staff was still here on that night by 6:00 p.m. But I'll help if I can..."

Annie tried to stem the flow, because 25 minutes was now 20. "Just a few questions, please. We're trying to retrace Commissioner Grossman's steps on the evening we believe he was murdered." That'll shut her up.

It did, though it did not shut her mouth. "He wasn't murdered here; tell me you're not looking at any of my employees. Do I need to..."

"Not looking at anyone, looking at everyone, at this stage," Annie said. "We just need to put together a timeline and a path by which it might have occurred, so we can look more closely."

Deputy Commissioner Cunningham nodded, "Closely," she said quietly. "Tell me how I can assist you."

Annie pulled out her notebook and looked at her notes. "If he left the meeting at around 6:00, and assuming that he came in his vehicle and so would..."

"Go down these elevators to the VIP parking level." Allison Cunningham's eyes were up and making a solar circuit from ear to ear.

That caught Annie's attention. Ms. Cunningham was recalling, scanning her inner surfaces to see the scene.

"Are you remembering something?" Annie asked quietly, not wanting to disturb the rapid eye movement.

"I was trying to remember, from...what?...the 5th through the 7th or so?"

Annie and John were sitting stilly, afraid to react, but John nodded slightly.

"Well," the woman finally said, "there would have been a janitor here, but..."

"Yes," Annie almost screamed. In fact, it came out as a slightly interested, slightly pleasant encouragement.

"Clyde Bunsen." Allison Cunningham said the name with a grimace. "I truly can't tell you if he was on duty or not. We had some real issues with him--he drinks. He sleeps in the restroom.

We're trying to 'document him out,' but these things take time. Yes," she said firmly, making the first eye contact in five minutes, "I suppose you have to talk to Clyde. We already talked to him, and one of those days, he was actually sent home, so it really depends on which night..." She looked at them hopefully, as though they were going to tell her when and where the Commissioner was killed.

Annie was writing. John was writing. "And is Clyde still an employee, given your efforts?" John asked. Receiving a positive, if slow, nod, he said, "and his schedule this week?"

So, Clyde Bunsen was supposed to work Monday night thru Friday night. There was a separate crew, one that cleaned carpets and sanitized bathrooms, that came over the weekend.

Back in the hallway, John called his partner about Clyde, although he vaguely remembered the guy. Skinny, flaky, fuzzy with dope on a good day. Didn't drive, went everywhere on a bicycle. Might have access to his girlfriend's car. Lived over on Douglas. There was a low-rent housing complex over there, and John had a vague recollection of some drug bust, where the cops came back with stories. John got transferred to a clerical, asked for the file on that bust to be put on his desk. The information might give the leverage often needed to get unwilling witnesses to be candid. For whatever it might be worth, they had to interview Clyde Bunsen.

"Hardly sounds like he could muscle Grossman around," Annie said.

"You know," John mused, "We have spent so much time on the dumpster, and the Dump, and the meetings, and the truck, we haven't gotten over here much. That's what you're thinking, isn't it. Could have started here. Would have, in most crimes."

Annie didn't want to offend John, who was a good detective and worked hard. "No harm," she said. "If you hadn't done that, we'd be out there doing it now. Just expanding the search, since we haven't got any other leads. Probably nothing. We should come back one of the next couple of nights, around 6:00, and see if Clyde is doing his thing and remembers Commissioner Grossman walking by. If he does, that's that, and it was an idea, is all."

They went down the hall, past a door labeled "janitor's closet" and the men's and women's restrooms. Annie went into the women's restroom and looked around. John went into the men's. They guarded the doors and switched, to see if anything seemed unusual. Both restrooms had locking stall doors, wide tiled floors, mirrors, multiple trash cans, and otherwise institutionally unremarkable.

"What is it with government buildings," Annie said.

When she said nothing more, John prompted, "they're...governmental?"

They smelled alike. They absorbed color. They looked cheap. They had too many right angles. Even the restrooms. "Here's what bothers me," Annie said, and smiled to herself when John actually leaned toward her as though there would be a great secret passed between them. "What gives anyone the impression that men like to look at themselves while they pee, and women like to look at themselves when they wash their hands?

"The part that really bothers me is that the doors open in on you, and you can't get out of the stalls. You can't hang your purse up because someone will reach over the top and steal it, but that's where they keep putting the hooks. Seriously. Who takes their coat off to pee, so what's the hook for?"

She was to the elevator, and turned around to see John staring after her, a bemused look on his face. Too much information, she guessed. Oh well. She stood in front of the elevators going up and turned 180 degrees to stand in front of those that, from here, only went down.

"So, these elevators go down to the parking garage, and these come all the way up from the street and go on up to the Library, and beyond?"

Annie gestured and looked at John for conformation.

John nodded. They turned toward the descending elevators and pushed the button. And thought about the layers of fingerprints that appeared to be on the button. Apparently not one of Clyde's jobs.

The elevator came, and grunted and complained them down to the third level, the VIP parking floor. All government elevators needed oiling, Annie thought. The lower garage levels were for the peons and the delivery people, she guessed, and the big guys got to drive "up" the ramp to the only floor open to the outside air. Aside from a too-bright light outside of the opening doors, the garage still looked dim and shadowy. People were coming out of their cars and walking toward the elevators, looking at their PID's, carrying various types of work containers, from archival boxes to briefcases. Staffers. Coming from the farthest spots from the elevator.

John and Annie walked out about four steps, looked up and down the pedestrian path between the cars and the outer wall. They both saw the possibilities immediately. Someone laying on the ground in front of a car--or even moreso in front of a pickup--couldn't be seen by people walking down the garage to their cars on the other side.

"Huh." said Annie.

"I know," John said.

They found Commissioner Grossman's spot. "Commissioner of Fish and Game" in big block letters. In a smaller space beneath the permanent designation, "Grossman," on a plaque with hooks. No one was permanent, even if their position somewhat was. Annie stopped in front of the vacant spot. John looked around. They both looked down. They looked at the cement barrier in front of the parking spot, where the front tires came to rest. They looked at the area by the driver's door, and the passenger's door. It had been a long time since anyone had cleaned this area.

Annie stood up, walked over to the retaining wall, looked out at Juneau, looked down. "I don't know what I expected to see," she muttered. "We need something, but I'm certain this place has a connection to the murder."

"Let's say, for grins, that it does," John agreed, "what might it be? A hair would be gone by now, or too compromised to be of any help..."

"Unless it matches the one on the headrest."

"Yeah. We need to get that back from the lab. Okay, we pick up any hairs we see."

"No, have your crime team come over and sweep this, vacuum it, all the way back to the elevator door. We wait here til they come. Take my car if you need to go. Have them remember the camera."

Annie stood like a tough little guard dog just outside of the parking place. This wasn't it, maybe, but it was the closest they had come, and she knew it. And something else, but she couldn't quite raise that to her consciousness. Let it simmer, she thought. Then it can *drop in and tell us what condition our condition is in.*

Chapter Twelve

Tuesday, October 15, 1998 - 11 a.m.

You always looked at the family first, but this woman sitting on the worn sofa across from Annie, who was perched on the edge of a small side chair, showed only unfeigned grief. Annie had seen every variety of real and manufactured surprise, sadness, disbelieving shock, and knew that if this woman was not devastated by the untimely death of her husband of 16 years, she was the best actress in the galaxy. A dangerous conclusion, but the evidence was before her.

"Mrs. Grossman, I'm so sorry to have to ask you questions at a time like this, but..."

"No, I understand. He would have wanted me to help you in whatever way I could."

The woman looked about, as though there were an apparition only she could see. Nodding briefly, she turned back to Annie and asked, absolute confusion informing her entire posture, "Why would anyone do this? Dick gave his whole life to public service. We moved, we uprooted the children, we just...we just..."

Annie almost registered her inner shock. In the days she had been here, and the people with whom she had talked, this was the first person who had used the Commissioner's first name. No one even referred to the Governor's first name. These power people didn't have first names. Here, he wasn't a celebrity; he was a spouse, a father.

"Take a moment," Annie said softly. "I need to ask you who might have disliked your husband enough to do this."

Eyes red with weeping shifted up, over, down, finally settled on hands clutching one another tightly. "No," she said, "no. He was the boss everywhere he went, so I suppose...no. No one." Then, "Why do you think it was someone who disliked him?"

Tread carefully here, Annie thought, and finally said, "The specifics of the crime, and some of our interviews seem to indicate that it was...personal."

Carolyn Grossman looked up sharply. "What do you mean?" Her voice was stronger, affronted, combative suddenly. How could it be personal to anyone but her? How could it be personal and she not know about it?

Ah, here you are, Annie thought. "We can't say any more at this time. You and the children...boys? were in Sitka? Did Mr. Grossman call you on the evening of his disappearance?"

"My daughter was staying with friends. She didn't want to miss the trip to the museum on Monday. So just the boys and I. Yes, he tried to call. I missed one call and had a message on the home phone. We were in Sitka, in a gymnasium. I had a message from the school secretary that he had tried to call. Then I called his mobile but it went to voicemail. He may not have even had it with him. He hates it. So I went to the pay phone and called our home answering machine, and picked up his message there."

"And what time was that?"

Mrs. Grossman thought about it. "Nearly six, I think. He was finishing some kind of meeting, he said."

"Can I hear the message, please?"

Clearly the widow did not want to share the call. "Can I say no?"

"Technically that wouldn't be helping us, would it," Annie said with a disarming smile. "We are trying to find out if he was nervous or upset about something. We can get a warrant if you like."

"No, I was just curious." Carolyn Grossman almost smiled, but not quite. "Meetings didn't make him nervous or upset. Here." She walked to the message and punched the button in for Annie. Then she went abruptly into the kitchen, saying over her shoulder, "I'll get us some water."

It was strange to hear the dead man's voice. It sounded jocular and firm. *Hon, I just stuck it to another budget meeting. Hope you and the boys are there. Tell them to remember to play hard. That's the only reason you play. Love you. See you tomorrow. Bring dinner on your way home, will ya?*

Huh. *Stop and pick up dinner on your way home* from the ferry terminal after three days with a group of high school boys somehow just fit with what Annie knew about the dead Commissioner from her interviews thus far. A bit of ego to the exclusion of others' needs or feelings.

"Thank you," Annie said. "I would like to ask you not to delete the message. I'm not going to confiscate the tape, under the circumstances, but it may be important at some point."

"You don't have any suspect, do you." Carolyn Grossman suddenly seemed to have all of the air let out of her recent indignation. "It could have been..." She stopped.

"Yes?"

"When he came here as Commissioner, he found some examples of people whose jobs were 'vestigial,' I think he called it. Like they weren't needed. So some jobs were eliminated, but I think those people got jobs in other departments. I don't know. He didn't like to discuss work. He said I didn't really...He said it wasn't important."

"But it could be, couldn't it," said Annie, inviting Mrs. Grossman to share more with her by seeming a little confused herself. "We have to consider everything, everyone."

"Oh my god! Me? The boys?"

"No, of course not. You weren't here, you have an alibi, the boys are not considered suspects. There were no difficulties here at home..." She waited.

The indignation was back. "I can't imagine what you mean."

"Really, Mrs. Grossman," Annie looked straight at the other woman. "You are an educated, informed person. You no doubt know that most murders are committed by family or someone close. We have to ask these questions. If we don't, they will be asked in court. More to the point, we, the investigators, will be chastised publically, probably by the judge, for not asking them. Do you understand?"

There was a multiple personality here. Back to grief. "Completely. I'm sorry. So, no difficulties. We were a loving family. Professionally we had quite separate lives. I was an art docent til we moved here from Anchorage, and I am an art teacher shared by two elementary schools here. We seldom discussed our work. We concentrated on the children and being together when we were together."

"Did Mr. Grossman have friends with whom he played cards, hunted, fished, and so forth?" Annie asked. She found herself actually interested in the answer, trying to fill in the shell.

"He did not. I don't mean people weren't friendly, but he was an administrator, and they get to the place, he always said, where you can't trust social situations. People are working an angle, he said. People are looking for things to use against you, here, he said. I didn't ever realize it would be so political. The other jobs, they were like jobs, and he would occasionally fish or hunt with other people he knew. Of course, when he was a guide, that wasn't recreation. No, he didn't have friends here yet. He hadn't been here long enough. We didn't entertain. As I said, we were a close family and we did things together."

"What about--the family originally came from Missouri, is that right? At Mrs. Grossman's slow nod Annie went on, "did he have friends or family from there? I'm trying to determine who might have known him well enough to know something about his personal habits."

Whatever grief Carolyn Grossman had felt when Annie came in, it was sucked back inside now, on the way to being battened down. "No. He said the family was enough. He spent a great deal of time with the boys." Then, something clicked. "Murder. This is being investigated as a murder."

"Yes, undoubtedly."

"Murder." Like it was a foreign word. She had not applied it to her husband or the circumstances of his death, about which she showed remarkably little interest. "For some reason, I thought maybe...one hopes, just an awful accident, but..." She stopped. Her demeanor shifted. "No, I don't see how I can be of any more help."

"Oh, but you can. We found some hairs in the front seat of the truck..."

Clearly disgusted: "Yes. I refuse to ride in that truck. He takes the dogs to run out by the runway, and they both shed terribly. They aren't allowed in the house here."

"Can I see the dogs? And is it possible that I might have a sample of their hair...to eliminate them as suspects?" Annie tried another slight smile. Mrs. Grossman said only, "of course," and "come this way."

They walked through the kitchen to where two large dogs, a shepherd mix and a lab, were pad painting with mud on the glass door. Annie took two plastic evidence bags from her pocket, marked them with the dogs' general descriptions, and petted each one, securing ample hair with one swipe down their backs.

"Thank you," she said, as they both backed away from the still-open door. She noticed both dogs sat obediently without trying to enter the house. On an impulse, she made a surreptitious hand gesture at her hip and one dog took a step forward. Mrs. Grossman's sharp rebuke caused it to hunch and flatten its ears as it backed out and actually dropped to its belly on the porch. Mrs. Grossman shut the door.

Huh again. "And where are the children?"

"They are back in school. It seemed that if they wanted to go, I should let them," Carolyn Grossman said as she led the way back into the living room. She did not sit down. "Surely you do not need to talk to them. The boys. I forbid you to talk with my daughter. She is inconsolable. I'm just getting her to eat again."

"No, I don't need to talk with them, but perhaps you could ask them, when you feel up to it, if their father ever mentioned anyone who might dislike him?" Grossman was shaking her head violently, but Annie handed her a card. "If you do, even if it's later, anything might be helpful. Remember," she added, "we're trying to catch an elusive and apparently careful person who has hidden his trail well. We are not the adversary, here," she said gently. "We are trying to bring an evildoer to justice. To find justice for your family."

"It's just not a good time to talk to the boys."

Nevertheless, she took the card, looked at it and then at Annie, and put the card in her pocket. "If there's nothing else?"

"I think that's everything for now. Oh," Annie said, and then, as though as an afterthought, "Did Mr. Grossman have a home office?"

"He didn't like to work at home. He had a computer that only he used, of course. The Detective took that, but said we would get it back." She looked hard at Annie as if to be sure.

"Yes, we are looking at it for any evidence that someone might have sent him a threatening email."

"So the Detective said. But I'm sure there was nothing. He didn't believe in personal emails. He said it was 'dangerous' to put anything in writing when you were the boss."

No doubt. "Ah," Annie said. Then, "No calendars at home, no Blackberry, nothing that might have shown any meetings or appointments?"

"Why would he have those at home? His work had nothing to do with us." Mrs. Grossman seemed genuinely surprised that anyone would, in fact, bring anything into the home that didn't belong there. And as convinced that there was a sharp demarcation between home and work, in a state where virtually anyone of Commissioner Grossman's position would be on call from, if nothing else, the Governor's Office, on a moment's notice.

"We may have a few more questions, and if you think of anything, anyone who might have a grudge, anything else that might be remotely connected (Mrs. Grossman was shaking her head again), just call me."

They walked to the front door, and Annie turned to face the woman who would now have to decide how many of her husband's rules to continue following. "Mrs. Grossman, I know this is too new and raw for you to completely understand our investigation's twists and turns, but we will do everything we can to bring you the closure you deserve."

"Tell me when I can bury him, that will be the closure we need."

Because there was no answer to that, and Annie did not want to raise the specter of the autopsy at this juncture, she only nodded, and stepped out into the persistent rain. But she hadn't left the porch when she remembered the overcoat John had told her to ask about.

"One last thing, please," she said, and waited while Carolyn Grossman rearranged her face to accommodation. "Did he commonly wear an overcoat?"

"Of course! Who in Juneau doesn't wear rain gear?" There was no dissembling, only a sincerely confused look.

"We didn't find one. In any case, in order for us to find it, can you tell us anything more about it?" Annie waited, hardly daring to breathe, as Carolyn Grossman thought, stepped back inside and opened the hall closet, shuffled through coats and jackets and said, "It's the London Fog. I bought it for him for Christmas last year, because his Anchorage coat was too heavy and the lining was sewn in. The lining of his new coat zips out, and that's still hanging here for the winter." She stopped, and her eyes filled with tears. "That taupe color that's so popular now," she nearly whispered.

"Thank you, Ma'am. We'll be in touch. You've been helpful," Annie said. "Did I give you my card already, in case you want to contact me?" She knew she had, but she was hoping to give Carolyn Grossman something to be snippy about. It worked.

"Of course. I'll have it by the phone. Thank you for working on this for us. I understand what you have to do. I don't like it. He was...we are...private."

163

"I'm sorry for your loss," Annie said, because it was, like "aloha," a beginning and an end.

Back in the car, Annie made notes, used the clunky phone to call John and have him to get a warrant by the end of the day to confiscate the answering machine and any personal papers or other devices kept at home, regardless of what the woman knew. She recognized a rigid division between these "loving" spouses and yet it was not unusual. Perhaps his choice, certainly reinforced by his reported personality. Perhaps her agreement, acquiescence, even comfort. In any case, though there may be a time Mrs. Grossman would have something to offer in the investigation, it was not now. More the pity, because the longer she refused to entertain the possible persons who might have a vendetta, the less chance their search might be narrowed from everyone in the known universe to actual suspects.

Chapter Thirteen

Tuesday, October 15, 1998 - 5:00 p.m.

Annie needed to organize. She could feel, in the recesses of her mind, the impulse forming. She didn't want to forget pieces that might not become important until some time in the future. Especially a detail that would need to be re-investigated in Juneau. She had found that just writing something onto a sticky note kept it alive.

Back in her little apartment over the garage, listening to the local oldies, she had the beginnings of a murder board in front of her: bulletin board, easel, stick pins, string and markers courtesy of K-Mart closing last year. Appropriately, in the background, a doo wop group sang *don't know much about history...*Which was about what she knew about this murder.

She stared at the board, looking at what she had so far, what should be connected to what. She actually had striped yarn to use when she was not completely sure of the connection. Right now there was a good deal of striped yarn. She had strings running from the dumpsters behind Fish and Game to the Dump where Grossman was found. From the parking garage to Fish and Game. There were notes of interviews under a big question mark, and a red "X" with an envelope of notes under a red stick pin for people who were not suspects or valuable witnesses. She was trying to decide where to put the afternoon's serendipitous interview with the former employee at the top of Harlan Roberts' *disgruntled* list.

She decided to add a label "bully" and put the interview there.

She thought about Carolyn Grossman. Her experience told her something was there, but it could be nothing and she was simply misreading the clues. It was certainly a strange interview. Generally, at this level, family was all cooperation. Was there a point to the hostility? It was a little bit like playing hearts. Every so often, even when you were playing all of the cards carefully, correctly, someone dropped the queen on you out of nowhere. Only, to them, it wasn't nowhere, it was strategy. But you didn't get to know what the strategy was. You only got to see the last trick.

Back to "bully." She wouldn't put that word on the board in her office, but this hadn't been a nice, or likeable, man. That didn't mean that someone needed to kill him, and it didn't mean that Annie would begin dragging her feet through the snow, though winter would come and soon, with no suspect and no genuine theory of the crime.

There was an interpersonal battle here, somewhere. Someone had been hurt. If Grossman had been the bully as a child or adolescent that he had been as an adult, the list of people who could have been pushed just a bit too far to recover their balance might be spread out, might include people who had been out of his life for some time, might include relatives of those who had been bullied. Revenge was looming larger and larger as a motive, but if you were a certified jerk, the list of those who might want revenge was long, with shadow veins like Aunt Nellie's thighs.

Though they were often portrayed as big at an early age, Annie knew bullies came in all shapes and sizes. She remembered ones she had known in grade school--the two boys who had chased her home from school, throwing apples at her from the sour apple tree on the corner of the open lot she crossed. Every day for weeks. She wasn't allowed to change her path home, and they seemed to know it. They terrified her; they were older, bigger and remarkably accurate with the hard little missiles they aimed at her bare legs. She didn't tell her parents, but later, when one of the boys turned up as one of her father's graduate students, she couldn't bring herself to speak to him. To Annie, he was still the schoolyard bully, hurting her across the years by teaching her to be afraid of male violence.

So, if Annie had these bullies still firmly with her, someone probably had Commissioner Grossman in the psyche. Male or female? Young or old? Big enough to subdue a large man and put him in a dumpster, that was what she knew at this point. Oh, lordy, what if there were two of them, and they had to work together to get him over the edge? She shuddered, not wanting, at this early stage, to even consider that.

She replayed the afternoon's interview in her mind. After talking with the grieving widow, she had been fortunate to catch Cathy Munson at home, and relatively close. Munson was number one on the Deputy Commissioner's list of potentially "disgruntled" employees, which didn't automatically mean to Annie that there was no valid reason for her resentment. Munson had been the supervisor of the IT wing of the department. The word "bully" had been hers.

They had been through the facts about when Cathy had come to the department, and when she had left and under what circumstances, how long she had actually worked under Grossman, how she felt about being terminated. The responses had been crisp, blunt and nearly snarled.

"It sounds like you didn't like him," Annie offered, in a neutral tone, ready for backpedaling or denial.

"No one liked him. He reveled in it." Cathy Munson's voice was flat.

Annie raised her eyebrows.

"I know, I know," Munson sighed. "He did away with my position. I'm a disgruntled employee. But you know what? That doesn't make him a nice person. He had a way about him—like a bully. That's a good word for him. He was a bully. Anyone more powerful than he was, either because they had political power, social power, information power, to them he was almost friendly. Especially if they were women. But he was also really cold to both men and women, especially in meetings. He spoke, they listened. He yelled, they ducked. He raged, they stopped making eye contact with anyone. All behavior that says to me lots of people were afraid of him, he knew it, and it was his *modus operendi*.

"He wasn't a friendly guy. He occasionally made things happen for others, if he liked what they were doing, I suppose. It's a mystery who he liked and who he didn't. After the reorg, there were still employees there whom he couldn't fire, because of the union, so who knows. I, personally, don't think anything he said in the first year was real. He was all "help me understand." He might be positive, ask you all kinds of questions and even offer assistance with negotiations with other departments. Or he might just ignore you, and then you find out he's asking other people about how well you do your job and how important it was. He would ask general questions like anyone new, about what you thought could be sundowned or cut. No one should have answered that, but we didn't know then." She seemed more thoughtful than argumentative.

"You've thought about this," Annie said. "You have perspective."

"Sounds like something he would have said. Spuriously flattering. Sorry, him, not you. Like a snake, tasting the air, and your size, before deciding to strike. If you didn't have power, or worse, you didn't have power and you disagreed with him, he'd actually try to scare you—yell at you, have a philosophical tantrum, call you names to your supervisor…"

"Can you give me some concrete examples?"

"Sure. Anyone at F & G could. Most wouldn't, last week, but they might now. Career government employees are afraid of the politicals, who reshuffle everyone based on whom they like, and then leave them vulnerable to the next political, who assumes that anyone in a position of any authority is still loyal to the last guy. The ultimate power a political has isn't to hire or fire, or even discipline; it's to reorganize, eliminate positions without any hiring or firing, just lop you off like you had no worth to the organization, no job that was worth doing."

Annie knew this political lesson, and it wasn't what she was after. Any "political," as Munson said, could and would do that. Whether Munson meant anything that was specific to this political, and whether it would be useful remained to be seen. "And so an example of the bullying would be..."

"Okay, there was a woman here, who had come to work with a project she knew a great deal about. We recruited her. She was darned near famous, had a network of successful programs. Technically, she worked for me, though I wasn't her immediate supervisor. I was her supervisor's supervisor. She was supposed to give a presentation to the State Fisheries Board on the habitat project at Seward. Grossman is there, and I'm there. We were the Municipality of Anchorage Board room, built in projector and all that, and for some reason, she couldn't get her laptop to display. Now we're talking about five minutes, all told, to trouble shoot and complete the set up and granted, this should have been practiced before the meeting.

"Anyway, he sat there looking at his notes, not a comment, not a look. I went into his office then next morning on something else, and he just exploded on me. She was an idiot. She should be fired. She was a cretin. She was too stupid to ever be in a public situation, ever again. His face was red, his neck was flushed and looked about twice its normal size, his eyes were all *go to war*, and he was clenching and unclenching his fists. At first it scared me, but I had a desk between us, so I just said the first thing that came to me. I told him I didn't have time for such hatred, and he said 'good.'

"I should have known that did it, but I wasn't thinking, I was so shocked and angry that he thought he could talk about people like that in a professional setting. As soon as I left the office, I knew I shouldn't have said anything. Within a couple of weeks, I was gone, and she's still there because there was no cause for termination. She's not allowed to speak in public."

She looked at the ceiling for a moment. "You could hear a similar story from lots of people."

"And how were you...terminated?"

"Not right away, as I said. Two weeks later, early, when no one else was there, he walked into my office, sat down in the chair by the door and said, 'I can get into your email any time I want.' I told him I had a recipe for Tiramisu in there, and he should go ahead and try it. He stared at me for a really long time, and then he got up and left.

"In retrospect, not the most political of comments under the circumstances, but I guess I thought I had more value to the department. Two commissioners had given me amazing performance reviews, and raises. As if that made any difference to him. I felt like he was waiting to see how I reacted, and I played that wrong." Cathy Munson looked out the little window behind her, seemingly rethinking the exchanges that had, apparently, led to being fired.

"I watched a special on coyotes on the Discovery Channel once. About how they have stopped being focused on wild game, perhaps because of the difficulty. About how they have come into the cities, and now they kill tame things, like cats and small dogs. They're successful by looking like dogs, watching people's habits, learning to kill in the hours when people are gone. But some of them kill right in front of people, who don't realize the danger, just sit there and watch. Coyotes--Alaska Natives call them 'the tricksters'-- mask what they are.

"I remember this one scene—a coyote had a big sheep by the throat. The sheep could have run, but it didn't. It was bigger, and probably stronger than the coyote, but it didn't try to use that, either. It just kept turning away from the coyote, but the coyote hung on, and they went in this bizarre circle until finally, the coyote had killed the sheep. It fell, it quivered, and that was it. All the coyote had done was identified the jugular and hung on. That was it. Do you understand?"

Annie nodded, slightly, as Cathy Munson seemed to want a response. The woman was looking down, at her hands, then at her book case, then out the window. "So the next day he announced a reorganization of the department, and said he was bringing in a consultant from Anchorage, someone he knew, to upgrade the department's communication system. They would eliminate unneeded layers of exempt employees to pay for it. I am exempt. I serve at the pleasure of the governor. Left the university to take the position eight years ago."

She gestured around her home office. "I have an adjunct position at UAS. Maybe a position next year, if someone takes leave. The kids are in high school here." Her voice faded, and her face became stone. "Probably I will never work in state government again. That's how it is: some secret code is written into the register, and they won't even talk to you.

"People who were connected to Juneau, not just the pols, or the one-time administration hirees for key programs, they're safe."

Though Annie thought she knew what Munson was talking about, she played dumb. "People *connected to Juneau* would be...?"

"Born here. A member of a powerful political family. The Admin Commissioner, for example, is the grandson of a famous Juneau legislator. The woman who is the longest member of the Fisheries Council is the great granddaughter of the first mayor of Juneau. Then you have the Old Juneau clique, and the Fishermen. You have the Loggers, the local Gay community, the Douglas Islanders, Native groups. The people who run things aren't from outside, and they certainly aren't from Anchorage. Their descendants will also be safe from firing. It's a skill to listen, watch, and figure out whom to leave alone. And whom you can dominate, reorg out of existence, or just fire outright."

A smart bully, Annie thought. She remembered person after person independently stating that Grossman sometimes yelled, often threatened, and wasn't above using name calling to try to back down an opponent or an underling who showed contrary views. She thought about how she would have felt if he had called her a cretin and said she couldn't appear in public again. If she was new to town, and didn't belong to one of the cliques. Apparently the employee in question knew about her pariah status; Cathy Munson must have told her. Should she interview that person? She checked in her notes to see if she had a name, and she did. So she would make that call and see if there was anything there. She made a note on a calendar sheet. Linda Hurtsen.

She looked at the little local phone book, found the name, and called.

"Ms. Hurtsen?"

"Yes, who's calling?"

"This is Annie Brewster, Special Investigator from the State Police. I'm conducting interviews related to Commissioner Grossman's death. Would you have some time to talk with me tomorrow?"

"No. I mean, not at work. Do you do interviews in the evening?'

"Yes, I do. Would I meet you at work?"

"Oh no...someone might...I mean, it wouldn't be good at work. I'm really busy tomorrow. I get home about 5:00. I live in the condos beside the A&P. #3C. Can you come to my home?" Her voice was hurried and slightly breathless, as though she was involved in sex or exercising. Either was fine with Annie, and neither pertinent.

"Sure. How about 7:00, so you have time to take off your coat and unwind."

"Sounds good. Uh, how will I know you?"

What a careful person. Or a scared one. Annie made a comforting noise, as though she were considering what she might be wearing. "Short gray hair, brown pants suit, big badge and bigger ID." She chuckled, hoping it sounded authentic.

"Thanks. I'll see you tomorrow night. The porch light will be on."

Annie hung up. Why did everyone sound so nervous? Except Commissioner Doyle, of course, but it seemed that that was just his normal demeanor.

And Rearson. No phone number in the book. She'd have to use the state directory and call in the morning. Rearson still seemed like a possibility to her. Humiliated in front of everyone, put down, and so forth. However, the strict pecking order in the exempt positions, and Doyle's statement that Rearson shouldn't have even spoken, told her that it might be another blind alley. Or dark alley. They were everywhere.

After she had talked to Munson, she had seen the secretaries, who, to a woman, played dumb. They were in new positions, good secretarial skills being one of the few things that would get you moved over, not out. These were employees with strong unions, and in the highly stratified system of government hiring, there were few in their category. They were quickly transferred and back at work for someone else who was at a sufficiently elevated level to merit a highly skilled clerical. But they didn't make any points by talking poorly of their previous boss, and they knew it. The only thing Annie saw in common among the interviews was that none of them wanted to talk, none of them smiled, none of them remembered their time with Commissioner Grossman with any clarity.

Duck and cover. You live in a political town, with a political job, a good salary, excellent benefits, great retirement--why not keep your head down? As a matter of fact, what was wrong with those who did not, and how long would they last? Tomorrow she would talk to Rearson, and Linda Hurtsen. One more pass through the Dump in the morning, and a debrief with John, and then continue the slog through the reeds, hoping to find something floating...no, go to bed.

She dialed Fred, and felt a rush of warmth at his voice. "Hey! How are things?"

"Oh, just a mess," she said. "How was drawing?" It was their private joke about what architects did all day.

"I'm thinking of becoming a cartoonist. Took Bones on the Coastal trail. Saw three moose, one little bull with two cows. Don't know who was more scared, Bones or the bull. Everyone squatted and peed."

"Did you?"

"Yeah, after. So when you coming back up here?"

"Oh, Fred, soon. This one is just--well, I know it's too early to be saying this, but it's so shadowy and there are so many ways out of town, the dump and the rain have just taken any clues we might have had. John Sullivan says we won't solve it." With Fred, Annie allowed herself a full range of optimism and pessimism, because he was her other half, and they talked about everything. Fred was the only living soul she absolutely trusted. Bones was in on it, too, but he seldom offered anything of importance.

Fred, however, often did. Useful angles and thoughts that she had yet to have. As now, "I'll bet whoever did it was from somewhere else, and is long gone."

"Huh. Like, a serial killer type?"

"No, I don't see that, but someone who is passing through, maybe coming, maybe going, but had some issue? I don't know. I just bet they're not there any longer. I know I wouldn't be. You do know how easy it is to escape Juneau and get somewhere else fast, darlin'."

Annie smiled and wrapped his mental arms around her tired shoulders. Rain always made her achy. "So John said. He ran through just the staggering number of ways someone could have left town that evening. Everything but a train and a dogsled."

"Hear that, Bones? You're off the hook," Fred told the dog, who whined, heard Annie's telephone voice saying "who's a good suspect," and rolled over to show his belly for a scratch.

"Boy do I miss you guys when I'm out of town. I'm going to come home this weekend, I'm sure. Sunday night at the latest. I will have interviewed everyone in town by then, and don't get me started on dumpsters. Hoping I'll have it solved by then is just ridiculous. This is one of those that has so many possibilities I'm presently unable to draw straight lines."

"I can do that. I can even show you how."

"Ha! Then I could show it to the judge..." They both laughed softly. "Good night sweetheart. Sleep well. Want me to call in the morning?" Annie yawned hugely.

"Not tomorrow. Bill and I are going to meet for coffee, and I can always wake up when coffee is involved."

"'Kay. Say hi to Bill for me. Night. I love you."

"Love you too. Be safe."

Annie turned down her covers, cast one last baleful glance at two days of work, and turned off the beside light. Through the blurry, rain-washed window, an equally blurry street lamp gave enough illumination that she had no trouble seeing her way to the little bath and back to bed. She lay back on the pillows and tried to think, but the soothing sound of pattering rain finally drowned everything, and she slept.

Outside of the little house, people walked by, even this late, because it could be a walking town, it was that small. Outside, cars pulled out of parking places, to be replaced by someone who had been circling the block, just trying to get home for the night. And somewhere, out there, there were answers, but they, too, were blurred by the rain, and by no end of comings and goings.

Chapter Fourteen

Wednesday, October 16, 1998 - 9:00 a.m.

The Dump was open, and Annie knew her way around now. She drove directly to the barn where the detritus from the location of the body was strewn about on the tables. She reminded herself to give the license plate numbers to John to see if someone could run them down. She wanted to see if there was any home garbage that connected the Fish and Game dumpster and the trash surrounding the discovered body.

In the back of her mind was the emerging belief that knowing into which dumpster Grossman was pitched would yield nothing. Possibly a smelly raincoat covered with dog hair. Once again she tipped her figurative hat to the careful, clever murderer.

There were a few new things. Most of the paper trash picked up around the body was either Labor or Fish and Game, actually, so that was good. Whichever truck picked up one would pick up the other, they were that close. Hopefully. That needed to be checked out. There was a disturbing bunch of budget sheets, which could be from Admin. Annie scanned through the dumpsters, trying to remember where Admin would have put their trash. On the loading dock? She remembered a big trash receptacle with wheels, now that she thought of it, in the parking garage. Go back and look, after she saw Hurtsen. After they talked to Clyde Burner, she remembered, which was set up for 6:00.

Of the few things they had found or found out so far, there were no murder weapons. Annie looked over everything on the plywood display table. What about these keys? Where were the truck keys? John's report had said they didn't have keys, had gotten one from Mrs. Grossman, and assumed they were in the pile somewhere. "Ask John to have these keys tested," she said into her tape recorder. She put the keys into an evidence bag. There was an overcoat, but it was ripped, and navy blue, and seemed too small. Nothing in the pockets.

There were several juice bottles. She put on her gloves and looked at each one in turn. Was that gunshot residue on the inside of that one? Was it a home-made silencer? How hokey would that be, and how coincidental. *What if the hokey pokey was really what it's all about,* she wondered. Looked like mildew, or mold. It smelled really strange, again, like musty bathrooms. All three bottles had mildew or mold, black and grainy. She laid them back down and moved on, then went back and picked up all three, put them into three evidence bags, and set them to one side. It might be important, and if it got buried again, mentally or physically, it might be forgotten.

No weapons, unless you counted the fish club, hanging on a leather thong, just above the table on a peg. She turned to the uniform who was standing at the opening, subtly watching her. "Was this always here?" she asked.

"Yup. Apparently they try to take anything useful and hang it on the wall." He gestured to several clothing hangers, a shovel, some old towels and a rake that were on the wall at the other end of the building. "Want me to ask?"

"Sure," Annie said, knowing the young man would probably like a break.

There was no blood on anything. That wasn't unusual for the rain, but you would think there would be something on a paper, somewhere. However, Annie wasn't sure what that would tell her.

The sheer volume of paper from Admin, Labor and Fish and Game was impressive, and roughly three times what had been sifted on

Monday, so they had hit the mother lode. Annie nodded, reassured that she was somehow making progress, and waited for the uni to come back, which was right away.

"Got the fish club about the time all of the chum came in, end of September. Someone apparently went fishing and then threw the evidence in the trash." They both smiled. You had to be pretty desperate to fish chum, unless you were going to feed them to dogs, but people couldn't seem to resist. Fred and Annie preferred Sockeye. Bones was eclectic.

"Thanks. Hey, I'm Annie. Brewster."

"Jack Sitka."

"Seriously?"

"Yeah. I had to move to Alaska."

Okay, nothing more to see here, as far as she could tell. She would remind John that there should be pictures, and samples of what was collected in the way of identifying paper, just in case they needed it for a warrant or evidence later. No one would expect them to keep the actual garbage, but pictures would convince a jury if they were good. She had to hope they wouldn't need this, but in the absence of a suspect, they had to keep everything.

Having arranged a meeting with Rearson for later in the morning, Annie was temporarily without anything specific to do. She had all of the copies of passenger manifests packed away, and without a description of a suspect, there was really nothing she could find out by asking carrier personnel who had come and gone.

Something about *come and gone* poked at Annie. She got into her car and drove back to town, back through town, and out to the cruiseship dock. There being no more ships, everything was pretty much closed up, with staff apparently sent...where...to Hawaii for the winter? She made a note on her tape recorder to find out what ship had been there, what passengers the ship held. As far as she knew, these were all people who had originated in the lower 48, probably Seattle or San Francisco, but it wouldn't hurt to ask. The timing might be right. Long shot. Actually, with several thousand people--passengers and crew--on these hulking hotels, Annie sincerely hoped it would be a last resort to get into that can of worms.

She walked up through town, getting a feel for things. She bought fudge at the little candy store, because Fred liked it so much. Then a bag of "nutritionally balanced, gluten-free" bones for the dog. What happened to milkbones? Who knew dogs had celiac's disease? She looked at the sweatshirts, on sale now but still outrageous, and wandered through the bookstore. She bought a copy of "Murder in Juneau" to read on the plane.

Who was she kidding. She couldn't read on the plane, and whatever happened in the book, it wasn't germane to her case. Unless it was. Do your research where you find it.

Rearson's office was in Community and Regional Affairs, a low brick structure a few blocks below the Capitol Building. Didn't look new. Looked repurposed. Annie parked in the tiny lot in a clearly marked visitor's spot, and put the little "police" card in the window. Parking was sincerely the most contentious thing in this town, and she didn't know whether a police vehicle could park in a visitor's spot or not.

Rearson was ready for her. He was a thin, short, balding man with red cheeks and a white beard. Looked like about half a Santa Claus. He was the polar opposite of Deputy Commissioner Roberts: he smiled, stepped toward her and held out his hand in welcome. Annie introduced herself, disengaged her hand from a slightly warm and moist palm, and followed Rearson into his office.

If he was a knuckle dragger, he certainly had every type of computer and peripheral she had yet seen in Juneau, all in his office. She looked at the various machines, most blinking green on a black screen, but two, on a table under the window, showed the bright screensaver that came with the new Apple machines.

Without thinking, she said, "I thought the state was all IBM."

"Yeah," he said. "These are personal. You can't really buy an Apple on the state's dollar. What with all of the schools in the state using donated or subsidized Mac labs, it's hard to understand. The state procurement process is pretty committed to the lowest bidder, even if it's a 1957 Desoto.

"So, how can I help? I assume this has something to do with Grossman. I was at the last meeting. Word is you're reinterviewing..." He sat, tipped back a bit, and stared at her intently, but with a curiosity and openness that she hadn't seen.

"How long have you been in state government?" Annie asked, comparing the difference between his demeanor and that of every other person she had interviewed.

"Came last term with Phil, and how much longer is anyone's guess. I was hired from the communications sector, because we don't have good data to back the initiatives the Governor and Commissioner campaigned on. I did what I could to beef up the data Community and Regional Affairs collects and uses for decisionmaking, but I've hit a brick wall."

"So I heard." Annie had not missed that this was not a political employee per se. He called

Commissioner Flores by his first name. That, all by itself, was proof.

"Oh--you know about the 'knuckle dragger' comment. Pot calling the kettle black, if you ask me, but I got chewed for speaking up and for pissing him off. You know," he said, leaning forward, "I just don't get the whole chain of command/pecking order thing. I left a job with Alascom to come here, and I couldn't believe how people were afraid to speak to anyone above their pay grade. And all I did was try to get the group to consider upgrading the whole system at least to the norm of a decade ago." Again, an engaging smile.

"Huh," Annie said slowly. "So you're not put off by bad meeting behavior so much as by the social and political hierarchy?"

"And how it affects the ability of people to do their job. Government all over the place--you have this two-tiered system, and it encourages people who are career employees to hide. No one wants to offer any real ideas. There are no suggestion boxes; none are welcomed. Most Commissioners actually have no experience in their job. By definition, I guess. There's no school for running things from the state level. It's all about coming in and changing everything, 'draining the swamp;' but in most cases, changing is next to impossible because the general fund is gutted and most state employees, except for Admin and the AG's office, are funded by some grant that's their real main job. There's no one in the department, in way too many cases, to even enforce ongoing regulations. Sooner or later the whole system is going to grind to a halt." He ran down. He frowned. He looked away. He looked straight at Annie.

"Okay, that's done. You ask your questions. Sorry."

"I can certainly identify with your frustration. I've actually heard it before. And I really have little to ask you. So, after the altercation and the nasty comment, did that make you..."

"...feel like following him and killing him? Give me a break. That's like cutting the head off the hydra. No, it was embarrassing, because I have probably four times his background and three degrees in related fields, and I couldn't respond in any way--I accede to that much about the protocols around here. And I'm pretty sure I could identify the actual knuckle dragger in the room, but, no, I wasn't angry at him, and I certainly didn't kill him. If anything, I was just shocked that anyone would just try to shout down an idea, without any data or research to support what he wanted to have happen. Just prejudice and ego. How do you do business that way?" It wasn't really a question, so Annie just went on.

"So tell me what you did after the meeting was over, including any times you recall."

"Sure. Left at 6:30, because I spent some time with Schwartz, making sure I had the correct figures to share with the Phil, and asking about notes. She said she didn't take any, but she wrote the whole meeting. Another case in point. She wouldn't have said that to a Commissioner. But, okay, then I walked, in the rain, down to the Baranoff, met my wife and some friends for a drink before they were leaving on the Cruise Ship. At 7:30 we walked them to the gangplank, waved them up to the ship, and went to relieve the babysitter. I think that's it. Home for the rest of the evening. Drinks on a credit card, receipt available. Are we good?"

"Pretty much, thanks. I have to say, I'm surprised at your positive attitude, given what you really feel about the atmosphere. it's so different from other interviewees." Annie was not dissembling. She had no sense that this man was in any way involved.

"Well," Rearson said calmly, "I had a talk with Phil the first week we had a cabinet meeting and I met Grossman. On the way back to the office, I said something about Grossman's affect. Phil basically shrugged and said, 'You see that look, put it together somewhere in the back of your brain with centuries seeing males posturing and then knowing the instant things are serious. This happens in a second. If you see certain signs, you look hard and decide whether you're going to have to fight the guy. If you're not, you have to think everything is posturing.'

'He said he thought at one time, in the early meetings, that he was going to have to fight, and then he just disarmed it all by laughing, though Grossman, apparently, didn't join in. Phil basically has no use for the guy. Called him a doublecrosser."

Huh. Annie got it. And the idea that some Commissioner had actually considered whether he would have to engage in fisticuffs with this guy, and that he would then give this advice to a subordinate new to state government, told a great deal. She went back to what Cathy Munson had said, that Grossman didn't attack people who had power. Lots of kinds of power, and "You're no threat," communicated by an untouchable peer, was power. The peer's subordinate, not so much. And in any case, she thought the posturing was a way to find out who could be bullied. She'd seen the behavior before.

No, she saw Grossman more and more as a sly, intelligent man who did nothing by accident, and fired for effect, in all ways.

****

Back out on the street, Annie put a red X beside Rearson's name. She went back up to her car, drove to her little apartment, and thought through the questions she wanted to ask Clyde Bunsen. She took out the leftover chicken and chewed on a leg while she stood in front of her board. She wet the end of her marking pen on her lower lip and wrote:

- *Clyde's timeline on Monday night from 6:00 - 7:00; how late he stayed*
- *Clyde's normal route of cleaning*
- *Anyone Clyde saw*
- *Anything out of place the next few hours, the next day*
- *What did Clyde do with the trash in his bins*
- *Who empties the big trash can outside of the elevators?*
- *what else...ask John*

She called John Sullivan and asked him whether there was anything to the bust over in Douglas where he had first met Clyde Bunsen. She read him the questions, and got his feedback. They confirmed their meeting at the State Office Building, after which Annie said she was going to interview another disgruntled employee. John was busy, and finally said, "Annie, I know you don't want to offend us, but you've got this one at this point. I'm good with everything you're doing, and appreciate the courtesy, but it is what it is. If we could have nailed it right away, we would have. So go for it."

Which was "the signal," and that was what Annie had, basically, been constantly checking with John for. There was the pecking order, and then there were the collegial checkboxes any professional in this state had to keep track of, or you would be alone in the snow. Something inside Annie relaxed a little, but for this case, it had been crucial to have John's perspective and assistance. Hell, she probably wouldn't have gotten an interview if he hadn't been there first. There were the politicals and then there was the Juneau establishment. You really had to live here to get anyone to take you seriously on certain topics.

So, back to work, drawing and cogitating. *Right down to the real nitty gritty.*

It was nearly four when Annie had reread and organized and incorporated and drawn lines, circles, and question marks. She thought a moment about her own vulnerability and finally decided to put Rearson under the red "X" stick pin. Rearson didn't kill Grossman. He didn't have a motive. His credibility was the fostered by expertise, and it hadn't been harmed, because no one seemed to be taking the put down as anything other than "oops, don't stir that particular pile." His boss advocate was still in place, and he wasn't personally threatened, that Annie could see.

She decided to lay down for an hour and think. Because it was the daytime, she set her little alarm for 5:00. When it rang at 5:00 she didn't recognize the sound. Must have been tired, she thought, and got up to tidy up and comb her hair for the next meeting.

Chapter Fifteen

Wednesday, October 16, 1998 - 6:00 p.m.

Clyde reminded Annie of a character on a crime drama, the mysterious witness who saw things, but whose affect was difficult to parse. And who was no doubt wearing a disguise so that the next time you saw him, you would wonder whether you knew this person. Clyde was a handsome mixture of Alaska Native and African American, with long, curly hair, bright eyes and a well-groomed mustache. He was average in height, and a bit underweight. Annie knew that he was an unforgettable personality from the start. Glib, with attitude, he could switch from dialect to more standard English depending upon whom he was with, which argued intelligence and education, both of which he was right now striving to hide.

Annie and John had been given a conference room in Admin Services to interview Clyde, who was in a janitor's bright blue coveralls and had his hair carefully combed and caught in a rubber band. He was otherwise garbed up in rubber gloves, a nose and mouth mask hanging on elastic from his neck, and rubber boots, as he had been cleaning the bathroom where someone had had an accident, or "hurled," as Clyde had apologetically told them. He regarded them alternatively with lively dark eyes and the demeanor of someone innocent and put upon. They engaged in introductions, a bit of small talk about why Sullivan remembered Clyde and whether Clyde still lived in the same apartments. (He did.) And how bad it could be to have to clean restrooms.

He really didn't know why they were interviewing him. "You can ax me anything, but I don't recollect seein' nothin', actually. Regular night." Clyde looked hopefully at the door. "Which night was it again?" he asked, still looking at the door.

"Monday, is what we're asking you about," John Sullivan said. He had shared with Annie that Clyde hadn't been part of the drug bust that had taken place at the apartment complex in Douglas, but had been there, had demanded to be interviewed, had produced nothing. Just wanted to talk about it.

"Did you see anything unusual Monday evening? Would have been about the time you came on, or within the hour after that? Which would be, any time from 5:30 on. 'Preciate your being willing to talk with us," John said.

"Oh sure. Let me recollect." Clyde gave every appearance of thinking seriously about the question, but all he finally said was "nope."

"So," Annie said, opening her notebook, "You come about 5:00 or so, and then what would you be doing right around 6:00?"

"Rest rooms always first, then drinking fountains, then wastebaskets, then you vacuum. Copy room, always a mess, you just have to make sure there's room in the recycle bin. State got a recycling policy. Mean everyone recycle on the floor if the bin don't have room."

Again, that twinkle. Annie responded with a smile, and Clyde, who had been reciting his job description, not giving the information they were seeking, again looked at the door.

"Mr. Bunsen...may I call you Clyde?...Clyde, then," as Bunsen nodded, "What exactly did you do that night? You were in the restroom around 6:00?"

"No, before. Went into the closet, suited up, put supplies on my trash truck, like that. Had to go find the cone to put in front of the door so people don't come in to use the facilities," he said fastidiously. "Put on my boots and got the mop and bucket. Got everything into the men's. Took

198

some time swappin' out toilet paper. Men don't use much. Went in and out maybe three times. So didn't see nobody in the hall, ain't nobody in the restroom when I was cleaning."

Annie ticked through the timeline. He started around 5:00, he started in the restrooms, and that was it? He saw no one? "What time does most of the staff leave?"

"Mostly by 5:00 everyone is gone, but some might stay later, for meetings and the like, come back to get stuff. Leave later. Nobody much here by 5:30. For sure, nobody here by 6:00."

Annie was fascinated with the way Clyde's speech patterns bounced around, and she shook herself mentally. "So please go on, after you cleaned the Men's restroom?"

There was an incremental change in Clyde's demeanor. He looked at the ceiling. He looked at his hands. His eyebrows went up and then down. "The usual, I suspect," he finally said.

"Clyde," Sullivan said firmly, "We talked to Allison Cunningham, and we know that someone reported finding you sleeping in the restroom the next morning. Do you recall how that might have happened?"

"Oh, well, I was done, and I just got so tired, workin', that I sat down against the wall in the men's, and I rested. Guess I dozed off." Clyde rubbed his chest absentmindedly and made no eye

199

contact. After a period of silence, which they tolerated, Clyde muttered, "Don't recollect nothin' after that. Jumped on me for doin' nothin' else on the floor."

Annie and John stared at Clyde Bunsen, who peeled off his gloves and examined his hands. "Guess I must have had a blackout or somethin'. You been told I was there in the mornin' tryin' to wake up. Must have been sick."

Or drunk. Or on drugs. Or lying. John Sullivan weighed in. "Clyde, would any of that be due to, say, being drunk?"

"What that woman been telling you. No. Hell no. I don't drink at work." Clyde put on a great display of affront.

John said, somewhat to soothe him before the interview was over, "Yeah, I just have to ask, given some past complaints. We don't care, in any case," he added for emphasis. "We just want to find out if anyone saw Commissioner Grossman before he was killed. Please go on about your evening."

Clyde eyed them suspiciously, made some kind of decision, and said, "Didn't see no one, like I said. Did go to sleep in the restroom. Got reprimanded for it." He stopped, then his brow wrinkled. "Onlyest thing was..."

Both Annie and John sat forward, and Clyde, who realized that he had given some kind of signal, sighed, and said, "woke up not knowin' what I did with my trash truck. Finally found it. Nothin' missin'." The last was nearly in a whisper. "Found it where we dump the bags at the end of the night, but don't remember puttin' it there, or anything else."

Though she wanted to find out where he really found the canvas-sided wheeled cart, Annie backed off, not wanting to disclose interest in any particular at this point. "So, you didn't see anyone, and other than your cart, which you might have left accidentally by..."

"By the elevators, end of the hall."

"...at the end of the hall." That wasn't what he had just said, was it. Annie smiled. "There was nothing that you found out of place?" she asked, fixing her eyes on her notepad as though there was something important there. "Let me ask you, Clyde, where do you put the trash bags before you go home?"

"Dumpster out on the loading dock the closest one."

"Do you ever go into the parking garage?" she asked, as casually as she could.

"Nope. Why would I?" Clyde appeared to think a second, maybe surprised at such a question, but again, the instant of indecision or dissemblance flickered, and Annie caught it.

"And you did not, that night, go down to the parking garages?"

"Said nope, meant nope. Don't go down there." Clyde wasn't sure about something, but he was firm in his answer. His face was like an old-time view master, snapping from picture to picture.

They tried more questions, but he held firm. He hadn't seen anyone, nothing out of the ordinary happened. They took their leave with the standard "please don't leave town," which caused Clyde to snort and laugh. He walked out, pushed his trash cart down the hall, and left Annie and John staring after him.

"Huh," John said. "When we were here before, no one mentioned him, we didn't talk to him, and we should have."

Annie said, "I have trouble seeing him as the murderer, which I don't like, because he could be, he has the best opportunity. However, he slipped there, if you heard it. He said he found the truck by where they dump the trash bags at night..."

"...And then he said he found it by the elevators. I don't see him being involved in the murder, but I think he has more information than he's giving us. I'd give my eye teeth to know if he really slept in the restroom all night, and what he was on. Not that I mind he doesn't have anything specific to contribute. Can you imagine him on the stand?"

That got them all the way down to their cars, safe this time of day in the visitor spaces for the State Library, reminiscing about witnesses who just morphed on the stand into ticking bombs. You couldn't possibly predict what this man would say. More to the point, he was so inventively loquacious, jurors might just hear something that was only speculation, but the prosecutor wouldn't necessarily catch it.

Still, Annie had to consider him a suspect. This was the most opportunity she could imagine. She tried to visualize Clyde bopping down the hall behind Commissioner Grossman, who would turn with a withering stare and dare the peon to get in the elevator with him, and then it just all dissolved. It didn't work for her, but stranger things had happened.

****

Annie pulled into the condo's lot and found Linda Hurtsen's number. She called on the bread loaf phone, and when Hurtsen answered told her she was through early, and would this be convenient. It was. She went to Hurtsen's door, which was opened before she got there by a tidy little wren of a woman, in no shoes, the shirt and skirt of a power suit without the jacket, which Annie saw on a chair, and a glass of wine.

"How do you do," she said, with great courtesy and just a suggestion of a nervous slur. This was her second glass.

"Thank you," Annie said, taking the offered dining room chair, opting for water when a glass of wine was offered. "Maybe a little later. Still working."

"Of course. How can I help?"

Annie walked through, carefully, what Cathy Munson had said. Hurtsen's eyes positively flashed. "I have to tell you, it was in no way, my fault. What an awful, odious man. He hated women."

"Wow. What makes you say that?"

"The evidence just kept stacking up. Of course, there aren't many men in the Department, though there are so many out in the field. There were three women who got reorged or fired, and the stories were horrific. I was just sidelined, which is in some ways worse. Here I build a program that documents stream flow, they hire me because of it, and he forbids me to even answer questions about it. I had a little party afterward, just the three of us, and we ate Ugli fruit and made rhymes about uppity women. At least, I did. We had some laughs about all of the words around 'uppity' in the dictionary."

"And who were these other two, should I talk to them?" Annie asked.

"They left town. I have two years to retirement, and I have to hope the next two are better than the last four." Linda Hurtsen rearranged herself on her chair, with a foot up under her and her skirt bunched around her thighs. She sloshed her wine back and forth in the large glass she held. "You know," she said finally, "no one is surprised when a new commissioner cleans out the exempt or supervisory employees. Nobody likes it, but they all do it. That's where they put cronies. But to go after the rank and file--we have a pretty strong union, and Grossman just ignored them."

Annie knew the "let 'em grieve" type of boss, who accepted the bargaining agreement, but really only saw it as setting up the areas in which management could act til the unit objected. She made a note to talk with HR, see what type of complaints there had been. She really didn't expect to get more information out of 20 disgruntled employees than she had gotten thus far from the six to whom she had spoken.

Nevertheless, she took the names of the two women of whom Hurtsen spoke, and they were on Roberts' list, she recalled. She listened for a bit more to Hurtsen's rambling description of the "fun" they had had trashing the new Commissioner who had just rearranged their lives. She looked up abruptly when Hurtsen said,

"...she said it was the most artificially stressful job she'd ever had." That was a telling line, and she wrote it down.

"And where is that woman now?" she asked casually.

"Oh, she went back to the Cook Inlet Native Corporation. If you're Native and college-educated, you can get a job easily. But in Fish and Game, there's just not that much turnover, and no one wants to hire anyone the administration doesn't want. It can mean, down the road, you don't get any contracts. The Department is a flow-through for lots of grants, and gets to make decisions about where the grant money goes. I can see that you are disbelieving," she said, scrunching up her nose and peering intently at Annie, who was shaking her head. "Yes, you are. But look at the Arctic Associates. They applied for a grant to study stream flow, and flat out told me they had been told on the q-t that if I was part of the bargain, they wouldn't be getting the grant."

No wonder this woman was bitter, if sloppily so. Annie made interested and soothing noises, extricated herself with difficulty, left her card and nearly sprinted to her car, lest she get some of it on her.

One block toward her little apartment it hit her. Where were the people who were happy with Grossman? Too much disgruntlement. She needed balance. If Grossman had brought people from Anchorage with him, or hired them later, who were they? They might be privy to conversation that never bubbled up to the Deputy's level, but could reveal someone who had a serious issue with this Commissioner, or a threat he felt. He might have hired someone to watch Roberts. Smiling, Annie went up to eat something and decompress.

Chapter Sixteen

Thursday, October 17, 1998 - 9:00 am

Annie and John went into JPD's videoconference room, set up for them to communicate with the medical examiner, who would join from Anchorage. They talked about the case.

"I think it's not a disgruntled Juneau employee," Annie said. "I don't get the impression that any of them have enough moxie, or personal power, or whatever else you want to call it, to actually carry out this complex crime. Of course, it could be someone who knows Juneau and the Commissioner's habits and traffic pattern.

"It could be Clyde, for that matter. There was something about the way he kept doing some mental fidget. Did you see it? And the business about where the trash cart was left, that seemed to bring it on."

Sullivan appeared to be considering, but he was actually on another thought. "I don't see it being any of the people who were in the meeting with him. One of the things that keeps poking me is that they all knew him for what he was--even Rearson, as you know since you talked to him--and they weren't going to war over it."

"If they weren't, it's because, if you put everything together, none of his peers, or near peer with a protector, are actually afraid of him. They are more like embarrassed by him, or for him. They recognize that he can be dangerous, but they don't sound afraid. He can't use his normal methods to fire them, he can't reorg them out of existence," Annie offered. "No, if it's anyone who knew him, it's a direct underling. I would say if I know anything at this point it's that he did his character assassination face to face.

"And another thing about that meeting. We agree, I think, that this is a carefully planned crime; it has all the earmarks, including no evidence. This was a budget strategy meeting, according to Schwartz, not the final cut. Who at that meeting would have had time to plan to kill him? Or if they planned it before, how did they leave at the same time he did, and all of that? I don't know, it just doesn't fit for it to be someone from the meeting."

Annie was quiet while a technician came in, made the screen of the monitor light up, got a green screen on the Anchorage feed and left the room. All over Alaska, meetings were held by audio and videoconference. Pretty much a necessity, she thought. "The thing we're not saying is that it could be a stranger. Opportunity by the dumpster? I don't know, John. Let's see what the ME says, and then I'll go talk to HR at Fish and Game and see if there are any other candidates."

"Seriously? You think it might be a stranger?"

"What else have we seriously got, excluding Clyde for a moment? Could be Clyde, I agree. He works alone, he comes alone, he leaves alone. But motive? I've been around the barn on that one, and I just have to let it sit for a bit," Annie caught herself before she hummed *"You don't mess around with Slim,"* because Croce was her least favorite earworm. And anyway, this was more appropriately *woolly bully.*

The screen flickered. Someone said, "testing," and suddenly Dr. Maria Hernandez, the ME, appeared, straightening papers in front of her. Behind her was a green wall, not Autopsy. Apparently she wasn't going to show them anything. Annie would go and see her in Anchorage, as she had yet to see the actual body. Find out *who's behind the Green Door.*

The ME was a woman in late middle age with a perpetual frown (who wouldn't have one, Annie thought) and a nearly visible "ticking" to do list that seemed to take up the space around her. She was gowned and had what looked like a mop cap from a Carol Burnett cartoon cleaning woman pushed back to reveal salt and pepper bangs and wisps of curls in front of her ears. She was semi-friendly on a good day, and all business today. Annie liked her.

"I will begin by saying, don't send me anything like this again. I'm too busy, and this guy was too dead." She waited a short breath and seeing only something like stillness on John's and Annie's faces, said, "Kidding. Morgue humor. Annie, hello. Detective Sullivan, I remember you. Shall I actually begin?'

"Yes," said Annie. "I haven't seen the body yet, so I need to come in to see you, and the victim, when I get to Anchorage next week. In the meantime, anything you can tell us will help. Trying to look at everything down here that might be related. We've got a lot of nothing relevant yet."

"Oh, there's a lot of that going on here, too," Hernandez said. "I faxed a preliminary report to you...you don't have it?"

Sullivan was huffing and on his feet. "I'll find it; where is the damn fax machine in this place?" He left the room.

Annie apologized. "Sorry. They just moved to this building, and they don't know where anything is. Of course, crime like this puts everything else aside, so they are still working out of boxes. John's pretty stressed about the mess. You can jump right ahead to the cause of death if you like. He'll be back in a minute."

Hernandez appeared to object, remembered it might be humor, and frowned into a small grin. "Well, no jumping, actually."

"Oh, no," Annie said immediately. "No cause of death?"

"Or several."

"Crap"

Sullivan re-entered, put a still-warm copy of the faxed autopsy report in front of Annie, and sat down with his.

"I'll just go through it. Stop me if you have questions," Hernandez said. "Starting with **EXTERNAL EXAMINATION**, top of page 2."

They all read. Annie asked, "Was there any evidence bagged and sent with the body that would normally be on the body, would be my only question about what the Funeral Director did." Sometimes, people tidied up. If they did, they did, but Annie wanted to know.

"No, not that I identified. Mr. Sessions bagged the hands and feet, in case there was something on the bottoms of the shoes. We've worked with him before. He's good, and careful. Respect for the dead, would be my guess. Professional hazard?"

Annie remembered at least two cases in which the work of Mr. Sessions was uncontested by the DA. That was always good, when the body had to go through more than one site. They read silently while Dr. Hernandez read aloud, and everyone made little notes in their margins.

EXTERNAL EXAMINATION

Autopsy began at 8:30 am on October 13. Prior to autopsy, on October 6, when the body was received, fluids were collected by standard procedures and sent to MedLab Toxicology in New Jersey for analysis. Attending at autopsy Assistant Medical Examiner Francis Preston and intern Norton Bellevue.

Preliminary preparation of the body was conducted by Juneau Coroner and Funeral director Mathew Sessions of the Mt. Lemon Family Funeral Home. Body was not embalmed or otherwise cleaned. Hands were bagged. Feet, in shoes, were bagged. Time and date of death were not speculated upon. The body had already passed through rigor at the time of discovery. M. Sessions recorded body

temperature consistent with exposure to wind, rain, overnight low temperatures. Additional information was nether available nor provided. The body was presented in a black body bag.

The victim is dressed in a dark blue suit with coat partially on one arm and partially folded beside and under the body. Suit pants do not have belt loops. No belt is apparent. Other clothing includes long-sleeved white shirt, red tie, shoes, socks, v-necked tee shirt, brown boxers. All clothing is damp. Jewelry is limited to gold wedding band. No watch.

The external, clothed body shows signs of having been in an area of waste, as reported. Paper pieces were extracted and other non-relevant materials, including apparent egg shell, were collected from hair, ears, under arms and pant legs.These were bagged, labeled and set aside. A police evidence bag contains the victim's wallet. Prior to examination of the wallet's contents, the victim was identified as Richard Grossman by a statement from the widow, Carolyn Grossman, included in the initial police report. The wallet's contents corroborate identity. No foreign material was on the wallet, which the evidence bag and accompanying picture show in the victim's pants pocket with a button flap in tact.

John said, "Contents of the wallet were listed and signed off on by myself and Sessions. Everything normal."

"And all still there. No fingerprints on the wallet but his." She read on:

Clothing was removed and set aside for further examination. Areas of the body are swabbed and submitted for detection of foreign agents. The external body is that of a normally developed white male measuring 74 inches and weighing 190 pounds. Appearance is generally consistent with stated age of forty-eight years. Some bruising, in random patterns, is apparent on the front of the body. All lividity is on the front of the body and fronts of the legs and arms, indicating position at time of death was on the stomach. Eyes are open. Irises are blue and corneas are cloudy. Pupils are pinpoint. Hair is blonde, approximately 8 inches in length at the longest point, and wavy.

Examination of the head and hands reveal bloating of fatty tissue due to moisture, similar to drowning victims. There are no marks on

the face associated with trauma. Fingernails appear clean, but any contents under the nails were, as stated, scraped and available. All teeth are present, with minimal dental work apparent. At this point, teeth will be x-rayed, but identify is not in question.

A small-caliber gunshot wound is apparent on the upper left neck, entering close to the spine, exiting through the neck at the anterior midline below the laryngeal prominence. No blood is apparent around the wound, beyond that seen on the shirt collar and referenced above. Minimal bruising around the wound is apparent. Two hairs were removed from the wound, which appear visually similar to the victim's own hair.

"Did you deduce that the lack of blood had to do with being in the rain?" Annie asked.

"I did not deduce anything to the contrary," Hernandez said fastidiously. "Though it was somewhat like performing an autopsy on a drowning victim, yes. There may have been more blood, but it would be unusual for this not to have shown on the clothing. I must say, however, the abrasions elsewhere on the body appear to be from...ur...the garbage truck? Shall we go on?"

Annie nodded, finding it slightly fascinating that an ME, who saw every kind of injury possible, didn't want to think about the compactor function of a garbage truck and its interaction with a body. She apparently shared John's active imagination.

Upon removal of the shirt and suit coat, the body is turned to reveal a second wound, entering below the clavicle through the ribs on the left side. The wound will be x-rayed but appears to enter at an angle pointing toward the armpit. The wound is smooth, with the opening of about one inch, consistent with an extremely sharp, but thin-bladed knife, similar to a fillet knife. Neither the shirt nor the suit coat are torn, further indicating a sharp weapon. Further examination is appended below.

She looked up, but Annie and John were both writing, so she went on.

The genitalia are that of an adult male and there is no evidence of injury. There is, however, shrinkage consistent with a natural or synthetic trigger.

"What does that mean?" John asked. Annie had seen it before. Several drugs, but especially Adrenaline, or speed, did that.

"Any number of causes. The Fight or Flight response triggers hormone surges to protect the genitals, I believe. Violent deaths, you see it," Dr. Hernandez said.

Violent death. And at some level, he had been aware of it? Was the reaction ever triggered in an unconscious victim? Were there drugs in the victim's system that triggered it? Annie decided to hold her questions, but she wrote them in the margin. Dr. Hernandez waited to see John look down again at his notes, and then continued.

Pubic hair is normal. Limbs are equal, symmetrically developed and show no evidence of injury beyond probable compacting. Nail beds on fingers and toes are slightly blue, consistent with prolonged exposure to damp and cold, though this does not rule out other causes. Hands are extensively photographed after this observation is made. An old scar, consistent with a bullet wound from a high-powered rifle, is apparent on the lower right shin. Approximate age of the scar is twenty years; beyond the apparent age of the wound, no further information appears to tie it to any

permanent injury or to the current investigation.

"Vietnam," John said. When Annie looked at him, he shrugged. "He was introduced as a veteran when he was appointed," he said. "So nothing that would indicate any real external injury to the lower body?"

"No, just a few abrasions, as I said, consistent with having been...whatever," she said. "I expected to see more, actually."

Annie again noted the ME's discomfort with the garbage truck's compacting process vis a vis a human body, given all of the horrific injuries she must have seen. 'He was cushioned by paper products, is our theory," she said. Annie made a note to talk with Hernandez about it again in Anchorage. The last thing they wanted was an ME testifying on the stand that all injuries could be due to the garbage compaction process.

"That would do it," Hernandez agreed. Anyway, no real injury to the lower body. So. **INTERNAL EXAMINATION**, page 3."

SKELETAL SYSTEM: No evidence of damage beyond some compacting.

RESPIRATORY SYSTEM - THROAT STRUCTURES: throat area impacted by path

of the bullet. substantial blood in trachea. Overall oral cavity shows constriction. Mucosa of the lips and the interior of the mouth is bluish-gray, distorted by moisture and compacted areas of what presents as small clumps of foam, consistent with vomit or other discharge. Mucosa otherwise are intact and there are no injuries to lips, teeth or gums. Victim bit the inside of his cheeks; scars are old. Teeth and gums are normal.

Airway is constricted by compacting and partially filled with blood and fluid. Epiglottis, glottis, piriform sinuses, trachea and major bronchi are observed to be somewhat compacted, consistent with pressure, but no signs of strangulation are apparent. Pressure presents as postmortem. Shadowed pressure marks also appear on the chest and rib area, but no bruising or tissue damage are apparent. Knife or sharp implement wound is now apparent and measures 1.75 inches at entry, .2 at the tip, and 8 inches total length. Path of the wound is observed to be in tissue not consistent with a cause of death.

Lungs weigh: right, 380 grams; left 396 grams. Lungs appear to be compressed, but

are otherwise undamaged. Death was not caused by drowning.

Remembering the pool of water in which the Commissioner's body was found, Annie actually snorted. She received a stern frown from the ME, but a big smile from John. In the silence, something was not being said. Annie looked closely at the ME, but she looked back at the autopsy report. "Anything there?" Annie asked. The number of things that were not the cause of death was expanding.

Dr. Hernandez would not be hurried. "Not yet," she replied.

CARDIOVASCULAR SYSTEM: The heart weighs 270 grams, and has a normal size and configuration. No evidence of atherosclerosis is present. The heart itself shows signs of recent "incident," cause undetermined. Death by Myocardial infarction is not eliminated.

Annie put a big question mark in the margin and circled it. John watched her.

GASTROINTESTINAL SYSTEM: The mucosa and wall of the esophagus are intact and gray, without lesions or injuries. The

gastric mucosa is intact and pink without injury. No food is found in the stomach. The mucosa of the duodenum, jejunum, ileum, colon and rectum are intact. Some coagulated blood is apparent in the body cavity, exclusively on the left side. Lividity indicates body was not level when bleeding occurred.

URINARY SYSTEM: Kidneys weigh: left 125 grams, right 122 grams. They are anatomic in size, shape and location and are without lesions.

TOXICOLOGY: Samples of right plural blood, bile and urine are submitted for toxicologic analysis. Vomitus or other foam-like substance on the edges of the lips, and dried nasal discharge are sampled and submitted for toxicologic analysis. Tissue from constriction of the airway is sampled and submitted. Heart tissue is sampled and submitted. Stomach tissue is sampled and submitted.

SEROLOGY: A sample of left pleural blood is submitted in the EDTA tube. Level 2 Toxicologic studies were ordered, requesting identification of any foreign substances in the fluid samples.

"Huh." Annie didn't like where this was going. They had done nothing to check for drug use in any of their questioning. It was possible that, when tox came back, there would need to be some new interviews. "Any estimates on when tox will be done?" she asked, circling that section of the report.

"Two weeks, maybe," Dr. Hernandez said. "I have to say that that's what I'm looking for as cause of death."

"Wait, what?" John said.

Annie merely sighed. "Shot in the neck, stabbed in the back, and we're looking at tox. Is this inefficiency or affect? What about the damage to the throat? The possible heart connection?"

"I would not say that the damage to the throat, though it did cause bleeding, was sufficient to cause death. There was no blood in the area around where he was found, am I correct?" When both Annie and John demurred and spoke of the rain, and the garbage, she said, "The same is true for the knife. There's a little bleeding around the wound, but indications are he was possibly already dead. The knife did no catastrophic damage, nor was the body cavity filled with blood, as it often is with a torso knife wound. A slash wound is definitely worse in that regard. If asked, I would say that neither of the weapons in question struck fatally."

"Huh," Annie said again. She hadn't really expected the knife was anything other than symbolic, but most people couldn't stick a knife in without causing damage, and here was one that did almost nothing. A conundrum. Still, she had expected the gunshot wound to be the cause of death. The throat was so full of things that bled. That said, she had seen people survive a slashed jugular, if it was sloppily done and help was rapid. Why hadn't the shot been to the head? Unless, unless, the murderer thought the victim already mortally wounded or dead, and the wounds were for effect, or something else. She acknowledged that since the first day of this investigation, she had viewed the gun and knife as symbolic of a personal vendetta.

She made more notes, then said, "Anything you haven't written yet, off the record, that might help direct us?"

"Bluing around the lips, a little residue of something on the mouth, pinpoint pupils, and I'm looking at possible overdose. I don't want to put anything down until we see tox, and then I hope it gives us something."

Annie and John sat forward, surprised into silence. Overdose? Annie suddenly went back two paragraphs and said, "did anyone look at the shirt front?"

"For what, beyond the blood on the collar?"

"Let me ask it another way. Was there any evidence of a neck restraint, anything that could have been a struggle..." Annie's voice trailed off, because she really didn't have a coherent question to ask, just a feeling that something was not right.

"Possibly. Not on the body, but maybe on the shirt. There were some scratches there, actually. On the shirt. I thought...you know, the truck."

"Taser," said John, at the same time Annie said, "Tased," with a finality that made Dr. Hernandez look hard at both of then.

"We've maybe been looking at this wrong," Annie suggested. "If you can find any evidence of a taser at all, it changes things. As you know, they can leave scratch marks on fabric. If he was tased, we don't have to look for a person who could subdue a big, healthy, physically fit man. Though he would still have to be able to lift him."

"I don't know," Hernandez temporized. "There is a little mark on the shirt. Nothing on the skin. There's some discoloration around the bullet wound. But..." Hernandez, normally the voice for sticking to the evidence, had apparently reached the limit of her ability to speculate. "We'll look at everything again. Maybe under a microscope, the taser holes through the shirt might be there, or they might be in the tie. Or there might be none. There were none on the body. If it is a taser, we may not see any body effects, I don't think, after so long. One must suppose...was the body transported..." she stopped herself. "Of course it was. I mean, was the body moved prior to death?"

They all thought about it. A taser could kill. If it was used in the chest, and full on, it might cause a heart attack. That had been the "heart incident" Annie had looked back at. But it took a person skilled with a taser to know how much juice to use to stun, how much to kill.

"If the killer used a taser, then we go back to the gun or the knife as the cause of death, right?" John asked. "Pending the tox screen? No signs of strangulation or suffocation in general, right?"

Hernandez shook her head slowly, making notes, reading, making more notes. "We'll check. Annie, when you get here, I'll have better information. As I said, don't bring me this kind of body any more. I'm too busy for this. Why would anyone do all of these things?"

"These are all good questions," Annie mused. "I guess we wait for tox. Too bad we don't have a lab in state. Nothing is shared with anyone until we have a final, right?"

"The Governor called. Himself. But I'm only going to tell anyone what we're sure of, and anyone I tell is only going to be you. I don't like the pressure. He shouldn't have called." Dr. Hernandez was a strict by-the-rules kind of professional, and she had that medical degree that commonly shielded her from politics.

Annie thought she should be so lucky. No one, not the family, not the press, not the Governor himself were going to hear this until there was absolute proof. She said, carefully, because Maria Hernandez could get testy and Annie appreciated her theories as much as her facts. "You looked for needle marks? I'm sure you did, just want to write it down."

"Of course. No sign on the arms, nothing that I could see between the toes. Actually, we all looked--meaning my assistants and the intern--because the condition of the body would obscure some kinds of marks. Tissues were swollen. Tox will show us something, but whether it will be an answer, or more questions, we don't know. And you may be a long time proving what we theorize to a jury."

They thanked Dr. Hernandez, terminated the connection, and sat. John seemed particularly pensive. He said, "I don't know what AIB's solve rate is. I know it's good, that you're good. I'm happy to turn this over to you. This is the tar baby, and I'm thinking you'll never solve it. I know, if we worked it down here, we never would. Too many weapons, no sure things. No crime scene.

No time of death. Seventy-two ways out of town. Years of people who might hate him. We are, pardon my french, screwed. We have to hope he was doing drugs and not paying, but I don't think there's an iceberg's chance in hell that he ever even used."

Annie replied, "That's why we call it 'fishing' and not 'catching,' as my old daddy used to say. Or 'investigating,' or any of the other euphemisms we use. I'll go over and talk to HR at Fish and Game, and I'd like to see what came off of Grossman's answering machine, so we know exactly what time he called. Then, I thought of another thing. When someone goes back to use the fuel pump behind Fish and Game's, do they clock in? I thought so," as John nodded. "So let's try that, and see what the unis got on the follow up on the license plates. Someone might have seen something. We need the exact time of pickup at the two dumpster sites. We need the hair comparison. We need the coat. I've got a bad feeling about the coat.

"At this point, I just don't want to go back to Anchorage and suddenly realize I needed to talk to someone else, or again, or whatever. So if you can spare the time, I know you're busy and I'm supposed to be taking this, but anyone you think I should talk with, shout out."

They parted, Annie to her loaner car to go down to Fish and Game and talk with the HR Director, who was a pleasant woman who said she would make time for Annie whenever she arrived, and John to his neglected desk.

On the way to her car, she walked out to the bay where the victim's truck still sat. She walked around the truck. She stood behind it and looked through the undercarriage to see if she could see the wall on the other side. Nope. Transmission and drive shaft mostly in the way. Shocks in the way from some angles. Big tires in the way from some angles. Big hulking double cab with a canopy, like a van in some ways. Certainly in length. All of JPD's notes and pictures needed to be packed to travel. Perhaps she should take more pictures. She went back in to talk with criminalistics and see what they actually had.

Chapter Seventeen

Friday, October 18, 1998 - 11:00 a.m.

Annie woke to the sound of silence in her little apartment, because for some odd reason it wasn't raining. It might, to be honest, be snowing. There were so few sounds that Annie wondered if she had overslept. There was a little natural light at the windows. She went to the bathroom, turned on the coffee, and got back in bed.

Immediately, the earworm world awoke. *Jumped back in bed it was the middle of the night* began an irritating loop. She pushed it away. What to ask Fish and Game's HR Director, now that the ME's report had basically upended any tentative theory she might have concocted. She looked at her little clock radio. 6:30. Not exactly the middle of the night. She missed Fred's little snore, and she missed Bones at the edge of the bed, a coiled Springer, waiting for either of them to move so he could begin to dance about, ready for a walk, an outing to the refrigerator, anything. They had a slightly hyper dog, but he was so loving.

She thought about Clyde Bunsen. Some link to drug use. Certainly to alcohol, but that wasn't what was going on here. Suddenly she had a thought. Clyde had slept all night in the restroom, and he didn't remember falling asleep. He lost his cart, which was unusual, and found it by the elevators. He didn't want to talk about it. What if he, too, had been tased? The vision rose: Clyde rubbing his chest, during their interview, while thinking about his lost cart. It might be nothing. Why would a killer tase a janitor, who might then wake up, but do nothing else? Was he trying to see how long it took someone to fall? She took her little tape recorder from the bedside table and talked about it for a bit. Having recorded her concern, she got up. She might as well.

Later, showered and dressed, walking around with a coffee cup and a ball of string, she thought about the biggest "missing piece." Who. If there had been a person who had been at the forefront of suspicion last week, it would have been someone at the meeting where the confrontations had been. Who lost? Who lost big? And how would killing Grossman change that? From what Schwartz said, this was early in the budgeting process, but there was certainly some indication of where the cuts might be. Still, cuts or no, she didn't see any of these political appointees sneakin' and creepin' and murderin'. Possible. She just couldn't see it.

She thought about Cathy Munson and the Juneau cliques. She reviewed the list of disgruntled employees. Maybe the HR Director could tell her which were protected Juneauites. Munson had said that if you messed with someone politically and familially connected to the actual Juneau residents, that wouldn't go well for you. Still, murder? It was more likely that someone like Grossman would simply be told, "you can't do that, and here's why." He might actually see that power thing that held him in check, and turn away.

But it gave her something to discuss with the HR Director, and that got her seriously up and going.

She was there at the stroke of 11:00--an anachronism, Annie thought, since no bells rang. She parked in the public parking lot she had used yesterday, and went in the public entrance. She took the elevator to the second floor, and went in the door marked "Human Resources."

Grace Fleeber was the HR Director. She was a motherly woman of indeterminate middle age, hair and clothing neatly arranged, and modest jewelry. She had been showing something to the clerical person outside her door when Annie came into the reception area. When Annie introduced herself, she smiled, said, "Please hold my calls" to her secretary. They went into the inner office and close the door.

Annie had not met this woman before, had not, in fact, met anyone so welcoming. Must come with the job, the appropriate demeanor and so forth. But also used to directing people. She took her assigned seat. It was hard for anyone who had ever been called on the carpet not to react to the HR Officer with a little foreboding. They were the negotiators, they could hide. "I'm just doing some mop-up, and I hope you have time for a few questions," she said.

"Certainly! How can I help?" Fleeber folded her hands on the desk in front of her, all comfort and ease.

"This may sound funny, but everyone to whom I speak seems to be shrugging or ducking, and I know that there is a third category. I'd like to know two things from you, in general. First, did Grossman ask you to find a way to hire people he knew in his last positions?" She saw something instantly in Fleeber's eyes. So he had made such a request. Then, wait for it, Fleeber *shrugged.*

"That's normal, you know," she said. "For a Commissioner to bring people he can trust to solve problems. They are almost exclusively consultants, and often they come and go for particular jobs. Someone might come to write a specific set of regulations, for example, or to put out an informational publication that's politically sensitive. Someone might be brought in to design a new system, or program, or train employees to manage a certain kind of data. So, more 'expertise,' than 'find a way to hire.'

"There are also exempt positions, approved by the governor. Actually, there are public information people, supervisory people, and so forth, that the Commissioner can move out of exempt through reorganization, so that makes more room for employees whose productivity is a 'known' quantity from previous experience." Grace Fleeber thought for a moment, decided that she had answered the question, and arranged her face and body in a more open posture.

"I'd like to know who those people were, and if they are still here, or who they replaced." Annie knew there was information here, but Fleeber was shaking her head. It had been worth a try. "You know," Annie said, "this is a murder investigation. Roberts gave me disgruntled. He didn't give me anyone who held special personal status with the Commissioner."

"There was only the one man, from Anchorage, who came down after we lost...after the reorganization took...after we no longer had an IT supervisor."

Fleeber seemed momentarily flustered. Annie asked for the man's name.

"George Lightly. He's back in Anchorage, as of a few weeks ago. He was just here on a consultancy, and his family wouldn't move to Juneau."

"No others, in the whole first term?"

"Commissioner Grossman wasn't here the whole term. He came in the second year. And he wanted to bring his secretary with him, but that's a position on the register, not exempt. That I think he got changed. In any case, we've been trying to match him with...well, that's not germane now, is it. He didn't always like the secretaries who were available to him on the register."

"He did have someone who came and looked at all of the state game regs and made suggestions. Those were then turned over to staff to generate some proposed changes. So I remember those two. George and...I'll have to look it up."

"Did he come in and tell you there were people you needed to find a way to fire?"

"Oh, they all do that. They have to have a lesson on the contract. It's strong, here. This is a union town. The teacher's union is the strongest in the state. The State Employees are just about as strong. So we have to proceed with due process, and no one who is here under the pressure of making changes in one or two gubernatorial terms wants to move rapidly. No can do, most of the time. I don't react to it. They find ways, after a time, to do what they want to accomplish."

"Like a reorganization that eliminates certain positions?" Annie mused.

"Exactly like, I would suppose, although I haven't been involved in any such discussions."

I'll bet not, thought Annie. "As I've said, several people have told me that you can't mess with anyone who has certain historical connections to Juneau itself. Do you think that's right?"

"Certainly it is, and that's another thing Juneau newbies in power positions have to learn. They can't just go through the departments with a broom. The Union is strong, but the Juneau mafia, if you'll excuse the analogy, is stronger. Surely you've seen that. I think Alaskans are so used to short-timers that those who have to stay and mop up get testy about it." She laughed merrily. "Don't you have that in public safety around the state?"

"Oh, yes," Annie responded with her own laugh. "They'll even tell you about it. You don't go into Bethel and replace the public safety officer if it's someone whose family historically came from the village. But you might see why this interests me about Juneau. Were there any people on the 'disgruntled' list Roberts gave me who should have been protected?"

Fleeber frowned, chose words carefully, and Annie saw the particular skills of a successful HR person in state government. "I gave Deputy Co Roberts the list of employees who had resigned or been reorged under some conflict or pressure, but I don't know what list you have."

Annie thumbed through her papers and pulled out the list, which she handed over to Fleeber, who appeared to read it carefully and then frowned.

"I don't see anyone," she said.

Annie didn't buy it, so she tried once more. "No one there a life-long Juneau resident, for example?"

"Not that I see. But I don't know everyone's personal background. So," Fleeber continued, "that was one thing, I presume. What's the other?"

BS, Annie thought, and a skillful topic shift. As if this person, who could be a long-time Juneauite herself for all Annie knew, would be in her position and not know who was connected to whom. The woman was going to be polite, but unhelpful in the extreme. As a long-time, surviving HR director tiptoeing through a minefield of union contracts, political appointments and powerful people used to having their way, the woman probably wore her role to bed. She sighed mentally and then asked, "Did he have fans? Did any employees think he was doing a great job?"

Fleeber laughed again. "Fans. That's a new one. No, I don't suppose he did. How would I know? Do you know how popular the HR Director is walking about the floors of the building? All conversations stop."

Annie waved that away. "I would assume. But what about people who come in to talk with you about saving their job?"

"Certainly there are those. People coming in to say, 'gee, this guy's great!' not so much."

Annie tried to think of another way to ask the question, but couldn't. She finally said, recognizing as she did that Fleeber had a way of making people speak their minds, "The picture I'm getting is pretty one-sided. I'm hunting for balance, trying to get a fair picture of his management style, his staff relationships, that doesn't make everyone his potential enemy."

Fleeber thought about that. Annie could see her deciding something. Finally, the silence worked its magic, and Fleeber said, "That's great, but I can't help you much, I'm afraid. I see people who complain, who are hurt, scared, aggrieved. The ones who are happy and productive are pretty hard to tell from those who are studiously busy and politically careful. I don't suppose I would be able to point you at a single person. I don't think anyone was actively plotting his demise, but I don't think I would have known if they were."

"Any active complaints?"

"One. Wrongful termination from the man who used to sit at the reception desk talking to his girlfriend and doing crossword puzzles. Fortunately, he was the only person at his level in the entire department. Pretty much at that clerical level we're looking at filing and copying, mail distribution. No one wanted him. He was a long-time employee, but he had a bad work record that had been carefully ignored. He was two years from retirement. I think most people would have left him in place, but he wasn't a good face for the Department, first thing out of the elevator. There won't be anything come of it."

"Does the complaint make any specific charges against Grossman?"

"Just that Grossman told him he needed to go home and change, and maybe take a bath." Fleeber stared at Annie, who was obviously showing signs of shock.

"Can you do that anymore?" Annie finally managed.

"Of course not. I tap danced that one right back into vaudeville before we had a lawsuit."

"How?" Annie asked, genuinely interested, if appalled. "You must have skills on your skills."

"Actually, I told the shop steward we had documentation of previous supervisors talking to him about personal hygiene. I think we might. Anyway, someone in the copy center finally offered for him, and he was gone, so now we're just dealing with the slow-tracked complaint. There was no loss of pay, and now he's nearly to retirement, so I don't think there will be a law suit. It was also hearsay. He claimed someone *heard it said...*" Fleeber laughed at her little pun and shrugged her shoulders again. "Tempest in a Teapot," she concluded.

Annie rather thought so as well. "If you think of anything that might have bearing on the investigation, here's my card."

"Do you know yet were and how he was killed?" Fleeber asked.

"Ongoing investigation, but we do know some things. He wasn't killed at the dump, which is where everyone knows he was found. Beyond that, we can't really release any details."

"You're still looking at someone from his own staff?"

"We haven't ruled that out, actually."

"Okay." Fleeber took the card and looked at it. "If I think of anyone with or without motive, I'll give you a call."

That infectious smile. She really was like someone's favorite aunt. But she hadn't had any information that Annie needed, beyond one name which, Annie thought, would probably amount to nothing.

"I'd like to see his office. I have the JPD search warrant with me this time to show Roberts. I know that the JPD took his calendar, and some other things Roberts undoubtedly knows about, but I'm basically starting at the beginning to just see if another pair of eyes lands on something of use. Would you walk me up there so he knows I'm not skulking around?"

"Certainly. Since Deputy Roberts has been appointed Acting, he may be holding meetings in the conference room that is attached to the Commissioner's actual office."

They walked down to the opposite end of the floor, and to the corner office suite that overlooked the Channel. Annie thought to herself that all corner offices were the same, everywhere. Coveted, reserved for the most politically powerful, and at the end of a maze of cubicles that screened the aristocracy from the peons.

Apparently Fleeber was a non-threatening presence for the Commissioner's close staff. She was greeted by name, there were smiles and helpfulness. Roberts was not using Grossman's office. That would break protocol. The room was only for one person. If, in fact, Roberts' 'acting' status was actually confirmed to the real position, or extended while the Governor made another selection, he might move into the office, but not before. Therefore, only secretaries went in and out, the faceless, opinionless political spouses of the powerful. Annie had always wondered whether they could be excluded from testifying by way of their close understanding of the true activities of the powerful. In fact, most had non-disclosure agreements if they were in the rare air of top appointments. But Fleeber appeared to know the magic words.

Thus, Annie was given time alone, with the newly updated search warrant, and secretaries and ultimately the Deputy Commissioner hovering outside of the door. The desk had been gone through, but in the back of the lower, file drawer, there was something: she found cards which had fallen over and slid under the last files. They were blank inside; there were no envelopes. On the front of each was only a cryptic acronym. One said ESAD. She thought about that. Another said DYSTP. The third said DFF. Something told her to take them, and she was gloved, so she put them in an evidence bag, of which she always carried several on an active scene. Was this an active scene? Who knew. She would call the card company on Monday and see what the letters stood for. And try to figure out why they were where they were, if it wasn't an accident. Or a red herring.

Two pictures on the wall showed Grossman, first with a massive grizzly bear and then with a chubby senator from Washington holding a monster King beside a guide boat. With Grossman. The credenza held a scrimshawed walrus tusk, with a scene of walrus hunters in attigis, also polished for a cribbage board. And an oosik. It seemed everyone had to have one. It made Annie sad. Why carry around the genitals of something you have killed? She understood that they were valuable. It was just undignified, disgusting even, and showed a lack of humanity, rather like the soldiers who made tobacco pouches out of the breasts of massacred native women.

On Grossman's desk was another picture, of his wife holding their daughter, their two sons standing behind her. Next to that, a paperweight with "in appreciation" etched into it. There was a logo on it she didn't recognize, but she took it into evidence because it was an unusual, positive piece and might lead her to the friendlier former contacts willing to answer some questions. Chief among these was why this man, so adept at making enemies, would ever have been appointed by the current Governor. In any case, it was the only such plaque. Most Commissioners had several of these. She remembered the gilded gold pan in Commissioner Doyle's office, and the those that ringed it, from Native Associations, Regional Corporations, Foundations, Philanthropic organizations.

Other than these pictures and the plaque, there were few personal things. There were no books, only state maps on the wall, the credenza, a couch, and a conference table. Windows everywhere except between his office and the secretaries who sat in the more public area in front of it. If they wanted to see him, Annie thought, they must need to knock or call first.

Have to watch drawing that as a conclusion, she thought, but Annie never got the artificial status thing. You either had presence or you didn't. If you needed to build walls to enforce your importance, you probably were pretty shaky with it.

She finished the desk, she took pictures of the pictures, she made notes on things that should have been there and were missing. Like anything in the credenza itself. Totally empty. She needed to check with John about what was taken before. Personnel files moved into Roberts' office for safety? Or maybe it was purely a piece of decorative furniture, holding as it did a small drip coffeemaker, cups and various things to stir into coffee. None had been used.

She went back to the two pictures on the wall. She stood before Grossman standing beside a huge grizzly bear head. The bear's body stretched behind it like a rug. Posed, apparently. Grossman had his rifle, and one foot on the bear's head. Seemed strange to pose that way, for someone who ran Fish and Game. Disrespectful. However, you could look in any hunting magazine and on the walls of sporting goods stores and you would see the same type of thing. Why pose with a corpse?

Annie caught herself, hard. These were her values, not those of the victim. She was in serious need of recapturing advocacy for the victim, because everything she had seen and heard had been so negative. Collect the evidence. Bring justice to the family. That was the primary mantra, and she needed to be saying it to herself until it stuck.

Then she remembered where she had seen the logo on the appreciation plaque before. The Professional Guide's Association. Huh.

Chapter Eighteen

Sunday, October 20,1998 - 4:00 p.m.

The plane took off, did its abrupt directional shift with the temporary backing off of the jet engines, which jolted Annie's sensibilities and often triggered panic attacks. Properly medicated, she noted it and tried to breathe deeply to calm herself. Soon enough, they leveled out and what passed for comfort on a flight began to assert itself. Annie knew every sound that was normal, and how many seconds the jet's normal ascent took to get to every sound. Somewhere, she tracked them in her head. This time of year, they flew down the inlet, passed over the ferry terminal, rose over some distant villages and only then climbed between and above the mountains.

When the stewardess signaled 10,000 feet with the caution to stay seated, Annie noted the normal ascent at some deep level and calmed a bit. She took out her notes, which she had carefully gone over on Saturday, after talking one last time with John, seeing the truck for one more review of the evidence there, and talking once more with Clyde Bunsen.

Because the medication kept her from concentrating on anything too long, Annie bounced from clue to blind alley, from plausible to implausible scenario, from the disgruntled to the cold and calculating. There was the new information. After spending the better part of yesterday trying to pick the brains of both JPD detectives about drugs in Juneau and talking again to Clyde Bunsen who "don't know nothin' bout drugs. Nasty stuff, that," Annie had little that was helpful. Clyde had been genuinely horrified that anyone would think he had access to hard drugs. *Nasty stuff.*

She agreed. There was literally no evidence, according to Hernandez, that Grossman had ever been a user. They had his computer. Annie had looked at that in the lab at the Police Department. They did not have his phone; it was probably somewhere in the Dump. They had tried calling it, and got nothing. Roberts said that "The Co didn't like it," and there was no record of a call to Mrs. Grossman on the cell printout. So he must have used the phone on the reception desk outside the Governor's conference room. That fit the 5:30 timing better in any case.

The home computer was clean. Mrs. Grossman was correct, there wasn't anything personal, to speak of. Grossman had liked World of Warcraft, and that fit, somehow. He wasn't a presence on email. He didn't cast any kind of net using one of the nascent search engines. That also fit with what she had been told. The computer was now in the baggage hold, going to tech support in the Anchorage office, and they would identify if Grossman had anything of interest hidden away. Annie loved where the world wide web was going, she just wished she had the time to stop everything and learn more about what resources were out there. It was definitely the "wave" of the future, that and DNA, for police work. She had heard that England was going to put cameras on every block. That would have made the whole dumpster thing a slam dunk, but no such luck in Juneau.

His office computer had also been confiscated, because more and more, there was a computer link to every crime. But as far as she could cursorily see, there was nothing on that, either. She remembered Mrs. Grossman saying that her husband didn't believe in writing things down, that email was dangerous. Someone from tech needed to take a deep dive into what might have been erased, but the state email system was so old and rickety that she scarcely used it herself.

So, tomorrow get things organized, follow up some more leads, make appointments with Fish and Game staff in Anchorage's regional office, and then she needed to see the actual body. There were things she needed to check into evidence, and she wanted to get some pictures developed or digitized, or whatever Jason, the clerical who helped her and the other three investigators, thought could be done with them.

She had talked to John about the possibility of Clyde being tased. He had suggested she ask Clyde, because the JPD detectives seemed to make the man nervous. So she had. He had not recalled any unusual marks on his person, anywhere. He had no remembrance of falling, no bruises, just that he was cleaning the floor in the restroom and then he woke up on the floor in that same place. He recalled no sensations prior to waking up. He said if he had been "electrified" he would have known it. Annie was not so sure. Clyde had admitted to some personal alcohol problems, and occasional use of grass, which was decriminalized by no less than the Alaska Supreme Court, if it was in his own home. So, if he was a little "tooted," as he called it, he might have been oblivious to someone sneaking up on him in his labors. She now believed that that was what had happened.

Why tase Clyde? So he was not a witness, would be her guess. Why was Clyde's trash cart down by the elevators? What was he hiding about that scenario? She jerked into sharp consciousness. John needed to confiscate that cart, and check it for evidence. Why hadn't they done that? This wasn't exactly rocket science. It actually made sense, in her altered state. The cart wasn't where it was supposed to be, ergo, someone had moved it. She made a note, because she probably wouldn't otherwise remember to call John.

They bumped down over the Chugach mountains, made the big loop around Fire Island, and landed. She got her rolling bag out from under the seat and waited for the crowd to pass her, as she was clumsy and slow in this state. She wished that Fred could still come to the gate, but that had gone by the wayside. People had to stay with their cars. She made her way down to the baggage claim area, got a cart someone had left, and piled all of her baggage, including the boxed computer, to a satisfying peak, where she put her hand. Then Fred was there, putting everything in at the curb. They held one another for a moment.

"Let's go to La Mex," she said. "I could use a margarita." She hugged and wiggled with Bones, who was in the back seat on a rug, and then crawled into the front seat and rested against it for the first time in several days, with Bones as close to having his head on her shoulder as he could get from the back seat. Plane flights left her entirely drained, exhausted, and apprehensive about the next flight, as yet unscheduled. Fred finished loading everything and got in the driver's seat.

"La Mex it is," he agreed.

Over the years, they had done their best planning and thinking on the backs of placemats at La Mex. It was an old restaurant, now with three different sites, and they liked the oldest one with the slightly sleezy bar dominated by a picture of a woman with one huge breast in an equally huge margarita glass.

In the back of the restaurant were the old-fashioned, private booths, where you could safely converse without anyone else hearing you. And the placemats were printed with Alaskan animals on the front, but on the back, they were blank. She had several, covered with lists and diagrams, in her desk at work. Periodically, she pulled them out and laughed over the stages of her Alaskan career, and Fred's, or crumpled them up and pitched them in her desk's trash can.

They parked, assured Bones that he would get a "white package," which was the doggie bag *du jour*, and went in. In the dim recesses of the restaurant they found a corner booth that had no direct view of the rest of the room, ordered their drinks and settled in.

"This is a hard one," Fred offered. "I can see it all over you."

"Yeah," she agreed. "I can't see the threads coming together yet. I guess, because we really don't have a fixed crime scene, we didn't have the normal start of things. Most of the actual tech work didn't start til after I got there. I think the JPD did everything they could have, given the timing and all, but it was just a big, wet, nothing to me. Even starting everything over didn't really provide clarity." She was quiet for a bit, and reached for Fred's hand under the table as the drinks came. They shared a squeeze of mutual reassurance, and she sipped. "Good," she said.

"So," Fred asked, "you want tostaditos again? Or the deluxe burrito?"

"Burrito. With cheese sauce. My defenses are down."

"Burrito it is." Fred watched the waiter come to them, gave him the orders, moved the chips where Annie could reach them. When they were both crunching happily on the best salsa and chips in town, he told her how his week had gone.

"I'm going out to Anaktuvak Pass to see what might be done to the Borough Building there. It's sinking on one side, apparently. I was going to have to make arrangements for Bones, so it's good you're home this week."

"Glad to oblige. Glad to be home," Annie offered, smiling at his beloved and familiar face, so strong of feature, so open and approachable. "You know, if you had been Commissioner, there wouldn't have been a murder."

"Where did that come from," Fred wondered, smiling at what may have been a non-sequitur, but which he knew from long experience was not.

"Oh, you know, no one seemed to like him but his family, and he was not kind to subordinates. Scratch that," Annie said, taking a deep swallow and pushing the drink away until there was food to offset the alcohol. "He was mean. I hate to say that about a victim, and I'm hoping it has nothing to do with the murder."

Fred raised his eyebrows and looked at her.

"I know," she said, "I generally don't use that word this early. I'm using it with you. He was murdered, and we have no idea if it was a stranger or someone he hurt. It feels personal, but it feels like he wasn't aware of any threat. He was mean, but he was smart, and if there was a threat, he was tracking it. I can't find any evidence he was tracking this one." Somehow, unbidden, the cards in his desk flitted across her consciousness, and just as rapidly were gone.

"Still," she mused, "the way the murder may have been done, which I'm beginning to see, says someone planned it, carefully. Not a murder of opportunity. So motive gets more and more important."

Food came. They ate, they talked about the building in the Pass, that there was snow in Anaktuvuk this early, and what he would take for gear. You flew out of Fairbanks on a small plane for that village, and if the plane went down in snow, you wanted gear along. Fred had obviously been thinking about what Annie had said, however, and he asked, "Wasn't there anything to the janitor, the one whose name sounds like lab equipment?"

"Yeah, Clyde Bunsen. His nickname is Burner, actually."

"No."

"Yes. Anyway, he is a person of some interest, but he may have been targeted by the same murderer, perhaps for practice." Annie briefly outlined the taser theory, and said it was on the one hand totally uncorroborated by evidence, and on the other an increasingly plausible scenario.

Fred said, "Huh," which with Annie's recent experience made him almost eligible for Detective. Then he said, "So someone watched Burner the week before, saw his route and habit conflicted with the time the killer wanted to do the job, and decided Burner needed to sleep through the big thing. Probably took Burner's trash cart down to the parking garage and used it to haul around the body. Maybe looks like a janitor so no one...what?"

Annie was staring at Fred. Why hadn't they thought about that possibility? She began to scribble questions and names with lines on the back of the placemat, shoveling food in at a rapid pace.

Fred smiled and tucked into his plate. "Annie," he said finally, if only to smooth out the wrinkles in her forehead, "You gave me all of that, just in pieces. You just need to rest. It will come clear to you. You know you do some of your best connecting of the pieces when you're under the influence of one of your flight medication. So maybe now you'll find the clarity you need."

Annie stopped writing, rubbed her face with both hands, and took Fred's hand again under the table. "Maybe so," she said. "Maybe so."

She'd think about it tomorrow, after she set up her office murder board, and put everything into some sort of order. Suddenly, she just wanted to sleep. They got Bones' white package, including the extra salsa he relished, and headed back out to the Subaru SUV that was such a good vehicle for frozen streets. On the way home, she fell asleep.

When they reached their condo, a three-story affair with a double garage that was built into a slope so that you entered on the second floor, Annie told Fred to leave everything in the car but her rolling bag, because she couldn't cope with more. She just wanted to crawl into bed, a bed that smelled right and felt right, where Fred was at the end of her arm's reach. She left him packing for his own trip and showered, set out a few things like her toothbrush and the irritating magnifying mirror she now had to use.

But when she finally got into bed, feeling much relaxed physically, her mind churned. Saturday had been a strange day, collecting the recorded unis' interviews, making sure to rephotograph with her own camera, having the brief meeting with Clyde, and looking over the information the local crime scene tech had gathered. She needed to remember to call John right away about the trash cart, and to check again to see if the hair from the headrest in the truck had been analyzed yet, beyond just looking at it. Not human hair, they said. A wig? It was a wig. Where were the wig and the coat? She had brought the hair with her in an evidence bag for Trace to look at or send to a lab somewhere.

Apparently, she dozed. Fred was in bed beside her, warm and comforting. She snuggled into the curve of his shoulder.

"Going to be able to sleep?" he asked.

"I think so, but there's one way to be sure."

Later, they held onto one another in the dark, both slightly out of breath and satisfyingly smug.

"Do you ever see Bones watching us from the end of the bed when we make love," Annie asked, "because I do. I can hear him breathing."

"I just didn't need that image, hon. Let's lock him out of the room."

Both of them knew how that would go. Bones would pitch an immediate fit, or whine persistently, or put his nose under the door as far as it would go, and inhale deeply. That always made them laugh. Making love as you aged was an art, Annie mused. You had to keep focus, you had to be inspired, you had to be careful not to hurt yourself. You had to innovate.

And on that note, she innovated, and then all three of them finally went to sleep.

Chapter Nineteen

Monday, October 21, 1998

Annie took Fred to the airport to catch the first of his two flights required to get into Anaktuvuk Pass. With luck, weather permitting and pilot willing, as they said in Alaska, he would be home in a couple of days. Til it snowed, Bones could spend the days in the little grassy fenced area behind their condo, where he had a cozy doghouse. She needed to put in some extended time in the office for a couple of days, so Fred being out of town worked, even though it wasn't her preference

The Police Administration and the State Troopers were in downtown Anchorage, near the big old hotels and next to Earthquake park, where the streets had fallen during the mega-earthquake of the 60's. Annie liked to tell people her office was on the faultline. She thought it was funny. Mostly it elicited blank stares.

Like many law enforcement agencies throughout the country, here in the late 90's hers was discovering they didn't have enough room, didn't have the right lab facilities for the increasingly sophisticated criminalistics that were the core of an increasing number of cases, needed to rethink the way in which they approached Alaska's dispersed and remote crimes.

Their facilities were co-located with the state courts, but those didn't have enough room either. Anchorage had good staff and facilities for a small "big" city, but everyone needed newer technology. When they had anything requiring state-of-the-art machines for spectroscopy and toxicologic analysis, evidence had to go out of state. It took weeks, which affected the cases themselves. By the time the results were back, perps were in the big wind. The Gulf Stream.

Admin was preparing a big capitol budget for the next legislative session. For the time being, Annie and other members of the Alaska Investigation Bureau were housed with the emerging major crime and the Troopers, both of which were also in need of space and laboratory access. Actually, things weren't so formal, and they all helped one another out, except those who didn't, but they existed in every organization.

Annie mostly ignored, sometimes at her own peril, all of the political stuff. And here she was...right in it.

The Morgue wasn't anywhere near law enforcement. It was in another area of government offices closer to the Hospital. Annie drove there first, pondering the difference between the popular police shows and the actual spaces in which investigators worked in most cities and states. Like the police offices, the morgue needed updating. There were morgues, mostly one-room facilities, in several of Alaska's larger towns, but they were basically cold storage. All complex cases came to Anchorage.

Most population centers had only a cold room, or perhaps a funeral establishment. Bodies might be kept frozen through the winter until grave digging was possible. There were still vestigial remains of a more frontier mentality, where the doctor appeared occasionally and the preacher passed through once a year and married all the couples living in "sin."

Corrections oversaw the public safety officers, troopers, prisons and jails, and that was Annie's branch. They had a fledgling crime lab that mostly dealt with fingerprints and the ilk, but collected specimens from both departments were sent to labs outside. The state's Coroner was actually part of Health and Social Services, so

Hernandez was both that and the ME. Why, Annie didn't know. Someone with power at some point in the past had decided that it was a social service function, hence Maria Hernandez's full plate. The coroner position was morphing into one of medical examiner, with the name change coming first, and variably used. Some states had them widely separated, but as sparsely populated as Alaska was, it wasn't a problem yet. They, like all of the other aligned professions, had to rely on their network of colleagues in a state where more than one person in any specialty was rare.

Annie pulled into lowest level of the parking garage, where the Morgue entrance was, and took the lower door into the bowels of the building. Why was the Morgue always on the bottom floor, like a dungeon? Annie wondered. A wide space in front of the "freight" doors (*no admittance, please, key required*) allowed an ambulance to back up and disgorge contents directly inside. When you went through the man door to the side, there was a short corridor, and then the double doors into the Morgue itself. The doors were heavy, designed to swing open for gurneys and close themselves slowly, so that nothing was knocked about that was passing through. Humming the intro to "Monster Mash," Annie went in through the office door and told the staff member who was pulling something from a file cabinet that she was here to see Dr. Hernandez and view the Grossman body.

Hernandez came out and got Annie, wiping her hands on a disposable towel. They went back to the cold room, and the Medical Examiner pulled out the drawer. "Do you want me to stay?" she asked.

"No need," Annie replied. "I'll come out in a bit and look at the x-rays, if I can, and then maybe we can talk a bit?" At the ME's nod, Annie laid back the sheet and looked at the victim.

Over the years, first as a beat cop and then as a trooper, Annie had seen many bodies. It wasn't like war; there generally wasn't carnage. The dead were often alone and there were few, if any, visible signs of cause of death. Part of the autopsy was a thorough cleaning of the body after trace was gathered.

You thought about that, but you developed a distance, or you went into some other line of work. You needed to shut down your emotional response, hardest when victims were children, and do your job. In Alaska, the remoteness, weather, dark, led to police spending a good deal of time at accidents. Uniforms had to stay on the scene until someone else came for the dead, unless they were in a village, and then they were EMT, Coroner and Investigator. You got as used to viewing bodies as a person of some compassion could get.

Annie looked at him. She needed him to stop being "the victim" or "the Commissioner," and see him as a person. He looked deceptively normal. Medical Examiners everywhere worked on that. It was for the families, who didn't need the vision of their mutilated loved one to pop up whenever his name was mentioned. Most people had, in Annie's experience never seen a dead person up close, life having evolved away from that. They needed to look...deceptively normal.

There were no particular marks that said, "taser" on the deceased's chest. Tasers seldom left a mark, but it was worth looking. Some scrapes and bruises on the chest, and these stood out against the pallor. She looked at the neck wound. The experienced eye said it was definitely an exit. She would see the angle of the entry when she saw the x-rays. She didn't touch the body, though she wanted to see his back. She walked to the other side of the tray and looked at the body from the right side. Nothing there that she could see. Everything was on the left. Standing on the right of the body, she shut her eyes and visualized how it might have gone down. The murderer was going to be right-handed like most people. She could see an amorphous figure grabbing the

Commissioner with a strong right arm and...what? Wrestling him to the ground?

Okay, that didn't work. The murderer walked right up to him, and that put the right arm on the Commissioner's left side. Suppose the taser is in the left hand. Reach out to shake right hands, tase with the left? Taser in the right hand would have to go across the body. But the murderer could have walked past, whipped around and tased him in the back, using either hand. Or the neck. Suppose the bullet wound was there to obscure the sign of a taser?

They needed to look at the front and the back of the shirt, but if he had had a suit coat on, and probably an overcoat (where was the coat, damn it?), it might not have been effective from the back. And where were the principals? Annie was more and more convinced that they were in the parking garage, but there had been nothing in the crime scene sweep, nothing in the truck. Had anyone looked in the back of the truck? Annie needed to remember to add that to the call to John.

Looking down at the body, Annie was certain the murderer was big, or of similar size and fit, and it all said "male" to her. Somehow, even if Grossman wasn't lifted into the truck here, and it took some strength to maneuver a body into the seat of a vehicle as big as his...wait. Fred's words were coming back to her. Hauled from the elevator in the cart to the back of the truck, put in there for the ride to the dumpster.

Fred could be right: Annie was beginning to put together the bits and pieces. But some things in a jigsaw puzzle looked alike until you got them next to where they fit exactly. She wasn't going to force anything. Her mother-in-law, for Pete's sake, took a scissors and made the pieces fit. She had actually known cops like that. The dumpster was pretty high, and it would be difficult to get a body as big as Grossman's up and over the edge. Unless you were standing on the tailgate of a pickup.

Annie looked at the rest of the body, spent a few more minutes with the head, covered him again and pushed the tray back into the drawer. There was no head trauma beyond the neck wound. Annie was again struck by the fact that someone had made this look amazingly easy. No defensive wounds, no physical trauma beyond those non-lethal wounds. The murderer was either insanely lucky or smooth as ice.

She walked out and waited, thinking. Maria Hernandez finished what she was doing and gave directions to her assistants to continue. They both went over to the x-ray system on the wall. Maria put Grossman's x-rays into the slots and turned on the backlights. They started with the neck wound.

"You can see that this is the entry, and it's a pretty clean pass-through, though it's obviously a small caliber," she said. "This is the pathway, so you can see it wasn't going to be lethal."

"Probably not designed to be," Annie mused.

"So, what? Just personal?" Maria asked, genuinely interested.

"I think...we have to wait for tox. But I've been giving it a lot of thought. If it was the metaphorical *coup de grace,* wouldn't it have been in the head? Why wasn't it in the head? No, I think it's something else."

"Camouflage?"

"Possible."

"There may be something in the tox. I don't have to tell you, but a bullet this size would seldom exit the skull. Just not powerful enough. So then you would have the ballistics; this way you don't."

"Huh." Again with the skillful murderer thesis. Didn't that argue for someone who had done this before?

They looked at the knife wound. Annie tried again to visualize how the wounds occurred. "My guess is that the body is on its stomach, in the bed of the pickup or the dumpster already, and the killer is tall enough to reach over, striking the side of the body which is closest to the edge of the dumpster. That makes the murderer right handed, right?"

Maria Hernandez though about it, positioned herself over a hypothetical body, and tried the angle of the knife entry using each hand. "I agree," she said. "I'd testify to that."

"You're undoubtedly right about the fillet knife. Smooth entry path, probably new. But we didn't find anything in the garbage.

"Would someone else dumping garbage have picked it up? I mean," Maria asked, "what if it was laying right there on the edge of the dumpster, or on the ground?"

"Possible. I don't think so. We have a careful murderer," Annie said. "Didn't make mistakes that we know of. We don't have witnesses. Unless you count the janitor, who said he was 'sleeping off a drunk' in the men's restroom at the time of the murder."

Maria raised her eyebrows. "Sleeping off a drunk."

"Yeah, and he doesn't remember anything about how that happened. One minute he's awake and then it's morning. We talked to him, after our meeting with you, thinking if the Commissioner had been tased, maybe he had as well. He said he would have known if he had been 'electrified'. But we don't think that he necessarily would have, if he was using something at the time. Maybe he'll remember something, at some point." Annie listened to herself. The theory of the crime was emerging.

"At any rate, you can see the wound paths, and there's nothing else. We wait for tox, as I said."

"Okay," Annie said, "let us know as soon as you hear anything."

"You do the same. At this time, we don't have much. Even when we have COD, we won't have much." The ME put on a new pair of gloves and turned back to the tables behind her, one of which was in progress.

Annie thanked Maria and nodded to the others on her way out. She got back to her car without thinking much about where she had even put it, and then stopped. Here she was in a parking garage. There was no one else in sight. She could take off all of her clothes and roll around on the pavement. No one would see her. No surveillance cameras. She was away from lights, which were only at the stairwells in any case, and there were plenty of places to hide. The dumpster sites were all too open. The parking garage had to be it.

She drove back to the Police complex on 4th. She parked in an AIB spot, and went in to get a cart for all of her paraphernalia. It took her the better part of an hour to say hello, check in with her boss, set up a time to debrief him, drop the computer off with their techie and sign everything into evidence, about which she was fastidious. She hated to compromise anything that might come back to haunt her, or anyone in the office, in the future.

There was a big white board behind her office door, with active cases in columns. Half was empty, so she put packets of notes in the tray, everything else on her little table, and went to check her mail and email.

The first thing she did was send an email to John. Have someone check the trash cart, was the first request. Reflexively, she looked at the calendar. Two weeks. After all of this time, might there be...drool? The carts were canvas. It was a stretch, but it was possible. Anyone call on the tip line? She would love to return those calls for John. They had used a local line because Juneauites were funny about calling Anchorage. So insular.

By noon, she had debriefed the boss, a short, muscled man from Georgia with the demeanor of the retired military officer he was. She was pretty sure he was Army, though she hadn't asked. There were more military in Alaska, per capita, than any other state--DEW line sites, two Air Force bases, two Army bases and Coast Guard installations. Every other person in a position of authority was retired military. No one particularly talked about it. It was double-dipping in retirement systems.

Beau Beatty was a competent administrator, but he was too reactive to what he perceived to be "the chain of command" for Annie. He wanted a response for the Governor. Annie gave him everything she had, which wasn't a response.

"So we can't release the body. Toxicology may reveal a cause of death, is what you're pussyfootin' around. Don't have a killer. What, exactly, do we have that I can tell him?" Beatty rested his hands on his little pot belly and regarded her fiercely over his readers.

"You can tell him it's a complex investigation, and that we don't want to alert the murderer to what we do know by releasing any details. How's that?" Annie wondered what the boss was after. He knew what she knew.

"It will do for a few days; then we'd better have something else."

"Beau, can you say *cold case?*"

"No. Don't you, either."

"Right. I need to use Carson for a bit, see if I can connect some dots," she said, alluding to the investigator to whom they assigned all manner of small tasks involving research into existing, but as yet cumbersome, data sources--driver's licenses, travel manifests, tax records, that sort of thing. Carson was a good research assistant, if he didn't bury himself in the data til someone had to reach a hand in and drag him out.

"Sure. Whatever you need. I'm taking you off of the McKenzie case. It's close to done, and Manfort can handle it. Just stay on this, and see if you can get it organized. Was what JPD had helpful?"

"They were great, but they are in an uproar down there, with the new offices. The best thing I can say is that they have security on everything that might be a clue. They are helpful if I need someone interviewed. Seriously, Sir, if you can imagine finding a body in a dump, delivered by a garbage truck...what can they do but sift through garbage for days? Beyond the weapons and possibly his coat, no one knows what we're looking for. Still, they were really careful, and we can take it from here."

"Good to hear. Been thinking about trying to get that John Sullivan up here. Phil Barnes is going to retire."

Annie nodded, said that would be good, refrained from saying that Phil Barnes had always been retired, from what she could see. "John's thorough, and good with interviews," she offered. Beatty began straightening papers. Annie took that as a signal that she might back out of the room, promising vague things about updating.

She got her files on the McKenzie case and took them to Darin Manfort, an Asian American man whose broad detective experience belied his youthful demeanor. He was taking increasingly complex cases on his own or with the third detective, Jamalia Hendericks, a retired MP from Fort Richardson, out after 20 years and working on her second, retirement.

Annie asked Jason Williams, AIB's clerical, about seeing if Carson had space in his schedule. She put her lists up with sticky spacers made for cabinet doors, durable and moveable. She liked the system. It was semi-permanent, like life. Instead of striped string, she now used colored dry erase pens. She tried to construct a timeline across the top, since there were, as yet, no suspects.

Huh. There were not a lot of actors in this. It was secret. It was personal. It was disconnected from the Commissioner's daily life. She thought about that. She hadn't said it to herself until now. It sounded and felt correct. Whoever had killed Grossman in this solitary and stealthy fashion was, at this point, a ghost. No footprints. No fingerprints. No obvious connection to anyone. Or some connection to all underlings, all vulnerable to an abusive boss. But whom?

Annie drank a cup of tea and was reviewing evidence when the phone rang. "Brewster," she answered.

"It's John, Annie. We had someone call on the tip line. The assistant state librarian was coming down from the next parking level up, which only has stairs at each end of the ramp. She saw Grossman, in his truck, leave the parking lot at 6:15 or so. She was going back to get something from her office, she said, for an early meeting. She just lives up the street. She left her home at six, and that's how she got to 6:15."

"She saw him clearly?"

"Says so. She said blonde curly hair, big man, alone in the truck, coat pulled up around his ears."

"Crap. I was just starting to think he was killed in the parking garage and dumped later...John, check the back of the truck again. What if the person in the front seat wasn't him? Raining, dark, curly wig, the coat...all of these would cause any witness to see a familiar shape and call it Grossman."

"Check the back of the truck?"

Annie told John she was exploring a theory that the murderer had used the cart to get Grossman to the back of the truck, and then took him back to the Fish and Game dumpster. "What if the murderer had already, by that time, put on a similar wig and put on Grossman's coat, which is why we haven't found it," she offered. "So the suit coat could have transfer from the back of the truck, if it wasn't clean."

"Huh. What if. We'll get on it. We did look in the back of the truck; it appeared to be where you put wet dogs. A muddy mess. We just left it. His suit coat could be muddy, but would we be able to tie that to the crime?" John was quiet, and then mused, "If his jacket wasn't muddy during the meeting...The clothing is at the Morgue, right? Have them hold the jacket. We'll take samples from the back of the truck. I'll call you back if we get anything. I think if we do, we could get it to you on the late plane, send it up with an officer who's coming to testify. She's on that flight."

Thank you jezus. "Thanks, John, you're a lifesaver. Good tip, actually. Any others?"

"None you even want to hear. Aliens, and like that."

They hung up laughing.

Annie called Hernandez and told her to hold onto the suit jacket before sealing it into evidence with the rest of the clothing, as there was a possibility they needed to establish "similar mud." After she hung up, she thought all that would really tell them was that he was in the back of the truck. Which, given the state of the vehicle's cleanliness, might be eaten alive by a good attorney. But it might be something.

Eli Carson knocked on her door. She really liked Eli. In his late twenties, he was smart, thoughtful, and resourceful as an investigator, and his computer skills were a serious increment above hers. "Eli," she said, "come sit and hear what we're doing."

Like most Alaskans, Eli was from both here and somewhere else. His father had come with the military, and his mother was Athabaskan, from the interior. He was a beautiful coffee color, with wide, brown eyes and prominent cheekbones. He wore his straight black hair in precise braids. He slid easily into her side chair and took out a notepad. "I'll be on it by tomorrow. Just finishing up for that drug bust on the Kenai, where they needed the aliases deciphered. Whatchu got?" he asked.

Annie ran through the connections she had made so far, outlining her emerging understanding of how the crime had gone. "I have a feeling that we need to grab some things before any more time passes. Mostly, names, I guess. JPD compiled a list of the transports of various kinds that went in and out on the day of the murder, the day before, and the day after. I feel like we need all of those times and manifests.

"We have incoming up to the murder time, which appears to be after 6:00 p.m. on the 7th, and outgoing for several days after that. We need to see if any passengers stayed in Juneau motels or hotels. We need to know where you can get a new fillet knife, but that's a low level. I'm guessing they're sold pretty much everywhere. All we know is new, and we may never find it.

"We need to know rental cars, same time period. After we get that going, and of course it will take a bit, put it into a data base so we can...I'm telling you your business," she said with a bit of chagrin. "Especially because I couldn't even spell 'data base' til you got here. Sorry."

"No problem, thanks for the cred. So you can cross the passenger lists with the postals. I mean, if it's a disgruntled *previous* employee...etc."

Annie was nodding, distracted by the possibilities. Eli was making notes on his notes.

"Right. As usual, you see where we might have to go. Also, for the lists, criminal record, arrests, any records outside of the state on Fish and Game employees, all offices, all locations where Grossman previously worked."

Eli rolled his eyes. "You're hunting for the ones toting around a loose canon," he said.

Annie laughed. She got a kick out of the juxtapositions of cliches that Eli favored. She had to admit it made people pay attention to what he said, because he was famous for them. "Feel free to follow any such trail of ordinance," she agreed.

Eli went away with his list and notes, muttering about where he might get these things. Annie stared out the window, then at her murder board. She walked up to it as though in some kind of trance, and drew a little figure in the corner of the board. In a curly wig and a winter coat, holding a knife dripping blood.

Chapter Twenty

Monday, October 21, 1998 - late evening

Clyde Bunsen was in the break room, having a cola from the refrigerator, which he could have put there. The spare trash cart was outside the break room door. Clyde glowered at it. It didn't have things in the right place, and even though the police had said he'd get his back, Clyde couldn't figure out what they wanted it for. He didn't like it. He was having a serious issue with getting to work with all of the dang bottles full of the various types of cleaner being in a different order, and no trash bags so he had to go get them. And it didn't roll right, which was, after all, why it was the spare.

It needed a spare. Clyde smiled at his cleverness. He was looking at the cart as though it would morph into something familiar if he just stared at it, when Ernie came in, leaving his cart by Clyde's. "Burner," he said in his big, deep voice. Ernie spoke slowly. Clyde was nice to him, but some of the building's other janitors, not so much. He didn't like it when others were unkind to people like Ernie. Ernie couldn't help that he wasn't smart. He had a good heart. He worked hard. Loaned Clyde things and covered for him on occasion.

"What happened to your cart?" Ernie asked, immediately noticing that it was not the same. They had their names on their carts, though it wasn't anything official. Ernie, like Clyde, was protective of his.

"Police took it."

Ernie swung to look at Clyde. "What police want with a janitor's cart?" he asked, apparently sincerely confused. "Don't their janitors have their own?"

"Well, things been goin' on," Clyde said, switching to the dialect he used with Ernie, which was, in its way, an important piece of the smoke screen he used at work. "Want a coke?"

"Not supposed to drink all that sugar," Ernie said in a voice that mimicked someone else's. He did, however, sit down next to Clyde and pull a bottle of water out of his coverall's side pocket. "What's the things been goin' on?" he asked, perfectly mimicking again, this time Clyde's cadence, but not unkindly.

Clyde didn't take offense. There wasn't anything mean about Ernie. He felt a little protective of him, truth be told. "Somethin' creepy been goin' on, is all. Now don't be scared. Was two weeks ago, someone was here who shouldn't have been. I'm still workin' it out."

Ernie was thinking hard about something. "In the Janitor room?"

"Maybe. Why do you ask?" Clyde looked at Ernie with a new interest. "Lose somethin'?"

"My old coveralls. Took my new ones home to wash cuz they got, you know, that sick guy, and the old ones weren't there the next night. I know I hung them behind the door, so I wouldn't get them confused. I needed them. Someone took them. Had to clean in my jeans and that's not allowed," he concluded piously.

That was a lot of words for Ernie. Thinking, Clyde decided that this was related somehow to his trash cart being missing, and where he found it, and what else might have happened that night, which he was not about to tell anyone. Ernie was a big guy, a little overweight, and there was no way his coveralls fit any of the other janitors, most of whom were Filipino short women. "Where was you cleanin' that night they were gone?" he asked.

"Up in the Library. Got my cart, bags, towels, some more soap and toilet paper, and went up.

Never came down til I was through. Went to take it off that door hook and put it with my cart and it was gone. I can't believe how much toilet paper women use."

"Unhuh...they do that. So at the end of that night your coveralls was gone."

"Yeah. Do you want to eat lunch now?"

It was 8:00, and though they took breaks every two hours, they didn't eat til 10:00. Ernie had forgotten the time, which he didn't track well.

"Naw, I'll eat at 10:00 like normal. Got a power bar if you need somethin'."

Ernie eagerly accepted the power bar and ate it like candy. With his mouth full, he said, "Police been talkin' to you, everyone says."

It was hard to know if Ernie had actually participated in any conversation, or simply walked by someone talking, or made it up. He had an active imagination. Clyde said, "Not so much. Wanted to know about when that Commissioner dude was murdered, did I see anything. I said no. Wouldn't tell 'em if I had, actually. You just get into trouble. We supposed to be invisible, right, bro?"

Ernie had talked to Clyde a lot during his first few evenings about how not to make anybody mad at him, because in his last job, someone had been. Real or imagined. Clyde had told him no one here paid any attention to janitors--they were invisible once they put their coveralls on. Ernie had been intrigued, and had made little comments about his invisibility from time to time.

He remembered, and smiled. "Indivisible," he said, then corrected himself. "No, that's from the flag salute. Invisible. That means they can't see you if you have your coveralls on, right? Reason we don't clean in jeans."

"Right. We're invisible. People treat us like we're not here. So if I talk to the police, tell 'em what I see or don't see, then people start lookin' at me. Noticin' how I dress and how I act, comings and goings, like that. So if they already doin' that, must be because when the police talked to me, I wasn't invisible."

Ernie grasped that. "Stay invisible," he said softly. "Not like you knew nothin' anyway about that, right?" Clyde's speech pattern again.

Clyde nodded. "Not like I do. Not like I'd say if I did. None of my business."

He went one way and Ernie went another, back to the elevators. Clyde had done the desk baskets earlier--a change to his routine, but more people saw him at work. He was so careful now that he sometimes checked them twice, walking the floor in the opposite direction, making certain he hadn't missed one. There weren't many men on his floor, so he did the women's first and then the office trash, and then went to finish the men's restroom.

When he put out the cone, opened the door and switched on the light, he had a powerful sense of deja vu. He stood for a moment, then he looked under the stall doors. No one. He wasn't having that happen again. He rubbed his chest absentmindedly, then his lips. He looked at himself in the mirror. He looked through the mirror to see if anyone else was looking back. Had that happen once in a police department when he scratched himself and heard a laugh. Mirrors weren't always mirrors.

He'd had a dream about that night, after the cops had talked to him. Had he been tased? Or just tooted. Or both. Anyway, he didn't like doing the restrooms now, and he didn't really know why. World was just creepy. Too much on TV about all of the crime stuff. You just about had to watch it, and it put all sorts of ideas in your head.

Tuesday, October 20, 1998 - 9:00 a.m.

The janitor's cart was dirty: streaks of dried cleaning fluid, permanent pieces of gum stuck to the bottom and mysterious bumps and dribbles of various colors. Both wet and dry garbage from desks and restrooms came in bags that ripped. The dregs of food and drink containers collected in the bottom of the cart. The evidence tech who worked with the JPD didn't see anything that could be swabbed and analyzed. There was the tiniest bit of something dark on the rail, but it turned out to be fruit juice which had dripped out of a bag, apparently. The recycled paper bag hung on the end, emptied nightly.

The top of the cart's frame was bent a little on one side. Like many such carts, this one was an empty frame with a removable canvas bag dropped over it. The cart wasn't level. There was an actual bend, about in the middle of one of the sides, the weakest point of the frame. The tech photographed the cart. The frame wasn't meant to bear weight, and heavy bags occasionally bent the upper bars.

Detective Sullivan came out. He asked about the bend. Could it have been made by a body? They all shrugged. They had a bag of salt for the winter, and they tried laying it on the edge. It didn't bend with one, but it bent a bit with two sacks. There was obviously a weak spot in that limb. So it was possible something had hung over the edge that was heavy, but it was also possible that the cart frame had been bent in the distant past. Who was careful with a trash cart? Detective Sullivan said, "good work," and left. They put the cart in the garage with the truck, but they weren't sure why.

Detective Sullivan called Annie Brewster. She picked up on the second ring. "Annie, John again. We don't get anything from the cart, except a possible bend in one of the cross members at the top, right where something heavy might have been put on it. Are you there?"

"Good morning, John. How are you? I am fine." Annie was chuckling. "Know you're busy and want this one off your plate. Thanks for the info."

"Yeah, sorry for the abruptness. We don't see anything there."

"Thought it was a long shot. Document looking at the cart. And anything else someone might drag it out of a file in 10 years and say, 'What's this?'" Annie said. "I'm doing that. I have Carson working on inputting all of the passenger manifests from whatever source, for the same reason. Yesterday, I talked to several people who worked with Grossman in his last jobs. No one wants to talk, actually, so I'm going out to the Fish and Game here and see if I can talk to someone in charge. That's all I've got."

They exchanged a bit of frustration, but John was distracted. Annie sympathized, and held back the smaller pieces she had learned since they last spoke. Ultimately, after they had given it another week, there was nothing in the trash, no connections through any of the license plate numbers, and nothing from anyone who refueled a car that rainy Monday night when Grossman went dumpster diving.

She looked at notes Eli had prepared. Grossman had worked for Fish and Game briefly, in the field offices in Delta Junction and then in Anchorage, but in between and before he had been a River Guide, on the Copper and then on the Big Su. He had been president of the Guide's Association; he had lobbied on their behalf. He had been appointed to the Game Board, and there had gotten to know the man who became governor. Had taken him fishing--she had found a newspaper clipping. The Governor was a "wounded warrior," and walked on a prosthesis replacing his right ankle. One weekend a year, the Guides took wounded veterans free. Apparently Grossman had impressed the Governor.

There was a divide in Fish and Game around the state--the commercial fishermen with the guides or not, depending on the issue, versus the conservation interests. Alaska wasn't a Sierra Club state. It was conservationally complex. Alaska natives wanted to protect subsistence hunting and fishing rights, the Regional Corporations--what passed for reservations in Alaska--wanted to develop resources. Tourism and the Guides wanted to promote hunting and fishing to the world. Any kind of development caused some backlash. Had his posture supporting sport fishing and hunting caused a rub somewhere along the line?

She made a note on her blotter for Eli to get lists of all of the employees in the sites where Grossman had been the supervisor. Were there lists of complaints against him either from previous employees or the public? Annie's earworm wanted out. She could just barely catch the refrain from *How Long Has This Been Goin' On.*

The Fish and Game field office on Raspberry was a one-story building with a small warehouse and weigh station for people who had come in with an animal that needed "sealing"--the process of weighing, measuring, and certifying the game as legal.

The receptionist directed Annie to Bart Starkinson, the regional manager of a huge area including the Kenai Peninsula, with its millions of summer tourists, and the most of the fish guides. In the many tributaries off the inlet, big fish runs began in May and continued through September, so this office had the most contact with Fish cops, as they were called. While the actual rangers who issued citations for too many fish or illegal bear baiting were under the state troopers, which was the Department of Corrections, there were many people in Fish and Game who played a part in their work, contributing information about illegal activities they had witnessed or for which they saw evidence as they did field work.

Starkinson had been an employee under Grossman, but not a direct subordinate. He agreed to see Annie and gave her the time readily enough, but said that he barely remembered that far back, and didn't know that he could be any help.

Annie waited in a chair outside of a secluded office area, walled off by portable dividers. Virtually all state offices seemed the same: the important people were closed away. The rest of the staff worked in cubicles that gave the impression of spaciousness, but were really crammed full of paper of all sorts; furniture too large for the space; and so many computers, peripherals and cords that it was a rat maze to get to one's desk. The faceless "organizational man" or woman was still a theme for bureaucratic or other repetitive work. The person seemed to disappear, and everyone looked vaguely alike. And right on schedule, a gray, nondescript man emerged from the office door.

"Bart Starkinson, how do you do?" The man who held out his hand looked like all of the color had been leeched out of him. He had a firm handshake.

"Annie Brewster," she responded, following him in and sitting in a side chair, which was her apparent assigned seat in this investigation. "I won't take too much of your time. This may be a wild-goose chase, but if it is, I guess I'm in the right place." Wildlife humor.

To which he didn't react. "I'm happy to help. What is it about this death that brings you here?"

Annie said slowly, "I don't exactly know. Grossman was killed with elements of a personal connection with his assailant." Seeing the quizzical look that met her statement, she added, "I really can't say anything more than that we are trying to look back into Grossman's work history to see if there is someone who might have information..."

"Or, a grudge? I see. I was not a close associate. He sat where I am, and he was here for only two years. He had been a guide, then had worked in the Delta Junction office. Some years ago. I looked up his personnel file."

Annie felt her heart do a little thump. "Are the personnel records centrally located?"

"Yes, the newest are digitized, archived here. Some probably qualify as fossils by this time. You need a warrant, but when someone...passes...those files are removed from the system and put in the archives."

"I have a warrant coming, and will serve it as soon as I know where the records are. We're trying to save time, as the window to solve this may be short." Annie was aware that the man in front of her could be her murderer, silly as it seemed, and was tiptoeing between the facts necessary to get answers and not give anything away.

"They are here, as we have the most computer capacity and the most space. Besides the file, what else can I do for you?" Starkinson was moving papers about on his desk, as though the file might be right there, on the blotter. Maybe it was.

"Co-chronological employees. Anyone who worked directly for him. We're looking at lists, at this point."

"I see. We have those, too, but it will take a bit to retrieve them. I can have someone get you a hard copy of those. Many are no longer here. Do you still want those?"

Especially those, Annie thought. "Don't you think?" she asked. When Starkinson nodded, she asked for the specific chronology of Grossman's time in both Delta Junction and Anchorage, which Starkinson said was in the personnel file. Which he actually had copied and ready for her, without the subpoena. Someone had authorized him to cooperate, and Annie's built in "crap detector" immediately went on red alert. What had already been eliminated from the file?

She assumed a bored face. "I don't know about taking anything until the subpoena is done. I'll have everything in it that we need, like any employee complaints, and so forth."

Starkinson looked up sharply. "Those would be in a separate place," he said. "Depending upon the resolution of complaints, they are either destroyed by mutual agreement or kept in Human Resources at the state level."

"So Bart," Annie said casually, using the man's first name to nudge compliance, "if you wanted to know if there were employees who had filed complaints, what language would you use in a subpoena." Starkinson's face turned white, then red. "Never mind," she said, "just kidding."

They talked about the structure of the field offices, and how they related to other entities, such as the state office in Juneau, the various Boards that oversaw or provided advocacy for regulations, assisted in public relations. Boards received gubernatorial largesse. Between per diem for meetings and actual stipends for participation, some of these board positions were quite lucrative. Some of the members were there to dismantle what they saw as unfair regulations, which generally translated to those they personally found to be unfair.

It was a safe subject. Annie was given some history documents about Alaska Fish and Game, and a state directory of current employees. That gave her an idea. She could check back with the State Librarian and see if those directories were kept for the last two decades. She knew they were somewhere. She asked Starkinson about that. Yes, he assured her, they were somewhere.

"So, have I answered all of your questions?" Starkinson asked.

"Just one more. Did you, personally, have an issue with him?"

Silence.

"Did you and he ever have disagreements, something which lingers in your memory?"

Silence. Starkinson was not making eye contact. Annie waited. In the silence, she was horrified to see Starkinson's eyes begin to fill.

Finally, he looked at her, having sucked whatever betraying moisture she had seen back into his defenses. "He was abrupt. When he first came, he asked my supervisor a lot of questions about everyone's position here, and then, out of the blue, he fired my supervisor, the woman who had hired me. My mentor. Then he called us all in and said that he was there to see the office become more efficient, and he now had the information..." he paused, cleared his throat. "Sorry...necessary to make some personnel decisions. He said he would be watching us, and interviewing each of us, to see who would stay and who would be transferred. We were all terrified of him. I was not familiar with how rapidly things could change. It was my first office job. I had been a field biologist, and I developed some medical issues so I needed to get out of the field. The opening here seemed perfect. I spent the next two years in total paranoia and stress.

"That said, I don't think he knew I was here. I never had a conversation with him. I made myself useful on every project. As others were eliminated I somehow stayed. Then he left. Rather abruptly, actually. He went back to guiding. I don't know why, but maybe he just wasn't cut out for administration. Then he was appointed to the Board, and it started all over again. He circulated a list of people who were 'dinosaurs,' as he said--it was on the record--and I was on it. I don't know what happened, but no one was fired at that point."

That much talk seemed to exhaust him. Annie made a list of what to put in the subpoena, asked Starkinson for his opinion on where the various records would be so that she could make certain the subpoena covered all venues, and said, "That about does it. I'll get back to you, I'm sure."

Annie went to her car and sat. So the pattern was not just in Juneau. That was what she had predicted. Now, there could be someone who had wanted this man dead in Anchorage, in Delta Junction, or in the groups who had been slighted in recent regulations. She sighed. She cursed her tendency to see these investigations as expanding, rather than contracting. She saw the connections between too many things.

In fact, that kind of reductive thinking was what got detectives in trouble, and made the window of fresh evidence and accessible witnesses slam shut. She saw it all the time. By the time AIB was called in, there were cases that had been so narrowly investigated that they were already partially cold. At some point, she thought, she should look at the actual statistics that compared Alaskan cases and solution rates to the time when AIB was actually called in. Programs on television, and even statistics in the academy, set most solution rates as 48 hours or less. This one was so far beyond that when she started that it was almost intimidating.

Starkinson would need an alibi, if Eli's various lists and cross lists included his name. She didn't think that was possible. No one could be controversial and survive, would be her observation. These smaller offices were far from the toxic politics in Juneau, but they were at the ends of the chains that could be pulled from there.

She spent the rest of the day running down the few potential clues and leads. She called Presto Publications, and after a bit of a runaround, happened upon someone in the legal department (when you say you are the police, what do you expect?) who actually laughed.

"You don't have RTTT?" the lawyer, who had the richly smooth voice of a black woman from the South, said, "I have that one in my wine cabinet."

Annie waited patiently, and the lawyer said: "ESAD is Eat Shit and Die, would be my guess, but you will never find any proof. It's just how I translate it. In fact, the cards don't say, and they weren't advertised that way. It's part of a game of *whaaaa?* when you open them."

"Okay," Annie said, "I get the ESAD. What about DYSTP?"

"Do you squat...a way of making fun of a guy, I suppose."

"Okay, I get that too. DFF?"

"Dear FuckFace, would be my guess, pardon my french."

"Can you tell me, or direct me to someone who can, when these cards were produced, and when they stopped being available?"

"Sure, there is a file. Some people didn't like them. They were only issued for one year, and mostly no one ordered them--the reps gave them out as souvenirs. Issued in 1989, withdrawn by 1991. So parts of each year."

"Thank you."

"Uh, can I ask, off the record, why you're calling about them? No one has mentioned them in years.

Since the woman seemed only genuinely curious, had given her exactly the information she needed, Annie answered, "I found them in the deceased's desk drawer. No envelopes, just the cards with nothing else inside."

"He wouldn't be the first person who bought them because they expressed what he thought about someone else, and then didn't send them because they were uniformly offensive."

"And who was the rep for Alaska while they were active?"

"Hallie Burton," the woman said without hesitation. "She probably wouldn't have gone up there; most reps did everything online when expensive travel was necessary. They had to pay their own travel, as quasi contractors. Hallie was one of our best. She died a year ago, but there's an outside possibility her records are here. If she had the cards and gave them as samples, there wouldn't be a record, though."

Annie said she would appreciate the attorney looking at the sales records to make sure, and let her know. She thanked the attorney, hung up and

and went across the room to the chronology she was building. It took a vertical column and was separated by years, starting when Grossman came to Alaska in the early 80's and coming forward to his death. A few people were plugged in here and there.

If Grossman had received the cards, that was different than Grossman carrying the cards around so he could throw darts at someone from the privacy of his office. She decided to have them dusted for prints, just in case. She put "suspicious cards" on the timeline in the appropriate years. She took a big green marker and entered Grossman's various jobs on the timeline. Starred the two years referred to by Starkinsky.

She was staring at the board when Eli came in. He had a few sheets of paper in his hand, and gave them to her when she turned toward him. "This adds to his work history, everything I could find. I asked Claudia to check all of his driver's license addresses and we put those in to the timeline. Guy was a mover the first few years. If I see any pattern, it's Republican versus Democratic Governors. When he was working for the state in the two field offices, there was a Republican administration. When he wasn't, it was Democratic. So maybe it was just a political thing that had him moving around."

Just a political thing. That about summed it up. Annie was dead certain that this was related to office/political work. "Guiding" didn't fit. Of course, guiding could be political. Guides had hierarchies, too. They were fiercely competitive, keeping their best spots for fish, moose and bears so secret that their family didn't even know. For just one "hint" about where a trophy animal would be, someone could reap thousands of dollars in tips and more in subsequent trips. Guiding might include jealousy and infighting, but if that was the case here, it was later in the investigation. She might hear a name that got her to a name. Like that.

Eli left his lists. Annie set them aside. She called the Delta Junction office, left a message on the administrator's voice mail. She would wait for a call back there. Should, but didn't want to, drive to Delta. She called the State Librarian and was told there was a cache of state directories in the Legislative Office in Anchorage, she should call there first, and call back if they didn't have what she needed. Directories weren't digitized, and though loosely tied by retiring employees to another data base, they were more like phone books. You could get left out of it, if you missed the printing window and left before the next edition. Nothing on this case was easy. Humming *Blue Moon,* Annie called the Uni in Juneau who had interviewed the man dumping garbage illegally and the city and state employees using the gas pumps. She had cleared the cars in the big parking lot by the Fish and Game Building.

Corporal Townes had, yes, he had finally talked to the man dumping personal garbage, who had been defensive. A one-time thing, and they couldn't prove otherwise. Hadn't been there the week before, and had an alibi. He got a stern warning, but that was it.

It happened, however, that a maintenance worker filling a truck with gas so it would be ready to go in the morning vaguely recalled seeing the Commissioner's pickup, which he recognized because it was always parked back by the building. It was there at 7:00 when his stub said he had gotten gas. Annie was pretty happy with that, and told Corporal Townes "who's a good investigator," which made them both laugh. She had him put the interview and copy of the time-stamped stub into an evidence envelope to send up to Anchorage.

What did she know now? By 7:00, his truck was parked, but he had never gone into the building. Annie wanted to put that part to bed. Grossman was already in the dumpster. If his truck was in its parking place, someone drove it there.

The courier came in and gave her a sealed envelope that she found contained a couple of mud samples from the back of the truck. She immediately got her coat and took them to the ME, to compare with the mud on the back of Grossman's jacket. If they were a match, at least the manner in which he got to the dumpster was much clearer.

She looked at the clock as she left the Mortuary. Quarter to five. Where had the day gone? She called Jason and said she was going home, and not to call her unless it was urgent, she was that tired. It wasn't just jet lag, it was persistent frustration and, perhaps, a small break.

Chapter Twenty-one

Tuesday, October 22, 1998

Annie asked Jason to find George Lightly, which was quickly done by calling his last known place of employment. They knew he was now working with Cook Inlet Regional Corporation as a consultant, helping them with village connectivity. Some villages were on the road system, and some were across the Inlet, a million connectivity problems away. Some were in the footprint of the satellite, some were in the shadow, and some were just not going to get there until another satellite was put into orbit. Perhaps not then. It amazed Annie how this pattern repeated itself everywhere she had been--if you were in certain places, with a certain income, it was all open to you. Everyone else, not so much.

She made an appointment and went to see George, who was working from home, as most consultants did. He lived near the University, in new condominiums along Lake Otis. There was something about the area that appealed to Annie. It seemed like real woods in the midst of the city.

Nice place. She parked in the generous driveway and went up to the door. George had the door open, and she could see him through the screen as he came in response to her knock. "Lt. Brewster?" he asked.

"George Lightly?" she responded. They both smiled, and went into the living room and sat down. "You have more computers than Kivilina," she observed, looking at the four different computers, apparently wired together, and the variety of peripherals that crept away from, or toward, them.

"How can I help you?" he asked. He had the disconcertingly high-pitched voice of an Irish tenor. He looked like the one on the Lawrence Welk Show.

"I'm investigating Commissioner Grossman's murder," she said, and waited for him to show something. Grossman's death had not been discussed in the paper as a "murder."

"Of course," he said. "You wouldn't be here if you were not."

So much for any element of surprise. "And let's just get this out of the way. Where were you on Monday, October 5?"

Lightly looked at her for a moment, and then burst out laughing. "I'm not going to ask if I'm a suspect. I was in Seattle, waiting for a plane to get me to Anchorage. Took a bump so I can take my daughter to Disneyland. I actually got back into Anchorage on the morning of the 8th, around 11:00. And I did not come through Juneau."

"Sounds like an alibi to me," Annie said. Eli could check the manifests he had. "So let's go to why I'm here." When Lightly nodded, Annie continued. "Grossman was killed by someone who left some clues that this might be personal." Lightly snorted. "We are waiting for toxicology."

George Lightly abandoned his pretense of boredom and sat forward. "Toxicology?"

I have your attention now, Annie thought. "We had some strange results, is all I can say at this point, from the autopsy. Probably nothing to it, but we're checking all of the boxes." She looked down at the questions she had prepared for this man. "Can you please tell me how Commissioner Grossman approached you to work temporarily at the Department?"

Lightly described Grossman, a former colleague, a former boss, as someone who knew a great deal about computers, though he had certain "blind spots," in terms of the type of hardware he thought should be used exclusively. He hated MacIntosh. Lightly actually laughed at that. "He probably had stock in IBM or Microsoft," he suggested. "Or he wanted you to think he did, and they knew something Steve Jobs didn't know. But mostly, it was just prejudice. At any rate, so long as you didn't say *MacIntosh*, you could talk to him all day about computers.

"So when he got to Juneau, he had a woman in charge of IT who argued with him. He was really pissed at her. He called me and asked me to take a month and get myself free, he had a big contract for me."

"Isn't there a state contracting system?" Anne said casually, camouflaging her interest by writing as she spoke.

"Yeah," Lightly said, "Not my concern. Anyway, 'expertise' trumps the system. If you write the RFP in such a way that you need particular expertise, there generally aren't two people available in Alaska who will even apply."

"And how long were you in Juneau?" she asked.

"Just finished up," he answered. "I hate that place. My family said 'hell no,' so I went back and forth."

"And for how long..."

"About a year and a half. Things weren't as bad as he thought, but I went through everything and he told me how he wanted things changed. I got that done for him.

"Did you have any sense while you were there that he was under any pressure or threat?"

Lightly looked hard at Annie. "Grossman and I were cordial. Knew each other in Prudhoe since the old pipeline days. Not buddies. He didn't have buddies. He didn't talk about anything personal, beyond saying pretty personal things about the incompetence that surrounded him."

Annie could see that. Lightly had the power of his expertise. Grossman knew him and had paid for specific things to be done. Since Lightly could do them, and did, there wasn't any reason for conflict. But Annie asked, "No problems of any kind?"

"Still with that, huh. Of course. Everyone had conflicts with him. It was his management style. Evolved into 'shock and awe' after a couple of years. He tended to move on when he pissed off too many people. Some liked that. He was a bit of a black hat, and some liked that, too. I didn't kill him. I don't know anyone who did, or would want to. That said, I think he could have gone down like that guy in some town in Oklahoma. Everyone shot, and no witnesses." He pursed his mouth to avoid the smile that was in his eyes. So, not serious?

Annie remembered that actual murder. Murder by town. Everyone was a suspect, everyone alibied everyone else. Some similarities, actually. Had Grossman been murdered by multiple former employees? That would explain the various wounds, wouldn't it? She remembered Linda Hurtsen's women's group. And dismissed it. Temporarily. She wanted to stay with Lightly for a bit more.

"Mr. Lightly, did you observe employee interactions while you were working for the Department that discussed threats to Commissioner Grossman?"

"No, but I'm certain that they went on."

"You are."

"Yes, of course. Everyone knew I was there to take Munson's job, at least temporarily, and having seen her go, the others in her area were really frightened. They must have talked. They were cooperative with me, however. No signs of sabotage. Grossman told me to be on the lookout for disloyalty, so I told them I was, and they all looked at me like I was speaking Greek. No one talked to me. But body language is important. When he came around, they hunched, like dogs that are afraid of their master."

Lightly laughed at that. Annie could see why Grossman and he had gotten along. She hadn't really thought there was anything here, but she was looking for what kind of person Grossman did hire when he had a position of importance that he could fill. "I think that's everything." Annie closed her notebook. "Can I give you a card, and if you think of anything, or anyone who might have information we can use, I would appreciate it, and the Governor would be grateful."

"The Governor, actually, might have information."

"How so?"

"The Ethics Complaint."

"And when would that have been?" Annie hadn't heard anything yet, but knew she was getting some complaints from Fish and Game on Raspberry when she got the search warrant over there.

"Seems like it was way back, but it was famous when it happened. Governor would have had to do something to explain it when he appointed Grossman, or he'd never have been confirmed. Behind the scenes, I would surmise."

"And the complaint was about?"

"I remember little. Something from an employee, though. A whistleblower complaint?"

Lightly obviously knew. He wasn't saying more. He had probably said more than he intended. Or he was giving her a red herring because he didn't want Annie to investigate anything more recent. Annie had come into Alaska in 1991, done a couple of years with the Troopers to get some state credibility, and then had been switched over to Detective and then AIB because, with a masters in criminology, she was destined to go there and she was needed. She had no recollection of the "big deal" of which Lightly spoke, but in those early years, she might just not have recognized it if it did surface in the papers.

Lightly was, and wasn't, a bust interview. How far back to look? Revenge may well be *a dish best served cold*, but in Alaska, that might mean permafrost. How had Grossman and Lightly interacted in Prudhoe that led to Grossman calling him these many years later? Was it relevant? Since this was the first and only person who had known Grossman a long time and survived, as it were, it was interesting.

It was early afternoon, and Annie drove over to pick Fred up. He had eaten in Fairbanks, so she just took him home to recuperate and indulge Bones in a group nap. "I've got stories," he said. "I'll do dinner and be ready for show and tell whenever you get here, babe," he said as she let him off and ran up the garage door so he could go in. She could hear Bones' excited barking all the way on the other side of the condo. She wasn't sure how much of a nap Fred was going to get.

She was barely back to her office when the ME's office called. The tox results were back, and they had slides of the mud to show her.

Annie decided to take Jamalia Hendricks with her, as the woman was relatively new to AIB, and would need to have the personal relationship with Hernandez that Annie and Manfort had developed. Hendricks was keen to go, so Annie swung by and picked her up.

Jamalia said, "Thanks for the invite. You know ME Hernandez pretty well, Manfort said."

"I do. She's great. Keeps us from jumping to conclusions because she won't. It's a good tension. We respect her, and she respects us. I'll be glad when they get her better access to a crime lab."

They talked about the McKenzie case, which Annie had once been on. "You left really good notes, and I think we're close." The case involved two little girls who had disappeared in a part of Delta Junction that was home to many Russian immigrants, including some with mafia ties. The man who had taken the girls had been apprehended, but he said he had passed them on, and though they were close to the head of the operation, they weren't there yet, but he was talking. They had his bank account. They had a solid lead to the girls.

"Best of luck. Let me tell you what we have so far on this one, so you can put tox in context." Annie ran down chronology, weapons, COD, and what had bubbled up from the interviews. Jamalia asked good questions. Annie handed her notebook to Jamalia and had her write them down. Were any disgruntled ex-employees big enough to pass for Grossman, and had there been any really low tides in Juneau along the channel's edge, so they could look for "thrown objects."

"We've only recently decided on the dumpster," Annie said, musing. "I'll call John Sullivan. They might want to check the tide table."

"And you're sure it was a man?"

"Pretty big for a woman."

"Assumption?"

"Yeah. I'm not ready to go there. I have known a few big women who could have done the job."

"I remember when I was in the MP's here in Anchorage, at Rich, there was a big Samoan woman. You didn't mess with her. Men would think that they could, because she had long hair and there was no mistaking she was female, if you take my meaning. They may have tried something once. When they got out of the infirmary, they probably didn't try it again."

They pulled into the Morgue parking area, and Annie took her notebook back and said, "big women. I'm open to it. So, before we go in, this is a paper review, but if you want to see the body, sing out."

"Can't carry a tune, thanks. I can't think of why I'd like to see an old white guy dead two weeks. Or...let me think about that."

They walked in laughing, and Annie thought how quick-witted Jamalia Hendricks was. Smart, well-trained, approachable, she was a great addition to the team.

Maria Hernandez was waiting for them, in her office this time, her desk so inundated with loose paper that Annie had no idea where to stand or sit. She introduced Hendricks and Hernandez, and then they all went to a little round table, the mess on which Hernandez scooped into an archival box, which she held, turned a full circle, and put on the floor. Then where there was actually room to read what Hernandez had ready for them.

"First off," she said, "I believe that Carfentanyl was the cause of death."

"That would be a show stopper. Carfentanyl. That's an elephant tranquilizer, isn't it?" Annie asked.

"Yes," said Hernandez

"Was," said Hendricks.

Both women turned to her. "It showed up in Georgia when I was training there. More and more overdoses. We got briefed on it. They're trying to find an antidote. It's nearly always fatal. People don't know they're getting it. Sorry to interrupt."

"No, that's great. We haven't heard much about it up here." Hernandez thought for a moment. "I guess it doesn't change anything. I talked to Vice, and they don't have any record of street use here."

"Please go ahead," Jamalia said.

"Okay, Carfentynl is the presumed cause of death. Large dose, big enough to kill, certainly enough to cause a heart incident. That is the actual death incident, but they are co-indicated. He would have been incapacitated, entirely, and may have actually been dead before he was transported. That would explain the lack, basically, of blood around the two wounds."

"This is an injectable, right?" Annie asked.

"Yes. Injectable. Undoubtedly, if we didn't have a bullet wound obliterating the path of the syringe, we would have seen it right away. That's where it went in. There were no needle marks anywhere else."

"Where did it come from, if it's not a street drug here?" Annie mused.

Jamalia was looking hard at the results. "If it had been a street drug, it would have been in the blood stream with something else, we were told. Was there anything else?"

"No, actually. Pretty simple tox, with a big, red warning that we shouldn't touch it, or the stomach contents, without gloves. Nasty stuff, but that was pretty much it. No signs he was a user. Therefore, we must assume someone injected him to sedate or kill him. Anyone with experience with the drug would know it would kill him." Hernandez was reading and rereading, as though she thought there would be something clearer come out from between the lines.

Annie's mind was buzzing. If it wasn't on the street much, yet, then it came from someone who had used it and would know it was dangerous to handle.

"We're looking for someone who had access and may have experience. Is this only a safari drug, or Is it used here? Wait!" Annie said, sitting up suddenly. "It replaced Ketamine, on Kodiak, for grizzly tranquilization in the early 90's, if I remember correctly, because some really big bear--they wanted to know what was in his stomach, which didn't sound good--blazed right through the Ketamine. The biggest grizzlies are hard to dose, apparently."

Hernandez said, "There you go. It's here, it's been here, someone got it, someone used it, case solved."

Hendricks looked rapidly at Annie, who was nodding, and then back at Hernandez, who said, "what more do you want?"

"Uh, a suspect?"

Annie was now openly laughing. "Oh, yeah, that. Jamalia, this is Maria being funny. I encourage you to laugh. She'll only get subtler if you don't." Everyone was laughing now. "So, can we say anything conclusive about the mud?"

Hernandez pulled a single slide copy out of her pile. "This is the mud from the back of the truck," she said, showing them the magnified copy. She laid another next to it. "This is the mud from the back of his coat."

They were an obvious match. Right down to the dog hair, the mold and the tiny tidal creatures that were part of the beach where everyone ran their dogs.

Annie felt an outsized relief that one thing seemed clear now: "Grossman was killed in the parking garage, put into the back of the truck, taken to the dumpster by Fish and Game, and pitched in, after which he was shot and stabbed, in obfuscating and personally meaningful ways. Because we have a witness to 'his' leaving the garage, we now know that the murderer had a wig or similar curly blonde hair, and wore Grossman's overcoat as camouflage."

It was a rush to say something definitive. "All of our evidence points that way," she said. "The only part I don't like is that we don't have a *by whom.*"

"Oh," Jamalia Hendricks said, "I got that for you. It was done in the parking garage with a syringe by the Invisible Man...or Woman."

"Thank you for that," Annie said dryly. "Let's bag everything and make sure this box of evidence gets over to me."

****

Before she went home for the day, Annie stopped in to tell Beatty the results. "You can call the Governor. However, sir, this needs to be embargoed."

"No Shit," Beatty said. "We're not going to put out that he died of a drug overdose."

"No, of course not," Annie agreed. "In fact, he didn't administer it, so there's no whiff of his using any drugs. The drug is the probable, though indirect, cause of death. The heart attack was probably brought on by it. He could have had a weak heart; people do without knowing it. That makes the actual murder dicey--the weapons didn't kill him. You can tell the Governor, *murder most foul* and we're still working on it."

"What about the other: *Commissioner of Fish and Game killed by elephant tranquilizer?*"

"Oh, let's not go there yet. I know that the sources of this drug are few and far between, and we'll be all over that to try to narrow down from where it could have been taken, try to match that with disgruntled employees, but..."

"Don't you say it. I told you not to say it."

"Sir, I have been *not saying* it, but it's creeping up on us. If we don't get something soon, it will go cold and you know it."

"Oh, Annie, someone could come forward with a clue. You may have a break with the ethics complaint thing that Lightly talked to you about. You may have a break just knowing COD."

"Most assuredly so, sir. We have more, exponentially, than we had two hours ago."

"So, I'll call the Governor and say you're closing in on it."

Annie shook her head. She wished she felt that way, but it was possible someone, or something, would give them the break they needed. "Sir," she said, "what do we tell the family? I think we're not going to get more from the body. We could release it. Does it go to Juneau?"

"Don't think so. Governor said something about Missouri. Family plot. Anyway, yeah, we can let him go if you're sure we have everything documented. I know that you do," he said when Annie started to object. "That was a gotcha. You'll get it. I have faith in you."

Annie didn't know if that was positive or not. She didn't like optimism. Something kept telling the optimist things would turn out, right up to the time it said, as Beatty had done, "*that was a gotcha.*"

Chapter Twenty-Two

Tuesday, October 22, 1998

Home smelled comfortingly of spaghetti. Bones ran to leap about her at a respectful distance, deliriously happy. She wanted to dance around Fred the same way.

She walked into the small, pass-through kitchen where a spot at the bar was ready for her with the light wine she preferred and a dish of popcorn. "I don't know who owns this bar," she called, "but I wish to propose to the bar tender!"

Fred emerged from the laundry room with a stack of folded towels.

"I would like to revise that. I wish to become the love slave of the bar tender," she amended.

They danced around the kitchen a bit. "Boy, have I missed you," Fred said into her hair. She felt her whole body relax. If it wasn't for Fred, she would work until she fell into bed, and then toss about restlessly until she got up to work again.

"Oh, I've missed you, too. Can you sit and have a glass with me? I'm sure you've already got everything done."

"True that. And I already have a glass in the fridge." He took out the vodka he preferred and they sat in the bar chairs, Bones with his head on Annie's knee. Annie snaked a slobber-catching napkin under his chin when he turned his head to make sure Fred had not gotten away from him.

"Bones thinks things are moving toward normal," she said. "Tell me your funny story."

"Oh, Elijah. You know the old guy who owns the soddy where Warren lives? I called Warren and asked him what he needed, and he said a box of .357 ammo and a sack of grass seed. Seemed like a strange order. Warren is a bit bushy, you know. Anyway, the ammo was so when he's laying on his back in bed, he can shoot lemmings off the ceiling. Elijah told him he needed to patch any holes he put through the sod..."

"So you brought him the grass seed to repair the...roof? Didn't anyone tell him that sod as in *soddy* isn't grass as in *lawn?*"

"Of course not, though Elijah couldn't quit laughing. Asked if they could eat it, like cereal.

I've been totally unable to get the vision out of my head of Warren shooting lemmings from his bed."

"What was wrong with the Borough Building?"

"They haven't had normal 'freeze up' for two years. I took soil samples. If we extended the sonitubes another five feet, that would probably prop it up for a time. It seems temporary, but the only alternative is to cut the building in half, like we did in Point Hope, and drag it to more solid ground. I think everyone wants to go with the sonitubes. When we finally have freezeup, we can come in and jack up the sagging spot, drill the sonitube hole right next to that, and see if it stabilizes over the winter. How long that'll last, I don't know. I occasionally have nightmares about all of the village buildings and schools built on permafrost beginning to lean like the Tower of Pisa."

"Which is, you know, straightening up," Annie said. She mused on the sloping buildings on the Slope, as the north slope of the Brooks Range was colloquially known and went from there to *hang on, Sloopy, Sloopy hang on.*

"And so, how's your dead Big Guy?" Fred asked, after they had shared the popcorn, including a handful for Bones which they dropped, by mutual agreement, onto the dark brown carpet, purchased by mutual agreement when they got Bones.

"Tox says Carfentinal killed him, precipitated a heart attack. Looks like the killer injected him, then shot through the area to disguise the mark of the syringe."

"I don't know that drug."

"It's super morphine. Thousand times stronger. It's an elephant tranquilizer."

"Wow. Isn't that overkill?"

"Yeah, overkill would be about right. Fish and Game has used it, off and on, and only for Griz, for maybe 20 years. Mostly, they use Ketamine, but for the really big, dangerous animals that have to go into deep sleep and stay there, I'm told, Carfentinal is the drug of choice. You apparently have to be careful of the dose, and not get any on your hands. Powerful."

"Hmm." Fred sipped his drink, and gestured with it to somewhere on the ceiling. "Find out who has used it, and narrow the list down to that?

"At least that. Tomorrow, I'm reviewing a whistleblower complaint with our Asst. AG. It's been sealed; I can see parts of it. There may be something. I've been thinking former employee, but probably we need to expand that a bit. Veterinarians. Guides. I don't know."

Fred nodded, checked the hot water on the stove and then pronounced, "it's time to put the pasta in."

He did, and Annie went up to get out of her good clothes. She settled on a lounge gown, and came back down barefooted. Fred was stirring pasta into boiling water. She set out three plates, one of which would be for Bones, and collected silverware and napkins. She put the little salad Fred had made into wooden bowls, along with a generous helping on Bones' plate. Dogs were omnivores, Bones said. Once they had begun fed him what they ate, he had stopped begging.

Homemade spaghetti with moose meatballs, salad, warm rosemary bread, Annie didn't think she was ever any happier than this, unless it was having such a meal in bed. Fred was just the best. He was a perfect foil for her in some ways, keeping her centered and calm when her job was at its craziest.

They had no children, but some people couldn't, and they had gotten past it. They had settled for Springer Spaniels, and the rambunctious dogs fit into their lifestyle. They walked the many trails around Anchorage, including in the winter. They enjoyed road trips into the interior, when Bones could put his head out the window, goggles in place, and bark at everything. They fished, drifted rivers, hunted occasionally, and spent comfortable evenings reading aloud in front of their fireplace. Alaska suited them well.

As they were cleaning up, Annie said, "I don't like the idea that someone would have hated this man so much that they plotted for years to kill him. It would just consume your life, wouldn't it?"

"Or it might give your life meaning, purpose?" Fred's voice was muffled as he bent over to put the spaghetti pot back into the lower cabinet. He stood up. Annie was looking at him quizzically. "I mean, if your life had been ruined by something this jerk did, not saying he deserved to die, you might feel like you couldn't trust anyone, couldn't see people, couldn't do anything--like everyone was looking at you, laughing at you."

"Fred," Annie said, putting her hand on Fred's arm, "that's awful. Have you been thinking about this?"

"Yeah. You and me, we're there for each other. What if this person only had work? When work is taken away, what if they had nothing, so revenge was at least purpose. I can't imagine going to work if I had been held up to ridicule, let alone socializing with people from work if I had been fired. I can't imagine how lonely it could be."

Annie thought about that. "That's assuming that the killer doesn't have a spouse."

"Yeah, I guess I think this is something you'd want to hide from a spouse even if you had one."

It was interesting how much Annie always felt she learned from Fred in an investigation. He always gave her something to think about. It also kept her humble. She needed more details about the little figure in the trench coat at the bottom of her murder board. It would be a great help to have a better profile. In fact, that was what Fred was doing, whether he knew it or not. It helped. She would contact the FBI office and see if they would loan her a profiler.

They watched the news, whose 20-something weather women and 50-something male anchors always made Annie mad. Weather was coming down. For late October, that was normal. They had always had snow by Halloween. She and Fred had already frozen their allotment of salmon, and Fred had successfully gotten a small moose with his bow on the Air Force base. They had meat for the winter, and to share.

But Annie couldn't keep her attention on the coming winter. The killer was still out there, Annie mused. What did the killer have now that he--or she, thank you Jamalia--didn't have before. Closure? And would that mean the case was also closed, in his or her mind? Because it wasn't. But if the killer considered it over, he would go quiet.

It would be one and done. There might not be another clue, another tip, another connection.

****

Janet Beck, the Asst. AG assigned to Fish and Game, was temporarily in Anchorage. A competent, no-nonsense woman in her 60's, she actually remembered the complaint. "The whistleblower," she said, reading around redacted text, "who shall be unnamed, witnessed Office Administrator Grossman breakfasting with three guides. She was at an adjoining table and claims she clearly heard Grossman say, 'I can get you that.'" Beck looked up. "Then the next day he went to the silver data analyst, and asked for projected strength and dates of the fall run. The whistleblower sat in the next cubicle, apparently, and heard this conversation, too. Asked the data guy if Grossman did that often. He said, 'all the time,' that he didn't like it, but felt he couldn't refuse.

"Any employee is prohibited from giving information to guides. It's an ethics violation. The commercial guys and the subsistence fishermen bring this up every couple of years. Not just Grossman, I would guess.

"The complaint calls it a pattern, and says employees don't feel free to refuse. It was filed toward the end of the time Grossman was here. He'd already put in papers. Complaint went

324

nowhere, and yet, at about the same time Grossman left, the data guy was transferred to counting fish in Copper Center, with no explanation. He's still in Copper Center. Don't know what he did, but that's a place you go to die, when you're in state government."

"Just politics," Annie said. "Nothing personal. Guy pissed someone off, and I think we can say 'who.'"

"I expect," Beck said. "Of course Grossman was interviewed, but he said the guides were friends from the Copper, and had asked him what the limits would be for the coming year. Claimed that he was asking the data guy for information on the runs to see if they needed to delay the season. Then, if I remember accurately, the whistleblower withdrew the complaint."

"Just like that?"

"Woman was terrified. I tried to get her to tell me what had happened. She didn't want to talk about it. I couldn't get anything. She requested the complaint be sealed, but the newspaper had been sniffing around, they knew it had been filed, and they wanted to see it. It was redacted and sealed, eventually. New Governor's orders."

Annie tried to get her to a name, to no avail. "Let me ask you this, then" Annie said, a bit frustrated. "Was the whistleblower a large woman?"

Beck snorted. "Five feet. Ninety pounds soaking wet."

"Thank you for that detail. We're pretty much convinced that the murderer is a big person, likely a man. I'd like to follow up on this complaint, see if anyone involved wanted revenge, if they ever mentioned it, if they have unusual activity in their bank accounts that might extend to hiring a pro."

Annie was more forthcoming with the Assistant AG than she had been with others. It was like talking with your lawyer. You could say what you needed to say, and they didn't react.

"I'll talk to Burton and see if there's more I can give you. I don't think the name of the man who was sent out to Copper Center was sealed, as a matter of fact. I'll find out and call you. I have that search warrant you wanted, by the way, and that's why you're seeing this. You can take it out to Fish and Game and see what else is buried in personnel."

"I want to see Grossman's file. He goes from Prudhoe to guiding, to two state offices not as a grunt but as the boss, quick turn back to guiding, State Game Board and then Commissioner. Right?"

"He's had a connection to the Governor for a long time. That's the gate for that path. The Admins all over the state, and the Commissioners in Juneau, aren't hired because they have real expertise. That's left to employees who may have to hide it. Top guns are hired because of who they know, who they took fishing, whose sister they married, what district they can pull votes from, how good they look on television. And the big one for Alaska is how constituent groups feel about them. The guide lobby is huge. Big money tourists will come back again and again if they get trophies.

"Actually," she mused, "the first time I ever heard Grossman's name, was when he took the Massachusetts Representative out to Kotzebue where the bozo picked up a walrus tusk. Grossman apparently didn't know anything about it. Guy had it in his luggage. What a mess."

Annie would pretty much bet Grossman knew exactly what the congressman had done. There were several elements of the relationships between guides and clients that irritated her. Helicopter hunting being top of the list. She thanked Janet, went back to her office, and called Eli.

He came in with his notepad and stood looking at the murder board. "Carfentinal?" he said, gesturing at the board. "That's an elephant tranq, isn't it?"

"Yeah. Eli, on that, we need to find out who is qualified, how you get qualified, how you get access, to use that drug legitimately. Then we need to ask Vice how you could get it illegally, and whether they're seeing it at all and where. We asked before, but ask again, please. Then canvas the veterinarians in Anchorage, Palmer, Wasilla, Juneau and anywhere else there's an actual vet, about how they would get it and if they ever use it."

"Right. Anything else?"

"Actually, that's not why I called you. I've got to a redacted whistleblower complaint from the AG. I want you to look it over carefully, get any dates you can, and check for the employee who got immediately transferred to Copper Center."

"Copper Center. That's cold."

"Literally."

"So, they transferred the whistleblower?"

"No, they transferred the person who facilitated the person about whom the complaint was filed," Annie said carefully.

"Okay, do that in English," Eli said, writing.

"Grossman asked a specialist for information the whistleblower says was given to guides. Then the specialist is transferred. Just want to now why."

"Okay, got it. This might be the killer. Someone transferred me to Copper Center, I would start plotting right then and there."

They laughed, but neither of them wanted to live in Copper Center. Strange place. Definitely a long way from Costco.

Eli had marching orders and left. Annie stared at the board. Years were starting to fill in, names were proliferating, the theory of the murder was taking shape. Maybe now they had something.

Chapter Twenty-Three

Friday, October 25, 1998

Eli was a careful, inventive investigator, with plans to be a cyber CSI. As the field of computer forensics expanded, he saw the trend and how to prepare himself. He had a confidence that made others value his opinion beyond his years and background. And he was seldom wrong.

So when he couldn't find the transfer of Melvin Bright from Specialist III Salmon Data Analyst to Specialist I Specimen and Water Quality, he dug deeper. State salaries were public record; Bright hadn't taken a pay cut. Interesting. Eli knew there was something in his personnel file, for which Search warrants weren't carte blanche. Too many contract protections. He thought by the end of Monday, when they had Bright's and Grossman's files, he could identify the whistleblower. His radar brain told him they needed to get to the files before something went missing.

Personnel files were purged when employees made major job changes, left the state, or died. Few files contained sensitive materials. In a transfer's file, there would be a notation that something had been received, a memorandum, and put into the file at the request of the Office Admin, but there would be no memorandum. There would be notes about a request for transfer, but it wouldn't be an actual meeting, it would be hearsay. "Requested lateral transfer." Some bosses took offense if you tried to get a different job. The timing was correct. So the personnel files could be interesting for what they didn't include.

Bright was a current employee, and his actual file was with him.

Eli found Bright's name in the state retirement data, used to form actuarial tables for the generous pension system. Aha. Bright had been transferred late in 1994. He was, at that time, 45, starting on his 17th employment year. To retire he needed 20 years in the system, or be age 55. If he went quietly, he had three, perhaps four years to full retirement, depending upon his actual hire date. He called the Copper Center office on a hunch. "Melvin Bright," he said when the receptionist answered.

"Mel's in the field," she said. "You can have his voice mail."

"Thank you," Eli said, waiting for the beep. "This is Melvin Bright, salmon specialist for the regional Fish and Game Office in Copper Center. Please leave your name and number. I will call you back."

Strange. Melvin wasn't the salmon specialist for anywhere. Was that his job title? It had been four years. Maybe he had his old job back? Eli left his name, said he was calling on behalf of Annie Brewster of AIB, that they would appreciate talking with Bright about a current investigation.

He went on entering names from passenger manifests into a spreadsheet. Some matched current employees, who frequently went back and forth to Anchorage. They also went out of state for meetings related to the grants that supported their positions. He had the lists of former employees, and on a hunch, looked in 1994 for the employees at the Raspberry Office of Fish and Game. Too many women for him to guess who might have sat next to Melvin Bright. Melvin would know. He crossed that with the retirement data and got five women who had retired in the intervening years. He made a detailed list, and, based upon where they worked last, found that three of them had not moved and the other two had gone somewhere south. All five might have something to say. Monday to do list.

The other task Annie had given him was interesting. He liked variety. Three Fish and Game offices had used Carfentanyl since 1990. A bear was darted on Kodiak, because it kept tearing doors off of remote cabins and laying waste to their contents. A Polar bear was darted in Kaktovik because it had killed three chained dogs and was spending time watching the children get off the school bus. Every village, no matter the size, had a school bus. The Delta Junction Office had darted a big bear that would not leave the park visitors alone, having been trained by them to follow them about for food.

Yes, there was a year-by-year list of who had access to the darts, but it was in the procedures manual by position, not name. No certification required. He didn't know how far back to go. Annie had told him to investigate the complaint from four years ago. On a hunch, he expanded the lists he was looking at and saw some possible matches from Kodiak. Some current State Troopers had experience with darting. He'd have to ask Annie about that one.

He developed a list of veterinarians and started calling. On the fifth call, a veterinarian in Fairbanks said she had used darts on the bison around Delta. They had darted an injured, farm-raised bull elk. "Carfentinal? No, use Ketamine. Carfentinal is for rhinos," the Fairbanks Vet had said. Did she know the Fish and Game people who did the darting for the state?

Yes, of course. Used to be a woman, now it was a guy named Hilton, or something like that. They had actually attended some training the drug manufacturer had provided. Yes, Hilton was still around. He worked out of the Delta office.

There were many more Anchorage vets, specializing in small animals. One catered to horses, of which there were now a surprising number. The Zoo's veterinarian had two assistants, and all three of them had used tranquilizer drugs. The veterinarian had had to put the Zoo's elephant down twice. "It was really difficult to decide on dose," he said.

By the end of the day, Eli had a short list of people who had occasionally used Carfentinal. All were wary of it. All said, yes, Fish and Game used it in situations where they had a large, hostile animal. It wasn't good for transporting. Animals tended to die in transit. No one wanted to talk about that.

Nor did they want to talk about any past employees who had been involved. Mostly because it was AIB calling, Eli supposed. He didn't know what this list would do, beyond being put in the box with everything else. Perhaps at some time it would be useful.

Just as he was about to take the results to Annie, Bright called back.

"This is Melvin Bright. I believe you rang me?"

Tired white male from Nebraska was all Eli saw when he shut his eyes. "Thank you for calling back, Mr. Bright. Do you have time for a few brief questions?"

"Depends on what they're about. If it's about Grossman, no comment, beyond that I was in Copper Center, repairing a broken pipe with crap parts."

"Actually, we're trying to run down a person who used to sit next to you in the Anchorage Fish and Game Office. Just trying to complete the directory for those years. There was a six-month period when it wasn't published."

"Sounds like a bullcrap job. I'm sorry for you. Don't remember anybody who sat next to me. Male or female?"

"Uh, female, we think."

Melvin Bright was quick. "If this is about the whistlesblower complaint, that's sealed."

"And what complaint would that be?"

"I don't see how I can be of any help. Maybe ask Annabeth Wilson, who was the office manager. She would remember before I would."

"So how are things out there? Is it winter?"

"Getting there. The drive to Anchorage is probably icy. Can I do anything else for you?"

Eli though how to ask this. "Yeah," he said, shuffling papers audibly. "You went out there in 1994, at the end of the year, right?"

"Yes."

"And you had requested a lateral transfer, but this doesn't seem lateral to me."

"Give you a prize. Look. I don't talk about that period in my life. I moved on. I moved here, and in a couple of years, I'll move back. That's what State Employees do. They needed someone, I could do the job, and I get travel compensation when I come back to Anchorage to see my family. I'm a positive person. I choose to see this whole thing positively."

Eli didn't know where to enter that narrative. "Excuse me, what 'whole thing' would that be? Your transfer?"

"No one wants that, no one wants to have...it doesn't matter. It's nearly over. Really, I don't see why you're asking these questions. I don't want to talk about anything personal, do you understand?"

"Thank you, sir, for your time," Eli decided it was best to cut and run before the man became hostile. "If you remember who that might have been that sat by you..."

"I tell you, it's sealed. Let it go."

"Again, thank you, sir," Eli said, and hung up.

He thought about the call on his way to Annie's office. Annie was going to back to Anchorage Fish and Game Monday to look at the archived personnel files. He guessed he would like to go along. Sometimes he acted so unofficial that people said things.

Annie was entering names and notes on the murder board. "Eli! Tell me you have something."

"Actually, I do. I have all of the lists in the machine; next step, program them to query one another. I talked to all of the veterinarians, expanded to Fairbanks. Zoo vet being the only one who's ever used the Carfentinal. They're all afraid of it. There's no certification for the darters, but someone named Hilton at Delta is considered experienced. Melvin Bright, who transferred to Copper Center, says to leave him the hell alone, he's just puttin' in his time on this space station."

Eli could always make her laugh, and Annie thought laughing was a good thing at this stage. "So, ho hum day, huh?"

Eli grimaced, "Melvin plainly doesn't want to talk about the person who sat next to him. Plainly doesn't want to hear 'whistleblower.' He did let two things slip. Primary motivation for taking the position appears to be that he wasn't given a choice. He knew exactly how long he had until retirement, and he's got his eyes on that prize."

"Retirement?" Annie prompted.

"He was 45 when he went out there, 10 years away from retirement age, but he had 17 years in the system. That means, probably by next July, he can retire. He has no incentive to answer any questions, or to pull out the old calendar books and tell us how things went down."

"Huh," said Annie. "Second slip?"

"He named a retired Office Manager as a source of information. People who are already in that zone talk a lot more easily."

"Good thought. Anything else?"

"I want to go with you Monday. There's a minimum of a dozen archived boxes of files, and I've just been in all those names, so maybe I can help. Plus, I'll mill around and see if I can get any pictures."

"Yeah," Annie agreed. "That could be good. Meet me there Monday morning at around 9:00? I have another interview after."

Annie put Eli's work in her briefcase and got her coat. She still felt she needed to see Melvin Bright personally, but being in Copper Center during the murder was just about the best alibi she could imagine.

So far, this was like describing individual trees, and thinking that this would help you find who was hiding in the forest. It felt backwards, pursuing anything that might be of use before it slipped away. They had only a shadow of a suspect. An emerging concept was the relationship of Grossman's management history to how others viewed him, but no one at any level wanted to talk about that. Who among those with whom she had talked had the desire and expertise to commit murder, with its reliance on an exotic and rare drug?

Her phone rang. She put down her briefcase, took off an earring and put it in the pile on her desk, and picked up the phone. "Brewster," she said.

"Inspector Brewster, this is Allison Cunningham. Do you remember me?"

"Deputy Director of Admin Services, yes. How can I help you?" Annie asked.

"I don't know if this is important, but one of the custodians, Ernie Hansen, who cleans in the State Library, has come in and reported that someone stole his coveralls. Two weeks ago. The night the Commissioner was murdered."

"O...kay. And did these coveralls ever turn up?"

"No, and that's why Ernie came in. He needs two pairs. He has a real thing about wearing dirty ones, and he...he's a bit challenged, mentally. He's a great worker, dependable, and he's certain he hung his spare pair behind the door in the custodian's room. When he came in the next night expecting to have them to wear, they were gone. He was really upset."

Annie had a brief aha. "Is Ernie a big man?"

"Yes, he's really big. Six four, probably 250. So he can't wear anyone else's, and no one else really could wear his, they're so much smaller than he is. Why?"

"Just a hunch. Thank you so much, Ms. Cunningham. That's helpful. I'll make a note of it."

"Um, I've never had so many things that involve the custodians, and I just don't understand...were they maybe being pranked?"

"It wouldn't be the strangest thing I've ever heard of. In any case, has anything else been unusual--barring the Clyde's night in the restroom, Ernie's coveralls--anything else?"

"No, I guess that's it. I just put the two together, I suppose."

"I'm glad you called. Sometimes these things are related; sounds like this one is. So thank you, and if I have more questions about it, I'll call."

Annie hung up. She walked over to the murder board, took the pen and drew a second figure, to the left of the one in the curly wig and trenchcoat. In janitor's coveralls, a mask, gloves, and a hair net. And glasses. Because you couldn't exactly clean toilets in a ski mask, now could you? So you put on the fake nose and glasses, you hide your hair, you cover your hands, and presto, you don't leave anything behind that ties you to the crime. She shook her head, put the pen in the tray in front of the board, and picked up her briefcase.

There was no coat. Now there were no coveralls. Both coat and coveralls were plus size, big and tall, whatever. Both would make this a big person. But what if it wasn't? What if it was two midgets, one on the other's shoulders?

Chapter Twenty-Four

Monday, October 28, 1998

Eli and Annie met at Anchorage's Fish and Game office, served the warrant, found the HR supervisor, and asked to see the archived personnel files. He took them down a set of narrow steps at the back of the building, to a utility corridor, past a boiler area, electrical panels, archived and cold storage specimen rooms. Len Norton--nondescript voice, face and gray clothing, who would no doubt disappear at any moment--directed them to a small table with two chairs, brought them the two files they requested, and vanished.

Eli looked around. "Only one escape route," he said. "Don't like it."

Annie chuckled. "At least it's not on the back porch," she said. Funny place for archived files, though.

They looked together at Grossman's file. Administrator's files were notoriously thin. They could confiscate the files, but to Annie it was about paperwork. Everything they took had to be listed and witnessed. Find what was useful first. They took Grossman's picture, his work history, his pay grade, a merit raise, his hiring papers, his resignation letter: "I am respectfully resigning my position to return to the River Guide business that I love."

Annie stared. She hadn't heard Grossman's "public" voice, but she didn't believe a word of it. What had really led to his going back to guiding? There were no performance reviews in the folder, from anywhere. Why had he left Delta? There were no details but the date, October of 1994. "Eli, can you find anything, anywhere, that says why he changed offices?"

Eli flipped through the file. "Nothing," he said.

Annie used the desk phone to dial the HR supervisor, who was apparently sitting on the phone. "Mr. Norton," Annie said, "Do you know why Grossman came from Delta to Anchorage in 1994?"

"Wouldn't you?" Norton said, in what Annie supposed was humor. "Sorry, Fish and Game joke," he went on. "He came temporarily because the previous Admin resigned suddenly with terminal cancer. Grossman was the most familiar with procedures and staff functions. He was hired permanently in 1995."

"So he came as 'acting,'" Annie concluded. Just like his move to Juneau. She asked, "Why are there no performance reviews in his file here?"

"Performance reviews are not mandatory for administrative staff. They receive a merit increment from their own supervisor, if it is indicated, but other than that, the only things that would be in a permanent file are commendations or reprimands."

"And since I don't see either..."

"I would conclude there are neither. Administrative personnel files do not follow the employee; exempt employees are privy to confidential information that is not germane to the next level of the organization."

Bite me, thought Annie. "I'm not seeing any complaints from employees. Where would those be."

Silence.

"Mr. Norton?"

"Uh, if you are referring to the sealed complaint..."

"No, I've seen it." Let him chew on that, she thought. "I want to know about the others." She took a stab: "Where is the one from Delta Junction?"

Silence.

So there was a complaint from Delta Junction or Len Norton was afraid that there was. Eli gestured, and Annie punched the speaker button.

"We are aware that there was an issue, but there is no documentation," Eli tried.

"I know nothing about another complaint," Norton decided. "If it exists, it would be with the State Ethics Officer. They have to log them all, and they are public record. However," he cleared his throat, "We are not necessarily informed."

O-S-U-R, Eli wrote on the notepad beside the files.

"Thank you, Mr. Norton. You are certain we have Grossman's entire file? And Bright's?

Finally, "Most of the contents of Bright's file would be in Copper Center. What you have is entirely that portion relating to his work here."

"One more question, Mr. Norton," said Eli, using his 'respectful' voice. "Did Bright's job description change when he went to Copper Center?"

"Of course. Why do you ask?"

"Because, he definitely requested a lateral move and stayed at the same salary level, but the move wasn't lateral, was it? I'm just ignorant of how the state reassigns people, is all."

Silence.

Then, "Bright did request a lateral move. There was no open position in Copper Center at his pay grade. They had an opening and an urgent need, apparently, for someone who performed duties Bright had done in a prior position. However, since this was not a disciplinary move, he would have been allowed to assume some additional duties that eventually led to a higher position, comparable to what he did here."

This sounded like mumble in the jungle to Annie and Eli, who couldn't resist trying once more. "I see nothing in Bright's file that indicates why he requested the transfer."

"No, we wouldn't put anything like that into a personnel file. I might have it in my desk files. No, I don't see anything about that. Let's see, that would be back in 1994, I may actually have a 'request for employee action' file in the non-current personnel records."

They heard him shuffle through papers. He was apparently not at his desk. They heard a file cabinet's metallic click. He came back to the phone.

"It's just a form. Requests to be transferred out of the Anchorage Office to take a comparable position elsewhere in the state. You can't put where you want to be transferred to unless your family has made a move. His family stayed here, as I recall."

"Bright said he was compensated for a weekly drive to Anchorage, is that correct?"

Silence. Paper sounds. "Yes, apparently. It's in the terms of the transfer."

"Is this normal? Can you identify any other person who was transferred with this compensation?"

Silence.

"Mr. Norton," said Annie, "I believe that my search warrant covers any and all paperwork related to the employment of Melvin Bright and the late Commissioner Grossman. I believe that you have a copy of that search warrant. Will you please immediately take the file from which you are reading to the door and Eli will come and get it."

"But it has things about other people in it also, so I didn't think..."

"I will come up and help you to load them up for us. Normally, we go through the files and remove anything relevant, so we will conduct that aspect of the investigation, now, please."

In a half-hour, they had twice as many files, as well as relevant papers from the personnel office. Annie shook her head. The 'foot dragging' gave the impression that there was something being hidden. The people who were protective of these files had nothing to lose. Still, Annie thought, if the wrong person found out that the

347

HR supervisor was opening the personnel files to the police with inappropriate oversight, the HR supervisor would be the next person moving to Copper Center.

Annie and Eli filled out a list of documents they were taking, put them into two briefcases they had brought with them, and left. Eli said, "Wait for me in the parking lot," and stopped at the receptionist.

"When I was a kid," he said to her, "we had a family friend who was the Office Manager here. Big woman, name of Annabeth. She and my mom were friends."

"Oh," the young woman exclaimed, "That would be Ms. Wilson!"

"Yeah, Wilson," Eli agreed. "Thought I'd say hello if she was still here."

"Oh, silly, she retired several years ago. She's in the Pioneer Home!"

"Gee, thanks. I'll go visit her," Eli said, "Great. My mom will be excited."

He found Annie at the edge of the parking lot. "I'm going to the Pioneer Home to talk to Annabeth Wilson," he said. "See if she remembers the name of the whistleblower."

"Eli, you just keep on keepin' on," Annie said approvingly. "I don't know what we'll have then, but I'm thinking we might want to do a newspaper search for that time period. See you back at the office."

The Pioneer Home was in the middle of Anchorage, in the Denali Park Blocks area. It was an imposing old white building with almost no parking. Apparently, few residents drove and staff took the bus? Anyone who was historically Alaskan or who had been in the state long enough could live in the Pioneer Home, and there were stipends and increments in the retirement system to help with their benefits.

Annabeth Wilson was in the group television room. She smiled at Eli, appeared to be genuinely happy to talk with him and immediately led him to a small table in the corner of the television room where they could speak privately. She reminded him of his grandmother. Her satiny hair was white and arranged neatly in a bun on the back of her head. She had the warm, comfortable demeanor of someone who was going to break out, any second, in macaroni and cheese, fried chicken and apple pie.

"Ma'am, I would like to ask you about the time when you were the Office Manager at the Fish and Game office on Raspberry."

"Lands, honey, that was in the...let me see. I left in '96, just before I moved in here. I guess that's not so long ago. Seems a lifetime. What do you need? Do you want a cup of tea or coffee?"

Because it seemed normal and polite, Eli accepted coffee, and this led to his carrying cups, condiments and the carafe off the coffee machine to their table, where they shared bad coffee with bad creamer. They looked into their cups and grimaced simultaneously. Eli said, "We're investigating Commissioner Grossman's death."

"Oh, yes. I read something about that. Murdered at the dump, was he?"

"That's just where they found him. But, yes, murdered. Looking into this, we have to clear any past issues with disgruntled employees, because..."

"Because you don't have a suspect?" Like most people who kept things running, Annabeth Wilson had a lively interest in what was going on around her, even if her world had shrunk. "I have to admit, I wondered who kilt him. He wasn't popular, but he wasn't there long, so these things balance out."

"We know that he had some issues with employees. We're specifically interested in any complaints there might have been, just to know who might have a grudge."

"It's a long way from a grudge to killing someone. You know that, I'm not telling you your job. Don't shoot these messengers. Janet Barker was a complaint, I recall. And...wait, that was before Grossman came. Of course, there was the

Melvin Bright transfer. And Sophia Brower, but she left. So, hmmm. There might be something from Freddie Bointse. I don't know.

"The HR supervisor keeps a file in his desk that's just complaints and partial complaints. I know about it because he took one out in front of me and ripped it up. Sophia's complaint, as I recall, because she withdrew it. I don't know what happened to her. Anyway, you want to know about Melvin?"

"Certainly, if you think there's anything that relates to the investigation. *I've already got what I came for,* Eli thought. *Sophia is the sealed complaint. Desk drawer in HR, get it into the next search warrant. Find out when Freddie and Janet were here and if they are in the drawer.*

"I don't know that it does. He was really mad, but the thing you needed to know about Melvin, he was generally mad. He came to work frowning, and he left muttering under his breath. I can imagine how much he hates it out there. He talked to the shop steward about it, and I guess the decision was, if they didn't lower his pay, they could move him wherever they wanted. So that didn't go anywhere."

"Was Melvin actually a part of the complaint that was sealed?"

"No, he just had the information. Excuse me. I'm not supposed to talk about that, but I don't suppose it matters. Complaint wasn't from him; it was from the gal who sat next to him."

"Sophia."

"Yeah. She just got in over her head. People do that. Feel personally responsible for holding others to the regulations. You don't be telling the boss he can't have information he asks you for."

"So," Eli said slowly, "Grossman asked for some information from Sophia?"

"No, that's probably why the complaint was voided, as they say. Got the information from Melvin. Melvin had to give it to him. Then Sophia filed the complaint. Then something happened. Sophia quit, Melvin went to Copper Center. I don't know anything more about it than that."

"That's great. You've been helpful. Thank you! Can I come back if I have more questions?"

"Sure you can. But you best stop at an expresso stand and get us both a Latte when you come. This coffee is like left-over chewing tobacco."

****

Annie was on her fifth time through Grossman's file, and the transfer request for Melvin Bright, when Eli came in.

"Annabeth says the whistleblower is Sophia Brower."

"An actual witness. I hope you didn't frighten her."

"Nope, she's my new Grandma. Ordered a Latte for my next visit."

"Then you can go back. Sophia. Try checking the archives of both the *Anchorage Daily News* and the *Times*. See if there's anything on the business pages about movements, retirements. There might be something about state employees."

After lunch, Eli had made his calls and internet magics, as Annie called his search strategy. "Sophia Brower went to the North Slope Regional Corporation. That's a big family name up there. We need a strategy. She probably wouldn't welcome a call on a withdrawn complaint. Bright, nothin'. I don't think that level of state employee is 'business news'."

"So," Annie mused, "if you had to say right now..."

Eli hesitated, began, "Sophia was politically connected to a powerful family, and you said you were told in Juneau that he left politically connected people alone? So Melvin, who actually 'committed' the sin of telling Grossman where the fish were, Melvin had to go. But Melvin was savvy. First he argued he wasn't giving information Grossman couldn't have gotten himself by reading the spring and summer reports.

He wouldn't 'confess' to doing anything wrong, and he was Union. Beyond that, he wasn't about to lose his paycheck or his retirement. He needed to stay at his pay grade--retirement is an average of your highest three years. They tried to humiliate him, so he used the little power he had, all of which came from the Union, and worked a deal. He wouldn't leave unless he got per diem to see his family, got to keep his old title so it didn't sound like a demotion, nothing negative in his file."

"Sounds right. He was plainly a scapegoat. But it doesn't sound like he was going to murder anyone over it."

"Grandma Wilson said Bright was a pessimistic, grouchy guy. So he might sound like he's threatening, but my guess is that he wasn't. He was pissed, but he was always pissed. He described himself as *positive* to me, and said he'd moved on. Sophia has certainly moved on, and up, and you don't mess with the North Slope. Too much money, oil, natural gas, coal. I don't know. My guess is that it wasn't as big of a thing. I'd give money, though, to know if Grossman's resignation had anything to do with the complaint. Like maybe there was another one, somewhere, and that's why the guides loved him."

"Huh." Annie couldn't find anything wrong with that, but it didn't get them to a murderer.

"You might check back through Sophia's financials and see if she hired someone unusual."

"Did that before I came in here. Found just such a payment, traced it down to the payee. She paid a PI $400 to investigate someone snooping around her house. I talked to him--actually, I know him. Jake Jimson. Older guy, traditional PI with a stereotyped dingy office and a floozy answering the phone and doing her nails. He was pretty circumspect. Said that he was sure it was tied to the complaint, because when she withdrew it, everything stopped. Someone was calling her, sending her obscene cards, like that. When someone tried to jimmy the lock on her deck door, she got scared, stopped everything, resigned and moved with her husband to Barrow. Do you want me to find out more?"

Annie stared at the murder board. What if the cards she had found in Grossman's desk were the same Sophia had gotten? So, they shouldn't be talking to Sophia, but she would certainly like to know. She got up, went to the box beside the murder board, sifted through it, pulled out the evidence bag with the cards in it. "I found these in Grossman's desk."

"ESAD. What does that mean?"

"Eat Shit and Die."

"Woops. Any fingerprints?"

"Just Grossman's. I don't know--did he send them to Sophia to scare her into withdrawing the complaint? And did he then, when he couldn't destroy her, send Melvin to Copper Center? Seriously, Eli, these things just keep emerging-- he was mean, he was vindictive, he punished people, he fired people for expressing their opinions, he shifted people into shit jobs, he was the quintessential bad boss. Do I want to go pester Sophia if she's gotten peace? We already know Melvin has an alibi. What do you want to bet that Barrow's a better alibi than Copper Center?"

"True that. We just keep piling stuff up, and we put it in the box, and one day we open the lid, and there he is, on top, smiling."

"And who would that be?"

"That guy," said Eli, pointing at the two figures at the edge of the murder board.

"Tomorrow see if you can get the State Ethics Office to tell you of any complaints against him."

"Will do."

Eli walked out, whistling, and Annie wished she felt so lightened with what she had been doing. Which was, basically, making sure that when the case was stalled, everything was organized and key questions as yet unanswered were clear for subsequent investigators. She seldom had everything so complete, so labelled, so correctly and carefully filed until a case was over. She found it soothing, actually. It felt like progress, even if it wasn't.

Chapter Twenty-Five

Tuesday, October 29, 1998

Annie felt that when she had to subpoena what were, essentially, government records, the only real way to get them was a personal contact. Government lawyers were reluctant to comply with any records request. They led with "overly broad," which was lawyer for *tell me what you expect to find.* And then you generally found what you should have known or needed to know was there, but it wasn't listed. Politics played into all records requests. Depending upon whom the records mentioned, there would be a veritable wagon-circling before a record's release.

She left Fred finishing his coffee and Bones with all four legs in the air having a nap on his pillow. She stopped by AIB to see if her subpoena was ready. She hoped she didn't need it.

Marsha Buck was the State Ethics Attorney, a gubernatorial appointment. Most ethics complaints were funneled to the commissioners, so there was a chance that any complaint would have gone to the then Commissioner of Fish and Game, Alfred Hudson. Mr. Hudson was another person who Grossman had replaced, late in the Governor's first term. She might ask why, but she did not want to give the impression that she was blaming the victim. She wasn't. She just wasn't, quite, blaming anyone else

Buck's office was in the same complex as Public Safety. Annie parked in her regular spot and walked through the building and out the front. In the next building, the Law offices looked out over Cook Inlet. Annie walked up to the second floor and to the Suite labelled 200. So much of her job was getting from place to place. Marsha Buck was in, and at her desk. Annie entered and took the open chair and Buck finished her phone call.

"Annie!" she said, as though she was actually happy to see her. "I'm so glad they put you on the Grossman case. I can't believe there's no suspect yet. What can you tell me?"

"Marsha, and then 'sorry, no.'" Annie smiled and held out her hand, across Buck's desk, which was shaken warmly. "So I want to say right up front that we have swirling mists of suspects. We need clarity, and we need it fast." She watched the frown materialize and set itself into cautious interest on Buck's face.

"Here's what we do have," she went on, deciding that putting out some bait was a good move at this point. "He was quite probably killed in the parking garage in the State Office Building. The killer waited for him, possibly disguised as a janitor, and stunned him, we think, with a taser, followed by an injection of a potentially lethal tranquilizer, and then put him into his truck, from which point he was taken to the Fish and Game dumpster, placed there, given one possibly obfuscating and one symbolic wound, and the next we know, he's in the Juneau Dump."

"Whew." Buck was, despite her lawyerly reserve, obviously interested. "I read once that tranquilizers won't put anyone out fast enough to overpower them."

"Well," Annie said, slowly, "this one would put an elephant down."

"Jezus. So, how does the killer get him to the dumpster without being seen? It was, what, in the six o'clock hour, from what I've read, and people were all over the place, getting into cars, whatever."

"A really good disguise? We're holding details back, because we don't want them in the media. We don't know if this is a one-off stranger, a serial, a disgruntled employee, or what."

"So," Buck said, "you want to know if we have complaints from the disgruntled employees."

"Busted," Annie said, and smiled again. "At this point, I only want to know who filed one, because we're looking at a short list of people from a variety of sources, in the absence of any other leads."

"Let me see your subpoena, see what I can give you," Marsha said. She looked over the papers, which would have to be left here in any event. "Don't see anything missing from work history. So Delta or Anchorage, those are his state jobs before this one?"

"That's about it. Not a long time. Full disclosure, I saw the unredacted parts of the sealed complaint from the Raspberry Office, the one that was dismissed."

"Yeah, I know about that one, although the whistleblower complaints don't come here. At any rate, there isn't much. You know, employees seldom make ethics complaints. They tend to come from the public, or watchdog groups. There were two Ethics Disclosures from Grossman himself, once when he was hired at Delta, and once here. You have to file that if you come from a related business or leave to go back to a related business. Nothing else from Delta.

"There is one ethics complaint filed by a reporter at the Daily News, in 1995. I don't think anything came of it. That was the era when the previous governor was reeling in ethics complaints. By comparison, this was pretty innocuous. I'll get the file for you."

While Buck was out of the office, Annie thought things had been in a bit of an uproar when the previous governor had resigned. Everyone was affected somehow, whether they loved or hated him. Annie was indifferent. But the ethics complaints had bothered her, just by their sheer volume. She could see how a complaint about a low-level functionary for a state office could get sidetracked, or maybe put on a siding, or lost.

Buck came back in and handed Annie the file. "I want you to look at it, and then we'll make you a copy."

That was a smart move. If there was nothing, Annie didn't need the file. If there was something, Buck was demonstrating complete cooperation. Annie thumbed through the complaint, made by Allan Fields, who, if Annie remembered correctly, was originally with the *Times*, before the papers combined. He might still be there.

Fields had alleged that he had knowledge of information given by Richard Grossman, then Office Administrator for the Anchorage Field Office of Fish and Game and blah, blah, blah, to

Big Susitna guide, one Chuck Racer, owner of Chuck's Big Sue River Adventures, which was not yet available to the public. The complaint was after Melvin Bright had been transferred to Copper Center. Annie felt a mild spark of enthusiasm. She ran her finger down the other pieces in the file, to the disposition. "Complaint vacated, employee no longer with the State Department of Fish and Game."

So, if it was vacated, did anyone follow up at all? See, Annie thought, that was the problem with this guy who moved around a lot. He didn't stay in one place long enough to be caught in what appeared to be an inappropriate sharing of information, and then the Melvin Brights of the organizational world received the punishment.

"Okay," she said, I'll take this one, please have that copied for me, and I'll sign the sheet on it. Anything else?"

"There may have been. We log all requests for procedures and forms, and if you give me the list of dates, I'll get those logs and you can see them. I don't know what help they will be. Can I ask you something?"

"Sure."

"Why are you going hard at disgruntled employees? Is it because of the 'symbolic' wound of which you spoke? Because you might open a big group of suspects and spend all of your time running down alibis, for nothing."

Annie nodded in agreement. "As we both know, there's a lot of running down...for nothing...in our greater business. In fact, though, I'm working the theory because it keeps turning up interesting information."

"As in?"

"Marsha, no one liked this guy."

"I'm glad that's out in the open. I'm, frankly, surprised he was appointed Commissioner. I said so at the time. He must have given big to the Governor's campaign. I don't know. Do you have any other possible leads within the state offices where he worked?"

"Haven't looked at Delta, yet, but we've spent a bit of time in Anchorage. I think the HR Supervisor has desk files, but he's holding them back. We're going out again today to boot him out of his office and search it. Don't like to have to do that, but the previous receptionist told us he'd showed them to her, and when we were there yesterday, he deflected us to another set he had in a file cabinet, so if we hadn't talked to the retired receptionist, we wouldn't have known. We suspected. He actually said he had desk files, and made it sound like it was forms he used."

"You might look at Delta. I know it was a long time ago, but people who attract complaints from employees tend to get better at it as they go along. It's in the early years when they make mistakes. The farther up they go, the more circumspect they are. They *reorganize*, for example."

"And don't I wish I had a fiver for every time someone has mentioned that," Annie laughed. "Marsha, thanks. You see why we are proceeding carefully."

"Yes. Better you than me. I hope your boss has a good relationship with the Governor, because he's going to get into this at some point. He's not a suspect, is he?

Annie froze, instantly alert. What if it was a former supervisor, who didn't want his or her relationship with Grossman to become public? What if the former or current supervisor had plans for a "next step," and Grossman's toxic management style wasn't going to be supported. What if the Governor himself wasn't involved, but a political protector was?

"Earth to Annie," Marsha Buck said. "The Governor is not a suspect, is he?"

"Sorry. No. We've just been pursuing every semi-logical lead, is all. Could someone connected to the Governor have seen Grossman's style or past behavior as detrimental to the Governor's future plans?"

"Okay, I get that. Anyway, I'll get the logs for you out of the archives if you can get that added to the subpoena."

The women walked to the elevator together and parted amicably. Annie went back up the stairs in her building, passing the front desk, uniforms waiting in hallways, detectives in inexpensive suits going into and out of doors, and small groups of people on the benches along the walls. She went up to her office, put the copied files on her desk, and picked up the amended subpoena that included the HR Supervisor's office.

She had a feeling about this visit. She put her little tape recorder in her coat pocket, got a hot cup and lid to take coffee, and went back out to her car, signaling Eli to come with her as she went past his cubbyhole.

"So what did you get?" He asked when they were buckled in and going down 'C' Street toward the Fish and Game Office.

"I have an ethics complaint from Allan Fields. He filed under the '*Any person may file a complaint with the attorney general regarding the conduct of a current or former public officer whom the person alleges has violated the Ethics Act.*' He includes a statement that Grossman gave a Big Sue guide information that gave advantage. Names. Signed under oath. Not required to divulge his source, because he's a reporter. If it were me looking at it, I'd say that someone gave a tip to the reporter, who made the complaint, but wasn't exactly zealous in following it. Those were the years no one paid attention to anything but who was living in Juneau and who was living in Palmer, if you take my meaning."

"Hmm. All of that fits. Does the date fit?"

"Bright was just about to be transferred to Copper Center."

"So we have a whistleblower who withdrew her complaint because she was being harassed. The scapegoat bargained for himself when no one else would protect him, and the union came through for him. Bright, actually, sort of won."

"Seriously? Copper Center? Away from his family?

"He came out of it with his reputation and career intact, he didn't lose money, and it can't be an accident that Grossman left right away."

"Okay, if I buy that, and I'm not saying I do, that still brings us back to Bright, right? Do you want to check his financials? See if he could have paid a hit man?"

"Sure, I live to serve. But I don't think it's Melvin."

"Because?"

"You know, he's one of the grey men who labor in the dim recesses of institutions. They don't take action. They don't get into it with anyone. They do not plan or conduct complex murders. They die at their desks."

"Yeah," Annie agreed, "Nothing about the Melvin Bright situation seems to point to him as the murderer, or Sophia either. Why are we not going out to Delta?"

"We're just looking at the closest stuff?"

"We have to guard against choosing a path and then selecting evidence that corroborates our choice."

"Right."

They turned in at Fish and Game. Annie put her badge on the belt of her suit pants, pushed her jacket back casually over her holster, and took her briefcase. Eli watched all of this. "You think we're in some danger here?" He was grinning, but stopped when he saw that Annie was serious.

"You never know why people lie to you, or what they will do to hide strange things. I went to see a guy once who had been a principal in a village school. Teachers were in revolt, details unspecified at this time. kept hearing about candy he sold as a real issue. A colleague and I went to his house, after hours. We asked about it, and at first they said, no, they didn't do any such thing. Then they wanted to know if it wasn't legal. Then they hemmed and hawed until finally they have us a box. We got outside, opened the box, and it was all genitalia."

"A genuine lapse in judgment, no?" Eli was laughing again.

"A lapse in something. So I prefer to see what Norton is hiding. I don't like having to come out here again."

Norton was not at work. He was home with heart palpitations. Annie hadn't heard that word since her grandmother died. Starkinson came in, read the expanded warrant, and unlocked Norton's desk. The deep, right-side file drawer had a number of files, all under employee names. Starkinson raised his eyebrows. He turned to Annie and said, "I was afraid of this. Norton is careful with personnel matters. I've talked to him before about having the files in more than one place. His explanation was..."

"...wait just a second, please," Annie said, taking her tape recorder out of her pocket and speaking into it. "*Tuesday, October 29, 11:30 a.m., Anchorage Field Office of Fish and Game, present are Chief Inspector Annie Brewster, Research Assistant Eli Carson, Office Administrator Bart Starkinson.* Mr. Starkinson, are you aware this is now being recorded?"

"Yes," he said, somewhat hesitantly. "What do I say now?"

"Please repeat what you said about Norton having personnel files in his locked desk drawer, and continue with Norton's 'explanation,' that you were about to give us."

Starkinson repeated himself, and then continued, "he said these were working files, concerns or complaints were just his rough notes, and when something was formalized, he transferred typed records into the actual personnel file or sent the complaint along as he was required to do, to the Commissioner of Fish and Game."

Annie was mildly disgusted that the state could think of no better way to handle complaints than to route them back up the same chain that had probably produced them to begin with. Rules was rules.

"*Record off, 11:45 a.m.* Under the circumstances I would need to look at everything in his desk, and Eli will make an inventory of the file cabinet and credenza. We'll call you through your secretary if we need anything else. You are, of course, free to stay, but you need to take a seat over there."

Annie went through the files, seeking specific names and otherwise returning the papers to the drawer. She pulled files for Sophia Brower, Melvin Bright and the two additional names Annabeth Wilson had mentioned, and scanned other files for pertinence.

In that process, she found two complaints stating someone was accessing the registries on employee computers after hours. This old system actually put everyone's files on two big drives, and anyone sitting at an office computer could access those in a given registry to which that computer was linked. She made a note of the two complaints, wrote down the dates, and the fact that no formal grievance had been filed. They were more in the mode of grousing about someone touching "their" stuff. Employees had no expectation of privacy, actually.

There were no files for Grossman, none that mentioned him. Annie went through the other drawers. Power bars and a pair of clean socks.

It was possible that something had been taken from the "desk files" since yesterday. It was more likely there was never anything relevant to their case. There was no security here. Norton had no ties to Grossman, he didn't seem to care what questions they asked about Melvin Bright, and aside from being what Annie would term 'unforthcoming,' he was a confidential employee. He was being confidential.

Annie spun what Norton could be hiding through her mind as she thumbed through the files farthest back in the drawer. All old, late 80's or early 90's. Labelled 'A' for active, 'R' for retired and 'S' for separated from service. Mostly R and

S files. She took out one and flipped through it. There was nothing unusual in it. The man had wanted to grieve the fact that he had seniority in a certain work unit and the new person got a corner cubicle. Give me a break. Why was that grieveable? And since Annie was pretty sure that it wasn't, why did Norton keep it? Was he keeping track of some kind of pattern?

So, if Norton had seen some pattern, but wasn't ready to talk about it yet, that didn't automatically mean it had anything to do with Grossman. In fact, there was no particular reason why it would. But that was another thing--what if Norton had been collecting something that now that Grossman was dead, wouldn't reflect well on Norton himself?

Better safe than sorry. "I'm going to take all of these files and see whether they have anything in common," Annie told Eli. "Are you about done?"

"Yeah, all of this is useless: procedures manuals and forms. Books about personnel management. Looks like Norton might have been taking some classes. Nothing relating to the investigation that I can see."

"Me neither. I'll fill out the form for these. Measure the stack, will you? There's a ruler in the top desk drawer, I think."

Annie stood and stretched, stacked the files neatly and took the list she was making over to the credenza. Eli pulled out the center desk drawer. "Did you look in here" he asked in a funny voice.

Annie turned toward him. He was standing in front of the desk, but though he was holding the ruler, he was looking at the wooden writing board that pulled out, like a cutting board, from the edge of the desk over the bank of small drawers. On the writing board was a taped piece of paper, on which was written in pencil, *ESAD*.

Well, well, Norton. "Check all the drawers, inside, above, underneath contents," Annie said. "Feel around below the files. That's where I found the ones in Grossman's office. Maybe other people use the same strategy for hiding these things."

Eli took the desk and Annie the file cabinet and credenza. They found nothing else. They took a razor blade from the desk drawer and carefully peeled off the piece of paper with the epithet and put it in an evidence bag. Annie gave the room a once-over. They went out.

"I believe we're done here," Annie said to the secretary, who glanced into the outer office where Starkinson was talking to another man. "Here's the list of what we took with my card attached. If

Mr. Norton has any problems, please refer him to the search warrant."

Annie was exuding excitement on the way to the car. "A clue! What does it mean? Did Norton send the cards to Grossman? Did Grossman send them to Sophia? Did Norton send them to Sophia? Did Sophia send them to Grossman? Okay, we have to think this through carefully."

"Yeah, but it also could be something innocuous, like, Sophia said she'd gotten this card, and she was scared, and she was going to drop the complaint. Norton is...oh, in love with Sophia, and he...decides he's going to find out who is harassing her...wait, are you laughing?"

"Eli, geeze."

"If Norton had sent the cards, there would have been an actual card, right? They stopped printing those cards a long time ago, and this guy seriously needs to change the paper on that writing ledge. Oh wait, wait! I know! It isn't his writing. He's newer than that. The cards have been there since the meteor hit the Yucatan, but were preserved in bureaucratic sludge from that time forward..."

"Now you're just being silly." Annie turned out of the parking lot, but she played it. Whose office was that? "Second thought, you should go get a Latte and see your Grandma. Ask her who had that office before Norton."

Chapter Twenty-Six

Wednesday, October 30, 1998

On the way to the Pioneer Home, Eli stopped at the Cafe Europa and got some fancy Halloween cupcakes. He drove through a coffee stand and got two lattes. Decided on half-caf, because maybe an old woman shouldn't be drinking too much caffeine.

Mrs. Wilson was in the television room. She looked up and stood as soon as Eli came in the room. "Told 'em you are my cougar conquest, so you have to play along."

Quick as could be, Eli said, loudly, "I don't know why you won't go out with me. If it doesn't matter to me, why should it matter to you? Here I've brought you cupcakes, and.."

"Get those cupcakes over here to our table, or we'll have to be giving them to everyone who's awake," she said, moving at a good clip for a person with a cane, over to the little conversation table. She took a long drink of her latte and sighed with approval. "Now, that's coffee. So, you're back pretty fast."

"One thing I forgot to ask."

"Okay, shoot."

"We found a thing in Norton's desk. Need to date it, is all. He wasn't in, so I thought you might know who was in Norton's office before he was, and what year he came."

"People have to be supervisory to get a door. People think seniority means you get a window. I probably spent more time trying to calm people down over their desk being in a new place than anything else. Bosses always think, let's move everyone around for efficiency. People don't see their desk that way. Hands off of my stuff, and so forth. So, let's see. Norton was always the HR supervisor. Doesn't supervise anyone but clerks, but that's neither here nor there. Has to do with the level of responsibility, who writes the annual performance review.

"After Starkinson came...no, that's not right. Grossman, then Starkinson, and he stayed, and... no. I get confused. No. No one else has been in that office that I remember. People swap out furniture when someone leaves."

Eli nodded, sympathy and understanding informing his every facial muscle. "So did Norton take anyone's desk?"

"Nope. Couldn't get it out the door without taking it apart. It owns that room. It was always there. Norton was always there, would be my memory. My guess, Norton will die in that office."

Eli and Annabeth sipped their coffee, ate a cupcake. She scraped the frosting off of hers ("have to watch the sugar, got the type A diabetes"). Eli threw a lure into uncharted waters.

"Did Norton have a thing for Sophia?"

"Eli, how would I know? What's the tie in there?"

"Trying to understand why he was so protective."

"Don't know that he was. Thought of himself as protecting the regulations, actually. Some are like that. No, I don't know as I ever saw anything protective. Again, why?"

"When she made the complaint, there was apparently someone stalking her."

Annabeth Wilson pursed her lips and looked at the rim of her cup with interest. "She was in over her head," she finally said. "She told all of us about it, whispering, one at a time. You know how toxic that can be. Grossman was fit to be tied.

"She was always given to fanciful notions, some said. Pretty much the women in the office knew she was having some issues with mail, or phone messages, maybe more. I told her get a gumshoe and let them hunt it down for her. Told her to call the police if she was that scared. Don't know that anything more came of it, but she left for Barrow all of a sudden, as I recall."

So Wilson had been the one who recommended the PI. How was Norton involved here? As HR supervisor, did he receive the initial complaint? At what point did Grossman know?

"Thing was," Wilson said, "Grossman knew the complaint was about him, and he never said anything to her, she told me. He acted like she didn't exist. He called Melvin Bright in, and they talked in private, but he never talked to Sophia."

"How did Grossman find out about the complaint?" Eli asked.

"Don't know. Seemed to know everything, from minute one. People got to taking things out of their desks that they weren't actually supposed to have at work, made sure files were put away at the end of the day, like that."

"Because?"

"Seemed like they could, I suppose. He had keys to everything, and it wouldn't be unusual to find him in the specimen room, in the personnel office, any old where. Got so you didn't have a conversation you didn't want him to know about, like you didn't call home, didn't take personal calls, and that. People would cue up things to print and then go stand by the copier. Anyway...we're off of what you wanted.

"The desk may have been built in that room. It was always there. We talked about having it taken apart and having a new work station ordered for him with more space for a computer and printer, but he didn't want a new desk. Said it had character and all sorts of hidey-holes. I had a roll-top once that was like that."

They finished their coffee. Eli asked her if she wanted him to hide the cupcakes. She did. She said, "I'll walk you out and put them in my room."

They went down the hallway, chatting about how she liked it in the Pioneer Home, and when they got to her room, she said, "How'd you like to come in?"

"I don't think we want people to talk, right?" Eli said. "I'd rather our relationship be mysterious."

"Okay, but 'mysterious' is for people who have lots of time to ponder things," she responded. "If you're embarrassed by the age difference, you just need to get over it. I have."

They parted, laughing, and Eli stopped at the desk. "Does Mrs. Wilson have family locally who visit here She seems pretty sharp."

"Annabeth? Yeah, she's sharp alright. And no, her children live in Iowa, actually. Thank you for coming to see her."

Eli left, thinking about this bright, vital woman. He liked her, but it didn't mean her memory was accurate. She may not remember exactly how things happened in relation to one another. He got what she said about gossip being toxic. All by itself, that would have eventually gotten back to Grossman and pissed him off. However, though they thought Grossman was behind the harassment of Sophia, they would never prove it. They needed to pursue the one lead they had; the cryptic acronym on Norton's desk blotter matching the card in Grossman's desk in Juneau. And to remember that it may not be related to the killer.

Starting her day doing paperwork, Annie's mind was also working on that. She took the cards from Grossman's office and the paper from Norton's blotter to the crime lab and asked that they be dusted for prints. She briefed Beatty. She talked with Manfort and Hendricks, telling them her progress, but mostly talking about the McKenzie crime, which would probably take more than one of them up to Delta Junction in the next week. Maybe they could stop off and talk with Hilton if she gave them the questions she needed answering? Jamalia quickly volunteered.

Annie breathed a sign of relief, because she didn't relish driving all that time to Delta, asking 15 minutes' worth of questions, staying in a bad motel and then driving back.

She and Eli came back to her office at the same time. He told her about the cupcakes and his conversation with Wilson. Annie told him sternly that the legislature forbid reimbursement for the cupcakes, but he could be reimbursed for the coffee if he had a receipt, and if she backdated the approval form, and then if Beatty backdated hers, and so on and so forth. Amid their rueful chuckling about food for information, Eli told Annie that the desk was born in that room, and at some time in the distant past, so was Norton.

Eli left laughing, and Annie put Norton on the board, humming *"I like mine with lettuce and tomatoes...*

The crime lab called, and she nearly ran down. The fingerprint tech was looking at two sets of fingerprints on a light box. He gave her a little magnifier and said, "want to look?"

"I want to have you bronzed. I can't believe you were able to get at this in such a short time."

"Oh, just started out with it, and it was pretty obvious. These are prints on file for Grossman, because he's been fingerprinted for three jobs over the years. These are prints on the cards. Here is the paper you got from the guy's office. Prints there don't match the prints on Grossman's cards."

"And? Are you seriously going to make me find this myself?" Annie was smiling, but she didn't...wait. "The index finger, right?"

"Yes. Grossman's. So the only prints on the cards Grossman had were his. Thumb and forefinger, like he picked it up. Partial down on the front, inside, like you were opening it. Pretty good print. There are no prints, or partials, except those which are consistent with his. Well, maybe one: a partial thumb on the back, like someone picked it up by the bottom of the fold, with just their thumb and finger. But my guess is that print was with surgical gloves on, or through a tissue. The really thin ones, if you squeeze hard, you can get a shadow of a print. You can never match them, because they'd never survive in court. Anyway, just the partial thumb, that's not Grossman's."

Annie said, "You guard that bad print like it's your passage into Heaven. I have a feeling about who might have left it."

"Yes'am, will do. Would be great if we could get prints through fabric, or plastic, or whatever. I'll make sure it's safe. Now, here's the sheet of paper, not Grossman's print as I said, but this is a really old piece of paper. Lots of unidentified prints."

"The only thing we're trying to find out is whether Norton has a readable print on that paper, which leads us to tying him to the acronym. It's a long stretch, and probably won't lead to anything. You can check, although I'm not sure why his fingerprints would be in any database. Len Norton."

"Norton, Norton, Norton. Nope. I'll see what I can find in the FBI database, or what we have for the rest of the state. So anyone who has been a teacher, anyone who applied to the police, so, wait, if I go back..."

"I'm going to leave these with you, and you see what you can find. Give me a call if you want to show me anything." Annie thanked the young man before he could show her the suspended library cards recalled by the Municipality, and left him muttering into his databases.

She hadn't expected Norton's prints to be on Grossman's cards. No--more likely, Norton and Sophia had talked, Sophia told him about the card, and he noted the strange acronym on the old piece of paper taped to the writing board on his desk. So Norton knew more about Sophia's harassment and leaving--indeed, the whole complaint--than he was letting on. It was possible that one of the files that *wasn't* in his secret desk stash contained his private conversations with Sophia.

Why would the same acronym intersect with Grossman at two points in his work for Fish and Game? Coincidence? But what about no such thing as? This was all tied together, she felt it. How?

By noon she was done with all of her phone calls and updated her notes. She thought about calling Carolyn Grossman and bringing her up to date, but decided she'd wait another day.

Maybe it was time to bring Norton in. He was clearly withholding, lying, obfuscating, thinking he was clever. He might actually be in violation of some state regulation or even law, putting private files in his desk when he was a supervisory employee. At least a contract issue. She really wanted to know why Grossman had left. That was potentially the only important piece of her puzzle she felt she could glean from Norton, and she knew that he knew. Maybe a latte. For the right beverage, would he spill? But he was not like Annabeth. Certainly not grandfatherly. More like your spooky uncle who was never right after Korea.

She called Starkinson and told him that they needed to depose Norton. The word "depose" made the most sense, as it did not imply arrest was forthcoming. She didn't give Starkinson an actual choice. Then she called Norton and asked him to come in voluntarily. He agreed, though he said he would have to clear it with Starkinson. She told him she already had. She asked, "We didn't see files for Sophia Brower in your desk files. Did you have a file on Sophia?"

"Whatever you saw is what I had," Norton said tentatively.

"If you run across anything, bring it along," Annie said, hoping to communicate that she didn't much care one way or another.

They set a time the next day for the deposition. Annie hung up. She made a bullet list of the questions on her blotter that Jamalia should ask Hilton, so they could go over them before she and Manfort left for the interior.

- *Record conversation*
- *Did Hilton ever use Carfentinal, note body language.*
- *Security for the tranquilizer drugs*
- *Years in job, background*
- *Prior job holder, timeline for previous employee*
- *Know Grossman? Body Language*
- *Ask HR person if files for DJ include any complaints against Grossman or Hilton.*
- *Grossman's predecessor, why left*

If they got these, what would they know? She called Sullivan, who was actually at his desk.

"John, Annie. Just checking up on anything you might have stumbled over at the Dump, and so forth."

"Hey, hi! We pretty much know what we knew. Found five fillet knives at low tide. No blood--human or fish--on any of them. Talked to everyone on the license plate list. One guy said he saw what sounds like Grossman's pickup pull into his parking spot from the channel direction, and saw someone he thinks was Grossman get out. Of course, he saw whomever was wearing Grossman's overcoat and a wig, would be my bet. Guy didn't have reason to pay any attention. Didn't see anyone go into the building, but wasn't looking. Was pulled into a parking place by that time. Guess that would be it. Oh--we talked to Ernie about his coveralls. He was pretty upset still. But he repeated the same story he told Allison Cunningham.

"So, if you ask me, it went down like you said: big man disguised as a custodian, Grossman ignores him because he's a worker bee."

"Yeah. Indicates to me a fairly sophisticated knowledge of Grossman's habits, dress, routes, and maybe attitude. Which keeps saying, 'former employee.' Oh, you'll never believe what we found in the Anchorage Fish and Game office."

Annie told John about the desk drawer in Norton's office, and told him what Eli was currently doing with the lists of passengers. "Eli tells me," she concluded, "that in a few years we'll just be able to put this all into a computer and it will spit out probabilities."

"Yeah, we've got probabilities now," John said dryly. "Got a funny call from Commander Beatty."

"Yeah, probability is he wants you up here," Annie said. "So watch your back."

They hung up laughing. Annie added another bullet point:

• *Talk to HR supervisor and see if he/she has desk files*

She was putting on her coat to go home a little early, as they were going to try to get a walk in before it got dark when her phone rang. It was the tech in fingerprinting.

"Thought you might like to know. On further review, one of the old sets of prints on the desk paper looks like Grossman's middle finger."

He would do that. Annie let out a long, heavy sigh.

Chapter Twenty-Seven

Thursday, October 31, 1998

Annie loved Halloween. They had pumpkins and cornstalks on the porch, with a witch in a camp chair wearing hip boots. Fred had carved his best pumpkin face in years. "Safe" candy was in a bucket inside of the door, where Bones couldn't reach it. He liked chocolate, but the vet said it was poisonous to dogs. She had tried to tell Bones, comparing it to bacon, tasty but dangerous. Bones refused to listen. Said he would like his bacon dipped in chocolate.

She put on her black suit, an orange shirt, some black beads and a black fedora she had in the back of her closet for just such occasions. Then, thinking the better of it, ditched the fedora and put on some high black snow boots. It was, after all, Halloween. That predictably, meant snow.

Norton's deposition was at 10:00. No lawyer required. Annie wasn't sure it was worth it. Grossman should never have been in Norton's desk. Damn. If this didn't quit being about Grossman, it would never be over. It was almost as though their hunt was being orchestrated, they were in a labyrinth, and there was a boogeyman around the next corner.

Plainly others thought *snow* as well. Johnson's Tires was inundated. Snowtires and studs. That was the surest sign of coming winter. The Chugach Range had had 'termination dust' since mid October, and it had crept down the mountainsides last night, for sure. Annie drove carefully, but didn't encounter ice. She got a coffee from the lobby and walked upstairs. She poked her head in and told Eli about the possible print. She went into her office, hung her coat, and went to see Darin and Jamalia.

"Sure appreciate you guys checking in at Delta for me."

"Oh, well," Darin said, "you pretty much finished the McKenzie case for us, so it's just *quid pro quo*, you know. At first, I was jealous of you being pulled out of this tar baby to go to Juneau, but after seeing what you've got, I don't envy you at all."

Annie grunted, sipped her coffee and nodded. "It's a bitch, on wheels, on skids, on a sled, in a plane...Hope you don't get snow on the way out."

"There's already snow. I hate that highway. We're going this afternoon, see about just staying in Glennallen and going up in the morning. Safer."

Jamalia asked about the Grossman case and Annie gave them an expurgated version that had all of them laughing, especially at Eli's new conquest of an older woman.

"Yeah, it would be funnier if I thought it wasn't serious. He took her cupcakes yesterday."

"Cupcakes? Wait a minute. He doesn't bring cupcakes when he does research for me," Darin objected.

"Knows better," Jamalia said, patting her thighs. "I'd have to throw them at him."

They all laughed again. Annie allowed she really liked the crusty muffin top of any cake-like thing that was unfrosted. Darin nodded gravely. Jamalia said, "give me your frosting, I'll handle it."

Annie went over her list of Delta questions. "Watch the body language. I need to know why Grossman really left, because I think there's a complaint in there somewhere, just like at the next place. The bigger the coincidence, the greater the chance that there's a reason in common. Get me the lay of the land so I know what to put in a subpoena."

"Okay, gotcha. Someone knows more than they're saying. Do agencies ever take pictures?" Jamalia asked.

"I would kill for a general staff picture, but I haven't run across any. Eli asked about that. Maybe there was a *going away* party for Grossman with pictures. Maybe in the local paper. Or not. See if you can find a friendly retired office manager up there who will give us the dirt. On second thought, take cupcakes. Probably don't ever get those in Delta."

Before she started Norton's interview, she checked back with the fingerprint tech, who had found Norton's prints in the FBI database, as he had been certified teacher in the 80's. These didn't match the partial from the back of the card in Grossman's desk, hazy as it was, so Annie didn't see where it got them.

Len Norton was prompt, nervous, sweating, carrying an old briefcase ad his coat, boots, and gloves across his chest. He said twice, "I don't know what you need from me."

Annie described the process they would use. Procedure required a second inspector. Manfort would be joining them. Norton asked if he should have counsel. Annie said that wasn't necessary, that this was voluntary, and if, at any time, he felt as though he were being accused of something or was uncomfortable, he could request a more formal meeting. Meaning, they were going to ask him these questions anyway, and he needed to suck it up.

He held his coat on his lap, as though he might need to run out the door at any moment, which would undoubtedly cause him to trip on his boots. Annie got him a cup of coffee, wished she had a donut of some kind, and read her name, Manfort's and Norton's into the tape recorder.

Manfort came in, shook hands, and sat. He said, "I'm just an observer. Please direct any questions you have to Inspector Brewster."

"Let the record show that we are interviewing Len Norton, Human Resources Supervisor for the Anchorage field office of Alaska Fish and Game. Mr. Norton is here voluntarily, in the full knowledge of his own supervisor, Bart Starkinson. In an on-site service of a subpoena on Monday, October 28, and in a subsequent visit to look at items covered in the subpoena but not provided to inspectors on Monday, Inspector Brewster found an item in Mr. Norton's desk about which the AIB has further questions."

Norton sat as still as a mouse in a dark corner, but his face was white and his lips were pursed. He said nothing.

Annie went on, "Mr. Norton, will you please describe your desk?"

Norton was frankly puzzled. "Describe my desk?'

"Yes, please, sir."

"It's old-fashioned, quite old. There are two small drawers and a locking file drawer on the right. Three deeper drawers on the left. A center drawer about two feet wide. Then there's a modesty panel under the desk, and...I guess that's all."

"And if you want to write, do you use the top surface?"

"Uh, I guess so. I keep a clipboard over at the side of the desk for people to use."

Annie decided to let that rest. "And can you tell me, as exactly as possible, your recollection of the incidents that led up to Sophia Brower leaving?"

Norton stared. His eyes watered a bit as he peered anxiously at her. "I didn't have anything to do with it," he finally said. "I don't know what caused her to leave."

"Were you in any way involved with either her resignation or Melvin Bright's transfer??

"Yes. I gave them both the appropriate forms and helped fill them out. Most people don't know how, and then the form gets kicked back."

"You did not put any notes in your desk about either Sophia Brower or Melvin Bright? We found none."

"I told you, Melvin's files went with him, and Sophia's were downstairs in the archived files."

"Yes, that's not exactly what I'm asking. I'd like to know if your 'desk files,' which we did go through, at one time had records of meetings you had with either person."

"I...threw away any handwritten notes once the employees were gone."

"I see. Can you tell me what you recall about that time?"

"I don't know why it makes any difference. I wasn't involved in the whistleblower complaint; it went directly to the AG's office. Sophia knew better than to talk to anyone in the office about it. There's a protocol that has to be followed, or the complaint goes nowhere. But I remember her being upset about something, and telling her not to let her personal life affect her work demeanor. She went home for the rest of the day, as I recall, and then everything was back to normal."

"For Melvin?"

"Uh, not the same. Melvin Bright talked to me about a transfer, and his contractual rights. I talked to him and the union rep twice, if I recall, and Grossman also spoke with him. I saw the terms of the transfer, all of which were done without my input. I thought they set a terrible precedent. I was never told anything about how the agreement was reached. Grossman took care of it."

"And did you ever hear any conversation, rumors, gossip, about Sophia's subsequent problems and withdrawal of the complaint?"

"Certainly I heard rumors. Someone sent her a nasty card, someone phoned her in the middle of the night and threatened her, someone tried to break into her house--that's what the police said. Then I heard she hired a private investigator. She came in just before she left and the only thing she ever said directly to me about it was she couldn't stand it, her husband was angry, and they were going back to Barrow. She got a good job up there, I heard."

I heard, I heard. So, Annie thought, I guess I just have to bite the bullet. "And do the letters ESAD mean anything to you?

Norton turned white. His mouth moved, but nothing came out.

"Mr. Norton?" Annie said sharply, "Is there something wrong?"

He managed a whisper: "They were written on the letter-writing platform on my old desk. I opened it one morning and there they were. I haven't opened it since. I'll never open it again. The hair stood up on the back of my neck. The fact that you found it means it's still there, but I have never looked at it again. I can't. It just appeared. It must have been the custodian; my office is always locked."

Somewhere in that was truth. "Did Sophia Brower tell you about the contents of the card she received?"

"No. Why?"

"Just curious. Oops," she said, consulting her notes and pretending to be flustered. "I forgot to ask you why Grossman resigned. Did you know? Did you help him with his papers?"

"Yes, I knew. He came in and got the boilerplate for the resignation letter. He took forms for his tax shelter and his retirement account. He never sat down. He didn't want any help figuring them out." Norton seemed a bit huffy that anyone would shortcut his important role. "He left, let me see, in the late fall, which seemed strange, if he was going to be a guide again. That's not a guiding season, but he told someone in the office that he had a lot to do to get ready for the spring fishing. And something about contract work. I told him that he should be careful to follow the ethics protocols and not do anything that related to his position here for at least a year. He said that was why he was leaving when he was. He also said, just before he left..."

"Yes?"

"It doesn't matter."

"It does, please finish."

Norton thought about things, looked at the ceiling, and then directly at Annie. "He said it wasn't any of my business to be telling him anything about his ethical responsibilities, and that if I felt it was, he would be glad to review my job description with me."

The same "threat" behavior when challenged that had emerged in a dozen interviews by now.

"And would you be willing to take a polygraph where you would be asked questions about information we have just discussed?"

"Am I a suspect?"

"No, we just would like to eliminate people who were proximal to Grossman during specific events." Which was cop for "*eliminate you.*"

He surprised her. "I don't see why not. I don't know why I didn't throw the thing away. Truly, I don't know why it upset me so. It was like being violated. Is it somehow tied to the investigation?"

"Possibly. So, do you want to do the polygraph while you're here or come back?"

"Now would be best."

"Interview off. I'll go see if the polygraph tech is busy. Thank you so much for coming in, and for the information."

Norton looked surprised, but Annie could see his whole body relax. Her mind was bouncing about as she walked. If not Norton, who? Grossman? The Murderer?

Later in the day, Annie went over the polygraph results with the tech. There was nothing, actually. Norton showed nervousness when asked about the acronym, and about the drawer, but no sign of actual prevarication.

She carried the polygraph results back to her office and filed them in the evidence box. She stood in front of the murder board. She followed each string out to the end.

What did she know? Practicing leaving out anything that was speculation was always a good strategy. Annie sat down at her computer. She made a list of what was absolutely or reasonably true about the case so far. Grossman's time of death, the parking garage, the disguised attacker, the dumpster, the weapons, the mud on the suit coat, the Carfentanyl, the missing coveralls, a list of interviewees and what they had provided, the complaints in the Anchorage office, suspects eliminated and why, and the greeting cards and fingerprint results.

And then she thought, shouldn't they call Brower and see if she did, in fact, get a card. That had slipped out of thought for a bit. But this had actually helped. She went next door to APD and found the detective who had investigated Brower's break in.

Tom Fillson was stereotypically overweight, medium height, his hair high and tight, and his shirt, if not exactly meeting at the buttons, well pressed.

"Tom," said Annie, reaching out to shake his hand. She had worked parts of cases with this man and got on well with him and everyone else down here. "I'm working on the Grossman murder, getting nowhere, and I wondered if you can direct me to an old complaint, made by a Fish and Game employee..."

"Sophia Brower. Yeah, I put it downstairs once it was vacated, but my notes are in there. Let's go down and see if we can find it."

Miraculously, everything was there. They were cards, not letters, and if they were fingerprinted, there was no mention of it. Brower had asked for them back when the complaint was withdrawn, and had destroyed them in front of Fillson. No pictures.

Tom apologized. "Sorry we didn't know to keep those. Sophia said she wanted to put it behind her, and she didn't intend to ever do anything more about it. We tried to talk her out of it. First the cards, then the phone calls, middle of the night, distorted voice. Finally, someone tried to get in the sliding glass door. We thought there was a crime.

"She was alone. Her husband was in Prudhoe. When the door was jimmied, she melted like a kid's ice cream cone. I don't think I've ever seen anyone so scared. She was sitting up all night. Her husband came down and went ballistic. We were relieved when they left town."

Tom Fillson flipped through his notes. "Guess I know now why we don't throw some of this away. Look through everything with our blessings."

Annie was turning the pages of the actual police report, asked, "Did anyone cast the footprints?"

"I think so. Tell you the truth, I don't remember. We did fingerprints on the glass door."

"Do you have those?" Annie held her breath.

"Yeah, I think." Tom paged through things, found an evidence bag with the information in it, and said they were copied into the database upstairs.

These databases. What were the chances, anyway? Any prints but Grossman's, what would be the point?

And later, when the fingerprint tech compared them, they did match someone, actually. They matched Len Norton. Annie threw her hands up in the air, got her coat, and went home to pass out candy.

Chapter Twenty-Eight

Monday, November 4, 1998

Annie started out the morning debriefing Beatty. Manner and place of death were really all they knew, and he needed to tell the Governor. AIB now had two new complex murders. Annie was frustrated with a full-time assignment on a case that had slowed to a crawl, or the following of useless "leads." Every time they took a step forward, they took a step back. There was a point when the best of cases came to a standstill. It wasn't an admission of defeat, it was a pause. Annie was hoping that she could go one or two days a week on the Grossman case and help out her colleagues on the other two, but that required Beatty's approval; he had promised the Governor his "best investigator" would be full time on Grossman.

Her colleagues needed her on other cases, especially the one in Kotzebue. PSOs in Kotzebue needed immediate help. A gay native man had been mutilated and killed. He was found in a snow bank with his genitals stuffed into his mouth. Booze was legal in Kotzebue, and there were bars. The victim was known to frequent them and proposition men who came in from the offshore rigs, fishing boats, and the DEW line site.

The Public Safety Officers in the villages existed in complex relationship with their community. They could arrest drunks, give tickets, quell domestic violence, and smash booze shipped into dry villages; but they were alone, their safe responses shaped by public opinion. It was better to get geographically distant backup on site before any confrontation. A murder required sensitive interviewing. Villagers might refuse to tell the PSO anything. Annie was senior, had been there, and felt she should go.

Beatty started out the debriefing visibly irritated. "I read your summary. I don't know what's going on, even after I read it. Give me a one-sentence that the public can have."

"Okay. Here goes: Grossman was a jerk, someone didn't like him, and after thinking about it carefully, they figured out how to murder him and not get caught."

Beatty stared at her. Then he finally smiled. "Annie, you're the best, but your sense of humor isn't something I want on public display. I promised the governor. This isn't the way it's supposed to be."

"I will get the guy. When have I not? Okay, the serial killer, but the feds wouldn't get out of my way. So, we want a delaying statement. We construct something reassuring and plausible, give it to the Governor, have a press conference in which we sound mysteriously hopeful, and then get Grossman buried."

"Right. Care to take a stab at language?"

"Beyond what I just gave you? Oh, that's right, we can't say that." Annie smiled and sipped her morning coffee. "I'd say something like this: 'Commissioner Grossman was apparently murdered by someone who knew his habits and routines well. This was a carefully planned murder. Details are being withheld in order not to alert potential suspects. Information has been provided by over 60 interviews and potential witnesses. Anyone who might know information pertaining to the case...' blah, blah."

"60?"

"It sounds good. Forty, for sure. Anyway, we can keep a lid on the evidence and the autopsy, keep pecking away at the possible disgruntled employees."

"And remind me why you're going there, exactly."

"Sure." Annie sighed. "We'd go after others but we don't have any others. Eli compared the passenger manifests for every transport going into and then out of Juneau in the weeks surrounding the murder. There are no matches, yet. Similarly, some of the evidence that was 'tossed,' 'buried,' 'burned' or *mailed*--shit, why didn't I think about that?--might turn up, be identified, and so forth."

"What happened to the guy at the Fish and Game office with the incriminating evidence on his desk?"

Annie didn't bother to correct the details of Norton's involvement. "We brought him back in after we found his fingerprint on the jimmied sliding glass door at Sophia Brower's. He says he went over there, at her request, because the police left without securing it, and she was terrified to be in the house. Says he worked on it, got the latch so it would lock, and then put a block in the track on the inside and a brace against the lock mechanism. Fillson says those things were there when he went back the next day. By then the husband was there. They withdrew the complaint, got stuff packed up, and went to Barrow to his brother's."

"Norton is nothing?"

"Not exactly. He isn't being completely forthcoming, but he seems harmless. No way he went to Juneau. Did he have something to do with Sophia's harassment? Not likely at all. Was he in cahoots with Grossman? Gives us a break if it were true, but there's absolutely no evidence. If Norton is telling the truth, and the polygraph shows maybe he is, the hand-written letters appeared on the desk with no explanation, no ties. At least Fillson's note documents ESAD actually on the cards Sophia showed to the police. The only print of relevance on the blotter...ahem...is Grossman's."

Beatty's eyebrows disappeared into his precise hairline. "You're kidding me."

"Yeah. Another thing we don't tell the Governor. The company that makes the cards said they were only made for one year. The rep might have given them to someone who was a client like the Book Cache, which went out of business. The cards were never actually sold in Alaska. The rep died.

"When Sophia got the cards, Grossman was still in Anchorage, still at Fish and Game, and knew that there had been a whistleblower complaint against him. It gives Grossman the opportunity to send the cards, and write the acronym to scare Norton, who is way too officious and zealous about doing all of the forms, and was trying, potentially, to interfere in the transfer of Bright.

"This just takes us back to Grossman, who didn't, respectfully, kill himself."

"Yeah," Beatty said. "Not going there with the Governor. Okay, I'll work on a statement, and you go to Kotzebue. Three days, max, or you call me."

"Right. This is me being enthusiastic," Annie said. Then, "If you have time, why don't you ask the FBI for a Profiler. Temporarily, just to help us with the gut check."

"Good thought," Beatty said. "It will help us with the Governor if the Profiler says we're on the right track."

Profilers had deep knowledge of the relationships between crime and criminals. They studied traits, patterns, intersections of patterns. Maybe they would see something she didn't.

She stopped to see Eli and go over how to organize everything. "Make sure you put every scrap of paper you've touched, signed and dated, into that box, please," she concluded. "And make sure that the autopsy notes get in there, too. And whatever else you found out about Carfentinal."

Eli was just staring at his desk blotter. "You know," he said slowly, "I think the killer went to Juneau and got him, and then just kept on going. You're not going to find the killer here."

"Yup," Annie said. "That's what I'd do. It's the opposite of the old Alaskan line, 'let 'em come up here and get us.' There's a lot of world for a killer who leaves the state to get lost in."

Manfort and Hendricks were due back from Delta Junction tomorrow. Then two of them would head for Kotzebue.

Rather than taking down the murder board, Annie took pictures of it and had Jason show her how to print them. She needed to learn some of this stuff. She printed the pictures, full sheet, made some notes, and stuck everything into one of the bankers' boxes. She had a lingering sense of irritation that she could feel a murderer out there, standing quietly, looking at her.

When she erased the two little figures at the bottom of her murder board, she felt the murderer smile. She bared her teeth. "You think you have won, but you haven't won," she said to the hazy shape. "I know these things I will not write down, but I will come and put them in your face. You and Grossman had some sort of problem, and he won. He did what he could to destroy you. You stole tranquilizer from the office before you left. You waited, made a long plan, and eventually, when you were ready, you went to Juneau. You followed him. You killed him. You dumped him. And you left town. You left Alaska, is what I think now. Eli will find where you went, and I will find you."

****

The next morning, when Hendricks and Manfort came in, they sat down together with Eli in the conference room, with discreet bowls of fun-sized candy bars everywhere, and a plate with four discounted Halloween cupcakes between them.

"So, are the Russians Coming?" Annie asked.

"Nyet, they don't know anything about little girls. Just ask 'em," Jamalia said. "Last night, after we left, troopers followed a tip and found the girls in a locked pickup truck. Alone. Local doctor checked them out, and released them to their parents. We are sending the DA from Fairbanks and a FNSB detective to interview them. Don't think they know much.

"Don't know where the mastermind is. The old man is apparently back east. The wife said she remembers the girls, vaguely, as friends of her granddaughter According to the troopers, neither girl knows her or her granddaughter. That's all so far, til we can talk to them."

Manfort grimaced. "Troopers are following the owner of the truck this morning. If its one of the two guys we picked up yesterday before we left, then we're pretty much done til we find who ordered this. Troopers are flying them down today, should be in lock-up by now and then we can talk with them again. We. Can talk. You know the Russian guys won't. The girls are home, that's where we are. It may be where we get. DA says we have plenty for a grand jury. on the snatch and grab.

"FBI may pursue the old man, since his prints are on the container where they were kept, but probably they won't find him."

"And did we go to Fish and Game," Annie asked Jamalia.

"Yes, we both did," Hendricks said. "We interviewed Hilton."

"Big guy?"

"No. Buffed up but about 5'8". Hasn't ever had to tranq anything with Carfentinal. Prefers Ketamine. Took us to the room where it's kept, showed us all of the safeguards. Said in the history of the organization, there had never been any of the tranquilizer drugs missing or unaccounted for. Could be just smoke, but he was pretty smooth. Didn't know Grossman. He came after Grossman left, and the last biologist left, *in somewhat of a snit*, the position went unfilled for a time."

"Body language?"

"Cool as a cucumber. Are they cool? Anyway, no stress."

"And what about the person who left...what?...in a snit?"

"Well, she..."

"Wait, she? Another woman?"

"Yeah. A biologist who had apparently been there for several years."

"Huh. Did she file a complaint?"

"No complaints. Whoever has the forms may have a note that she got one, if she did. Nothing we could find. You need a subpoena for personnel files there, too. Not sure you'll find anything. You know, in the bush, people purge...Wups! There it goes, into the fire..."

On that note, Annie, Jamalia and Darin ate their cupcakes. Eli filled the dead air. "I was told by a Fairbanks Vet in that the woman before Hilton was good. Any idea why she left?"

"Fired, but not fired, would be my guess. Hilton was vague. Hilton maintained he didn't know. Oh, here..." Manfort offered an envelope, inside of which was copy of a newspaper article with a picture of Fish and Game staff hosting an easter-egg roll for the community's children.

Annie scanned it. Saw Grossman, standing off to one side. The staff was arranged like a choir on risers, with the tallest members in the back. That row had three big men, one in a baseball cap and sunglasses, who might actually be a woman, now that Annie looked carefullly.

411

"Eli," she said, "I have this feeling that we need to date this picture, and get names on everyone in it. Can you see if the newspaper has more of the story that might include identification? Put whatever you get with your lists.

Annie looked again at the grainy picture. The sunglasses and hat reminded her of the drawing she had made, and that was actually creepy, so she shook it off and went over Jamalia's notes to make sure she didn't have any questions. "This part about the security on the drug."

"Yes?"

"Did Hilton lead with that? Like he anticipated it was a problem area?"

"Come to think of it, he did. I think it's the whole opioid thing. People want to know that dangerous drugs are under lock and key."

That made sense. Annie turned to Eli. "Carfentanyl is, one way or another, what killed him, so we'd better show we tried to run down any in-state source. Might as well check on how hard it would be to get it from out-of-state as well. Vice says it hasn't turned up on the street at all that they know of, so I'd just like to see the legitimate sources."

"I remember something about it only being available to veterinarians and field biologists, but that doesn't mean someone didn't bring it in.

Okay. I'll see what I can find." Eli made notes, flipped through to what looked like a multicolumn list. He made a symbol on that and a note to the side. The three Inspectors, fascinated, watched.

Eli left and they talked Kotzebue. They agreed that Annie and Darin would go, as they always went in teams. They chose the weapons they would take, picked up ammunition; checked supplies in the evidence kits, including luminal and plaster they would just leave if they didn't use it. They packed cameras and batteries. They had hard cases, because there was a baggage hold. It was a big plane, so they called the PSO's to see if there was anything else. A box of produce, heavy on the bananas. They would go tomorrow morning, and Annie would pick up the groceries on the way.

Back in her office, she warned Beatty this might be a "hate crime," depending upon details, and telling him to alert the FBI. Gay men were actually getting some protections. Then she called Sullivan, had him check the tip line for anyone who had miraculously witnessed the murder and had the murderer's name. No such luck. She went over Jamalia's notes, and, seeing the one line "Hilton says person before him left in a snit," she wrote out the things in the Delta office they needed to see, to get these included in a search warrant. She gave Jason her notes and asked him to use the boilerplate to draft one.

On a hunch, she went to Eli's cubby and asked him if he had a list of Delta's employees from the time Grossman was there.

"Yeah, if it's accurate. Someone could be missing, someone could be gone," he said, thumbing through his directories. "So there was a Steve King who was the IT guy. A Burton shows up in one, next says TBA, and the one after that an S. Parkinson. Don't know if that's male or female, don't know if it was a replacement for Burton. One old guy retired a couple of years ago, maybe still lives in Delta."

"Okay, put those names in the file and we'll see if we can find out anything more about the drug and security. We need to find that out here, too. Basically, that's all we have left to do on Raspberry. Just call and ask Starkinson if they keep any such supplies, or if they're all over at the State Troopers. I'm pretty sure that's what he told me originally."

"Will do. I'll actually go over and take a picture in the lab. You all be careful out there. Natives are relentless."

"Eli. The word is *restless.*"

"Right. That too. Be safe."

"I will. You know, the lab probably signs out syringes. Anchorage does. You might call and see if they had records for the years Grossman was there and since he left. I don't want to have to go back up there twice, but I think we need to see the Fairbanks vet and Hilton. Maybe after I get back from Kotzebue something will break."

****

Kotzebue looked tidy dressed in snow--rows of houses, an area of businesses, a small airport with a long runway. They banked and landed. Annie thought Alaskan pilots had more types of experience than colleagues in the lower 48. Weather was its own grave teacher. Everyone, passenger and pilot, had stories. Some commercial pilot had said that landings in typical Alaskan circumstances would simply not be attempted in most US airports. Might be true. She thought about these things when medicated.

Annie and Darin took the waiting taxi to the PSO's pre-fab home/office/jail. Burtie Franks and Ernesto Martinez were anxious to get the body out of the village. Funerals were huge, multivillage mourning events, already underway. Andy Pakuyurak wasn't the town's most popular figure, but native people were tolerant of his lifestyle in general, and he was theirs, in specific. Annie thought this civilized and humane. His body was in a flight bag in a locked cold storage area behind the building.

They looked briefly at the victim, who had obviously died in agony, his face was smeared with dried blood. He was not wearing pants. The gaping hole where his penis had been gave mute testimony to the rage of the killer. What was the matter with a polite refusal? Who was so offended that they would do this? She asked the PSOs that question, and Ernesto, who appeared to have no reaction to the body at all said, thoughtfully, "We don't know most of people who come in on the weekends, or off their shift."

Burtie said, "We talked about it. We figure this wouldn't be someone in the village--it's too public. We've been told Andy never approached anyone local. That leaves guys who are only here for the day waiting for the jet, to guys going on the next boat, to long-time clients where there was some beef."

"Or," Darin said quietly, "Someone who was threatened by being propositioned in front of workmates, even though he and Andy may have known one another before."

"Or," Annie added, "Someone who lives here and had been hiding out, and the proposition was public?"

Burtie sighed. "I suppose."

They went over the evidence collected, talked to the bartender who remembered seeing Andy that night, and sent Burtie and Ernesto to talk with companies whose workers were in town on the night in question.

They got a list of names, over half completely unknown to local PSO's, and all gone except two who had been taken from their boat to the hospital. They interviewed these two, who were actually helpful. One of the guys, they said, was really touchy and homophobic. It gave them a name to pursue. Unfortunately, he was back out at sea. They regrouped. They talked to people who knew people, talked to wait staff, found out nothing important. Checked in to the hotel and put their things in their rooms, and then Annie ordered room service, telling Darin she needed some processing time. Or sleep.

The next morning, they visited the site where the body had been found. Not the murder site. No blood. The PSO's had bagged Andy's hands, but nothing else. The AIB inspectors secured new evidence, having found what looked to be Andy's pants stuffed into a nearby burn barrel. To dispose of trace on the pants? There were many boot prints. Everyone wore boots.

Beneath a caribou hide hanging off a porch railing fairly close to the burn barrel, they found a large spot of frozen blood. They took pictures, and looked here and there for a knife or an ax but found nothing. Annie said it didn't look like that was where the caribou had been butchered, and there was no blood on the hide. It was not fresh, but freeze-dried like everything else left outside in the Arctic desert. They collected bloody snow out of an abundance of not wanting to come back and do it again.

Temporarily, they had nothing to do. All of their interviews with employers had been conducted. They had collected the passenger list from the airline and looked it over for males coming into town or going out in the window of opportunity and aftermath of the crime. Annie went into the cold room to talk to Andy.

There were a number of things detectives did that the public might find strange, and sitting with the dead, visiting them in the morgue, and in the cemetery, was one of them. She unzipped the body bag and looked at his face. She knew not to touch him, but there was a lock of hair in his eyes that begged to be moved, so she put on a glove and carefully set it back in place. "You rest in peace," she said. "I will find who did this. Rest."

And, as if there had been something between them, Annie had a sudden memory of this village that included having talked with the minister-- Father Balcombe, she recalled--about local people. He was a skilled observer, and a confidant of many local people, apparently. Telling Darin where she was going and why, Annie went to church.

In the early years of Alaska, and in a fit of fairness, the ecumenical council had efficiently divvied up the state among denominations. Nowadays, there were little Catholic churches in villages, too. But most had stayed as designated. Kotzebue was, as it had been since the 50's, Presbyterian.

Annie went down the aisle of pews to the church office, past offertory envelopes and hymnals she recognized from her childhood. Father Balcombe was still pastor, assisted by a ministerial wannabe teacher who had come to Kotzebue with his own vestments.

Balcombe was thin and tall, with salt and pepper hair and a neat beard framing a tanned fisherman's face. After brief small talk, Annie said, "What was done to Andy isn't something you want in your village, and it isn't something anyone should be trying to protect with silence. Do you have any knowledge that might help us find who committed this cruel murder?"

"I don't know of a local person who would murder anyone," he said firmly. "We have our share of violence, certainly. Bars do not help. Poor Andy was well known. He was here every Sunday, without fail. He sat in the back of the church, alone. He occasionally took something out of the offering plate, I am certain, to buy food and drink. Some time ago he tried to live in

Anchorage--I think he had a sister there--and he was apparently in jail for drunkenness when he was raped. He was never the same afterwards. He was in the hospital for a bit, and then came back to Kotzebue and began to make a living importuning the fishermen, basically."

"What a sad story." Annie exclaimed, horrified that this had happened in custody. "Did everyone in the village know this story?"

"Yes, certainly. The man who committed the rape in the Anchorage jail was tried and convicted. He served five years, and was apparently just released."

Oops. Annie asked for and received the name of Andy's rapist. Rape of native women was common. What was unusual was not that the victim was a man, it was that someone had been convicted. She thanked Balcombe and went back to the PSO Office. Burtie and Ernesto knew the name. The man had shown up off the plane asking if anyone had seen Andy, which had been greeted with raucous laughter.

"So this was someone who knew Kotzebue and Andy, and who was known by others here?"

"Not well, but he crabs out in the Bering, that's known. Don't know if he got his job back or what."

Darin and Annie exchanged looks. "Pick him up if you can find him," Darin said. The PSO's left to do that, although they weren't enthusiastic.

There was a startling lack of enthusiasm all around. It was truly a disturbing and horrific crime, and yet, everyone was going about business as usual. They all looked. They asked passersby if any had seen either Andy or the alleged perpetrator on the night in question. They got a picture of the man from the boat owner's office and showed that. No one had seen him.

Annie and Darin went back to the hotel. They ate in the bar, where they asked additional questions of the waiter and the bartenders. They went to their rooms. Sometime later, Burtie called, said they had "found the guy under a rock," and had him in custody.

"Let him sit a bit," Annie said. "We'll talk to him in the morning. In the meantime, get his records from Anchorage, anything on whether he was paroled, who his PO is, what evidence is already on file from when he raped Andy. Let's have those all printed out and ready to show him why he's in custody."

The next morning, though Annie suspected that they knew now who had killed Andy, she and Darin waited quietly in the conference room at the PSO building for Burtie to bring in Clive O'Gady. Finally, Annie said, "This might be too easy, but what if we tell him we have DNA, a handprint, clothing fibers, and whatnot. See if he folds."

Hours later, they thought it had, indeed, been too easy, though Annie felt it was just what she needed. O'Gady was in town, having tried to get his old deckhand job back, and was looking for other work. After they told him they had DNA, he said he didn't care who knew that he'd taught Andy a permanent lesson. It seemed that O'Gady had been treated to some of his own in prison, and he was permanently pissed off. He didn't rape Andy, he said, he just accepted Andy's offer of a blow-job, and then he wanted a more thorough experience and Andy didn't. He wasn't a homo. It was somehow Andy's fault. "Sometimes you just want to put it in, and it could be a hole in the wall. What was it to him? He was a certified freak. Wasn't like he didn't open up for anyone who wanted to poke him."

They really didn't want to talk to Clive anymore, so they put him in the cell in the back of the PSO building, and warned the airlines that they would be transporting a prisoner back to Anchorage on the late plane. Annie called Beatty and told him to alert the FBI that this was definitely a hate crime. Beatty would make an appointment for everyone to meet when they got back to Anchorage.

The family was distraught, but once they knew that someone had actually been arrested, they went from wailing to weeping, and then to planning. Annie liked that Andy would only be remembered, here, as a member of the family, beloved among his ancestors. She told them an autopsy was required by law, but that Andy's body would be back in a week. She suggested that they might want to arrange for cremation or a casket while the body was in Anchorage. She invited someone from the family to come along who could take charge of the body after the autopsy.

She said she personally would see that Andy was carefully and respectfully treated, and that the arrangements included the wishes of family members. Sometimes it helped for a female detective to deliver all of this to the mother. One used the skills one had, there being no script for grief.

All in all, it was over, because though they didn't have a confession, there had been no lawyering up, and O'Gady seemed unconcerned about what he had done. They had notes, a taped interview, and, with Andy in the hold and his brother seatbelted in beside Annie, went back to town.

Chapter Twenty-Nine

Thursday, November 7, 1998

Whitman Parfletch was terminally British, a brisk, thin, mustachioed Colonel Sanders. Happy to have something to do. It was his slow time, though things were picking up. The killing season was on the horizon. Snow meant more dark, fewer witnesses, buried evidence, buried victims. New snow could cover a body and it would not be found til breakup. Then there were the psychological effects of dark and cold. Criminals loved the long Alaskan dark.

When she had moved, Annie and her father had shared experiences with the peculiar ability of snow to hide the dead in plain sight. He described the trek to the Argonne Forest and the Battle of the Bulge, through the frozen and snowy landscape, where every bump covered by the snow could be a body, friend or enemy. In war, in death, the dead fell in undignified, grotesque or strangely peaceful sculptures. A blanket of snow made them unrecognizable as humans. So it was with the great wilderness of Alaska. The snow, melting, briefly revealed random victims or their belongings, and then gradually covered them again, until they were at rest in the permafrost like the mammoth.

This morning, the weather pronounced Winter with authority. Bones loved snow, running about and plowing through it with his nose. When the first snow fell, people and animals played in it. And then, shortly, it could be life threatening. Around the next corner, or in the back yard, was a lethally angry moose. A man was trampled to death on the university campus. The same dog who played in the snow could be frozen in it tomorrow morning. She had seen that in the Arctic, dead dogs still on their chains. In the urban homeless encampments, people went to sleep and never awoke. In the villages, an inebriated person simply sat down, went to sleep, and died. Winter could mean death in so many ways.

Annie went into the foyer, saw Whit in a three-piece suit and moon boots, and walked up with him. Moon boots were ugly white things, but the warmest, least expensive boots you could buy. If you didn't dress for the remote parts of Alaska on any regular basis, you could at least save your feet.

"Whit," she said as they made their way to her office, "How have you been?"

"I certainly cannot complain. And you? I heard you solved Kotzebue."

Annie demurred that it was good luck with the Minister. The FBI was deciding, Whit said, whether to take it. They were debating.

"Things are moving slowly on Grossman," Annie said. "Hopefully, you can review what we know and help us see what we might be missing."

"Hardly think I'll do that; hardly think you'd miss anything. But I will be glad to help. I read your notes, I looked at your murder board with Carson. He is a bright young man, by the way. I went back over the autopsy. Is there anything else you want to tell me besides what is physically here and in the file?

"I don't want to prejudice you, but I have my suspicions. So I'll wait. How's that?"

"Superb. How about I set up over here? I can look at the evidence and ask questions. By Monday, I'll tell you what I think."

Annie was going to run up to Delta, and to Fairbanks, on Tuesday. She wanted Eli with her, and he had some important mid-term exam on Monday. "Monday will work."

She arranged for Whit to take their open desk. She went back into her office, finished Kotzebue paperwork, and talked briefly to the

ADA who had the case, and who said the FBI was ambivalent. Yeah, the guy had been a male prostitute, but that didn't necessarily make him gay. AIB didn't need them, it was a courtesy. They had fingerprints, and semen from Andy's pants. Probably wouldn't need a Grand Jury.

Whit came back in, and stood looking at the murder board, muttering and making notes on a pad. Annie left him to his muttering, though she observed that he followed the threads in the same way she would.

"Man or woman," Whit muttered. He checked his notes. "How big was Grossman again?

"Over six feet, probably mid 200's. It's in the autopsy."

"So, someone strong, big, tall...let's see..." Whit left, muttering. Annie smiled. This case could make you mutter.

****

She didn't take anything home. Fred was going back up to Anaktuvak for at least a week to consult on restabilizing the building. They spent the weekend just being together. They took Bones to Kincaid Park, where he could run and they could walk and talk. The air was crisp, and they were dressed comfortably with good hiking boots. Midday, they came back to the public area and sat at a picnic table while Bones cleaned the packed snow from between his toes by, basically, chewing it loose and eating it.

They went to their favorite Saturday restaurant, the Peanut Farm, and watched football on the big television while they ate huge Halibut sandwiches. And fries. They went shopping. Then they took a nap. They woke up in time to snuggle in front of a movie with popcorn.

On Sunday morning, they read the paper, and Annie disagreed with the article on Andy Pakuyurak while she made them cinnamon rolls. Andy was described as a "native man with mental health problems," and Annie didn't like that spin. There were hints at Andy's "career" that Annie knew were true but irrelevant. Would they ever get past the time, she wondered aloud, when the background of the victim somehow relieved the perpetrator of a portion of guilt for the crime?

"Honey, juries get instructions now about not focusing on that. I did, anyway. Defense wasn't allowed to ask that woman anything about her past, the trial I was on. Hard to say, though, whether it wasn't in the minds of some jurors that she got what she deserved."

"Andy didn't deserve either of the crimes O'Gady committed on him." Annie took out the cinnamon rolls, put frosting on them and watched it melt down over the fragrant buns. She brought two to the table, took up her reading glasses, decided they were Fred's, took hers off of him and replaced them with his, and sat down to read the rest of the paper. "We should get different colors," she said.

"Of what?" Fred looked up, puzzled. "Hey, you have my glasses! Wow, I see better with these."

They tucked into the rolls, got sticky, got the paper sticky, licked their fingers, and decided that they didn't really need to get dressed today. They declared a snow day, turned on the gas fireplace, and settled into their chairs to watch "Face the Nation." Bones thought this was a really good idea, and after scratching about a bit, got his pillow in the right shape and crawled on to sleep.

But later, Annie thought about what she had said. Was Grossman responsible for what happened to him? Did his bad behavior have to be part of the solution? Irony was lurking.

****

Monday, November 11, 1998

Whit had an actual graphical presentation. In the conference room. Everyone sat in, as Whit said firmly that Annie could die tomorrow. She said she didn't think she would; Whit replied primly that no one ever thought they would.

He hooked his little computer up to a projection device that sat on a lectern, and opened to the first slide, which contained the five famous "w's" from journalism, in a scrambled order.

"These questions are not in the normal order," Whit said. "Most people like to start with 'who' or at least 'what,' but profilers like to start with the actual technique, as this is more likely to lead to the murderer."

Annie thought about that, nodded, even made a brief note about the order and how entry at any point along the list of questions subtly changed one's orientation. She did, if she thought about it, proceed from the *how*. It did, in fact, tell a lot. She refocused on Whit.

"*How* concerns weapons selected, use, degree of skill, and sometimes apparent force or care. These can all lead to motivation, emotional state, and possibly relationship. In this murder, for example, the *how* leads us to a personal relationship. A side question at this point is whether it is a ruse."

"For the *who* and *what*, we go directly to the victim and murderer, one of whom is known and the other unknown. If you add the *personal* elements of the *how* to the known victim, you can conclude with high certainty that this is not a crime of opportunity. This specific victim was the target.

"*What* did the murderer do? Again, in this case, there may be a ruse. None of the weapons appear to have killed the victim directly. Did the murderer know that would be the case? Undoubtedly.

"This crime required extensive knowledge of the victim's habits, careful preparation and precise execution." He smiled slightly. "What does the murderer have to know? *How t*o kill, *What* to use, *When* to carry out the murder, *Where* to do it, and *Why* wear a disguise*?* All related to planning. Then you go back and find the motive. Complicated, requiring more planning than normal for a single murder. I agree this is not a serial. Too personal, too detailed."

Eli looked at Annie, as though to ask permission to address a question. He was, after all, pretty low on the totem pole. Silly concept, given how helpful he was. She nodded.

He asked, "Sir, just curious at what point you decided this was an individual? Could it be two people, working together?"

"Young man, think about it. There are how many working pieces in the crime? One, find a day when he's coming to his truck at night. Two, develop a plan for getting him on the way to his truck. Three, observe the path his truck takes, on multiple days, and where it is parked. Observe his coming and going routines. Four, and these may be out of order, secure weapons. There were at least three, potentially four. Five, acquire disguise elements. Six, walk through the crime to see the timing. Seven...do you see where I'm going with this?" Whit stood back from the screen and waited.

Eli thought, but not long. "The more people you have involved, the simpler the plan needs to be. People forget. People improvise. Someone happens on the scene. People panic. People drop things. So, this plan is stealthy, complicated, and multi-step. At each step, you have to have contingencies. I get it. This is one person because it's so complicated, and with each step the possibility the next step may need to be modified."

"Keep this one," Whit said, nodding toward Eli, and going to the next slide, which showed key elements verifying preplanning. "The killer knew when Grossman's wife would be out of town, knew Grossman would be coming to his truck in the dark. The act is timed to the meeting. The final disposition of the body is timed to the dumpster collection schedule. Everything is on a timer, which, if you think about it, allows murderer an opportunity to rapidly leave town.

"This murderer is skilled in logistics. Flexibility and contingency are built into his plan. Either of the last two places Grossman could have been expected to appear would work. The Parking Garage has the privacy and gloom. The killer also has the elevator, the elevator lobby, the parking garage itself, the area around the dumpster and the truck as possible places to complete his activity.

"Finally," he said with emphasis, "most murderers do not appropriately secure and dispose of *all* evidence needed for crime solution. They may think they do, but this case is nearly unique for"--and at this point he flipped to the third slide--"the sheer number of evidentiary pieces which are not, as it were, in evidence.

"Including evidence of rage or passion. Certainly the knife argues for revenge. As this is such a careful, methodical crime, revenge that argues for a distant grievance."

Montfort asked whether the murderer could simply be fastidious. Whit said of course such killers existed. As a matter of fact, many serial killers completely cleaned their victims, for reasons other than removal of evidence. In this case, he felt "methodical" was more apt than "fastidious."

"The complete novice will always leave something, will frequently panic and do something stupid if the plan is interrupted. It does not appear any mistakes were made here. You may stumble upon some, but I think not.

"The serial killer will choose victims of a type, and though they may leave little evidence, bits and pieces begin to aggregate in subsequent crimes. Here there are no identified similar crimes. Given the idiosyncratic specifics with this one, I would conclude at this point he is not a serial killer, though he may be experienced, perhaps military. Experience with killing, but not with murder." Whit stood looking at the chart. EF Hutton was about to speak. Everyone leaned forward.

"This is the profile: 30's to 40's, male, quite probably ex-military, previously had significant contact with Grossman. Someone for whom Grossman represents betrayal, hence the knife in the back. Grossman would have known him, though not necessarily well. A former employee or someone supporting same is probable.

"The killer knew the drug and made sure that the dose was sufficient to kill. You don't use this drug unless you know its dangers. With it, you have a subdued, helpless victim who is going to die if he has not already. The gun is not the murder weapon. This person knows guns, and in this situation uses a gun with precision to hide the evidence of a drug being injected. The knife is almost delicately used, only to make a point. Sorry for the pun..." Whit smiled, so everyone else did. "He took everything with him, which indicates he is secretive by nature, and cautious.

"He is a loner, committed to something which he may think he is protecting. He kills Grossman in hand-to-hand combat, and then, from above, he humiliates the corpse. Dumpster, Garbage Truck, Dump.

"In his choice of setting, time, place, and method, he shows considerable thought, was probably in town for several weeks, or has been in town with the opportunity to watch Grossman's habits during the past year. He has worked by himself, even within organizations."

"That's what I have," he said abruptly, and sat down. "I would say, in summary, this murder has one special piece, and that is the drug. It being used primarily on wildlife. Which puts it squarely in Grossman's corner. I would be looking for a person who worked with wildlife, probably under Grossman's direction."

They all looked for some time at the bullet-pointed words on the last screen.

"We're in the ballpark with *disgruntled*, then," Annie offered into the silence.

"Most definitely. Against Grossman, I think, yes. It seems personal. It could be someone who has anger associated with his position. It could be an eco-warrior with an actual tie to Alaskan wildlife. No, as I speak, I think this is too personal. There is a previous employment connection, I would say. Not an ex-girlfriend or a mistress, that much is clear."

"And why not?" Hendricks asked.

"I'll bet I can't get away with 'because I said so,' in this group," Whit said, smiling and showing white teeth through his perfectly groomed mustache. "This is a crime that requires physical strength. Grossman is a big man. Ergo, the killer is likely a big man."

"Uh..." both Annie and Jamalia said in unison.

"I don't mean that women wouldn't have the strength to do specific parts of the crime," he said. "But think about this. From the minute a woman touched him, he would have fought, hard. Unless she was ready for that, she might be in trouble, fast. A woman's reflexes are different, trained differently. I go back to the complexities of the crime, how many times the body has to be subdued, moved, removed, and I come up with male assailant. On the other hand, the knife, that's more of a woman's thing. So, a big, careful man."

"Or Wonder Woman," Annie said. "That was helpful. We're going to do a couple more interviews up the road. We'll get back with you afterward and see if there's anything you want to add. Please debrief Commander Beatty, because he wants some specifics to share with the Governor."

"Oh, good grief. Tell me what you want me to say to him.'

They all laughed. "What you just concluded will be fine," Annie said. Someone was going to say "disgruntled" to Beatty and the Governor besides herself.

Later, looking at the profile, Annie thought two things stood out: ex-military, which they had not considered, and "protecting something." This fit a Fish and Game employee. Many of them felt aligned to the conservation initiatives and were anti-guide and commercial fisherman, because of by-catch. Many guides pressed as hard as they could to take the biggest fish, and these were inevitably the breeders. So, Fish and Game employee, ex-military. Think about Sierra Club, Green Peace. Maybe have Eli look into that. Grossman's ties to the Guide's Association were pulling her. Who didn't like that a favor was given to someone else? To what might an employee take deadly offense? Who felt the "duty of care" orientation to the wildlife, and saw Grossman's using their information nefariously or injudiciously?

"The other thing," Annie said, pointing with a pen to Eli's to do list, "is 'in Juneau for a couple of weeks.' I can see how it would take some time.

We went out one week, to check for names in and out, but maybe you need to go out three weeks?"

"Sure, I can do that. I'll need earlier...Oh Geez. Look at the time. Heading for my exam now, okay?"

Eli was finishing up two criminal forensics classes. Annie was supportive of his completing a BS and positioning himself to be their tech team member in the future. He found things they would never even think to look for. New technology didn't intimidate him at all.

"Go," she said. "So we'll leave pretty early tomorrow morning, and I have to bring the dog, so I'll drive. Remember to bring a sleeping bag and cold-weather gear in case we have car trouble. Also better charge up a phone. Talking to myself," she added, as Eli waved and ran out the door.

Chapter Thirty

Tuesday, November 12, 1998

Annie and Eli went up the Matanuska Valley on the highway that met the Richardson at Glennallen. The Mat-Su Glacier, one of the most beautiful and accessible to tourists, had receded so far that Eli told Annie he couldn't see it with the low clouds. The day was dark, overcast, and threatening more snow.

They would go to Delta first with their search warrant and conduct their interview, and then go to Fairbanks to see the veterinarian who had used Carfentinal. They would stay in Fairbanks, and drive down the Parks Highway home tomorrow. A big loop of incredible scenery.

Brewsters owned a four-wheel drive Subaru. Annie drove it to work, the perfect small vehicle for icy roads. With Fred still in Anaktuvak, Bones was in a bed in the back, restrained by a metal dog gate. In the second seat, safe from dog hair, was their emergency gear, and two small overnight duffels. From a sleeve of oldies CD's, they settled on the Eagles and sang now and then. Annie was perseverating on *lyin' eyes*.

The first snow had already been scraped and the curves sanded. They made good time. By the end of the third CD, a sad commentary on *life in the fast lane*, they pulled into the junction at Glennallen. They gave Bones a break, got coffee and gas, and headed up the road. The only people driving were locals, the tourists all having scooted over the boarder.

In Delta, they got lunch and then went over to the tiny newspaper office to see if anyone had names for their picture. In the archive, not yet on microfiche, was the original picture. No names. No help. The article mentioned Joe Brown, due to retire, tossing the ceremonial first Easter egg.

Annie put her warrant inside her suit coat, hooked her badge on her belt, put her gun in her shoulder holster. Eli watched her "suit up," as he called what she did. "Hope we're not going to have to use that," he said.

Annie adjusted her jacket. "Use what?" she asked. She couldn't count the times that she had been the only law enforcement officer wherever she was, and she was on duty 24/7. Eli knew it.

He was messing with her accessories. Jealous, probably.

Annie checked in with the Admin, gave him the warrant. They had known she was coming, of course, and Hilton was ready to meet them. Hyak Herman Hilton, blessed by his parents with a memorable name. He was a robust, middle-aged man with a startling shock of red hair that went in every direction. His handshake was bonecrushing. He was excessively friendly and oppressively healthy.

"What can I do for the police?" He warbled, leading them to his desk area, where there was nowhere to sit.

"We had a few questions for you, and will be executing a search warrant with the HR Supervisor. Hopefully, our calling ahead will mean that you have time for a few questions?" Annie paused and looked up, waiting. It was the few seconds she needed to see the frozen look on Hilton's face, possibly as a result of the two words, *search* and *warrant.*

"Certainly," he said, in a less ebullient voice. "You are most interested in our tranquilizer program? I assume that means you want to look at the security? I can take you back to the lab where everything is kept."

They went down a hall to the lab, to a locked refrigerator. Hilton took a ring of keys from the hook on the side and opened the door. *Strike One*, Annie thought. Inside, there were shelves of vials, several kinds of pharmaceutical products, some specimens, and bags of individually wrapped syringes and darts. There was a package clearly labelled 'Carfentinal' that still had the safety label on it. Two little vials and one long one in the same baggie, two labelled C and one labelled N, the antidote, Annie surmised. Jamalia had warned her. If you got this drug on your skin, you'd better *have* the antidote.

Everyone looked in the door of the refrigerator as though at an apparition. *Zool*, Annie thought, seeing Bill Murray and the rest of the Ghostbusters. Into the dead air, Eli asked, "which ones are used on bears?"

Hilton launched into a treatise on the strengths and weaknesses of the various drugs, with various sizes of bear. He spoke almost exclusively of Ketamine and Atro*something*. "We almost never dart anything," he concluded. "Maybe once a year, unless there's a grant that requires fluids more regularly. Don't like to put them down in the summer, but we have to find out the health of the population, and right now, they just won't come in for an appointment." He smiled broadly, then seeing no reaction, he said, "The bears. They don't come in..."

"That one." Annie pointed. "Carfentinal. Have you ever used it?"

"Just recently," Hilton answered. "I spent some time in Anchorage last month--at the zoo. Their elephant was going to a sanctuary in California and had to be crated for transport. We darted him so he could be safely confined."

"You used Carfentinal on the elephant," Annie confirmed for her notes. "How did you know how to figure dose? I understand that's a problem area."

"Yes. Based upon the weight of the elephant. We also had some African data telling us where to put the dose. It went right down. Can't say it was entirely subdued. You know this drug, apparently, so you know it's dangerous. Weight and health of the animal have to figure into dosage. We don't use it on bears. One died a few years back. We might have it along, but we don't use it."

"We're working on a case that involves its use," Eli said, looking around as though it were of no matter. "Do you guys have a system for dispensing and resecuring?"

"Yeah, as I told the other inspector. We put staff time, date, what is taken, and check it off when it's returned. When everything is back and verified, we throw away the top sheet."

Strike Two, Annie thought. "And do you have some record of when and how to reorder these tranquilizer drugs? Expiration dates? Vendors? Anything like that?"

"The purchasing clerk may have them. In fact, I'm sure she does. They keep everything else that relates to a purchase. I know they get it back east."

"Okay, thanks," Annie said. "One more question. Who had your position before you?"

Hilton looked into the refrigerator, rearranged a couple of things, closed the door and put the padlock back on. He hung up the keys. He looked around. There was no one else in the lab at the moment. He apparently made some sort of decision.

"You'll probably want to ask HR about that," he said. "There was a problem. I was never told what. When I got here, the position was unfilled, and it stayed unfilled til Grossman left. He and I didn't overlap. I was out conducting the fall Moose count. Then I had my Guard service. By the time I got back, we had a new Admin. I picked up innuendo about what had happened before I came, but no facts. Some dispute, closed-door shouting, and door slamming. The person before me was Parkinson, and believe me, you do not even speak that name around here. That's all I want to say."

Huh. "Thanks for that much. We will talk with HR. We'll come back if there's anything else. Oh, by the way, do you have Parkinson's old computer?"

"Hell, no. Rumor has it Grossman used it for a boat anchor. Ha. No, there was a pretty general upgrading of all of the computers right around that time, and I got a new one."

Annie and Eli went to the little HR office, one of the few with a door. HR supervisor, Florence Smith, and the present office Admin, Dirk Jonas, were waiting for them.

Jonas looked at the search warrant, flattened it on the desk and looked at it again. "I know that you are seeking personnel records. You know that these are the most protected files we have, and that we need to look at them before you do and make sure..."

"No, actually, you don't. We want to see files of a dead man, who has no rights to privacy, we want to know if you have any non-disclosures associated with the time Grossman was here. We want to know if there were complaints against Grossman. We want to see the file for S. Parkinson. We want to look at purchasing records for Carfentinal. I believe that you'll see all of those listed."

"The Parkinson file is redacted by written agreement. When that employee voluntarily resigns, most of the file is purged."

Give me another break, Annie thought. What now. "Okay, we'll see what's there. We need to speak with Steve Collins, the IT guy."

Florence Smith spoke, "Steve is here. I saw him. Would you like me to send someone for him?"

"No, we'll go to him. But thank you. Before we start, can one of you identify the people in this picture"

Smith took the picture as though it were something precious, and took out a large, lined sticky note and began to insert names. "Old Joe retired after this, I think. Maybe at the end of the fiscal year, in July. No, he stayed til the fall. I remember now. The back row is all gone, and I don't remember this guy. Who is that? Might be Parkinson. She left in August."

Annie wanted to know what had happened, but there was only a whiff. Like something on the air that was disturbing, but you couldn't quite put your finger on it. "And Old Joe's last name was...?"

"Brown. He lives up by Fairbanks, in the Pioneer Home. I think that's what I heard. He was the institutional memory, people say. I would say that if you get him started, you would need to have someone along to poke you every so often so you didn't doze off."

Smith made a joke. Wonder of wonders. Brown was definitely going to get a visit.

She went through the files for Parkinson and her predecessor, Burton, who did not overlap with Grossman. That file they didn't need. Parkinson was the biologist when Grossman came. As before, Eli and Annie read, identified pages to be copied, took notes. Parkinson's file was heavily redacted, toward the end. Before that, positive performance reviews, one commendation, three merit increases. There wasn't one word that was negative, unless one counted the heavy black ink, and the letter in which she said she was resigning for personal reasons.

Annie looked back into her original resume, tacked to the front cover of the file. There was no picture. AS in Biology, army MP with two tours in Iraq, final posting at Ft. Wainwright. A fellow cop. She would talk with the others about that, because it was critical.

There was a personal note at the end of Parkinson's resume that spoke to the importance of wilderness, protecting the balance between wild and tame. Close to the Sierra Club motto. Annie called the HR supervisor back in to the office where they were reading.

"Ms. Smith, can you tell me anything about Susan Parkinson?"

"No. I knew a little, but we were specifically told not to speak about it."

Annie stared at the woman, a little bit of a scrawny thing who reminded her of Miss Prissy of Foghorn Leghorn fame. "By a dead man, would be my guess. Look. I have sympathy with all of your rules and regulations, but I am the police, pursuing a murderer at the direct behest of the Governor. I am bound only by specific guidelines. I know what is privileged. I'm not going to try to catch you at anything. I just need to know why Parkinson left, and I'm certain this letter isn't it."

Florence Smith assembled her vertebrae, tucked her hair behind her ear and said, "Well. You may not speak of this outside of this office, because the file is legally embargoed on this topic. She left because she had, she said, *ethical differences with the administrator.*"

Annie and Eli sat stilly. Someone had finally said it. "Was an ethics complaint filed?"

"No. I spoke at length with Susan about it. She told me this was a he said/she said situation, and she was ready to go back to school, and she was just going to get on with her life. I thought that was an adult response to an uncomfortable situation."

"And what, did she say, was her 'ethical' problem with Grossman?"

"Did I say Grossman?" Florence Smith looked spuriously puzzled. "Let me look. It might not have been Grossman. Who was the admin before Grossman?" she called out the door to her secretary.

A relatively quiet, disembodied "Rice" drifted around the door.

"No, that can't be right. At any rate, I guess I'm confused, because I thought she left before Grossman, or right at the time, or something. I'll be right back."

Eli looked at Annie. "Parkinson's problem was with Grossman. He was here."

"Yeah, this woman appears to have said more than she wanted to, and is trying to appear flighty. There is no complaint. We need to find Parkinson and talk with her. You don't redact or embargo files for something like Smith described. Was there a Parkinson on your Juneau lists?"

"Not that I recall."

Smith came back and said rapidly, "Okay, she was here when Grossman was here, so she overlapped Rice two years and Grossman a year, or a bit more."

"And there were issues between she and Grossman?"

"Any new admin always has some employees who preferred the previous administrator's style..."

"But that wasn't so with Parkinson, right? Because she told you she had issues?"

"You know, I don't remember."

Okay, Annie thought, I'm not sitting here begging this woman to talk. "We will take Grossman's file, a copy of everything in Parkinson's file. Can you direct us to Purchasing?"

"Purchasing," Smith squeaked. "Oh My."

The Purchasing clerk, Helen Squibber, had records, and records about the records. The last Carfentinal had been purchased from a lab in New Jersey that specialized in Animal medications. It had been purchased in August of 1996 and had taken three weeks to arrive. There should be two doses in the refrigerator. They expired in November of this year. Helen had been told to hold future purchases, because it was so seldom used. In fact, it had been used only once by this office, by the biologist before Hilton, whose name she did not remember. Then she did. Burton. There had been a biologist after her, but that name she absolutely could not remember, and that was that.

Yeah, right, thought Annie. What would that do to you to be a name no one would speak--like you were dead? Anyway, the timing was okay if someone wanted to steal some, but there were two doses sitting in the fridge. She had seen them. She sent Eli to talk to Steve and took some pictures of the lab. They were not coming back up here.

They carried everything out to the car and gave Bones a run behind the office. They mused on the similarities among people in certain state offices, as though there were a "type" that was sought during hiring. "It's like, you know, *let's get us a human resources supervisor. Any ex-nuns or defrocked priests needing work?"* Eli opened the back seat and pushed the box of files in under one of the sleeping bags.

Annie took a thermos out of her cooler and poured Bones a drink. "They do seem remarkably similar. What gets me is the way they cling to these little pieces of information, like that is all that keeps them in their job, and if they let one slip, a great hand will come out of the sky and jerk them out of the building.

"So," she said, "what did you think of Steve?"

"I think he's Len Norton's doppelganger. He was pretty forthcoming, but he really didn't know anything." Steve Collins had described some ghost in the machines, and how Parkinson had had to make double copies of notes, and then Grossman went ballistic. Steve felt it was all a misunderstanding. People hit the wrong key, things went to the wrong screen, there wasn't necessarily anything nefarious."

"I guess it's no big deal at this point. I'm reconstructing what people will not say, summarized thusly: Parkinson had a run in with Grossman over something that was her responsibility, he wanted information, and then she quit over a difference of opinion about what he wanted it for. You know how he has reacted to anyone who disagrees. I do, anyway. I saw it over and over. We'll ask her. I take it she's in Fairbanks. She was going there to finish up a degree, Smith said. Eli?"

"Yeah. Just thinking. Look at this picture. Which one might be Parkinson? Seems like Smith would have known."

"She obviously did. Parkinson might have been a big woman. The file says ex-military. MP. They are generally big."

"Yeah. I took the picture with me to see what Steve thought. He agreed the tall guys in the back row were all gone. Didn't know if one of them was Parkinson because of the *disguise*. Does look like this one is in disguise."

Annie looked at the grainy picture. Three big people, one in a ball cap and sunglasses. She couldn't tell. "We need to find her and look at her, I guess. I'm just not going to get excited til I actually see her. Doesn't really look like a woman."

"I think we need to show this to Parfletch and see what he says."

"Okay. I called. We can see Brown at 4:00. He has yoga before that. Who knew Squarebanks had yoga? So let's get up there. If we meet with the vet in the morning before her patients begin to show up, maybe we can be home by dinnertime."

****

Joe Brown was simultaneously hearty and frail. He had a keen eye; he needed a walker. He laughed readily; he coughed frequently. Annie and Eli sat in his tiny private room, on kitchen chairs, with Brown in a recliner. On a tiny end table, as was true for most "chairs of last resort," was everything he might need: a carafe of water, another of something warm, a television remote for a small set half-way across the room, the day's crossword puzzle and Sudoku folded neatly next to a jar of pens, pencils and a letter opener. In plastic bags on the little table, carefully labeled, were medicines and some other things that looked suspiciously like specimens of expectorant. Finally, a jar of candy, which he immediately offered to them, and from which Eli selected a lemon drop. Annie abstained. Brown approved of Eli's choice which, knowing Eli, was probably why he took it in the first place. Candy was a non-threatening thing to share.

"Mr. Brown, we're trying to find out why Susan Parkinson left, and Florence Smith said you might know something. No one at Fish and Game will talk about it. Also, is this Susan, here in this picture?"

Old Joe squinted at the picture. Finally, "I think so. I don't see good, but that's about how tall she was, and she always wore a ball cap. I think that's her. As to the other, we were all told not to talk about it, but..." He stopped, and looked down at his hands. Annie and Eli were simultaneously horrified to see his eyes fill with tears. "She was a good biologist. Everything cataloged, all the specimens she collected just right and useable in the study up to Fairbanks. Always worked hard.

"Loved to be out in the bush, loved to follow the animals around. Only time she ever did anything...I don't think I want to talk about it."

Annie needed him to keep talking. "Mr. Brown...can I call you Joe?" When he nodded, through his handkerchief, she went on, "Joe, I know that you have a recollection that might help us. Please try to give us at least an idea of what happened." Annie waited for Brown to compose himself.

"Okay, Bastard is dead, so I don't suppose it matters. Sue...didn't go by Susan...Sue came back in August from a collection trip. She saw a huge boar, and now I know that Grossman was looking for one. He came and told me to have her report to him when she got back. I put the specimens away, saw the boar's scat. Looked like a small child's arm."

Something about the picture caused him to smile, but rapidly, his mouth fell and his eyes filled again. "She was so protective of the animals she studied. But careful, and thorough. There was already GPS in those days, and she wrote that all on the scat collection envelope." H paused, and breathed deeply, looking up at the ceiling.

Annie and Eli waited, knowing he had to go at his own pace, and that pushing would not be likely to change that. Annie made notes, Eli made eye contact. "Sir," he said, "you said Grossman was 'probably looking for one.' What did you mean by that?"

"Oh," Joe said, "he was always interested in big bears. Don't know why. But she no sooner went in to her desk than out he comes, asking about what she found. I thought he'd already talked to her by that time.

Annie said, "So Grossman asked her about the bear, and she didn't tell him, so he came out and asked you, right? Is that what you guess happened?"

"Yeah," he said softly. "Yeah. Wanted me to show him the scat, acted like he was surprised, but that was all. Didn't take any notes, just looked at it, at the other things in the freezer, and left." Brown was quiet for a bit. He coughed. Eli filled a little glass with water from the carafe and offered it to him, with a straw that was in the pencil cup. After Joe drank a bit and stopped coughing, he went on.

"There were rumors she found something wrong in her computer, and confronted him. She wasn't afraid of anyone. With her background, why would she be? She said she had proof someone had written down the GPS coordinates, on her desk note pad. And then they went through her computer and found her notes in a place where they shouldn't have been, and all of the references to the big boar were gone. Grossman came out to see the scat, saw it was gone but the GPS coordinates were on a new bag, and went ballistic. He did say he had some 'proof' about how it was her in his computer, manipulating records for some purpose none of us ever heard anything about. Not at all the Sue we had come to know, stickler for rules, protocol, ex-military and all.

"I don't know any more, except that she was asked to resign or told she would be fired. After she left, Grossman called us all in and told us that he would now be watching for any other employee who did the same thing. Lots of people actually went back through their field notes. Everyone was scared, and then, in mid-winter, he left. I did, too, because he told me it was time to go, and he had eliminated my position in the next budget."

In the stillness of the little room, and amid Brown's blowing his nose twice, Eli asked, "Were you and Sue friends?'

"She was a nice lady. She was real nice to me. She did her job. Something ugly happened, and then it was all put on her.

"I never told anyone that Grossman came out to see me, and I never told him that the scat samples had been mixed up. I saw right off that 'something big,' you might say, was missing, and the numbers on the scat of another bear had been changed, according to my list, but that's not an official list, so I...I was getting pretty confused by then...I don't know what Grossman wanted to know about the bear for, but I guess Sue did."

Annie and Eli were quiet, taking in the closest they had come to an actual motive, to the disgruntled employee whose life and occupation were truncated by what Joe seemed to be saying was inappropriate conduct by the boss, who had taken pains, apparently, to cover his tracks afterwards. Just like Janet had said--go back a few years, and he won't be as careful. They were unprepared for Joe's next comment, spoken softly to the ceiling.

"Bear was killed by a guy working with a guide. Non-resident. Just outside the park, in late September. It was my last week, so I remember that well. I couldn't...I didn't...hard to believe anyone would do that."

"Joe, what or who did what?"

"I don't want to say any more. I had a hard enough time sleeping for so long, end of my life-long job, and so forth. I don't want to remember it."

One last question, then. "Do you know where Sue went?"

"Ma'am, I wouldn't say that I do. We weren't buddies. I didn't have any reason to be in contact with her, and she knew that I had...I guess I didn't help, didn't know that he...he was the boss."

Old Joe ran down. Annie and Eli got up to go, and Annie said, "Mr. Brown, thank you for talking with us. I can't say that someone won't want to interview you in the future, but for now, that's all we need." It seemed silly to ask him not to leave town. He was never going to leave this room, Annie would bet. As she put on her jacket, she heard the old man whisper, "she didn't do anything wrong. She was just protecting the bear. Special, when they get that big. Something to save. She was a good person."

Annie didn't feel good about leaving him weeping quietly over what he had inadvertently helped Grossman to do to Sue Parkinson and a patriarch grizzly. He appeared genuinely remorseful, out of proportion to what he had actually done. As with other employees, Annie saw a loyalty to the job and its parameters that went beyond what these public servants were paid. She saw how they had been hurt by circumstances, by trying to do the right thing. She saw, finally, someone who must be considered a bona fide suspect, if they could find her.

****

They stayed in a funky, old Fairbanks motel on the highway, rather than weave though Fairbanks to nicer places. With the rest of their per diem, they ate well. Annie took Prime Rib scraps out to Bones, ran him around again, filled his water dish, and then went to bed. She wished she could call and see how Fred's trip in had been. They hadn't connected because of the weather, and she didn't know what he'd have for phone service in the Pass. Eli called his folks and headed for the bar to get "local knowledge."

They rousted out early, mostly because Annie could hear Bones' mournful howl from the car outside of her window. Apparently Eli could, as well.

Their Vet appointment was at 7:30 a.m. Patients started at 8:00, but the Vet had a helper who could take that. Dr. Sharpnack was in her late 60's, a homely raw-boned woman with big shoulders and gnarled hands with huge knuckles. Her face had a nasty scar across one cheek. She led with that.

"Never try to pull a calf unless someone has the cow's back leg," she said with a grin. "It gives you a funny face. How can I help you two?"

What a clever lead. As soon as she spoke, you forgot the scar and tried to picture "pulling" a calf, something Annie had heard of, but couldn't imagine. "We're trying to run down sources of Carfentinal, as Eli told you--was it you?--on the phone. We stopped through at Delta Junction and talked with Hilton..."

"Hyak. What a moniker. Parents must have hated him."

"Yeah, how about that. He talked about using Carfentinal with the elephant at the Anchorage Zoo. Said they didn't use it on bears."

"Hon, the difficulty is in getting the dose right. I think, back in the day, there were actually two bears that never woke up. It came on the market in the 70's, but it's really a drug for big animals, and if you don't know weight, or if they have a bad heart...what?"

Eli and Annie had inadvertently looked at one another the instant the Vet had said 'bad heart.' Annie said, "It appears Carfentinal was used in a murder we're investigating, and the victim appears to have had a heart attack at the same time. ME calls it cause of death."

"Well, I'll say this about death. You don't always know from *cause*. Some despair, unable to understand, and they just give up. Some so frightened their heart stops. Some won't breathe. Some won't eat. Some die of grief. I'm not just talking about other animals. I'm talking about people. I've seen it, and chemical studies of the immune system prove it to my satisfaction. So, Carfentinal and heart attack. I haven't used any for years, and I don't--aside from Fish and Game and the guys in the Safari Club, which is way bigger in Alaska than I care to even talk about--know of anyone who would."

Annie was getting used to Dr. Sharpnack's circular sentences. "Actually, I agree. I've seen all of that, too. In this case, we know it was in the victim's system. We're trying to find out where a murderer might have gotten it. You say you don't have it now. How long since you did?"

"Let me see. About three years ago, we got to the expiration date on the last of what we had, and I told my assistant to put it in the HAZMAT box. Too expensive to reorder just to keep in the fridge and not use. We have Ketamine, and Atropine. Besides, if you got the Carfentinal you need the Naloxone or whatever they call it, in case the animal stops breathing. My assistant and I used it on a bison up out of Delta, but we were super carful. Really careful."

"Your assistant would be...an experienced animal darter?"

"Oh, yes. Excuse me. She had some background, but I do too. We just worked it out. You estimate the weight, and hope the animal doesn't have any heart problems, then cut the dose a bit so you err on the side of safety. It's really too much trouble. Ketamine works fine. You aren't darting rhinos or elephants unless you work in a zoo."

They asked a few more questions about use by other vets, but got only negatives. Annie bought a healthy dog chew and they went out to the car.

"Eli," Annie said, sounding more positive than she felt. "What do we know now?"

"We know that we don't know. One thing I heard for sure was that this is the baddest drug in the arsenal, but no one keeps any particular security on it. You're the janitor, and you take it out of the HAZMAT box when you take that out to the secure disposal site. Think I'll check on how long it stays potent, what do you say?"

"Oh, yeah, Eli, you do that."

They drove over to the University and Annie went into the Registrar's Office while Eli ran Bones in the dog park. In a list of recent graduates, Annie saw a Susan Parkinson, who had finished a bachelor's in biology last winter term. Which would fit with what Smith had said. Graduated. No forwarding address, plans uncertain. Mail was forwarded to a post office box, but the university was a law unto itself, and they were not about to give Annie a hint at even the state without a warrant.

There was no mention of an S. Parkinson anywhere in the local phone book. There was an F. Parkinson. Annie called that number from a phone in the lobby. It was pretty obvious this wasn't the first time F. Parkinson had been called about S. Parkinson.

"Nope, no Sue. Wrong number. Tired of you calling, so write that down this time. No. Sue. Here."

"I'm deeply sorry to have bothered you," Annie said with a southern accent she hoped sounded like a pole dancer. "If you would be so kind, sir, do you know where she went?"

"Somewhere south, where all of us should go," was the grumpy answer.

"And how long have you had this number, sir?" she asked.

463

"You know what? Hang the fuck up."

So she did. It had been a long shot anyway. Apparently, if S. Parkinson had had a group of friends or acquaintances in Fairbanks, they couldn't find her either. But if S. Parkinson had left town, how would they find her? They called the Fairbanks police and asked about the name, but got nothing. They asked a detective to pull up the driver's license and they went over to the Trooper's to see it. The driver's license picture was typically bad. It gave her eyes as brown, hair brown, height 6'1" and weight at 220 lb. So, big woman. There was an address, because the DMV required a street address, but it was in Delta. She'd never changed it. They knew she wasn't in Delta. Annie had the license picture forwarded to her email in Anchorage.

While Annie and Eli were at UAF, the Veterinarian opened her desk drawer, found the little slip of paper and made a call to a number written there. She got a computer-voiced mailbox. She was fairly certain that the person who retrieved the voicemail would know what she was talking about, though they had never discussed it, and she had no proof of her suspicions. At the sound of the compelling *beep,* she said, through her wadded handkerchief, "The AIB police were here tracking the Carfentinal," and hung up. She stared for a moment at the wedding invitation on her bulletin board. *Leave her alone,* she thought.

****

The Parks Highway was a long stretch of incredible scenery, briefly punctuated here and there by someone's house, some trucks, a boat and two or three recreational vehicles. They ultimately came to a "scenic viewpoint," got out and found a safe place for Bones to run about. Annie let him off the leash and watched him mince up to some bear tracks, sniff them delicately, and back away. "Good idea," she agreed. Then, to Eli, "We found out valuable information. A good trip. The lack of security on the Carfentinal is important. Is it connected? I don't like coincidences. We go bippity boppity bing and bounce from an employee to a veterinarian, to a murderer, when we didn't even have a clue they might be connected when we set up the appointments."

"But you know," Eli said, opening the hatch back so Bones could jump back in, "There was something about that Vet after the Carfentinal came up."

"I agree," Annie responded, "but I don't know why. Could have been gas. You get to this stage, and you pull the thread, and things stand up out there in the fog. I'm pulling the thread, but for every pull, three things stand up in the fog, and I feel like I'm in a carnival shooting gallery."

"Well...that's cold," Eli said.

"Yes," Annie agreed, "it's cooling off fast, all right."

****

The next morning, Annie talked with Vice about Carfentinal. She knew more than they did. Fentanyl was just emerging on the illicit drug scene, and it was still relatively rare. Alaska had an abundance of illegal drugs, leading to inventive and deadly compounding, but Carfentinal had not yet become well known.

From what Eli could find out, the relationship of expiration date to long-term potency was unknown. Annie was now certain that the Carfentinal in Grossman's autopsy results had once been obtained legally, discarded, and picked up from the HAZMAT trash by the murderer.

She talked with the person who checked out drugs, darts and the special guns to Troopers. She said they had the drug, they kept it in the refrigerator, they didn't use it, but it was in the kit when they had a bear incident. It was such a difficult task to find a bear and then dart it, she said, and most of the Troopers asked someone from Fish and Game to come with them on a problem animal.

466

Annie asked about security, and was glad to hear the drug was carefully controlled here, with only one person having real access and signout sheets kept forever. She looked at the list of troopers trained to use it. There were two, one the Anchorage to Kenai circuit, and one on Palmer to Glennallen. Presumably if there was a problem in the Park, or up the Richardson, the Troopers would contact Fish and Game and Hyak Herman Hilton would suit up.

She made notes to have Eli try to find where Sue had lived in Fairbanks. Something else was poking at her that they should do, but she kept seeing poor old Joe weeping, and decided that was enough for the day.

Annie went to pick up Fred from the airport and give her thrashing mind a break.

Chapter Thirty-One

Intermittently, 1998 - 2000

They couldn't get Parkinson anywhere near Juneau around the time of the murder--or anywhere else, for that matter. Annie scanned manifests of incoming and outgoing transportation in the time window. Eli tried to find Sue after the graduation event in Fairbanks, which she did not attend. The ADL database showed she had a 1989 silver Toyota Corolla, which she had had in Delta, as all of the information was the same. She had left Delta five years ago, and had actually renewed the car's registration as though nothing had changed. Eli called the Troopers. They found that the address in Delta had been occupied by three different tenants in the last four years. They couldn't figure how that all went together, but as Eli said, anyone can walk into a DMV and renew a vehicle right there, nothing required but filling out the form. Frustrating, but true.

If she applied for a license in another state, that might help. So wait on that. Annie believed there was something too careful and intentional about Parkinson's "disappearance." And simultaneously chastised herself for developing a theory which had no proof attached, to the exclusion of any others. She spent some time each week going back through any other putative "suspects" if for no other reason than to eliminate them.

November went by. They got the logs from the two Fish and Game offices, which showed exactly nothing. There was no missing drug, in any year, as far as records showed. The Carfentinal, specifically, was all accounted for, both current stock and actual disposal dates, and they had purchasing lists for both offices.

In late November, Annie talked with Sophia Brower and put to bed the idea that the cards would get them anywhere. They were a strange anomaly that showed mean spirit, but on whose behalf? And toward whom? Sophia admitted she had received what she perceived to be a threat, and had asked Norton to find someone to secure her door. That was the extent of what she would say. In the back of Annie's mind was a lingering unease about Sophia's husband, but all protectors, boyfriends, husbands seemed to have alibis. So far, she had one or two "persons of interest" who weren't interesting, and a "suspect" who was MIA.

December brought serious snow. Everyone was shoveling for weeks, especially in Valdez, where people had to dig tunnels to get into their houses. December was a time of vacationing, family outings, wasted days with half staff. Annie and Fred didn't have family. Each was an only child with parents who died early. They typically went to Mexico at Christmas, but this year they stayed home. Fred was developing some new specs he didn't want to leave, and Annie was still trying to find that thread to pull. Bones thought it was all good, and took them for walks every day along the frozen creek where the trail was plowed.

Eli enrolled in a new term of classes with approval, support and leave time. He would be finished with his BS in two years, and would also have a special graduate level of courses in supervision of criminal forensics personnel. This would give him insight into the types of machines, technology, and staffing a state-of-the art lab would need.

Annie welcomed Eli's further education in criminal forensics, which was clearly his future. He had a gift for asking questions with spurious innocence, seeing connections between types of evidence, and making suggestions that did not offend his supervisors. Juries had begun to expect forensics. Criminals were learning to control what they left behind. Scientists were bringing to bear the sophisticated machines that had formerly been in manufacturing or research laboratories. They were being put to use exploring both old and new evidence. New developments in chemical and fingerprint analysis, in DNA, were emerging daily, now that the genome was not only sequenced but the databases of profiles increasing and the methods of analysis growing more and more sophisticated.

So Annie had hope, but it was mostly for the future. She continued to follow every lead. The Governor told anyone listening that the case was ongoing, and a solution "close." With a straight face. Aspects of the case were already boxed and in the basement. Grossman had been buried in Missouri, where the family now lived. Mrs. Grossman, taking a page from her husband's playbook, told Annie that she was incompetent, and not to call her again unless there was progress. Annie didn't take offense.

Carolyn Grossman was uncooperative, but she wasn't a suspect. She didn't stand to gain, which was somewhat unusual. Most men of high position had life insurance. Grossman did. It went to the boys. Apparently the daughter was not listed because the insurance was purchased before her birth. It was somewhat unusual, but not entirely so, that the wife inherited only personal property, according to the will. When asked about that, by a Juneau detective who barely survived with his head, Mrs. Grossman said she had her own retirement, thank you, and the money was for the children's' college. After that visit from the JPS, on Annie's behalf, the erstwhile grieving widow called the governor and engaged a lawyer to stop any further investigation into the victim's past. Nothing happened there, but Annie had been told to desist in that direction for the time being. Still, she wrote out some suspicions and future questions and tucked them away in the file of notes. The politics of this investigation kept getting in the way.

All of the license plates, all of the names in the staff directories, all of the lists and records and notes were cataloged and filed. The murder board was now a native woman who left North Pole for Fairbanks and never arrived. Troopers had looked, interviewed, given up. Her husband was certain it was their grown son, who was, like, whatever, Dad. Others had seen her in North Pole two days after she left, but no one remembered where. Annie didn't want to go to North Pole in the dead of winter, but there you were. She and Darin went up, spent a week, and were close to identifying a man in a red hoodie who had given the woman a ride out of North Pole in an old beat up Ford F250 with blue and white sides. The Fairbanks police had put out a BOLO, and the state troopers were watching for the truck. Fairbanks was a reasonably good place to hide a beat-up truck in deep snow, but in a state with so few roads, they would eventually find it.

By February, that case was solved by relatives, with whom the woman had been staying. Annie took out the Grossman file, reread everything and made a new list. Eli had found no matches for people coming into Juneau in the two weeks before the murder and leaving the day of, or after. All of the passenger lists from air carriers had been cleared, and all of the ferries. Annie was still working on the last cruise ship. She couldn't see that it would yield a suspect. The Cruise Ship company had a strange way of providing their manifests. Sometimes they listed family, with the number of persons but no first names, and sometimes they listed individuals. They were slow in providing anything.

Cruise ships were similar to airplanes. You had to have id anywhere you went, you got wanded when you went off or on, they maintained lists on their lists. Whether they maintained these for any length of time after the voyage was a complete gray area and seemed to require legions of legal opinions, translated from Norwegian.

Parfletch thought the women suspects were simply non-starters, symptomatic of Grossman's management style and relationships with women employees. He pointed out men who had been similarly harassed, fired, reorged, etc. He said, sure, it could be a big woman, especially one who had combat experience and training with weapons. He didn't think it was a reality, however. Most women in the army didn't have real experience beyond minimal combat training. Annie accepted that concept in general, having been one of the first women in what had been a man's profession back in the 80's. She carried around a cartoon of the then president whispering "nice legs" as the woman in uniform saluted him. The military was ambivalent about the participation of women. Real life wasn't GI Jane; it was more likely Nurse Jane. Parfletch hung with his "big man" because "big men" had the right "reflexes,"

Annie didn't argue, but questioned limiting the search to men, or even big women. In the absence of anything male to pursue, Annie was, in fact, only pursuing women at this point. So many could tell horror stories about what happened to them at work, or after work, or because of work. It was almost an underground conversation that women heard, like a bad phone connection. Men not so much. *Dude look like a lady* could probably hear it. So Annie was open to finding a damaged woman-- Brower? Parkinson? Munson? Hurtsen?--who had just gone off the rails in grief, embarrassment, shame, anger, whatever. A powerful boss made your life hell and shamed you on the way out.

She looked at the little unisex figures she had drawn and noticed that the second figure, holding a bloody knife, had more feminine characteristics. Huh. She closed her eyes, looked at her eyelids, and tried to imagine the figure. It obligingly appeared, walking away, getting smaller and smaller until it became a point of light. Eli said, "I just dropped in to see you, but I could come back after your nap."

"Nap, hell," Annie said without opening her eyes, "I'm visualizing the Grossman killer. I almost had he, she, it...and now I have to start over again."

"Well, excuuuuuuuuuuse me," Eli chuckled. "Just wanted to let you know that I got all of the Grossman notes entered, belts, buttons and whistling suspenders, and the interviews scanned in. I put the originals, labelled, in the box you gave me. Want me to take it down?"

"I'm actually loath to put anything downstairs. I've been thinking of putting things in this file cabinet. Why don't you box them and bring them in here? I'm taking a list down to the document room every day, and at this point, the box that's there contains few things besides that list, which tells anyone to come up here and see if they can get the key out of Jason. If we get a break I want whatever we've got to be there."

Eli nodded, and said, "I'll let you get back to your nap, then." And winked.

Cheeky. That's what he was.

Annie worked the guide services. Everyone in that group knew Grossman. Interpersonally speaking, the state was small. Though guides were individually licensed and generally worked out of the office of one owner, they also all belonged to guide's associations. These lobbied for extra openings, extensions of openings, and catch, weight and length limits. No individual would have enough clout to get Fish and Game to make any seasonal changes. The Game Board also preferred to hear from the associations.

Annie started with the group to which Grossman belonged, and which had later pressed for him to be on the Game Board. She talked with several guides. They were clipped and evasive, as well they would be, rather than admit to a law enforcement officer that they had violated the terms of their licenses. There was a young man on the Copper who remembered Grossman helping him early on, taking him on some trips to show him the river. Seemed out of character. However, she had only work-related information about Grossman, and was holding hard to her attempt at objectivity.

On the Little Su, a woman Annie thought must have had some type of ax to grind by the edge to her answers said that Grossman gave out favors, told *buddies* where to fish and hunt. When she had complained, she said she was ostracized by other guides in their section of the river system. That may or may not have been true. Women guides were rare, and full of attitude, having to prove themselves daily. Annie found it irritating and decided she'd have attitude herself. She knew of no evidence that said male guides put more people, per capita, on fish or other game. And she didn't believe "buddies," so there was the bias again.

What Annie heard loudest and clearest, however, was that everyone knew Fish and Game had information, and it wasn't unusual for a guide with a big client to call Fish and Game and "just talk" about a particular population. Hypothetically, these were public employees with public information. Everyone knew it pushed ethical. Everyone knew it wasn't fair chase. But as the female guide said, you have a senator here and he wants a big bear, for which he will pay you a $10,000 bonus, and you will do whatever you can.

Annie checked on the Governor's Wounded Warrior trip, and looked in the newspapers for VIP's coming to Alaska to hunt during the mid-nineties. She found, after some searching, the story about the congressman and the walrus tusk. The congressman was fined, and the guide was said to be unavailable for comment. Since that guide was Grossman, that was actually true.

She could get Grossman close to unethical behavior, but she couldn't find the elusive person who had made him pay for it, if in fact that was what happened. A search for similar murders yielded nothing. The papers quit calling her by March. In March, she and Jamalia Hendrix caught an ATM thief, who had gotten really good at hacking pin numbers, but occasionally got so excited she didn't hide all of her face from the ATM cameras. Jamalia, who had three daughters, caught a glimpse of flashing earrings, traced them to a store in the Dimond Center Mall, and actually found the thief buying the earrings on the store's old stock of surveillance footage. High Fives all around, and St. Patrick's Day Cupcakes.

In April, there was a big meeting. The Commissioner of Corrections wanted specs for next year's budget: a new Crime Lab, emphasis on cutting-edge forensics, and a co-located Morgue.

478

Everyone put in a wish list. Eli used it as a class assignment, and got raves for the design and attention to detail, which saved the department the cost of a consultant or three. He came over and spent a Saturday with Fred, talking about space and load and all of that. Annie made pizza. Bones was fascinated with Eli and spent the day with his head on Eli's knee.

Parkinson's sometime car was found in Anchorage, on a routine traffic stop. That caused a flurry of phone calls. The young man who had purchased it had driven it from Glennallen, didn't know anything about it being in Fairbanks. He said he bought it for $800 off Craig's List from a guy in Haines. Whose friends had driven it to Glennallen, so he never actually saw the seller. The signed title was virtually illegible. There had been two transfers, the first of which might have been from Parkinson to someone, but the signature was totally different from that on her license.

They confiscated the vehicle and dusted it for pints. There were prints on the registration, several. The car was a muddy, dog-decorated mess. Evidence techs did their best, but finally turned away in disgust. Besides, they knew it was Parkinson's car, so what would prints tell them? Much more important was "Haines."

Haines was a ferry ride away from Juneau, or a short plane flight, and the first transfer of title was dated September 15, presumably after Parkinson graduated from UAF and went into the wind. What she did from December to September was a total mystery, but maybe they could pick her up there.

The Marine Highway told Eli ferries from Skagway and Haines were part of the local 'bus' system, and they accepted walk-on passengers, for which they kept no lists. If Parkinson had come to Haines to sell a vehicle, it being the end of a route she could have taken down from Fairbanks, it still seemed like a stretch to then sneak into Juneau and kill Grossman. How, for example, was she to know that someone in Haines would buy the car? Hard upon that, Annie remembered you could sell anything in a village, even a car where there were no roads, and generally there were no questions asked. A car such as the elderly Corolla might spend the rest of its life, sans registration, title, anything, and no one would even know. Okay, it was possible.

In the meanwhile, their fourth investigator retired. Since he hadn't really helped for quite some time, having been out with one or another illness or using up vacation days, it didn't have a great impact. John Sullivan had put in his papers for a transfer to AIB, prompted frequently by

Annie, who kept telling him how desperately they needed help. He said no one in Juneau was interested in Grossman anymore. An Acting had been appointed and disappeared into the bureaucracy. The Legislative session was wrapping.

In May, Annie moved the files from her locking file cabinet to the evidence lockup. She spent some time with Jason getting things neatly arranged and labelled, because she knew she could solve this, and she wasn't getting a break two years down the road and finding that the files had been "misplaced" or some other euphemism for lost.

By the next fall, everyone was in angst about whether to get a new computer system before or after Y2K. It was a thing. Was the world going to come to an end, and all of the computers crash? Like that. Annie was sitting at the table in the conference room with lists in front of her, passenger lists she hadn't looked at for a year. They had a newly-sortable database that made comparisons a bit easier. This time, she saw Ferguson, C. coming in two weeks before the murder and Ferguson, C. going out on the jet to Seattle at 11:05 p.m. "Ferguson" was not a name they recognized; Annie followed it out of stubbornness.

Curtis Ferguson was an amiable sort, now an oil patch worker in Wyoming, where he was helping to set up barracks for the next big strike. Because Annie remembered the early Pipeline days, she knew exactly what he meant. He had been in Juneau because that was where he lived. The North Slope oil workers weren't allowed to declare Prudhoe a residence, as they would be able to, by sheer numbers, take over the Borough governance. The North Slope was a reservation in all but name. Workers did an extended shift and flew, free, to somewhere else in the state designated their official residence.

Ferguson had gone to Juneau to arrange a rental management agency, pack up and store his things, and head out for Wyoming. He said he had never heard of Grossman. Annie figured he was telling the truth. She asked if there was any point in her coming down to give him a polygraph, and he gave her a verbal shrug. She could if she wanted to. She didn't. She called the real estate office that managed his rental and his story jibed with their records exactly, down to a meeting the afternoon of the murder. Could still have done it, but Annie thought not. Notes in the box.

There were one or two others like that. Annie wondered if there was something wrong with that strategy. Suppose the killer came up from Seattle, or Salt Lake City, or anywhere else that was a good connection to Juneau. Why not come from down there? It was a whole new direction for looking, and she wasn't ready to open the case for that type of scavenger hunt. She still thought the name was on one of these lists, morphing into and out of focus. Like the few Parkinsons on the Cruise Ship lists.

She needed to compress those. She spent a few hours calling all Parkinsons where Eli had numbers and asking if there was a member of the extended family who had made the cruise with them. There was one Sue, who emailed her a picture of a cute little asian-american girl in a yellow dress. Nothing.

By December, the case was solidly cold. It fit, somehow. Annie and Fred let Bones stay with Eli, who was as delighted as Bones, and went to Cabo. They were sitting by the pool with some old friends, and Annie's friend Cherry, whose husband had been Annie's first Trooper partner, asked, "Whatever happened in the Grossman case?"

"You know, we can't get a grip on it," Annie said "I think there are people in Juneau who know something they aren't telling. I think there are people in Anchorage who know something. I know there are people in Barrow, Kenai, Delta Junction and Copper Center and Missouri who know something. No one will talk. No forensic evidence on the body. We know how he died, and that's it. The killer is just gone, and we're standing on the runway waving at the exhaust."

Cherry's husband George, a big, hulking man with a great smile, said, "Guy was an asshole."

"You knew him?" Annie asked, surprised.

"Yeah, had to ticket some dude who stood on the dock and caught a king. He had been fishing with Grossman, but was out of the boat, and he was damn sure keeping that fish, which wasn't legal. You've never seen a client dropped so fast and so completely. 'Our trip was over at noon, Mr. Smith. You're on your own.' Guy was an asshole."

"There's no real disagreement with that, unless you talk to his wife."

George snorted a laugh. They returned to their drinks. Fred took a dip in the pool.

Then George had another thought: "You know, doesn't have to be a disgruntled employee, although that seems the most logical. Some of Dudes have more money than God. Could it have been a hit?"

"Thought about a pro. Too many personal pieces. No, we'll find the killer, but it may be awhile. We've actually had solid leads, but at the end of each trail is some terrified, fired, transferred, intimidated employee who doesn't want to talk. I personally think it's a prior employee, and male or female. Planned this for a long time. Used the darts before, knew how. You would think that would get us to someone, but so far, no."

"All troopers take courses in using tranquilizer darts, you know. Did you do it?"

"No, George, but if you don't find a subject more appropriate to this beautiful sunset, I'm going to practice."

They laughed, they talked about something else. They listened to the tinkling synthesizer music on the patio and watched the sunset. Annie damped down the frustration she always felt when Grossman's murder was discussed. Maybe when she got back to work, she'd put in to go where Sue Parkinson was from. The military would know. It didn't make sense not to follow every little thing they had.

January, 2000

Y2K was a bust. Maybe somewhere it was an issue, but not Alaska. Everything was working when they got home. Even their digital clocks. They retrieved Bones with some difficulty, as he was now blood-brother to Eli in a number of significant ways that involved Eli's new female springer puppy.

Eli had made the mistake of telling Bones that this might be his mate some day. Bones couldn't have understood, but he tolerated the puppy from then on, Eli said. They could see it when the two were together--male dogs didn't often adopt puppies, but needs must. Come to think of it, Annie had seen on the new Animal Planet channel that there were other cases of males stepping up to protect babies. She thought it was anthropomorphic. Then she thought that she thought too much about most things, and it wasn't a good idea to extend that to dogs. Maybe the puppy smelled good. They always smelled good to Annie.

This morning, the first Monday back, Annie and her colleagues were completing required time at their indoor shooting range in the bowels of the police building. In the small towns and villages, troopers had outdoor shooting ranges. Here, on any given day, there would be a dozen shooters qualifying, working on comfort with new weapons, or just shooting for the fun of it. This included troopers, city police, detectives and others authorized or required to carry weapons

Annie, Jamalia and Darin were in their own lanes, aiming at targets that did not, in Annie's opinion, represent the most likely things she had to shoot. She was a competent marksman, and had consistently high marks in any of the scenarios used to train troopers in urban tactics, as well as the still shooting that she was practicing now. It was part of the job.

She finished her clip, cleared her 9mm Glock, and waited for the others. The targets rolled back to them. Her pattern was, as usual, consistent and tight. She could shoot a pistol, though she preferred a shotgun. She could certainly shoot a rifle. "Why don't I like them," she muttered.

"Because you just aren't a killer at heart?" Jamalia asked. "Whereas I, I am a..."

"...lean, mean, fighting machine, built to handle a squad of marines. I know," Annie sighed. "And I bet it's true. But I don't have the instinct. I've only had to fire my weapon in the line of duty three times in 20 years."

"That could be a record, if you're including shots at wounded moose," Darin offered.

They put their weapons away, collected their brass and dropped it in the recycling bin. They signed and filed their targets, and went back to the elevator that took them out of the bowels of the building up to their offices.

"So," Jamalia said, studiously looking at the elevator buttons, "What's up? Pretty quiet. Hope you had a good break."

"Yeah, thanks" Annie said, remembering her manners. "Hope you guys did, too. You worked hard last year." Then, into the silence that followed, "I'm spinning wheels on the Grossman case. It's going to be cold in about sixty seconds. Hell, it's cold already. I guess I thought occasionally I was close, and then it would just evaporate. It appears that it was a one off, so I don't know what even the profile gets us. Most of the cases we get there's some trail, some relationship, some former indication of intent. I have to say this would already be a cold case if it were anyone *but* him. Juneau has its own subculture, and Commissioners are temporary royalty. The Governor wants it solved."

They watched two floors go by, in contemplation of their own frustrations with cases that stagnated.

Jamalia said, into the quiet, "Do we all need to get together and debrief it again? Maybe someone will have an idea. John's first day is next week, and he might have..." Jamalia looked up, saw they were nearing their floor, and turned her head toward Annie, who had her eyes closed.

"I'm sorry, did I say something wrong?"

"No, I'm just trying to block out the elevator and concentrate on what you're saying. Don't like elevators. Yeah, I think a last look by everyone is a good idea. Including John. Now that he's joining us, I mustn't forget that it was his case first. Maybe I'll ask Beatty to sit in, so he can see what we're dealing with. I talk to him, but he doesn't offer ideas. That's what *I'm* dealing with, I guess, no ideas, but the expectation that I'm going to come in one day ringing the bell."

They got out on the AIB floor and trailed back to desks and offices. Annie hummed *Church bells may ring*, and then did a brief review of all of the songs with church bells, like Little Jimmy Brown in the Valley somewhere, Whispering Bells, and couples getting married before Vietnam, as couples had done in every war Annie had ever read about. Her own parents, who were strangers when they met after the war. She took her gun out of the holster, hung up the holster on her coat rack and put the gun in her top drawer. Made a note to remember to clean it.

Truth to tell, she *was* depressed. Jamalia and Darin were doing good work, clearing cases. John was going to be a strong addition, but he would have a learning curve on all of the cases, even hers. There was a difference between bi-weekly contact and being involved in a case.

She didn't want to be depressed. Reflexively, she thought of Fred, who was able to help her when something was bothering her, but this time, she didn't really know what it was. She had been in her current job for five years, a detective for three before that and a trooper for 10, in both Alaska and Washington state. She had known, when she accepted the transfer to AIB, the cases were more difficult, and some of them already in poor health with dead-end investigations and disappearing leads. She hadn't realized there were so many unsolved. She knew they were, literally, *down there*, in the evidence lockup, and some of them were her cases. Some were from the other police agencies or levels, certainly. Missing persons. Literally hundreds of them. They might need a "we solved these" evidence room, to boost morale.

They were short staffed, and Annie found it difficult to ask others for help when they were obviously working already. Her consistent pattern had been to solve in isolation, especially since they were still staffing up. When a case such as this one came to her, it was because she had the track record, which wasn't working so well here. Being her consistent "partner" was above Eli's compensation grade, and thus unfair to him. She knew she needed another detective, but she hadn't quite figured how to change her pattern without causing some alarm all around. *Wow, if Annie can't solve this, who can* or, worse, *Well, we wondered when she would go into menopause.*

Rationally, she knew she had made the progress that was possible, given the paucity of witnesses, weapons and...suspects.

Annie *saw* things associated with cases. She saw, and dreamed, connections. She visualized killers and turned out to be uncannily correct. It had played out in Kotzebue. So why couldn't she see this one? She was, of course, dreaming of the murderer. In her latest dream, the killer was huge, in a janitor's suit, with a wig and a smiley face mask. He literally picked Grossman up, threw him into a dumpster, and began to take off his own disguise. But wherever he took something off, there was nothing under it, until even his shape disappeared bit by bit into the aether. And then cartoon footprints began to move, and she followed them to the Harbor, where they ended. She would wake up at this point, and look at the harbor in her mind. When it should have been full of vessels (when was it not?), it was virtually empty.

When she needed to track down what her brain was trying to tell her it had connected, she bounced ideas off Fred. They both thought this dream meant the killer left on the water, probably in a private boat. It might also be telling her that once the disguise was eliminated, she wouldn't recognize the killer, which led her towards the "stranger danger" theory she didn't believe for a moment. So, search South, was what she was thinking, but where? She was not supposed to give up. It was hard to keep rattling that doorknob.

The killer was in the Lower 48. She didn't know why, but she was sure of it. The killer used to work for Fish and Game, or was the spouse or close friend of someone who did. It made the most sense. Or not.

Here she was again. There was no resolution. She got a cup of coffee and went back to her desk. Then she got up again and went out to tell Jason to set up a meeting about the case, for as soon as John Sullivan was here, in the big conference room, and to ask Beatty if he would come. "Actually, ask him what time would be convenient, and then tell the others." She went back in to look at her messages, which Jason handed her in a pink wad, drink her coffee and think.

The second message in the stack was from Cunningham, the Deputy in Admin Services, in the building where Grossman was murdered. "Nothing urgent," it said, but hours of availability were listed. She was in one, so she called.

Surprisingly, it was a direct line. "Annie Brewster," she said when they connected. "I see that you called?"

"Yes."

Silence

"Do you have some information, or do you want some, because I'm sorry, but we have hit nothing but dead ends." Oops. First thing they should teach any murder cop was to expunge such metaphors, but Annie had a great deal of difficulty with it. Caught you *dead to rights*. He's a *dead ringer* for his brother. We're *dead in the water* on this one. Allison Cunningham was talking.

"...and Clyde said, 'no, but I'll tell that blonde cop from Anchorage.'"

"Wait. We had a blip in the line. Please say that again?"

"I had a performance review with Clyde Bunsen. His work has improved. I asked him whether he had had any more blackouts, and he said he hadn't had one. I asked him about the night of the murder, when he spent the night in the men's restroom and he said he wouldn't tell me anything more, but he would tell you."

Annie suppressed a little thrill. Many old cases turned on these tips. "Should I come down?"

"With Clyde, the body language is so important, I rather think so."

"Okay. I'll see when. Appreciate the call."

"I wish I could be more help. I have a friend who moved outside, and we were talking the other day about how it'd never been solved. It's so *evaporated*, you know?"

"Boy do I. Some leads are still promising. I'll leave a message with your secretary when I'm coming down. Thanks for the contact."

Annie hung up, drank cold coffee, and went through the messages. Her mind wanted to fixate on *My friend who moved Outside*. She shook it off, and made the rest of her calls.

She didn't want to go to Juneau to spar with Clyde Bunsen. Maybe a video session? She tried calling the number she had for Clyde, and got an answering machine. "Leave a message. You *know* how busy I am. Better be important." She asked the machine if Clyde would be agreeable to having a video conference with her? Alternatively, would he give any information he had to Detective Sullivan, who was joining her staff in Anchorage? She would wait for a reply before making arrangements.

She didn't believe she would hear back from him. She wanted some detail about what he knew before she made the trip down. But she would sleep on that. Maybe it would be a good thing to talk with Cunningham again. Maybe not. She started on the list of people Jason should ask to the meeting.

Chapter Thirty-Two

January, 2000

They were in bed, with coffee and the Sunday paper. Bones was on his secondary pillow in the corner of the bedroom, gnawing on a rawhide bone. He tended to lick himself at night, which tickled Fred and drove Annie crazy. Hence the exile to the far end of the generous room. "You're next," was what Annie said whenever Fred or Bones complained.

The business section included an article on Bobbette Ellery, newly appointed Commissioner of Fish and Game. She hesitated, then read down the article, which listed Ellery's credentials as a member of the Fish and Game Board and a previous commercial fisherman out in Bristol Bay. Some things never changed, Annie thought. Fox guarding, developing policy for the henhouse. The last line of the article, however, went beyond straight news, in her opinion. "Ellery takes over the Department following the murder of Commissioner Richard Grossman, whose killer, apparently, is still at large despite the efforts at apprehension by both the Juneau Police Department and the Alaska Investigation Bureau. Extra security will be provided for the new Commissioner and her family. The AIB has indicated that it does not comment on ongoing investigations, but appears to now be working with the FBI on the case."

Annie sat up, threw the paper, threw back the covers and fell on her back. "You might as well have your way with me," she said. "Everyone else is."

"Now, Hon, don't read about the case in the newspaper. And it's unkind of you to put me at the end of the list." Fred said.

Still, he set down his paper and reached out his arm to pull her over against him. With her head on his warm chest, Annie murmured, "it doesn't make sense. This appears to. You smell good."

"Oh," he replied against her hair, "I am."

****

Monday morning meetings were the worst, because it was Monday. And a meeting. On the other hand, there was almost always food. People were generous, especially with something they knew they shouldn't be eating at home. There would be coffee, and occasionally water hot enough to steep a tea bag.

Annie brought bagels, cream cheese and pepper jam and put them on the table in the back of the conference room where there were already enough calories to sustain a refuge camp. It was hard to look on such careless plenty when so many people were hungry. And somehow it made her slightly nauseous as well. She filled her water bottle in spurious righteousness.

A murder board was set up here, somewhat expurgated to show only the more well-defined lines of investigation. She looked around. Everything was ready. She had rehearsed the agenda with Fred, and had a little note that said *Remember not to go over and over what everyone already knows, even if you feel you have to start at the beginning and go to the end. Don't be defensive.* She put the note in the pocket of her jacket, where every time she put her hand in, she would feel it.

Whit came first, followed by Darin and Jamalia, who both headed straight for the food. Annie was pretty sure neither of them ever got fed at home. Parfletch found the tea. Dr. Hernandez had walked up the stairs, from the glow on her face, and possibly with ADA Janet Beck, who worked most closely with the AIB and also glowed. Jason brought John Sullivan in, and Annie introduced him to everyone, though everyone claimed to either know him or have heard of him except the FBI Profiler. Annie had asked Beatty if it would be okay for Eli to come, since he had been involved with so much of the evidence, but he would be late because of an early class.

After everyone had something to eat or drink, and had found a place to sit, Annie turned to John. "New guy is it, John. Sorry 'bout that. Can you talk through the earliest details discovered about the crime, and where Richard Grossman was found?"

This was an interesting review for everyone. John had been deferential to Annie in Juneau, in October of 1998, but here in January of 2001, he was more at ease. They had, after all, just hired him to be part of this group, and he had been in Alaska a long time, which in and of itself offered credentials. He nodded and began, "We were called to the dump on a Wednesday morning because there was a body in the Government Waste." Straight faced.

After they were all through grinning behind their hands or to themselves, it being highly inappropriate to do anything of the sort, he went on more conventionally. "That was the exact appellation given to the area of waste in the

Dump. After it was determined that this could not have been the crime scene, it ultimately helped us to identify the truck which brought him there, and led us to one and ultimately two crime scenes."

They talked through it. Good questions, easily answered. Even Beck knew the basic details of the two crime scenes. She asked questions almost exclusively about evidence, and wasn't engaged at their level with the theory of the crime. She spent most of the time frowning and jotting down notes. When they got to the body, and developing evidence on the body itself, which Hernandez listed tersely, she perked up and looked at the reactions of others in the room. A drugged victim increased the jury's interest, apparently.

Annie took over for the rest of the stages of the investigation, gesturing to Darin and Jamalia when she came to the Delta Junction office. John, who hadn't heard all of the details related to the two possible Fish and Game office connections, took notes on his notes. Parfletch repeated his profile.

Commander Beatty had been brought in on most of the pivotal evidence, and he was accustomed to being somewhat in charge. "Let me ask," he said, looking at Parfletch, "why we are pursuing--in your expertise--a man, and yet all of the people with the clearest motive seem to be women?"

Parfletch appeared to consider that. "I see it that way," he said. "But a certain type of woman could have done this. An extremely physically fit woman, and perhaps one with an unusual life. Perhaps one who has been abused in the past, and maybe there is a record of that. I think, if I had no idea where to go next, that I would cross any female name you have, including the husband's or boyfriend's name, with domestic violence complaints, unsolved rapes, anything that went to the police so there would be a record of it."

"You think," said Annie, "that this could have been someone previously abused and pushed over the edge by the bullying behavior of the victim."

Jamalia asked thoughtfully, "If he had done the type of thing to me that he has done to the women and mouse men who have worked for him or around him, and I witnessed or heard about these situations, maybe I would ramp up my anger, is that what you are saying?"

"I suppose so, yes. I would not counsel you to avoid looking at women."

"And so we have not," Annie nodded. "In fact, the list of women we have interviewed, why, and what we learned is here if you'd like to look at it. I'll pass it around." She did. "They run to two sorts. First, we tried to find the obvious women (along with two subordinate men) who might have fit into the 'disgruntled' category, having been personally bullied, insulted, fired, misused and reorganized out of their long-time jobs. Some we found; *none* outside of Juneau would talk about it. That's a bit perplexing. Like the women in Juneau knew they were safe to talk because he couldn't do anything else to them, but the women in Anchorage or Delta Junction really didn't want to talk at all.

"Eli...and there he is! Eli Carson is known to most of you. Eli went with me to gather personnel information from the two Fish and Game Offices, and personally interviewed an older woman who had been the office manager in Anchorage. He's responsible for helping us to develop the data in this case, and is, as you know, working on being singularly indispensable to the investigation." Everyone smiled at Eli, who took an open seat and tried to look humble.

"The second category of women watched the bullying behavior, and in some cases were required by job title to facilitate that and aren't afraid to talk because they can't be touched by anyone due to retirement or interpersonal influence. We obtained information from HR staff, office managers, the state Budget Director who held the last meeting and timed Grossman's exit. They were consistent and forthcoming, but within the confines of their job descriptions. This is a political case, still, to these witnesses. Whatever they say is careful and expurgated."

"And can you review, following what Dr. Hernandez has already said, how the actual murder was accomplished?"

Annie sighed and looked at the ceiling. She could see Clyde Bunsen's confused face, all of a sudden. And said something that caused everyone to look up in surprise. "I believe the janitor in the State Office Building saw the murderer. This janitor spent the night on the floor of the men's restroom. When he woke up, he couldn't remember any details, but he kept rubbing his chest when we questioned him. Other details make him an unreliable witness. Though he does not admit to coming to work under the influence--and who would--that has been reported and even he hinted at trying to confine his use to outside of work. So...Janet...you know where that gets us with a jury. If he's a critical witness, neither John nor I think it would be a good idea to put him on the stand.

"There's a bit of a new wrinkle there, actually. Yesterday the Deputy Director of Administrative Services, the supervisor of this janitor, called and told me he had something to say, only to me. John, I don't believe this is anything other than what we already know, but it may make Clyde Bunsen a more credible witness. I'm looking at the ways I can talk to him. Maybe video.

"Anyway, back to the question. The actual murder employed a powerful synthetic narcotic, which Jamalia tells us we should begin expecting to see in the illegals trade, called Carfentinal. All legal sources in the state have been investigated, accounted for, theoretically. Vice hasn't found it in the illegals market yet.

"All official sources of the drug show rigorous disposal by the manufacturer's specified date, limited security on the HAZMAT containers in Veterinarians offices, the Zoo, and the Fish and Game offices. At this point, no wildlife parks in the state could order it, but the university could probably order it to do research.

"That said," she said slowly, "we are not ruling out the possibility that it was removed from a HAZMAT container and for the exact purpose of using it on Grossman. Security is an issue. We're working on this angle."

Parfletch asked, "When you interviewed in Delta and Fairbanks, you came up with a woman biologist who had quit because of an ethical complaint, is that right? She was trained to use the drug, right? What happened with her?"

Annie sighed. "She's in the wind. In the back of my mind, I know it could be her. Sue Parkinson. You'll see her on the board up here. along with Brower. These are the two people, along with a man, Melvin Bright, who were directly under Grossman, were apparently upset by him, and who, subsequently, left. Sophia Brower has a protective husband, who came and got her and took her to Barrow. I did talk to her, for what it was worth, which was just one click past zero."

Everyone was quiet and thoughtful. Beatty flipped through his papers, looked at the board, and finally said, "I had thought that additional staff might make the difference here, but now I'm not so sure. You've done a prodigious amount of work, and sometimes, that's what you've got."

"I'm not saying I'm giving up," Annie said quickly. "We may have Parkinson in Haines in September before the murder. It may or may not mean anything that I can't, currently, find her. Anyway, we're not here to hear my 'next steps,' as it were. We're here for you to recommend them."

Parfletch rubbed his mustache. "Alaska is a funny place, isn't it? Criminals can get in and out before we even know the crime was committed. Airplanes fly in every direction. I would recommend that you just follow the Carfentinal, because that's the one thing the killer had to have, and as a controlled substance, it has at least some chance of being traced.

"I don't think I have anything else on offer. I have nothing but praise for what you've done so far, but when there are no other examples, a Profiler isn't going to be able to suggest where to go next. I agree the killer is gone. I still think the likeliest killer is a man. Perhaps he's associated with one of the women, as you suggested might be the case, but perhaps he has grievances of his own. Maybe he lived where the drug is available, and brought it north with him. I can't begin to tell you all of the people who come here to practice crimes they can commit somewhere else where there is more oversight. The Mafia comes to mind. You have no 'comparables,' correct?"

Jamalia answered, "I ran a search when I first came, helping Annie out and learning the computer system. It could be done again."

"If this is a one-off..." Darin began, but Hernandez raised her hand slightly and everyone immediately stopped and looked at her.

"Men his age have heart attacks. If there hadn't been an autopsy, no one would know. Want to guess how many of those there are that are never branded homicides?"

Annie thought the faces in the room, all of whom had had some association with specifics of the case, all looked as blank as she felt. One step forward, one step to the side, two steps back. She didn't even know what to suggest, or ask next.

John, who had since the beginning of the meeting said nothing, cleared his throat. "It's tempting to go back to Juneau and look at the scene again, but I think we may know everything we can get from doing that. I know you're frustrated, Annie, but from the first I think I told you this killer isn't in Juneau, maybe isn't even from Juneau. That's my strongest feeling. The scene was just...empty.

"The people who didn't like this guy aren't necessarily murderers. He's an especially egregious bully, but he's not alone. Why kill him? And if he did something to you in one of the other places he worked, why kill him now, when he has this public position?

"If I were you, I'd stay really personal. In the past. He did something to someone, and it was so awful for them that they couldn't stand it when he attained this high position. It's just politics, if you're in Juneau. Career employees duck and cover, they do not rise up and strike. Maybe the rest of the state doesn't see it that way. We've already established that you can get into and out of Juneau, that the killer planned carefully and wore a disguise, that the murder weapons are probably at the bottom of Taku Inlet. It looks to me like the rest of state is where the killer was, and now the killer is in the rest of the country--or world."

"Thanks, John. I definitely want to keep hearing your ideas, and to have your help," said Annie.

Darin and Jamalia had heard all of this before. Annie valued the suggestions of her colleagues, although she was not quite so good at letting them know. She said now, "Darin and Jamalia went up to Delta Junction on another case, and interviewed staff there. Then Eli and I went up. All complaints, formal and informal, came from the two offices where he was the admin, excepting the one from the woman who guides on the Big Su. So, as John suggests, we have nothing in Juneau but those who seem to have witnessed the killer in disguise, and without them we wouldn't even have that."

"We have the wig hair from the truck, and the mud on the Commissioner's coat, indicating he was in the back of the truck," Eli reminded her carefully, unsure whether he should speak or not.

"Yes," Hernandez agreed, "and we have specific information, to which I could testify, of how he was killed. These paint quite a picture."

"Of everything but the killer, but you have probable height, dominant hand, vehicle of death, type of weapons used and a good theory of how the crime was accomplished," Beatty added. "I agree that you've hit a wall of sorts. But you could get a tip tomorrow, someone else who saw something. I wanted to ask, how hard did you look at the widow?"

"She was..."

"I know, in Sitka. But you agree that she might know something about it?"

"She definitely knows something, but she's locked down and the Governor is running interference for her. I agree that she was unusually reticent and controlling, no talking about the death, no talking to the kids, and the home computer was so clean it just had to be wiped. We even had computer techs look to see if there was lurking information, but there is no evidence anyone ever contacted him via home email. Personally, I think the man was paranoid about computers having information that could implicate someone or something. Both of the incidents at the Fish and Game offices involved computers, as you will see if you look at the notes."

Annie thought for a moment, and then added, "Mrs. Grossman has gotten harder and harder to contact and increasingly hostile in response to questions. I find that troubling. At first, I had the sense that she was in such deep grief that she couldn't talk. Then I evolved to the belief that she didn't want to hear any more about it, which is different than grief. That made her suspicious in my mind, but..."

"Yes," said Beatty, "The Governor just didn't want us to go there. As a matter of fact, she went to him for advice and he urged her to move the children back to their extended family and grandparents, because she didn't really have a connection to Juneau."

He sat back, put his hands on his thighs. "I would say, continue to pursue anything that seems promising, maybe to the end of the Governor's term, and I can't believe I just said that. I must be getting as frustrated with this as Annie is. Maybe a tip line with a reward would trigger someone's memory. Maybe put a general description of the killer in the missing person's database, along with a composite, if we could get one. Maybe that Bunsen guy is ready to make a drawing."

"Worth a try," Annie agreed. Tip lines generally produced hundreds of worthless calls, among which were the undeniably important, so you had to follow all of them. Long row for short dough?

"Regardless," Beatty went on, "When John gets moved and we find him an office better than the cloakroom, he can help you for the foreseeable." Everyone nodded around, and stood up when Annie did. Annie who collected her notes and started for her office. John carried the murder board behind her, and sat it back in its easel. "I don't know if that helped you," he said

"It is necessary to imagine Sisyphus happy," Annie murmured. "Thanks, John. Did you find your new office?"

"Yeah, and I have to tell you, it feels strangely like home."

Annie smiled. "Want to fly to Juneau?" she asked with a grin.

"Oh, why not," he said. "I happen to have a suitcase that isn't even unpacked."

****

Clyde hadn't returned her call and so was surprised to see them, but he was pretty happy that Cunningham had passed along his request. He did, indeed, want to describe someone he thought he saw on the night of the murder. He'd been thinking about it. "Clearing out" his memory.

His memory, once cleaned, yielded big, black-rimmed glasses, a ball cap and a face mask. He had had nightmares about it, he said. He was pretty sure it was the last thing he remembered. Did that help?

It might, Annie agreed, having had the same dream. She pulled from her bag a copy of the picture of the Fish and Game Field Office Easter Egg Roll and showed it to Clyde, without comment. Clyde looked hard at her, then hard at the picture, the at the picture again, then used his finger to go across the top row. He stopped on the picture that was, by process of elimination, assumed to be Parkinson. "There he is," Clyde said, "There he is, maybe. Looks like him. Wore glasses." Annie remarked to John later that whenever Clyde talked about what he saw, he rubbed his chest. John had noticed it, too. Nothing Clyde said gave them any indication that he had not seen someone. They were certain that he did, and that he had been tased like Grossman.

They praised him, asked him if he would sit with a sketch artist, and were surprised when he said yes. They gave the resulting sketch to the Juneau paper, with the tip line number, and got back on the next plane. But not before Annie told the sketch artist to give her a second picture without the mask and glasses, just the same face shape with a curly wig. He said he would work on it. When he finished, it looked surprisingly like Grossman, which wasn't, in fact, surprising at all.

The Cold Case - 2002

Chapter Thirty-Three

2001 - May, 2002

It was impossible to overstate the impact of the bombing of the twin towers on Alaska law enforcement, which was on high alert and hovering over the critical and vulnerable oil pipeline. Firefighters, a big group because the state burned every summer now, wanted to go to New York to help. Some had done so. Because Alaska was cut off from the rest of the nation by geography and its tiny population, yet had such an outsized military presence, there were reconnaissance planes in the air all over Alaska. The few DEW line stations that were still open were doing 24/7 patrols of their gadgets and dials.

By January of the new year, things began to calm down a bit, and by February the airport seemed normal, except for the uptick in security and the fact that no one seemed to have a sense of humor any more. Annie was glad that most trips of any kind were temporarily cancelled. It seemed a good time to do the work necessary to get the new Cold Case Unit underway. There being no current calls for reducing funding for law enforcement.

They had most of a new lab now, with more added this year, and were now going to add a fledgling staff to deal with the many cold cases that Annie referred to as "those down there we need to see to." Finally, Beatty called her in and said, "You see to them, and we'll get you some staff in the next go-round."

Accordingly, by Valentine's Day, Annie and Eli had the materials assembled that would allow some baseline decisions to be made on something other than the specific interests of a past investigator. It was time to get the AIB's newest unit on board. The last thing Annie wanted was a new guy from Homicide saying, "hey, mind if I look into this case," as seemed to happen over and over again on television.

CSI shows were popular, and had prompted a burst of students who wanted forensic programs. Annie felt it had brought forensics to acceptable dinner conversation. Fred wasn't so sure, but he was indulgent, and was developing a bit of interest himself.

She and her UAA criminalistics intern, Melissa, designed the meeting. There were guidelines, actually, in national publications. They needed a baseline of operating procedures that could be referenced in meetings, in warrants, subpoenas, court cases. Judges liked operating procedures, and wanted them followed. Annie knew she was going to participate in her job description, which made this meeting critical. She poured over recommended organization and key questions for case selection. The years had actually produced quite a national website of cases, with Alaska's among the most numerous. Not a surprise. Annie had gone to Seattle and Los Angeles, talked procedures and looked, on the q-t, for a person or two to hire once the unit was fully funded, which might be as early as April. She thought she had found a man in Seattle, and hoped he would come.

They had cold case data ready, numbering an astounding 278 in the last few decades. If you eliminated those too old for a living victim or perp, there were still 250 solidly cold cases. The intern put all of the unresolved cases, dating back to the history of the state, into a data base, one at a time as they brought them up and made sure what had been kept in the way of evidence, which also went into the data base.

Based upon this huge list, one had to decide where to allocate resources. Annie thought seriously about how the cases might be prioritized and how you had to have a minimum number of employees before you could prove you needed more. So some cases had to be solved in order for more funding to be forthcoming, and so on. Most cases were missing, raped or murdered women, predominantly native women. There were no serials they had yet seen, but perhaps the data bases would help with that. Many fewer men had been murdered, comparatively speaking. Of course, many cold cases were missing persons, with suspected crimes but no evidence or actual proof of death.

Annie invited her colleagues. John was helping Jamalia and Darin, learning the parameters within which AIB worked. The active cases were obviously his interest. Annie was fine with that--she wanted someone with cold case background. Representing the stakeholders, the AG would send someone. the ME would bring the new Coroner. Eli would bring someone he chose from the lab. She had UAA send a professor with experience in the types of evidence they had in the data base.

What is a "cold case" seemed a stupid first question, but Annie knew solid agreement, written definition, even, helped in court. All of the units she had contacted were willing to talk with her about how they had made their decisions, this being an emerging field where most established units were trying to help everyone else. The perpetrators of cold crimes could be anywhere, and the new technology was everywhere. The protocol, over and across units throughout the country, was that whoever had the case originally had the lead, and that at some point, an administrator had stepped in and said, "enough already, we have 10 new cases."

Occasionally the oldest adage in criminology--*if it isn't solved in 48 hours, it won't be*--was true, but less and less. With each new technological development that applied to evidence, a few cases needed re-examination. Annie was ready to propose that for any "viable" cases there would be a rating system that combined the potential for solution, the age of the crime, the existence of evidence, and so forth. That would lead to a prioritization that would ultimately lead to a list of cases. And a discussion of staffing.

There were political considerations. The unit had better produce. That might be left unsaid, but it was lurking. Those who had had their budgets shortsheeted, based upon money that was needed for the new criminological developments and their housing, were ready to pounce on an unproductive first year. It was unreasonable to think that the first year would result in many solved cases--there was a learning curve, for heaven's sake. But it was a consideration.

So, solvable, political, what else. There were those driven by new technology or the better application of older methods or where forensic evidence had been insufficiently processed. Eli entered a column in their Cold Case data base for the type of forensics used and evidence that could not be analyzed in any meaningful way due to the absence of an applicable test. And those where a test was available.

Bless Eli. Annie thought that most of the more recent cases might actually fit into the third category. She could see the stakeholder group prioritizing and blessing the lists of cases where she would "begin," and felt it was good protection for both her and Beatty.

She was cautiously excited about her new position. Cold cases meant less travel, actually, and more time trying to connect the dots, including communicating with other agencies out of state. There was something about these cases that drew her. She felt the irresolute dead all around her. It wasn't a spooky thing; it was just like being in a room of cobwebs--or maybe the bead curtains in an old 60's head shop. You walked forward slowly, and you pulled aside the curtain, and something beckoned to you through the fog of memory, perhaps showing you the way.

She saw the victims sometimes. Sometimes she saw the killers.

Lately, she had begun to see school pictures of the missing girls in that little village. Where did they go? Why couldn't someone look at school records and identify who was missing the next year? Probably, someone had done that, but Annie couldn't find any record of it. She hoped the case made it to the priority list, because her brain was apparently already working on it. She hoped that the Grossman case would be in the mix. Over the past year, she had become less certain that it could be solved, or that it was appropriate to resource the investigation unless the proverbial "break" actually materialized. But part of her didn't want to give it up.

Bones and Suzy were an item. She wasn't as old as Eli wanted her to be when she had puppies. Both Bones and Suzy thought that was hogwash, and flirted shamelessly.

****

The meeting went well. Annie watched people tend toward cases of personal interest, and once she confronted that by "confessing" what she knew was her own, there was relative agreement on the cold cases that should be pursued. There were six where the evidence needed to be immediately re-examined with the new technologies. Annie was delighted to see that the missing girls in the remote village, which had originally been about four "missing persons" cases, was moved up to the top 10. A case that surprised everyone had to do with pedophilic activity in one of the villages, and the perpetrator appeared to have been allowed to leave the state rather than face charges. The Alaskan victims had been children, some of whom wanted to know what had happened to the man who they now understood had abused them. Native communities might not view these incidents through the same lens, but he might be committing similar crimes in other states. That made eight.

A ninth case focused on a bizarre series of murders, the first found near the Naval Arctic Research Center, outside of Barrow on the way to nowhere. When the Center was decommissioned in the 80's, much of the contents of labs and apartments were put into old unheated Quonset huts, the military's go-to temporary structure. It was three years before anyone came to move the supplies and equipment to another location, at which time among the supplies the workers found four freeze-dried bodies, wrapped in white canvas and placed along the walls behind bedsteads and mattresses full of lemmings. Or perhaps they had been wrapped and then freeze dried. The Arctic did that. Bodies had been brought out, had been autopsied, and had been, since they were all native but one, who at the time could not be identified at all, given back to the Inupiat to be buried.

No one seemed to know if any of them had actually ever been definitively identified. All corpses were naked. Someone had taken great care to remove any identifying characteristics, teeth missing, the body hair removed, fingerpads gone. Annie shuddered to think how that had all been done, and whether before or after freezing, and so forth. Some body hair continued to grow after death, and since there was none, including on the genitals or under the arms, this was either done pre-mortem or the cold conditions kept any from growing. No beards or ear hair. No hair on the toes or tops of the feet.

They spent some time talking about this case. Eli said freeze-drying preserved some kinds of evidence, and thought he might get something if a body was exhumed. The unidentified man had been photographed, autopsied and buried in a John Doe grave, so they could try facial reconstruction and a public query with that. They agreed the Cold Case Unit should try, with some of the new DNA extraction methods, to match the four men with missing persons reports, and see if they could clear those cases of at least that much ambiguity. It seemed like a serial, but no similar murders were recorded. Annie couldn't help but wonder how many other Quonset huts around the huge state might be frozen crime scenes.

The tenth case was Grossman. Annie was relieved; she could not abandon it. She knew there were active, if hazy, leads. New x-ray spectroscopy, made it possible to restore latent prints off fabric, gloves and other surfaces that had previously shielded evidence.

Annie was able to get consensus on hiring another experienced detective, and a research assistant. Annie winked at the Intern, Melissa Burkhardt, who waggled her eyebrows in response.

Melissa was a middle-aged woman who had gone back to college after her children were in high school and more independent. She had good computer skills. She was sharp; she was able to see the relationships between the theoretical and practical. She wasn't much interested in the police work aspect of the job, but she was fascinated with the forensics and their application. The other would come, Annie knew. She was just as happy that there was someone, again, who would have a fresh perspective on old questions.

Annie followed Beatty out of the meeting. "Can I call Felize now?" she asked.

"Yeah. I did a bit of checking. We can fast-track it. Go ahead and call." he said. "Good meeting. I think if we could get something on three or four of these cases, we could get more staff in the next budget. Which one do you think has the best potential of the bunch?"

"Two categories on that. Eli might fast track those where the evidence needs a reboot, and that might give us some quick solves. The NARL murders will be the most staff intensive, so I would like to hold off on those. I think we can sniff around the village girls case--might be impossible to break through village silence. I don't want to sit around on anything, so I will try getting that one set up, and then go on with Grossman once Art gets here. I think, direct answer, the first group. Review the evidence and see where that gets us."

He agreed, and Annie went back to her office to call Arturo Felize, who she hoped was about to be her new partner.

Chapter Thirty-Four

September 28, 2002

Fall was nearly over in Juneau. It was a truncated phenomenon: one day of yellow leaves, one day of brown leaves, and then the cottonwoods were bare. Annie looked out her bedroom window at the big conifers dripping in their perennial midnight green, and thought about *farthest north temperate rain forest,* because it always seemed such a strange concept. The last cruise ship was parked at the docks. Passengers were moving through the town in their ponchos and under umbrellas, eating, buying and looking.

Annie met Arturo Felize at the counter-culture cafe called "The Fiddlehead," dead center between their two crime "scenes." With him was Beth Collinsworth, the new FBI profiler, who had asked to come along. Parfletch had retired. Annie had barely met Beth, but definitely welcomed her input. She made sure they both knew that there were great cookies here, and if they didn't buy a couple, there was something seriously wrong with them.

Annie really liked Arturo. They laughed a bit. They got on well. He was about Annie's age, and like her had been a Washington Trooper. He had done a decade in homicide, the last two years with the Seattle area Cold Case Unit, and needed to make a physical change, he said. He found that he really enjoyed the old cases, because they were like puzzles.

He was smart. Like Annie, he was not a great talker, but he watched everything, and he knew the law. He had commanding presence but he hid it initially behind an infectious smile and a ready handshake. By the time he had someone else's hand in his, he had you with his eyes. So Annie figured that was good for coaxing ancient witnesses or crabby bureaucrats. And she knew, though it irritated her, that many witnesses, especially native witnesses, would prefer to talk to a man with the warm brown skin. She had seen it over and over--anyone as pale as she was got used to it. She thought he would be great.

The search for Felize had started a year ago. As she went to other states looking at Cold Case units, she watched for an investigator who was clearly good, but wasn't Alaskan. Cold cases benefitted from new eyes, and with Alaska, anyone from the outside had those. Beatty had cleared the outside hire. Apparently the only argument anyone needed was "crucial experience." It basically trumped everything. Because they always had interns, they could entirely prove they were trying to build local capacity.

She could hardly wait to involve Arturo in the village girls' case. *New, experienced eyes.* Annie was tired of people shrugging and looking away from women assumed to be at risk because of "lifestyle." Thus far, she was totally happy with her new-found partner.

This morning They were going to walk the Grossman crime scenes. They had boots and raincoats and umbrellas, but the sky was temporarily mild and there was actually a bit of sun peeking through. "You know," she said over her rice and kale scramble, "I'm thinking we might start out up at the Capitol, and retrace his steps. It'd be a good idea for me to review the timing. John and his partner were good detectives, but they had nothing after a week, so I'm hoping that you see things I couldn't."

Beth had been quiet so far. "I read the files," she said. "I think another set of eyes is good, but more than that, we need to see the scene before we can comment on what happened. After reading all that was done, I'm wanting to revisit Whit's opinion." That much in a rush, and she returned to her omelet.

Annie and Arturo looked at one another, raised their eyebrows, and then looked down at their food.

Arturo said, stirring his gravy around, "I read everything twice. I have some notes, but I want to see it. I have to get a visual before I can help. I remember when the Green River Killer was active in Washington, we got so we all went to every crime scene, and you'd be amazed at what one person saw that another totally missed or just blew off as unimportant."

"I sure get that. You know, one of the things that still bothers me is that in the front seat of Grossman's truck, we found one hair consistent with a wig on the floor, and one on the headrest. Anyway, we built our theory around those hairs, and the fact that we believed that the killer was about Grossman's size and build. The one witness..."

"Yeah, the witness said she saw Grossman. But inside of the cab of the truck, right?" Beth was following.

"If it wasn't Grossman, it was the killer in disguise. We can't prove it either way."

They finished and went out to the front of the restaurant, paid and bought cookies. Ranger,

Ginger and Oatmeal, as big as saucers, soft and warm. Arturo put his in his coat pocket and continued eating small pieces until they got back to Annie's loaner car. Annie pointed up the street to the State Office Building that rose against the hill, and the parking garage beneath it. "That's where we're going. The Capitol Building is behind it, but you can't see it from here. Get in and I'll give you a tour."

They parked in a visitor's spot behind the Capitol Building. Annie put the "police business" sign in the front window. They went in through the back door and out the front, where Annie pointed the route to the parking places designated for legislators, appointees and key staff. It was only about a block, diagonally, across the street to the loading dock where Annie and John had stood four years ago.

Arturo asked, "Did anyone see him leave? See him actually walk this?"

"Saw him leaving, pretty precisely, but after that, no wits. The Capitol guard was apparently around the corner talking to people by the coffee machine. Hidden from sight. There are two corroborating pieces of information. He called his wife from the phone next to the conference room upstairs. He did that at 5:45 or so, according to her answering machine. He didn't call his office. He had access to one of those old 'loaf of bread' phones with the antenna, but he hated it, his deputy said. The deputy normally couldn't leave until he was given permission, but when Grossman hadn't called by 6:00, he called over here and was told Grossman was gone.

"The next thing we have is his truck in its spot at Fish and Game, so we figured he had to get there before the murder. Or close." Annie said.

They went back in and up the elevator to the Governor's floor, and Arturo took an old stop watch out of his pocket. "Wow. That's a collector's item," Annie said, looking at the winding spool, the stem and the little hands. Everything was becoming digital. Pretty soon, kids wouldn't know what those hands told them.

"Yeah," Arturo said. "My dad coached track. I wore it on a fob, but people thought it was a pocket watch and kept asking me what time it was." When they reached the Governor's floor, Arturo started the watch. They exited the elevator, sent it back down to the first floor, and watched it get there. They walked over to the receptionist, made brief introductions, turned and walked to the elevator again. It came, they got in, they rode down and they went out the front door. Arturo stopped the watch. "So that takes five or six minutes. He was undoubtedly out of the building by 6:00."

"That's the timeline. I'm told it was a normal pattern. We're walking..."

They followed a half-dozen people, some carrying papers and briefcases, some with newspapers over their heads, some talking on phones. Everyone went the same place. Up the steps to the loading dock (quick glance up at the glass skybridge), through the heavy metal door, and into the bowels of the building. Arturo stood on the loading dock, looking about carefully. A dumpster, a small forklift, two dollies of different sizes, an electric golf cart with isinglass sides and a little cart attached, six cement steps up to the dock itself, and the door. He watched person after person take the exact same route. Over half looked up at the sky bridge.

"So, did you think about whether the killer was up there watching for him? Seems like the timing is critical. It doesn't take anyone long to get over here, and if the killer isn't watching, how does he know the mark is even in the building?" Beth was atiptoe, stretching to see as much of the walkway as she could from where they were standing.

"That's a question. We didn't really talk about it much. If we theorize that he wouldn't recognize the murderer, that might be a strategy. Or if the murderer was in disguise. So let's time that one."

The corridor was empty. All of the doors into offices, the mail room, the rest rooms, were closed. They timed the walk to the elevator. They took the public elevator up to the State Library and walked across the Sky Bridge, past the latte cart, to the windows at the end that looked straight at the Capitol Building. They watched people walking both ways and timed several. Then Annie saw someone come out of the Capitol Building she recognized and knew, if she was correct, this person would be going to the parking garage. They started the stopwatch, turned and went back to the elevators, took the public elevator to the lower floor, picked up the other bank of elevators that went down to the parking garage, and stepped out into the safety lights and gloom.

"That's Grossman's parking place down there," she said. She knew the new Commissioner kept Roberts, who had filled in as Acting. She was pretty sure that was Roberts they had seen crossing the street. On cue, the elevator doors behind them opened and Harlan Roberts stepped out. Art hit the plunger on the stopwatch and wrote down the amount of time it had taken him to get here from the Capitol Building. They had barely made it before him. Waiting for the public elevator had taken too long. The murderer must have been waiting here.

"Mr. Roberts," Annie said, "Annie Brewster from AIB. We spoke after Commissioner Grossman was murdered?"

"Yes, of course," Roberts said, and then looked immediately at Felize.

Annie flinched and began with, "This is Beth Collinsworth, an FBI Profiler based in Anchorage, who is assisting us to make certain we haven't overlooked anything." Roberts looked at Beth, and back at Annie, and then neatly reoriented his body to face Arturo. Annie wanted to sigh aloud, but caught it just in time. "And this is our newest investigator. Inspector Arturo Felize, this is Harlan Roberts, Deputy Commissioner...is that still correct?...of Fish and Game."

The men shook hands. Felize smiled broadly. "We appreciated your clear-headed testimony," he said, pleasing Harlan, who began to preen a bit.

"I offered everything I could think of that might be of any assistance," he said primly.

"We need more people with good powers of observation," Felize said, patting Roberts' hand and then releasing him and stepping back. Annie resisted the urge to wipe her own hand on her slacks. Definitely Arturo was going to be a great complement to the unit.

"So the case is open again?" Roberts asked.

"It hasn't really been closed. We have followed nearly 100 leads; we know how he died. We finally have the staff and facilities to give it another hard push." Annie looked around the parking garage. Though she knew, she asked, "remind me which spot is the Commissioner of Fish and Game?"

"There, three down."

"And is this the same spot..."

"Yes, the same," Roberts said, staring down at the little compact that was in the spot. "I'm allowed to park there when the Co isn't using it. She's in Fairbanks at the Game Board meeting."

"Okay, we're just taking another look to see if all of our notes are still accurate. Art's going to look at everything with fresh eyes," Annie said.

"Good enough. Nice to meet you," Roberts said to Felize, nodded at Annie, and walked on down to his car.

"That is one cold SOB," Arturo said. "Wanted to wipe my hands on my pants after touching him. Like he was going to be slimy, but he wasn't. Snakes are like that."

Annie smiled, with a wry twist. "True that," she said. "He wouldn't kill a commissioner. He is a parasite on them. He drains their essence. He lives because they are here."

"Woo." Felize looked at Annie with arched eyebrows. "So, maybe you didn't like the guy?"

"Actually, that didn't enter into it. Just saw him for what he is. *Mean* isn't a negative to him. It's a sign of strength. He appeared in awe of Grossman, and he was most certainly intimidated by him. I've watched these deputies. Many of them are among the most astute political survivors you will ever find. No one elects them, but they run about 90% of everything. They know how to do it and not run afoul of the current administration. They know how to live through opposing administrations without being kicked out, and they will, literally, keep the ship afloat if everyone appointed by the Governor just leaves for two weeks, or a month. They have incredible day-to-day power."

"And yet, not a murderer?"

"Asked and answered. Think about it. He doesn't really care who is commissioner. He cares only that he is indispensable to the current and the next commissioner. Hire and fire the staff, sign the checks, keep the paper and pencils stocked, know where the budget can be manipulated to address the commissioner's priorities, and on and on. Occasionally, like Sir Thomas Moore or the elder Cromwell, someone else puts a bug in the Commissioner's ear that the chancellor has too much power, and off goes his head, but for the most part, these are lifers."

"Learning. Interesting running into him, huh. Okay, it's too chancy for anyone to be waiting on the sky bridge. And a stretch to say, *sans* particular evidence, that Grossman wouldn't have recognized some big guy looking down at him. But what about right here?"

Annie and Arturo looked around at the area outside of the elevator, and how quickly it slid into shadows and real dark, especially at evening, in the first stalls beyond the elevators. Behind the dumpster, slightly around the corner in one of the stalls by the elevator, or behind a car. There were plenty of hiding places.

Beth had been attending, but only peripherally. She was still looking at the scene, intently. "I've pictured it like this. Parking garages are all alike. Big lights by the elevator doors, and immediately places for people to hide--pillars, trash receptacles, big vehicles--too many places to hide."

"Yeah," Annie agreed. "No woman wants to go into a parking garage that I know of, no matter what time of day it is. Don't know if it bothers men that way."

She walked to the various places where the prospective murderer might be hidden. There was no reason to think any of the area was changed, even after four years. She bet it was the same dumpster. She looked back at Arturo, whose eyes had gone to some unfocused place she was beginning to realize meant he was working on how he wanted to say something. He began to mutter.

"I'm gonna kill this guy. I'm in a disguise. He doesn't know me. I blend in. What blends in? Why doesn't he have his guard up? No defensive wounds, why doesn't he fight? Or maybe, because of the disguise, he doesn't know he needs to until it's too late? He only sees a normal person who isn't out of place. What blends in? What should be here that time of day?"

Annie waited. She found this process fascinating. If he got to the same conclusion, she found it exhilarating. She resisted the urge to look at Beth, to see if she, too, was focused on Arturo's reconstruction.

He went on, walking back and forth between the Commissioner's parking spot and the elevator. "He was taken here, maybe even pulled around into the gloomy area there, and I'm going to say that it was a guy in a suit with a briefcase, waiting for the elevator. Zapped him with a taser and dragged him. Were there any drag marks on his shoes?"

Annie shrugged. "No drag marks. Taser, we think, but can't prove. Makes sense, though. Because tasers are registered, we hoped one might turn up in a pawn shop. Most of the shop owners were cooperative; nothing came of it. But we think a taser. Nothing else explains Grossman's not fighting back. He was a big, fit man, and he was, by all evidence, a wary and paranoid man. So, something was used to subdue him. The murderer may have used it on a 'trial subject,' before the actual murder. Remember the janitor Clyde Bunsen's interview. John noted he kept rubbing his chest. I think Clyde was tased too, in the bathroom upstairs. No proof of either."

"Yeah, I remember that. This seems the logical place for the murder, actually, and that witness, the woman who saw him leave the parking garage--"

"--or someone who looked like him. A big man, who could put on Grossman's coat and a wig and be Grossman, right?"

They measured a double cab with a canopy across the way, and, with chalk, drew the truck outline in the Commissioner's spot so they knew how much space was available around the truck on the night of the murder. It was obvious that the area to each side of the truck would be hidden from anyone in the elevator area, maybe from most of the people who might walk through to their cars. "Not entirely private," Felize said.

It was true, after all. Everything had to have worked just right for a such a public murder--no one sitting in a car listening to the radio, no one standing beside a car talking to a colleague, no one in the elevator with Grossman. So Arturo was right. But Annie didn't want to believe that Grossman was taken anywhere but here. She recognized the vulnerability of that for this case.

"Okay, not so private," she agreed. "How could it have gone down?"

"A quiz. I love it." Felize actually rubbed his hands together. He turned carefully 360 degrees. He walked up to the elevator and turned around and looked back at the parking space where Grossman's truck had been. "*Madre de Dios,*" he said suddenly.

He walked over to the rolling dumpster and opened the lid. There was a hydraulic arm, similar to those on a car's hood, that held the dumpster lid nearly straight up, so that things could be stowed or removed without the lid falling. The shadow formed by the lid, and the lid itself, rendered anyone standing behind the dumpster hidden. "I hide here, I wait for him to turn toward his car, and then I leap out and tase him. I grab him under the arms and drag him around this corner, do what I'm going to do with the drugs, and leave him here in the dark. I take his overcoat, put on a long-haired wig, get his truck, back it up here, put him in and presto, we're away safely."

Annie stared. A scenario she had never considered. She walked behind the dumpster lid, looked at how it formed a shadowed corner with the first parking space. A car drove in and came toward them, down the central driveway. Past the elevators. Into the second parking space, right next to where they were hiding their putative victim.

Felize temporized, "There could have been a car parked there, alright. That wouldn't have been good."

"You know," Annie said slowly, "tasers aren't as reliable through heavy clothing. Coat, suit coat? So we didn't consider an ambush from the back. We did consider that the murderer was disguised in some way. We considered that Grossman would have registered a person, but would not have been threatened, and would have therefore not known to mount a defense. All hinging on the idea of a nondescript disguise."

"Wait, I remember something," Beth said. "Wait. Someone called you about a janitor's outfit being missing. Was it ever found?"

"Nope."

"I see why you went there. Who pays any attention to a janitor?" Beth made some notes.

"Thought that, yes," Annie responded. "Big janitor. But that doesn't really change anything. Think about it. The murderer had looked at and spent time with the scene. During the whole day, probably, to see just how many people come and go. When the legislature is not in session, people don't come over here as much, so probably it would be pretty deserted on this floor by 6:00. Remember this floor is only for the VIP's. Peons park on the street or in lower garages."

They walked about the truck most like Grossman's, and back to his parking spot. "So," Art went on, "If I were going to use this place, I would take advantage of dark and shadow. Taser, hide him, stick him, leave him there, get the truck...or how could we get him to the truck?"

Annie essayed another small hint. "If it was a janitor, he would have a trash cart, wouldn't he?"

Felize narrowed his eyes. "You've already thought about this," he said in spurious accusation. "Okay, the murderer puts him in the cart, backs the pickup down here, opens the back and puts him in."

Annie shrugged. "One way it could have happened. Are you ready to see the next step?"

"Oh yeah. I'm into this now," Arturo Felize said, baring his teeth in a smile.

They retraced their steps. They went back up to the floor that went across to the loading dock, and walked down the hall. Felize ducked into the restroom, and when he came out, he said, "what gets me about this place is how everyone uses this passageway, and you and I have not been in this hall, or the elevator, with anyone. Where is everyone?"

"Working," said Annie reflectively. She looked in through the little window in the doorway to Admin Services. People were everywhere, moving, sitting, talking on the phone and staring out the windows. "Look," she said, and stepped back.

"Huh," said Art. "So we just use this corridor when we're gong somewhere, and the doors are self-closing. Strange."

"The longer you are part of state government in Alaska, the more this strangeness will begin to seem normal. Let me know when that happens, and we'll be giving you a vacation."

They all chuckled about that. Most people had no idea, actually, how state government impacted their daily lives. Perhaps the cubicles and long empty hallways were part of a giant Jedi scheme. Nothing to look at here. Move along.

They walked back through the Capitol. The security guard was now sitting at the little desk opposite the front door. Felize went over and introduced himself. "We're trying to go back over everything from the Grossman murder," he added by way of explanation. "Who do you think did it?"

The security guard, Devin Cooledge by his name badge, stared at Arturo, looked over at Annie, nodded and accepted an apparently genuine invitation to discuss his personal theory of the crime. He said, "I was around the corner when he left, but I can tell you he was never with anyone. If there was a group came out of the elevator, he might be in front or behind, but he didn't pay attention to anyone else. He never spoke to me but the once. 'You've got a job that matches your IQ'. What kind of thing is that to say to a person? I told one of the secretaries and they said everyone knew him for a mean guy. Hated women. Talked to them like they were stupid, and never allowed any woman who worked for him to speak out of turn. And he decided when it was your turn. Generally speaking, no one wanted to talk about him being murdered. Everyone just wanted to forget he was ever here."

Woo. Right there with most of the people she had talked to. Annie wondered how there was this much anger after all of this time. "You didn't actually work for him, correct?" she asked.

"You couldn't pay me. You know, it isn't that difficult to be pleasant. Y'all have a nice day."

They went through the back door to the Capitol Building parking lot, and Annie and Art sat in the front seat of their car taking notes and updating their backstory with Devin's information.

"Do you remember, in the 70's, there was a town..." Art began.

Beth picked it up immediately"...where there was a guy who had molested some kid, and he was found with 17 bullet wounds and no witnesses in the town, no match to anyone's gun, nothing. Everyone said, 'someone needed to kill him.' You couldn't arrest the whole town, and there was no forensic evidence."

They laughed their way out of the parking lot, and as she went down the street toward Fish and Game, Annie said, "With this case, everyone remembers it. Don't think we haven't talked about that once a month since Grossman was murdered. Nasty man. Does, in fact, treat women employees like shit, but will be an equal-opportunity asshole if there's a man he doesn't need. I don't think he deserved to be killed. But we don't have any sympathy from anyone, either, except his family.

"People filed complaints about him in three jobs. Wife claimed to know nothing--had never heard about that and was offended that I brought it up. She had to know. If there's something there, we can't access it. I don't think I've ever seen such a gap between the way a family perceived a person and the way everyone else, work and otherwise, perceived him. Here we are."

They circled Fish and Game on the asphalt, pulled back out in the big parking lot, turned to face the Channel, and parked. Annie pointed out the various buildings, the maintenance gas pumps, dumpster sites. They got out and walked over to edge of the Channel. "The evidence is out there, isn't it," Felize stated.

"It would be unusual if it were not," Beth agreed, "we don't know much about this killer, but we do know 'careful.' If you saw a deep, turbulent body of water, wouldn't you use it? Doesn't mean anyone will ever find anything useful. Profilers have a category where you begin to see any pattern break down. If you don't have a pattern, you can't come up with a profile that holds. A unique situation, a unique killer, a one-off, is hard to profile accurately. You all are obviously doing everything you can with what you have. Still, there is an actual murder. I'm hoping I can give you at least one small thing that helps.

"The thin physical evidence you have so far will, I am told, stand. You have speculations and suspicions based on strong circumstantial evidence. I am asking where these leads--like the janitor's coveralls, if they are now destroyed or sunk to the bottom of the inlet--will get you. I'm getting a bad feeling about how that." Collinsworth stopped, and looked about.

"I'll appreciate any suggestion," Annie said. "Anyway, back to the trajectory of the crime." They all turned toward the dumpster, piled high with bags of garbage.

Arturo cleared his throat. "This dumpster is pretty private. So, the truck came back here, I saw that. He's got to get into a dumpster or he can't get to the Dump. They found the truck in the regular parking place on the other side of the building. So, either he drove it here, or the murderer did, right?"

Annie nodded again, looking studiously away.

"Annie. You can talk. I get that you want my opinion, and you're going to be getting it for a long time, I hope, but I'm not likely to quit looking at things from all angles and as objectively as I can manage. Not how I'm made."

Annie thought about that. "You have come up with two pieces to the theory that John and I never even discussed," she said finally.

Arturo raised his eyebrows. Annie did too. They both laughed. "Okay, okay," Annie said. "Here's a compromise. You can ask me questions. How's that?"

"Is everything out there?"

"Yes. Undoubtedly. Just as Beth said. Too easy. Stand here, where no one can see you in the dark and with the building blocking anyone's view, throw things one at a time, and they're gone if you've got a good arm. Or, alternatively, take them out to the end of the pier and let them fall in the deep water in the path the cruise ship will have to exit over. That would churn up the water, cause some deep settling of muck."

"Has anything been found?"

"Four filet knives, at low tide. No human blood. Everyone near water in Alaska has a fillet knife."

"I did a little research on this Channel on the way up here. It's deep. No divers, right?"

"No. It took us too long to get back to here from the Dump But, clever, Art. It was a pretty broad question, wasn't it?"

"Yeah." Arturo Felize's eyes were sparkling. "Okay, Okay. We've got a place to hide all of the weapons. We've potentially got a place to get rid of the disguise. It would have been raining, safe bet, so I'm thinking the coat never reappears. It was part of the disguise, phase II."

When Annie looked at him quizzically, he said, "You know, the first disguise was to do the deed, and the second disguise accomplished the exit. So if you are going to get out of your disguise, you have, let's see, a coat, then the wig, then...what?"

Annie was beaming, congratulating herself, giving Art mental high fives. Maybe with some new eyes, they would solve it after all. "Let's see the Dump," she said, leading the way.

****

On the flight home, Anne was doing well enough with partial medication and so could talk. Art sat on the window because he wanted to see. Annie sat on the aisle because she did not. Beth was going over notes on the other side of the aisle. She appeared to be busy, so Annie turned to Arturo and led with her standard, "what do we know now?"

Art thought about it, looked out the window, and sipped his cola. "I believe I now understand that no one in Juneau was the murderer. All of those people we saw, all of the notes, all of the 'disgruntled' employees, no one appears to have been involved. Maybe it's more common down here for people to shrug and say, wait two years. It will all change.'

"I also think about the sheer number of Juneau people who said he was a jerk, a bully, and good riddance, without any real rancor--including the security guard no one talked to before. Among a huge number of people who seem to have some level of motive, I see no one with motivation. He was a complete known, and he may have gotten one or two employees when he first got here, but the rest just hunkered down."

"Someone in Anchorage, or maybe Delta, actually used those words," Annie said. "So where does that take your theory?"

"I no longer think it's a guy with a suit and briefcase. I think it was someone who knew him a long time, maybe had their life turned around or ruined by him, maybe even had an actual confrontation with him. They cooked this up over time. He got promoted.

"Hey, what about this? He was with Fish and Game, and there was hinky stuff about him and the guides, right? Then he goes back to guiding, and the threat is gone. So the ultimate murderer backs out of it, does something else, goes on with life. Then Grossman gets the mega position in the state organization, and the murderer raises his head, sniffs the air, and begins the hunt."

"I'm about to recommend that you expand your pronoun reference," Beth Collinsworth said, not looking up. Both Annie and Art whipped around and stared at her.

"Noooo," Arturo was the first one to find his voice. He may have done a fist pump beside his arm rest. Annie, who knew Arturo was ready to pounce where Parkinson was concerned, smiled, as Beth went on.

"Yesss. FBI profiler now agrees probably a woman. If you talk to the women to whom he did something, or even those he just scared, it's a list.

"The other recommendation I would have at this point, if you have the resources, is to reach out to other states, and I will too, for unsolved murders starting in parking garages and ending up on a dumpster or the dump."

Annie groaned. She knew they had done that early on. Doing it again was...probably necessary, given the time that had passed. Damn. But then again, they would look pretty silly if the same MO appeared in other states, or if they had even solved something. Where to start with that? No doubt someone, watching too much television, thought that was an easy task. It most assuredly was not. The fledgling communication with the national databases may help. She felt unaccountably sleepy.

Arturo just stared, and then closed his eyes. "I'd better look out the window for awhile and ponder that."

"Good idea. I'm going to sleep." Annie looked from one of them to the other. As plain as the nose on Grossman's face, which he stuck into others' computers. Almost all of the people Grossman had seriously "harmed" were women. One of them, at least, was a big woman with military training. She closed her eyes, and as she drifted off, she had a brief vision of a footprint appearing on a dark, rainy walkway. Shoes. There may have been a time when there was a shoeprint, but it was gone now. Purposefully, she turned away. Such evidence was consuming all of their energy, and when they investigated it, they had nothing.

Chapter Thirty-Five

October, 2002

Arturo had started his work by sequestering himself in his office with the top three cold case evidence boxes. Annie hadn't disturbed him, beyond to answer an occasional question. Then they had gone to Juneau. With Collinsworth's advice, they were now building a compelling argument to commit to the Grossman cold case. Including dropping any lead that wasn't Parkinson, who had the expertise with injectable drugs, the size and the training to commit the murder.

Parkinson apparently had opportunity, and that was no small thing. Try as she might, Annie couldn't think of how the other vague suspects could get access to the powerful drug, understand how to administer it, and carry out such an attack. That was the problem with hunting, as

Collingsworth had asked, for comparables. This was a complex series of dominoes that had felled Grossman, and she didn't see how they would automatically pop up in other states.

Sue had access. She could have lifted Carfentinal from a HAZMAT container on the way to a disposal site. This was the weak link in the provenance, as it were, for the drug. If the person who readies the HAZMAT container for disposal knows that the vials inside are unopened, she would also know that the drug was viable. She may actually have been the person who took the container to the disposal site. It was Alaska, where everything wasn't done entirely by the book.

The last access Sue had to Carfentinal was in Delta, as far as anyone knew. Grossman's common strategy when he terminated someone was to have them leave immediately--and to note to whom they talked and what they took. He had, according to Steve the IT guy, barred her from her computer. Had he barred her from the lab as well? It was a high probability.

Annie didn't know whether Carfentinal was degraded after the "use by" date. Some drugs did not seem to be affected. She made a note to ask Eli how best to find out, but she also made a note to ask Melissa to contact the manufacturer, hopefully not the legal department. One always got a different answer from the actual scientists, was her experience.

Arturo wanted to talk to Steve Collins again about the computer thing in Delta. He went over the notes from the Brown interview, and that with the veterinarian in Fairbanks. He wanted to ask what Joe felt Sue had done to bring down Grossman's wrath. Annie looked into the restroom mirror and said to herself, "can you say *deja vu*?"

Unfortunately, what had passed between Grossman and Parkinson had happened behind closed doors, and others could only speculate. Still, by his own admission, there were things that Joe Brown knew but would not say, according to the notes. Maybe if a new person asked him? Maybe get an additional detail or two. She didn't know where Arturo would get with that, but told him to go ahead on anything that he though might be productive. About the Vet, she was skeptical. Some people were not going to be helpful unless you asked the exact question that triggered their information, and some not even then. The woman had been so circuitous in her conversational style that they may have, indeed, missed something.

They needed small things first: where Sue had lived in Fairbanks, her bank, whether she had a local phone. It was time to move Sue into the primary suspect position. With that, they could get their subpoenas and see if there was any better contact information somewhere. They would be able to make some moves that had been postponed in the first year and a half after the murder.

Annie wanted to either clear or arrest her, because she was their best lead, but first they had to find her or an alibi supported by evidence. Sue left Fairbanks some time after classes ended in the winter of 1997, and they had not yet found her after that.

Annie followed up with the DMV about her car and found that Parkinson had apparently paid cash for it. Another dead end. Lienholders were helpful in locating borrowers.

No one had reported the car sold. The Alaska DMV may not be as zealous about following up on whether that was done--in most states, until someone actually applied for a new title, there might just be a piece of paper with a scrawled signature following the car around, or a registration in the glove compartment that would show the original owner's address and not much else. And since the address was Delta Junction, no real help at all. Was the car sold from Haines even hers at that time?

All state employees were automatically in the retirement system. Not yet vested, Parkinson had closed out her small retirement account.

Because she was out of the system, they were not communicating with her. From the University, eventually, they got a Fairbanks post office box, which led back to a Mailboxes Etc. Account closed. Again, no forwarding address. Ditto the military. If Parkinson had accessed any military benefits after her stint, they would need a warrant to find that out. The lack of forwarding was consistent across platforms, indicating some intentionality.

Annie thought that it was ridiculously difficult to just find Sue's address. Government and military information was closely guarded. How were your address and your phone number not public record, but available if one knew where to look? That was a cop's perspective. She actually knew all the arguments for protecting privacy including the ones relating to the newly ubiquitous identity theft. Annie's personal opinion was that expectation of privacy didn't entirely extend to those suspected of crimes. She accepted that courts felt differently.

At one point, Parkinson had just been a disgruntled employee. When they hadn't been able to find her readily, and when they had no solid evidence with which to pursue a warrant, they had set her aside. And then Clyde Bunsen had jumped on his chair just looking at her picture.

Was Parkinson hiding? Or was she just somewhere working, living, careful about privacy? If she was hiding, where should they start looking? Annie knew how to hide in the US, a myriad of mutating ways. At one time, you could just change your name, move and start over, like Annie's many-times great uncle avoiding the Civil War. It could be apocryphal, but she was certain that it was currently happening. The Internet could show you how to avoid having a social security number, a driver's license, or other "government issued" identification that could, increasingly, be used to track you.

Young people disappeared into the cash economy and stayed there until they needed social security, Medicare and health insurance. It was the country's informal witness protection program. You could go from state to state without official papers, which impressed Europeans.

Television shows pretended that if you had fingerprints or DNA, you went to some machine, inserted evidence, and got a suspect match. Emerging national forensic databases were not yet national. Some states still hadn't contributed data. What if the murderer was in one of those states? And if you wanted to use these new databases, the biggest impediment was that you had to have probable cause, an indictment or an actual arrest warrant.

That brought Annie back to the ways to hide. In this case, how would a relatively young person who had been in the "government" through a connection to Fish and Game--or in the case of Sue Parkinson, Fish and Game, the military, and a university system--escape all of that data?

Ft. Wainwright didn't keep fingerprint records. They relied on the FBI's data base for background checks. You could get discharge information. Sort of. You could, theoretically, declare the person a suspect, get a judge's agreement, and get some of a military person's file, but in most cases, the veteran was protected by a complex web of privacy laws, all of which began with "with the consent of the veteran," or "upon provision of a death certificate..." and proceeded to "subpoena" and "warrant."

She tried calling Personnel at Ft. Wainwright, where she got a tantalizing bit. Parkinson's biological father was deceased; her mother, listed as "next of kin," lived in rural Montana; and the mother's name was Mary Belmont. Annie called the Military Police to find someone who had actually worked with Sue. Major Buehler remembered Sue well. He wanted to know why Annie was asking the question, and she could literally hear him circling the wagons. The most she could get from was that Sue was capable of taking down a big man, had done so in the performance of her duties, and he would be glad to have her on his staff again, at any time. She was loyal, honest and had assisted in the solution of many crimes during her time in the service. Including two tours in Iraq. A Hero. Bronze stars.

The fact that the mother's name did not match Sue's was a possible clue. So the mother had remarried. Annie had Melissa search Montana phone records for a Mary Belmont, and found no listings, though there were scores of male-named Belmonts. Where to begin with that one? They could try police departments in cities, for a starter. They could try libraries and historical museums, and chambers of commerce. But if Mary Belmont was in the "seriously rural" part of Montana, there might be no such services. Much like Alaska. That was a set of tasks.

Surely Sue's mother would know where she was, if they were in contact. But there existed the possibility that she was actually hiding, which took the search into different terrain. Annie fiddled with a list. Change your name. Move. Change professions. Steal someone's identity. Go off the grid. Use burner phones, mailbox stores, postal boxes. Go abroad with Doctors Without Borders or help African governments preserve their wildlife. Maintain a repository of cash in a bank or credit union that agreed to let you open an account without a social security number, or give them an assumed name for the bank account. You could, by painstaking preparation, get yourself into a position where you had credit, safe places to put money, and even insurance under an assumed name. Cash would get you black market licenses and even a passport, which was always done in the movies. You could have plastic surgery. It was amazing how people could change the way they looked.

In the case of Sue Parkinson, however, she couldn't get smaller.

They needed to pursue the financial angle. Finances were attached to addresses and phone numbers. That meant finding the bank Sue had used, which might well be one in Fairbanks, or the popular military credit union. Annie made notes for a financial search warrant, called Janet Beck to double check the standard she had to meet, and drew a line from Parkinson to a big dollar sign.

Melissa had arrived, Annie could hear her talking to Jason. She stuck her head out the door and asked Melissa to come in. Annie gave her a list of things to track down, including whether the Driver's License database in Montana contained a Susan Parkinson or a Sue Belmont, or a Mary Belmont. And to contact Montana Fish and Game to see if anyone who fit Sue Parkinson's description had applied for a position there. Annie liked that avenue, suddenly, and told Melissa to try to run down to whom Annie would need to speak to get more information. She hated to start with HR. It was like it gave them time to plan how to obfuscate. There probably wouldn't be an ex-office manager who liked cupcakes.

****

Eli was constantly busy. He had two techs and three University interns who worked with him regularly. Most of the new machines were up and being used by the APD and the Troopers. The old crime labs were co-located now, which Eli believed would up everyone's game, or ante, or flagpole, depending on how Eli felt that day. The spreadsheets were humming through algorithms to match up what might have seemed like obscure connections in earlier years, often never seen, occasionally stumbled upon.

One such connection quickly popped. Mary and Robert Belmont had been on the Cruise Ship that left Juneau the night Grossman was killed. Eli was trying to get a home address through back channels, as the Cruise Ship company didn't seem to have one that they would give. Or, said another way, they didn't want to give the one they had? Who knew. There wasn't an age for any of the passengers--or, again, it was buried in privacy protections. They had been in a suite, a two-bedroom cabin with a sitting room. They must have money, Annie mused, because she knew what the cruises cost, and a suite was really expensive. There was nothing to establish that this particular Mary Belmont was the woman listed by the military as Sue Parkinson's next-of-kin, but Eli would try to find out what he could get legally. A person's expectation of privacy was governed by such a complex web of federal and state laws that sometimes information was forthcoming if you just knew a path through the maze, as it were.

Annie went through the rest of what Eli had discovered. There was some information about the wig hair. It was consistent with an inexpensive synthetic piece sold in places that dealt with hair accessories, and also marketed to breast cancer survivors. A trip to a local Good Will yielded up several such wigs. So this might not be a productive avenue of research. She found one which was blonde and curly, a little like Julia Roberts wore in *Pretty Woman,* and that was just another clue that the wig would probably not get them anywhere. If they had it, maybe. But two hairs, not so much.

Arturo came in with his coffee cup and looked at the murder board. "I talked to that reporter who filed the ethics complaint," he said. "He had never heard of Sue Parkinson, but he wanted to know if there was something there for him to pursue. I told him no.

"You know," he said slowly, looking at the people in Delta, the people in Anchorage, the lack of lines between them, "It's like the Asst. DA-- Beck? said, go back and you'll see the bad boss makes mistakes. By the time he gets to Anchorage, he's learned something, and then the thing happens again, but this time he's already got an exit strategy and a friend in the Governor's office."

"And your point would be?"

"Let's just let Anchorage go, for now. I think anything we need is in Fairbanks. Let's concentrate on finding Sue, and plumbing anything from Fairbanks that will help us understand where she went. See if she got to Juneau in time to plan, practice, enact and get out."

"On that note," Annie said, with enthusiasm, "Eli found a Mary and Robert Belmont in a suite on the cruise ship that left the night Grossman was killed."

"Wahoo! Arturo threw his cup in the air and caught it by the handle, with Annie suitably impressed.

"Do you juggle?"

"Constantly. Well, well, Susy, we might be getting close to you. Let's see if we can find Mommy."

On cue, Melissa came in to tell them that she had found a death notice for Robert in the Missoula, Montana newspaper. Longtime husband of Mary, no children. No children. Sometimes stepchildren were listed, sometimes they were not. So they might look for Mary in Missoula. They did. No phone number. No indication of where Mary might be even hinted at in the obituary. No indication if Robert had been ill for some time. It wouldn't hurt to call the Missoula hospitals. Melissa was getting good at pretending that she was not bright and would someone, anyone, help her so she didn't get in trouble with her mean boss. Waggling her eyebrows at Annie, who had to guard against laughing out loud. Arturo left in good spirits. Melissa sat down to use Annie's phone to call the Missoula Chamber of Commerce, hoping for local knowledge.

And found it. They had a real obituary. Robert Belmont had died of cancer, a helpful woman in the Chamber of Commerce had been glad to offer, and the American Cancer Society was a good place to donate, under the circumstances. Mary had moved, she thought. Mary had Alzheimer's, if she was thinking of the right Mary. Would Melissa like a local phone book? She'd put it in the mail right away. Melissa gave her a home address, because "please send the phone book to the police" didn't seem like a directive that inspired the sharing of confidences. By the way, could the woman recommend a real estate broker who was currently doing well in Bozeman? Why, yes, she could. Her son-in-law was doing quite well.

All in all, Mellissa had several promising leads by the time she hung up. She left saying she would get a list of retirement homes and care facilities in Missoula from the Chamber of Commerce and begin calling them to see if Mary was in one of them. Annie was pleased and humming *Something good...*as she left for the day.

****

Annie and Fred occasionally went to the movies, especially around the time that the award shows reminded them how out of touch they were. Mostly, they saw fewer and fewer new movies, unable to stay interested in the newest Star Wars iterations which had become so militaristic. They had settled on the Bourne Identity, even though the tickets cost less than the popcorn. They were driving home when Fred saw a billboard in front of a church. "Wait," he said. "The wages of sin **is** death?"

"It's in the Bible."

"Doesn't matter. *Wages* is a plural noun and..."

Annie had a sudden idea. "Wait, wait," she said urgently. "Say that again."

"The wages of sin is..."

"Right. Now the federal data base that links wages and hours to the social security number--how would you get around that as an employer?"

Fred was momentarily confused, shrugged, and answered, "You could contract. You know, one time I was working in Sitka, and they paid my fee and per diem in a check made to me personally. When I asked for an invoice, they said they didn't keep that kind of thing for contractors. They assumed the contractor would be filing his or her own tax records, and they didn't report it anywhere."

"So what did you do?"

"I reported it, of course. Gave the check stub to the tax guy, and...why are you looking at me like that?"

"Oh, you're just great. You have given me such an idea. Thank you!" Annie pulled Fred's hand, which led to a prolonged kiss in the front seat at the next red light.

"The light has turned, buddy! Get a room!" A young man yelled at them from the next lane, but the older woman in the front seat beside him gave them the thumbs up. Annie was so happy all she could do was smile and wave.

****

Annie asked Melissa to research contractors who worked with endangered wildlife worldwide. As soon as African nations got some semblance of peace after colonial and civil conflicts, their governments recognized that tourism was lucrative. And the wealthy required stability and visible animals. Definitely an emerging field, perfect for someone like Sue. Annie called until she found one security service that liked to hire ex-military. Yes, they knew about the jobs, more all the time. Biology and law enforcement would be perfect qualifications. He said they checked military contacts, and did extensive training and background checks.

But he knew this because of articles in his paramilitary/soldier of fortune magazines. He gave Annie two websites that might do recruiting. She looked at them. It all made great sense. Though the idea of *contracting* was intriguing, the IRS might be the gatekeeper to that avenue, and they were the undisputed champions of obfuscation. In any case, Montana was first.

To connect Mary Belmont to Sue Parkinson, they needed to talk to Mary. Back in her office, Annie looked at a source of morbidity and mortality statistics by county. When deaths were reported, there was a census-like data base that recorded marriages and births associated with the deceased. Nothing more there. Who else. The

American Legion. She searched. There was also an obituary in the VFW newsletter, and it was more complete than anything they had so far. Robert Belmont was survived by his wife of many years, Mary, and his beloved stepdaughter, Sue.

Annie ran down the hall to tell Arturo and to get Melissa to search the Montana DMV database for Sue Belmont. And there she was. Or rather, there she had been. The records were years old, from before she had gone into the military. She had gone to the local community college under the name of Sue Belmont. That meant that they might find a picture that was better than the DMV's grainy example. Who looked like their DMV picture?

There was public record of the sale of the house. Robert's death certificate was available. The homestead had been sold, the realtor said. The money was transferred into savings, and attached to a trust, with Sue Belmont as the trustee. The realtor said that he had talked to Sue, who was going to move her mother into memory care and was glad that there would be enough money to get her the best treatment. He wasn't sure where they had gone, but he thought it might be somewhere other than Missoula.

"What do we know now," Annie asked herself on the drive home. She picked up Chinese food and headed for the barn, muttering.

Chapter Thirty-Six

March, 2003

Annie and Arturo pulled their rented Toyota 4-Runner into the Bozeman Best Western. Annie had taken advantage of a rare calm landing to look at the town, in its bowl of snowy mountains. It was pretty, from the distance, not large. It reminded Annie of Fairbanks, til they landed and there were no piles of dirty snow. It was mild, as well. Definitely spring down here. In Anchorage, not yet.

They had an appointment tomorrow morning at the Brogden Memory Care Facility, where the elderly Mrs. Belmont had been accepted as a patient in early 2001. They didn't know what they were going to find. They wanted a dutiful daughter visiting her mother.

They assumed that Sue was working, so they were also going to visit local vets, based on the week's newest clue. Arturo had pressed the Fairbanks vet, Dr. Sharpnack, who finally admitted Sue Parkinson was the assistant of whom she had previously spoken. She didn't recall anyone having asked her for a name at the time of the initial interview. She had no idea where Sue was. Arturo felt he could have gotten her on the record saying that Sue had access to Carfentinal, but something in her voice stopped him. His impression was that if he had pressed, it would have negatively impacted future testimony. That could be done through a later deposition. Critically, Sue had worked for a vet there, she might be working for one here.

Annie told Arturo it was common for interviewees in this case to refuse to answer questions. Arturo said it was obstruction of justice, and Annie had just looked at him. Finally, he had said, "Alaska," like it was a bad taste after drinking milk that was about to sour. Then they both laughed, but ruefully. It was going to be part of Arturo's ongoing irritation with learning the subcultures in Alaska, and how little people were willing to get involved in the business of their neighbors. People Came into the Country for a variety of reasons, but, apologies to John McPhee's wonderful book, to up the numbers of their social media "friends" wasn't one of them.

Here, Annie and Arturo were going to talk to a few Vets. They might come up with someone who knew where Sue could be.

Their evening ended at the motel's little restaurant--close, boring, video games at the table. Arturo liked games. Annie casually mentioned Grossman's video gaming. "He was one of the early ones on some popular war game. Played it at home. World Warfare, or something like that. It was pretty much all we could find on his computer. It's still a mystery to me how he could be such a computer geek and then there's nothing on his office or home computer."

"We might check into with whom he played. I don't know how we would recover that, but I'll bet Eli does. As to the other, he could have just been functionally computer illiterate," Arturo offered. "There are people like that. They can play a game, but get confused when they try to download something or check email. They really only have skills in a narrow band, and then they extend that to liking or hating brands or operating systems, with little evidence to back their prejudice. That kind of fits Grossman. Hated Apple. What's to hate? Understood how to operate a PC, is how I read it. Wanted government investment to go in the direction of his comfort."

"Rearson, the Deputy Co of CRA, said much the same thing. He's a genuine techie Grossman called a knuckledragger. Rearson felt it was an epithet that should have been...self-directed?"

"Yeah. Anyway, as I read through all of the paper, all of the interviews we have about this man, I'm not sure that outside of a guide boat he had expertise in anything. He wasn't a good manager. I can't find him doing anything. He didn't even set policy. He seems to have gotten all of his power, and I agree he had power and knew how to keep it and wield it, from gathering information and either using it against people or garnering allies."

"He was into politics. He led with that. I haven't thought about it being his actual profession. Do you remember that creature in *Monsters, Inc.*, who was always eavesdropping and then leaping in and taking the best doors to the bedrooms of terrified kids?"

"Must be a gringo thing. Don't think I saw it. What about it?"

She saw the squiggly animated character lurking and said, "I think the point might be that he was watching around corners for something he could exploit to gain more power?"

"Okay. Didn't realize it was a law enforcement movie. I'll watch it. So, we go first in the morning to the Memory Care Facility. I'm for hitting the rack. I don't know what it is about flights into and out of Alaska, but all I want to do when we arrive anywhere is go to bed."

"Tell me about it," said Annie, pills still swimming in her system. "Glad we walked over here. I don't think I could drive, and that means I couldn't supervise you either."

They walked out in good spirits, and the motel's beds were making small cooing sounds when they got to their rooms. They agreed to meet in the breakfast room at 7:00 and parted company. Annie called Fred.

"Hey! he answered cheerfully. "I take it as a good thing that you can talk. How many flights did you take to get there?"

"Three. One big, one small, one bigish. Not too bad. How was your day?"

"Hon, it's pre-spring here, and the snow piles of melting dog feces are wafting on the breeze. Bones is beside himself with memories. I gather the puppies could be born by the time you get back. Eli had mom to the vet, and they did an ultrasound. Seven puppies!"

"Hopefully I will make it back before they're born. If not, you know, you have to take Bones over and introduce him."

"Yeah. We've been talking about appropriate shower gifts. He just keeps saying 'milkbones,' or something like that. I told him this might call for something more special, but he doesn't get it."

"I expect that men don't, but then, I don't much either," Annie said. "We're going tomorrow to talk to the care facility--see if we can talk to Mom. Then we'll canvas some vets. We've set aside some time to look around, talk to the local police, like that. We'll leave Wednesday."

"Let me know. We could try the text thing--you send me a message about when you're coming in and I see if I can find it, after I figure out how to turn on the phone and so forth."

"Oh Fred. You can do it."

"Yup. You too."

"Indeed. We will not become dinosaurs. We may have to take a class."

"Yeah. I know how that would go. 'Mrs. Brown, you have your garage door opener. Mr. Brewster, you have a pager. Those of you who do not yet recognize a cell phone, please step to the rear of the room. Those of you who are part of the 21st century, step forward...'"

As they did at the end of many phone calls, they laughed, sent warmth in to the aether, and slid down into the sheets and pillows, comforted by the contact.

****

The Brogden Memory Care Facility was hidden behind bright green bushes and the first of the spring flowers. The walk was well maintained, there were handrails everywhere, and the foyer exuded polish. No residents visible.

They had called ahead, and were shown into Director James Claymoor's office. He was Chaplinesque, middleaged, with dark hair gray at the temples, and a tidy black mustache. He introduced his assistant, Alice Whatter, a woman of similar age with a bright dress and smile, and shook hands and exchanged cards. Claymoor offered, "I understand that you are not really looking at anyone in this facility in connection with the crime that you are investigating. Because if that's not accurate, we have some procedures that we routinely use. It may not be an issue since Mrs. Belmont passed last January."

Annie digested that. "To your first question, no. To the passing of Mrs. Belmont, that is a bit of a surprise, but It's really her daughter we're to whom we're try to speak in connection with an ongoing investigation. In a death, next of kin is generally a matter of public record."

Alice Whatter, the Assistant Director, looked at Annie, and then Arturo, and back at Annie. "I knew her daughter relatively well," she said slowly. "She was attentive. She visited her mother every day. And then...James, how much can I say?"

"Oh, please don't worry. We're just following a person who may have information about an old crime. It's not anything to do with this facility," Arturo said in his calming, gentle voice. He leaned forward, establishing eye contact with both of the people across from him, holding his relaxed posture until they relaxed, marginally, as well.

"Alice, say whatever you feel they should know," he said. "Alice does most of the contact with individuals and families," he explained. "She kindly keeps track of who gets visitors and who does not. Go ahead, Alice."

"One gentleman was close to death, and his son, ironically, had been a friend of Mary' daughter in Iraq. In the same unit! Big surprise when they first saw each other. Anyway, they got on, and became a real source of support for one another as their parents went slowly into complete withdrawal. It was so nice, that they each had someone. They saw one another here, and eventually they timed their visits to be here at the same time. Then, before their parents were actually gone, they announced that they were getting married, and we had a 'party' for them, and Mary was able to "be there," because we had the actual ceremony at her bedside. She cried and cried, but she was so happy. The young people were happy. It was a special time for all of us. New life, life going on, right under their bored, lonely noses. It was just wonderful." Ms. Whatter took a tissue from her pocket and dabbed at the corners of her eyes.

Annie sat back. Sue Belmont, Sue Parkinson, Sue...whom?

"Do you feel you can give us the name of the man she married?"

"I can do better than that. I can show you the invitation." Alice Whatter left briefly through a door between her office and the Director's, and returned with a cream-colored invitation. "I don't know why I kept it. It was just such an unusual thing, such a lift for everyone. These two young people, finding one another, it seems, and taking one another's hands just at the time each was suffering such loss and grief."

"I can certainly see that." So, Sue married Peter Vanderberg. They would look into his military records, see if he was in Alaska when Sue was there. See if they were in the same unit in the Iraq deployments. See what they could see. Annie thought about it briefly, while she was writing something, more to avoid staring at Ms. Whatter than anything else. "Best to them," she finally said. "Do they live here?"

"No...at least, I don't think so. I remember before Mary came, Sue and I had a long financial discussion. Sue went back to--somewhere outside of Missoula, I think--and sold the house and acreage, and with that there was plenty to support her mother here and some left over for Sue to rent in the area. Sue worked somewhere locally in the year Mary was here. Oh! I remember! For a Veterinary. Apparently she had some experience with that in Alaska. After the wedding, I don't know. Why don't you look in the newspaper? The wedding announcement might say what they plan to do next."

Whatter sat back, folded her hands in her lap, and fixed a smile. She might as well have announced she had nothing further to say. She had a bit of a stiffness to her lower jaw, as well. Annie sensed that the woman had some emotional connection to Sue, and would move into protecting her if pushed. That seemed strange, but then the people who didn't want to talk about Sue Parkinson were a large group by now.

"I think that's what we came for," Annie said. "I sincerely hope that you will call us if you can think of anything else," she said.

Of course they would.

Or not.

As they walked out, Arturo said, "She knows where Sue is."

"Yes," Annie agreed, "and is suspicious of us. What I saw, again, is that her priority is to protect Sue, not to give us information."

"I expect that's true. I want to call that vet in Fairbanks again and yell at her. You could have been here two or three years ago. When did you first talk to her?"

"1998, November, I think."

"You might have gotten to her that much sooner. Anyway, let's try to find out where she worked here in Bozeman. Any reason to go to the University?"

"I wondered about that. She may have settled on Bozeman, which is far from the family homestead, because she wanted to take classes. We can try all three names and see if she's enrolled recently. It might help us find her, or her husband. Yeah," Annie said, "let's go see the Registrar, which means the Registrar's assistant, which means we should go first to the Bozeman police, because that's the first place they'll call to see if we are legit."

So they went to the local Police Department. By protocol, they spoke with the Chief, a hefty blonde woman with tightly curled hair and the arms and hands of a ranch worker, no nonsense, patient and smart. The Chief asked the necessary questions: why were they in Bozeman, did they need assistance locating their person of interest, like that. "I can tell you now, the folks at Brogden's are straight arrow. They felt you hadn't pressured them to cut you any favors, or they would have already called me. In any case, I'm happy to give you whatever you might need. Want me to send someone with you to the vets?"

They did. They got an engaging young detective named Jerrod Redfeather, who rode along with them and narrated the route. "This is the oldest veterinary establishment in Bozeman," he said as they pulled up to the fourth clinic. No one in the previous three knew Sue.

The Bright Eyes Clinic was, in fact, old. Real trees were the first clue. There was a large-animal pen to the side of the facility, holding a horse with a bandaged hip and a goat who was eyeing the bandage with interest.

The Veterinarian was currently with a patient, who turned out to be a pregnant pig in a horse trailer. The pig having the greater claim, they waited in his office. He came in drying his hands, took off his lab coat, wadded it up, and threw it in a box under his desk. Annie resisted the urge to ask why. Probably a substitute laundry basket. The Vet was short, bulky and bespectacled. "Glad to meet you," he said, extending his hand to each of them in turn. "Denise said you had a question about Sue."

Annie sat up. "Yes, sir." she said. "Did she work for you?"

"Yes, for the time her mother was in Brogden's. She was a good, consistent and dependable worker. Way overqualified. I told her she should go to Vet school; she said she was too old. It was like having another Vet here. I'd hire her again."

"We just want to ask her a few questions," Arturo offered. "She worked for a guy whose murder we are investigating, and we need to know about a related ethics complaint. "

"I don't know anything about that. I knew that she had lived in Alaska, ex-military, had worked for Fish and Game. She was pretty candid that a government job wasn't for her. She wanted to help game animals--poached, trafficked or injured and needing rehab. She took some classes in that at the U. Not sure which ones, but she actually got some questions answered by a professor that led us to be able to save a Golden Eagle, even though we normally don't do raptor rehab. It was interesting. We had to operate and insert..."

Annie didn't want to go to sleep, but the other end of the spectrum from "I don't know anything" was definitely Dr. Christensen. He was loquacious. He was forthcoming. He had little information that related to Sue. Finally, he seemed to run down a bit.

"Did you know the man she married?" Arturo asked.

"Sure. Knew his parents. He went to the local high school. Huge guy, great football player.

Actually played at the U, and then went into the army. I think he was an MP. Anyway, great kid. He finished up a masters and they went to his new job, after Sue's mom passed, and Ted Vanderberg, his dad. Funny, that--both parents died within a month of one another, right after the kids got married. I tell you, it was quite a thing, their hooking up again after all of the time since their military days. Anyway, I do think they moved, but I don't recollect knowing where. Vanderberg was in a master's program up at the university about protecting wildlife, and they might know where he got a job."

They took their leave. In the front seat of the car, Annie said, "I don't like this. I don't know what I don't like about it, but I don't like it. We do not want to catch this woman in Montana, or we'll be the least popular people here and lucky to escape with our hair."

"Yeah." Arturo was making notes. Finally, he looked up. "This is the most sympathetic killer I've seen. I've only just gotten to saying that. If you put all of this on the witness stand, the jury is going to go for the kleenex box. We really have to find her, but we also have to come up with something that makes her a little less virtuous. I mean, decorated war hero, cares for her mom, sterling employee, kind to old guys who gossip about bears, and on and on."

Annie nodded. "I get the impression that people we question are hoping that a woman did kill him, and that he finally got what he deserved. You don't want that on the stand, believe me. I don't know. Let's drive over to the U and see if we can find where we can't find her next."

****

Annie loved university campuses, even small ones. Bozeman was home to Montana State University, with programs in wildlife ecology, preservation and biology. They easily found the right building. Popular program. In addition to undergraduate courses, there was a Masters in Wildlife Ecology, graduate courses in forensic biology, wildlife management, and endangered species. Annie was impressed. This was beyond anything she had seen at UAF.

They spoke with the department secretary, who hailed a passing professor. Yes, everyone knew Pete Vanderberg, and yes, he had just married. He had finished his coursework and taken a job in Oregon, at the forensics lab there that dealt with poaching of endangered and threatened animals. Did Annie and Arturo know about that lab?

Dr. Featherly gave them a brochure from the little kiosk by the front door. "The only one in the world," he said. "Our graduates are passionate about protecting wildlife. Someone is hired there

582

nearly every year. Pete was going to run their microlab. He had training on spectroscopic interpretation." He tried to talk more about that, but Annie and Arturo were both thanking him and backing away. Some people knew too much.

They went the motel, organized their notes. They put brochures, staff directories, and phone books into a box, along with copies of the real estate trust, which had a good signature for their suspect. Annie called Eli and asked him to make contact with the lab in Oregon, establish a conversation with their director about their most valuable technology, somehow insert Vanderberg and see if they were actually in Ashland. They packed. It took them most of the day Wednesday to get back to Anchorage. The distances were disgusting. Especially since, Annie knew, she just had to turn around and fly out again.

Chapter Thirty-Seven

March 2003

It was still winter in Anchorage, dark and cold.
January, February, March. The worst months, in
Alaska. "The Crazy season," they called it in the
bush. People did go a little crazy. Maybe this far
south it wasn't dark for most of the day, but if it
was dark when you left in the morning, dark when
you went home at night, how was that not dark?
The wind blew wetly off the Inlet. Annie brought
out her snow gear just to get to and from work.
All parking lots were reduced by fifty percent,
because you just couldn't plow them clean, and
lined spaces disappeared. The first car made a
decision, and all other cars had to follow.

Annie was at her desk, a little heater behind
the modesty panel drying her boots and socks.
Like most people working in Anchorage, Annie
kept "city shoes" at work. You had to have

outdoor boots. She had taken some spectacular falls before she figured out a flat, gripping sole was mandatory. She felt that way about most things, actually, and explored the concept of a griping soul, a gripping soul, a griping sole and so forth, as she went through phone messages.

She mused on the conversation she and Fred had had on the way home from the airport. They hadn't gone to La Mex, because Fred had been home making soup and waiting for Eli's call about puppies being born. Soup had sounded so good. But Annie had really wanted to talk with Fred about her emerging fear, and see how a regular citizen would react, as it were.

When they were sitting with the remains of their soup and bread, sipping a red wine, Annie had tried to put it into words. "What if this woman isn't prosecutable? What if no jury is going to convict her?"

"Why would you say that? You have all of the evidence. He was definitely murdered."

"Oh, perhaps. A skillful prosecutor might say, murder? When none of the weapons were lethal?"

"The drug..."

"Could be the cause of death. No DA wants 'could be' anywhere near a case."

"Something else is bothering you."

"She's apparently everyone's idea of a kind, heroic, principled, good to her mother...are you seeing where I'm going with this? This doesn't sound like a murderer. It isn't like I'm putting Anne Bonny on the stand. Oh, shit..."

Annie had been hauled up short at that point by a vision of Sue as a pregnant defendant. "Fred, she's newly married. Both of them are older. What if they have decided to start a family?"

Fred's eyebrows scrunched together. "I wouldn't be putting this woman on the stand pregnant. That was enough to acquit Anne Bonny, as I recall."

"Yeah, you used to be able to 'plead your belly,' but that was for capitol cases. Women weren't declared innocent. They just weren't hanged until after the baby was born."

"The Anne Bonny's of the world may not have been, but what about the heroic, kind, good-to-her-mother, takes-care-of-puppies, Madonna and child?"

Hours later, Annie was still replaying this conversation. She was waiting for Arturo and Eli to come in, and she kept picturing Sue, now that they knew her face a bit better, smiling from the witness chair, holding a baby. Annie looked at the newly reconstructed murder board.

Something in her rose and settled. Sue had taken the Carfentanyl from the Sharpnack Vet's

HAZMAT box. That would have been the easiest place--no organizational functionaries looking over your shoulder at disposal, no bureaucratic procedures requiring you to have witnesses or signatures. She wanted to know what Eli had found out about the expiration vis a vis the potency of the drug.

Eli and Arturo came in, laughing. Annie moved to her conference table. "Eli," she asked, "did you get anyone at the Ashland Lab?"

"Yeah. Director was really nice. Said everything we have is useful, and that we also need a Transform Infrared Spectroscopy. I agree. They use that a lot to get chemical information off paint chips, compare dyes in carpet, and so forth. I have some literature coming, and probably, from what it would cost, we could get a rep up here to demonstrate."

"And does Vanderberg work there?"

"He does. He and his wife...Sue...have been there for about a year and a half. Sue works cataloging and preserving specimens. Vanderberg is in charge of the microlab, which is just looking at all of the smallest stuff using the comparison microscopes, and so forth. I gathered it was a big operation, because most of what we have in our lab, they have separated out into individual departments with multiple staff members. Four guys look for prints and DNA left behind by the poachers, for example. I was really shocked. Did some background research. They actually do forensics for the whole world."

Eli's eyes were shining. Annie stared at him. "Eli, you aren't leaving us, are you?"

"Oh," he signed, "I could never leave Alaska, it's home. But can you imagine all of those toys?"

Arturo was laughing. "I can imagine a microwave, dude. Stop there. So we know that the Vanderbergs are there. We can go talk to them. Eli, what we learned was that for every person who thinks Grossman is a jerk, there is an alternative universe that thinks Sue Parkinson-- Belmont, Vanderberg---walks over hot coals to save Mother Teresa."

Eli stared. "What does that mean for our investigation?"

"It means we need hard evidence," Annie said. I can go down and ask her questions and see if she confesses. What are the chances of that? Other than an interrogation that probably goes nowhere, we lose the element of any surprise, and we might lose them. They have some pretty marketable skills in other countries."

She thought a bit. "No, I think it's not a big deal. In fact, we're closer than we've ever been to an actual suspect. Before we contact her, though, we tighten down everything we have. Anything on the fingerprint on the card and desk blotter?"

"We raised the old print through gloves with the new machine. It was amazing. We now have Sue's prints--military 'found' MP's are fingerprinted to eliminate those who accidentally touch evidence. The index finger is close. Shares a couple of points. I don't see it being anything we could use in court. Nothing on the blotter that matches her."

Annie waved as though swatting a fly. "I don't see us using the cards. We can't prove where they came from. We have to be careful not to introduce anything that is a possible red herring. A grand jury will ask how it ties, and we would have to say it just goes to the general maelstrom that surrounds Grossman and into which the various pieces of evidence of his management style get dropped and eventually disappear."

"Gee, Annie, exciting metaphor," Arturo said. "I remember reading something in Comparative Lit about descending into a 'maelstrom,' but I couldn't save my soul by recalling what it was."

"Whirlpool." Annie said.

"Big water, like the sand thing in *Star Wars* where..." Eli agreed.

"Whoa, whoa. I get it. I'm for quickmud. Anyway, I agree. No on the cards for now."

"I've been on worse runs--we have motive, we have opportunity, we have drug access, we have "escape" the same night. Right?

"Did you have someone run down potency for the old Carfentinal?" Annie was getting used to Eli having knowledgeable staff to whom to delegate, and was sensitive to not asking the lab's director to run errands.

"Right, the potency. Sales rep referred me to the manufacturer, just like you said. I made the call myself, because here I am in a lab, with an actual title. The lead researcher was nice. Says they don't know. They've used it 10 yeas after and it still has a kick. You just need a bigger dose. They don't have any idea how much bigger. He said it was possible an old drug would still be lethal five years out. He said they never touch it without being garbed up. I guess, if I had to translate, I'd say no problem with it still being potent after it's expired, and especially if Sue picked it up from the Vet where she worked until the fall of 1997, and used it in 1998. Right? It's going to be viable, no doubt."

Annie made a sticky note to add the information to the file. She folded her hands and looked at them.

"The other thing," she said slowly, "is that I'm afraid, genuinely afraid, no jury anywhere will convict on what we have. She'll just look like a good person on the stand, especially if we have any of the people we've interviewed testify. We have to decide how much we talk about Grossman, because that evidence all leads away from the killer and to the victim. Sue has allies. She has a life track record that's arguably better than yours or mine. As I said to Fred last night, the only thing worse would be if she were on the stand pregnant, and then we would have zero chance of getting anything other than involuntary manslaughter."

"We need to have a sit-down with the Beck. Maybe we can identify a specific piece that would make an indictment more of a possibility?"

"Maybe. Arturo, when you go back out, will you ask Jason to get an appointment with Janet for us--your convenience. Eli, can you give me that government staff directory for the 90's? I want to look up the back story on Allison Cunningham."

"The Admin Deputy Director? You think she was involved?" Arturo asked.

"No, but I remember something that kind of dinged in my belfry about some friend she had who'd moved outside. I don't know why it's bugging me. Probably nothing."

Eli found the directory. Allison was, back in the early 90's, in the Fairbanks North Star Borough office, the equivalent of a bureaucratic quartermaster. Fit right in to the Admin Services business. She had come to Juneau in 1995, apparently, according to a little date by her name.

Annie looked at the dates, looked at the murder board. Nothing ventured, as they say. She called the number Allison had given her, and got a voicemail. She asked Allison to call her back and hung up.

She was almost out the door of her office to go and discuss possible travel to Oregon with Arturo when her phone rang. "I've got a call to patch in to your phone," Jason said. Annie went back and picked it up.

"This is Allison Cunningham. You called me?"

"I did, and thank you for calling back. Silly little piece of information I need to make sense of before I put it away in the evidence box."

"Sure. Anything I can do to help. Do you have a suspect?"

"Perhaps. This isn't about that, though. This is a cold case now, and I don't want there to be something in my notes that some detective, in the future looks at and says, 'I wonder what she meant by that?' You know?"

"You bet I do. I walked in to piles of that sort of thing, especially about problem employees, when I came here. Anyway, what's the question?"

"I'm reading along and you said that you had a friend from Outside who wanted information about the case? Is that right?"

"Oh--I guess, but it was just the one call. I had a friend in Fairbanks who stayed with me the week before the murder, and left on the cruise ship with her parents before there were any details released. That's all. You know, there's been almost nothing in the papers about the case."

It was difficult not to breathe when struggling to affect disinterest. "There's just so little to tell. We followed him around to see if there were former employees who might want to murder him, but we really didn't find anyone." That much, as least, was true. Annie said, carefully, "Your friend might want to know that we have put it in the cold case queue, and we are looking at all of the evidence again."

"I'll pass that along. I'm not sure where she is now. I haven't heard from her since the wedding."

Annie suppressed the urge to shout. "She got married Outside? Did you get to go? So many of my old friends just send invitations, but they know we can't make it, and its amazing how little people know about the cost to try to get to these things. I miss 'em, though."

"Me, too," said Allison. Someone asked her for a signature. "Sue was a good friend," she said. "Apparently met the love of her life down there.

Lucky her! I need to attend to something, here. Is there anything else I can do for you?"

"Oh, I may get back with you, but I think that's it. Thanks for the information."

She got off the phone. She got up. She walked down the hall. She stood in the doorway of Arturo's office until he got up and came toward her, she looked so strange. But she turned and went toward Eli's lab, gesturing over her shoulder for Arturo to follow.

In the door of the Criminalistics lab, with its glistening tables and humming machines, Annie stood and looked for Eli's shiny hair over the tops of the protective gear. He turned, lifted his face shield and walked over to them with a concerned look on his face.

"Annie, what is it?" he asked.

"Allison Cunningham's old friend, from Fairbanks, visited her the week before the murder and left with her parents on the cruise ship."

"Wow," Eli said. You want me to..."

"Eli, Arturo, the old friend's name is Sue."

****

"What do we know now" became a flurry of "what else can we find out quick?" "She took the ferry from Haines." "She must have dumped everything and gotten on the ship." "Her parents probably didn't know anything at all--she shows them around Juneau and says she has to take care of something, and later joins them in their cabin, already paid for, no other record. All arranged in Seattle." They needed to prove that.

They called the Seattle cruise offices. The Belmonts had paid for a third person to join them in Juneau. Hallelujah. The path was now Delta to Fairbanks to Haines to Juneau to Montana with Mom and Stepdad. Arturo followed each step carefully. "She was at Allison's for at least a week, assuming the date she signed the title in Haines was when she moved on. There's a ferry every couple of days. Come down, sell your car, meet your parents and spend a week while they're sightseeing and Allison is working researching how and when to kill Grossman. She was there. We've got her."

"Hold on, cowboy. She's potentially there and we've potentially got her. We have her in suspect status and we can get a warrant...for what? At best, we can force her to talk with us. We have to get Cunningham to confirm the dates and hope that she doesn't circle the wagons around Sue like everyone else has."

"Is Cunningham obstructing?"

"You know," Annie said, "I wouldn't go there. I remember...let me look at her first interview. Here it is: *I was in Fairbanks for a meeting...*' She was gone for several days before the Cruise Ship left. So Sue wouldn't have had to work around her, right? I don't believe Cunningham puts the murder and Sue together. Why would she? I think no one who knows Sue will.

"Most of the evidence we have Cunningham actually helped us get. We never put out an APB or anything of the kind for Sue. Cunningham will tell us when Sue came, but my guess is that Sue was as careful with her as she was with the murder--listen to me convicting her already--and didn't do anything that might have made Allison suspicious. On the contrary, she might have been so careful she can actually alibi herself, and there are no parents to interview, remember? I say identify those things we can never prove, and set them to one side, build up what we can prove, and make the circumstantial case as tight as we can get it."

"Are we going to Ashland?" Arturo asked.

"I vote not yet. Too much interest too fast. We'll spook someone."

They went to their various desks, though Annie wanted Beatty to know there was movement, and went to tell him.

Chapter Thirty-Eight

March - May, 2003

They met with Janet the next morning. She wasn't reassuring. "If you can bring her back and get her to confess, yes, it's a case."

Annie mused on that. "Not likely, although it is possible she's so straight-arrow she may refuse to lie. We've never interviewed her. We only know the peripherals--people everywhere, mostly women, who have what seems almost a universal reaction to refuse to answer any questions. From Old Joe who went on and on about how kind she was, and how she cared for animals, to the Vets in Fairbanks and Montana, to the facility staff in Bozeman, to her past military supervisor, we hear nothing but praise. If she had pressed her ethics issue in Delta, she might have won."

Arturo shifted in his seat. "I'm newer on this than Annie is, but I agree. I feel like we don't have

DNA, we don't have weapons, we don't have the disguise. We basically have almost no physical, lots of circumstantial, evidence. Annie, John and Eli came up with nothing, though they found the killer, when I would have said, early on--as I think John did--we'll never solve this one."

Janet raised her eyebrows at Arturo's conviction that Sue was Grossman's killer. She looked back over her notes. "I don't have any trouble with you getting a warrant to look at her more closely as a person of interest. Financials, probably, which might help with specifics of time and place. I'll call the county DA in--where is Ashland? That's the county that has Grants Pass, it says here in my national directory. Probably a DA over there. Tell him or her that you're going to come down and ask some questions that may lead you to have to make an arrest. Let's talk about those questions." She waited for Annie's response.

"Was she in Juneau during the Grossman murder, for a starter. We believe that she was. No witnesses. With proof of a 'convenient disappearance,' so we don't want to tip her friend in Juneau by asking any more questions there. Might cause her to warn Sue, whatever. We're going to need to call Allison as a witness, and it needs to be a surprise.

"Then we need to ask Sue about the *ethical difference* she had with Grossman, as that will be a pattern we can show we have asked so many others, not singling anyone out. At that point, I think we could arrest her, depending upon what she answers."

"Annie," Janet asked, "are you sure you're ready to go there?"

"Frankly, Janet, I don't know," Annie said. "The last thing I want is a trial that just circles all of the circling we've been doing, and then begins to unravel."

The ADA thought a minute, flipped through notes. "My recommendation is to reduce what you want to give a grand jury. Present your theory of the crime, the witness list, and then, if we can get her back up here, the grand jury can question her. Stops there if they don't like the evidence."

They agreed. The actual visit would be delayed a month to prepare the grand jury presentation and to see if anyone alerted Sue. They didn't want her disappearing again. After that, Annie would make a "sham" visit, ostensibly to get more information about lab procedures and equipment. Arturo would hold down the fort in her absence. If she needed to make an arrest, Oregon Troopers could go in with her. Annie didn't see an arrest being in the offing, but one didn't know.

Annie thought Vanderbergs weren't going anywhere til there was pressure. After all, they had said everywhere they went that they wanted to talk with her but not as a suspect. Beatty called the Oregon State Police and they said they would let him know if it looked like the Vanderbergs were leaving, using "unobtrusive" techniques. Annie tried to picture how you would unobtrusively determine whether a family was going on the lam. See if anyone was mowing the lawn? She guessed, in places other than Alaska, just watching unobtrusively might be a strategy.

****

Annie and Arturo brought bad colds back from Bozeman, and spent a week apiece at home recuperating. Then there was catch-up, and finally the currently empanelled Grand Jury was given the case to determine whether an indictment was possible. They heard the theory of the crime, and agreed that questioning Sue Parkinson was crucial. The DA was now ready to so indicate, though no one was presenting any potential murderer at this point. Parkinson was designated a "person of interest" who had or "reasonably could be seen as having access to critical information about the crime."

In early May, Annie finally stood in front of the Wildlife Forensics Lab in Ashland, Oregon, just outside of the tiny town decorated on an

Elizabethan theme to further encourage visitors to the Shakespearean Festival. The Lab was attractively landscaped, with a prominent American flag waving on the pole beside the front walk. A plaque on the building proclaimed the joint work of US Fish and Game Service and the local lab, the only one in the US that focused on identification and prosecution of those trafficking endangered animals.

Annie had been briefed by Eli. She knew the Lab worked with an international organization, and it was a legitimate and respected collection of scientists who aided law enforcement immensely. She got that--you couldn't pursue anything about wildlife without identifying the origin of plant or animal ostensibly poached.

Poaching was the fourth highest illegal activity in the world. Here and there, animals were actually being taken with governments looking the other way. Annie had asked several colleagues who worked in Wildlife Crime, rangers from Washington and Alaska, about the contractors who were around the world, but chiefly in Africa, trying to stop poaching. It was, indeed, an emerging field. Annie no longer thought Sue was involved in it. It had been a brief possibility, maybe would come up again.

Annie was ready with a story about why she was there. State Police were on call to assist her, but she had not involved the local PD. Her strategy had been to deal with the Director. She had requested to visit and have a tour of its sophisticated equipment to determine which AIB should put into their next budget request. She had a list of the equipment Eli had, and what they were doing with it, and she had a list of the equipment Eli told her to ask about.

Inside the public door was an impressive employee directory. Annie scanned rooms, offices, names, divisions. Under "Evidence and Law Enforcement Relations" she saw what she was looking for, Peter Vanderberg. Third floor, 37A.

She took the elevator, which was filled with beautiful pictures of wildlife from around the world. There wasn't a receptionist on the third floor. A short, elderly man with the badge "volunteer" on his beige jacket asked politely if he could help her. She introduced herself, said she had come to speak with Vanderberg, if he was here.

She waited on a little loveseat next to a coffee machine. The room smelled of ashes and burnt coffee. She readjusted her pocket tape recorder, made sure that she had badge ready if anyone wanted to see it, and silenced her cell phone. A door at the end of the hall finally opened, and there appeared one of the biggest men Annie had ever seen, outside of Pro Wrestling or an NFL team meeting. He had on a lab coat, protective glasses pushed up on his forehead, and blue gloves which he stripped off to shake hands with Annie, who stood perhaps to his shoulder. He smiled kindly. "Get this look all the time. Let's go into my lab and sit down so you don't get a stiff neck."

"Gee, thanks," Annie said, as they settled in two chairs, with a small table between them, just inside the door. The lab was pristine, ferociously busy. There were several stations where complex machines were already at work, with two lab assistants moving about among them and adjusting dials. There was an air of efficient activity.

"We have a few minutes before everyone else gets here. I come in early and check the day's schedule. Techs warm up the machines and get out chemicals we'll be using. And we have the law enforcement deadlines and priorities on that board over there, linked to the cases we're working on during the day, so that if there's a break, you can walk over to the board and identify who should hear about it, or find where a specimen was collected." Vanderberg stopped. "Tell me what you would like to know, or I'll just talk your ear off," he said.

The Director had told Vanderberg about Alaska's interest, and had left him with the impression it was a courtesy tour to get his opinion on the best forensic technology for animals. That, all by itself, seemed to be interesting to him.

"I do want to hear what kinds of cases you get that involve poaching. I know that you have game animals, and trophy animals, and those..."

"On the road system, generally our own animals, not trophy size. There are no doubt people killing black bears for their organs. You have those too. Troopers occasionally follow *wasted animal* complaints, and illegal bait stations. So many of the trophy animals, you have to fly to hunt, and that takes poaching out into the wilderness where it can be hidden. Fish are really difficult. Too many fish, wrong species, it can be frustrating for people who have a limited time to fish."

Annie paused, but Vanderberg was sitting forward with interest, so she decided to just go on. "The perhaps illegal taking of a trophy bear appeared in a cold case I've been working on. The rug from it is back east in some senator's office, but I'd like to know something how to track it back to a hunter. Don't expect you to give free advice," she smiled.

"We do all kinds of ballistics, and we do dental DNA. Somewhere in the hide will be a bullet hole and we can pretty much trace the animal back to where it was taken by the DNA of the species. In your case, you would know it was one of your bears right off, but most of what we get is taken from shipping containers.

"Don't legitimate kills have to be 'sealed?' If so there's a stencil on the hide. It's not good that it's currently out of state. There's generally a local taxidermist in the loop--no one wants to take a raw hide across country. You can pursue the taxidermist's records. Do you think it was a crime? Of course you do, you wouldn't be investigating it otherwise. How is it a cold case?" Vanderberg looked at Annie expectantly.

"We're investigating the murder of a man who had been a guide, and then went to Fish and Game, and then back to guiding. Fish and Game employees filed complaints against him because there was a pattern of sharing information with other guides..."

Vanderberg's face was frozen. He looked at Annie, hard. "I know this case," he said slowly. "Long time ago, right?"

"Quite a while, yes," Annie said. 'Were you in Alaska?"

"Haven't had the pleasure."

"There's a tension between guiding and conserving there, to be sure. I expect you have some of that in any country with tourism. People focus too narrowly."

"We hear things, any investigations with wildlife attached. This guy was investigated more than once, right?"

"True, leads have been scarce, but we have one. Thought we'd go back to the bear and see what was there. Our Crime Lab Director, Eli Carson, wants to know what you think is the best technology to trace hair. We have lots of haired animals and sometimes, a pile of hair is all we have."

"We like to use polarized light microscopy for that. It's the best for hair, fibers, and so forth. I have some specs I can send him."

"Could you? That would be great. The hair on the bear may give us all that we need, assuming he still has his teeth."

"Better than hair, for certain...Oh, high Hon. Inspector Brewster, this is my wife, Sue."

The woman in the doorway was in every way a physical match for Vanderberg. A big, attractive woman with dark eyes and long brunette hair pulled back into a clip. Hugely, radiantly pregnant, beautiful, almost fragile in her pregnancy. She looked like the Madonna in a lab coat.

"How do you do?" Annie said "Didn't you work for Alaska Fish and Game at one time?"

"Hey," Vanderberg said, "Do you guys know one another?"

"Oh, no," said Annie. "But in Alaska, there's the name familiarity, so it feels that way. I can't tell you how many years I have looked at lists and lists of employees of Fish and Game. I would love to never have to do that again. Nice to finally meet you," she said.

And to herself, *What do we know now?*

Coming Soon...

Distant Early Warning
An Alaska Cold Case Mystery

Prologue

February, 1980

In the middle of winter, in the middle of the day, it was night. He stood for a moment by the fence where the resident wolf pack slept in the snow, tails covering their faces. In the beam of his lamp, the Alpha's eyes glittered blue. Big, soft lights glowed in the ice crystals wafting around the long building. On the horizon, a crease of faint light outlined the distance. The Naval Arctic Research Laboratory was going to stop their animal research. The big polar bear, Irish, had been promised to a zoo and would be transported this week.

He had been out the back way through Irish's cage room many times, but he did not relish it. He had had to take this path to get where he was going without being observed. The bear had been at the far side of the enclosure, shifting weight methodically between his huge front paws, looking at the closed door into his sleeping chamber. The cage was a concrete pad surrounded by 2" black metal bars, with a four-foot "safety walk" outside the bars and between them and a concrete wall. At the far end of the cage was the door outside to the wolf enclosure.

He had waited in the walkway looking at the 10-foot bear, who had been in this cage most of his life. Then he had looked away from the bear and started the long walk down to the outer door. Irish had attitude, and signs warned visitors to keep their hands and arms out of his cage. The bear would pretend not to care that some human was standing and staring at him, and then just that fast, pick up his bowling ball and hurl it against the bars not 6 inches from his watcher's face.

Which the bear had proceeded to do to him. BANG! Impossible not to flinch. At that point, Irish's human voyeur had walked halfway down the path between the outer wall and the bars, realizing every step of the way that a bear's paws could fit between those bars. As the bear had moved toward him, looking the other way in disinterest, he had timed his walk down the pathway to match the bear's pace. It sped up, he sped up. Then he was out the side door and looking back through the glass, at Irish, staring at him, not three feet away.

That had been interesting. Don't speed up. Don't change your pace. Don't stare. Cultivate a disinterested look; it fooled most prey. He could see where he could make some improvements in technique. This was a predator to learn from, as they were reputed to be the only mammal that routinely stalked and ate humans. Irish definitely saw his visitors as prey, and treated them as though they knew the rules.

Human males, especially, had forgotten the rules. They didn't see themselves as prey. Sometimes they behaved more like the old, dying caribou that just lay down and gave himself to the wolves.

What would happen to the wolves? He expected it would be difficult to move a whole pack, though he supposed they had been studied enough and could just be released somewhere south. Likely they would no longer fear humans, be killed for their pelts.

His boots made no sound in the snow, because it was so dry it was like walking in baby powder. It did not stick to his soles or resist them in any way. Just as the men had not attached themselves to his soul. They also had not resisted. Cold was a mighty asset.

NARL was about two miles outside of Barrow, through Browerville, past the incinerator that didn't work, past the last houses. The village lights didn't come here. The pack ice was like a mountain range in the dark distance. He looked about, walked around the end of the wolf enclosure, and, when he was sure no one was watching, dragged the sled he had left behind the building to the farthest Quonset hut. Just another load of storage boxes, a barrel, and a long wooden crate that had once held rifles and ammunition.

Everything stamped "Property US Government." The ongoing projects associated with NARL were being distributed among other interested organizations, and the Village Corporation was going to actually take over the facility. This Quonset hut was long-term storage.

He warmed the deicer inside his gloves and worked the door lock until it thawed and disengaged. Locks in the Arctic were a problem. Even the de-icing gel froze. Once inside, he set the lantern on a table, and in the cool blue light made notes on the inventory sheet which did not remotely reflect what he had on his sled. He began to offload his cargo.

At the far end of the hut, there were several mattresses standing against the wall. He flipped over the first two in the stack of six to make a platform of sorts, and used a little saw he had brought to cut a three-sided hole about two feet by six feet in the mattress still standing. He laid back the flap of mattress cover, and used metal sheers to clip off the coils, which he dropped down inside the mattress itself. Now he had a useable hole. He opened the big, wooden rifle crate and dragged and then tipped the object wrapped in a sheet onto the platform he had created. He put on his gloves and took out the veterinary shaving tool.

When he was through, the corpse before him was bare of hair and smoothly beige.

He reoriented it on the sheet now covered with hair, and rolled it onto a clean one, carefully peeling hairs off with the big roll of tape he kept inside of his coat. He wrapped the soiled sheet in on itself, and again and again until it was a little package, which he put in the trash receptacle by the door. Once more, he cleaned and rolled the body onto a new sheet, folded the soiled one and put it in the trash. He inspected the one just used for tell-tale hair. He picked off two. He went over the body with a soft brush, and then with a canister of pressurized air from his pocket.

Finally satisfied, he used the sheet to move the body into position, and pushed it into the hole in the mattress. He picked up scraps, used the tape again, and stood back to look at his work. All of the mattress sarcophagi held other treasures. For this burial, he pressed items personal to the victim far down in the recesses made accessible by the hole he had made. He straightened the mattress material and laid it over the body, smoothed it down and secured it with a staple gun. Then, approving of what he had accomplished, he stood up the three mattresses he had flipped forward, wadded the used tape into a ball that went into the trash with the sheets, and unloaded most of the rest of the sled. He was giving everything a once-over, straightening the mattresses and picking up any tiny bits of trash when, right on schedule, the door opened.

"Are you 'bout done? I'm ready to go, if you want a ride."

"Perfect! Yeah, I'm just putting these cartons over here. Cartons are empty, so I'll just stack them here in front of the mattresses, out of the way. Help me with these two and I can go." His co-worker became his alibi and his accomplice.

They muscled the cartons into a neat stack, with the big one on the bottom. As they went out the door, he picked up the trash can, emptied it into a plastic bag, and put the bag on the sled. He got his lantern, turned it off to save the battery, and locked the door again.

No one opened the door again for three years.

Chapter One

May, 2003

Arturo Felize had nothing but contempt for people who abused children. Every cop had something that tweaked his tail. For Arturo it was crimes involving the helpless. The case spread out before him on a conference table was just that-- girls, perhaps killed, perhaps trafficked, perhaps runaways, perhaps dying by natural causes, all gone from about second grade on, in a ten-year period in one of the Alaskan bush districts. The case was 20 years old. He was in the mode of turning all of the pieces over and trying to find the parameters to establish the frame of the puzzle. He knew already that no one had really followed the one or two leads, and he needed to find out why.

Felize personified the diversity most police departments wanted, and he had been highly recruited in the last two years. At forty-eight, divorced, with a grown daughter in college, he had decided he needed a change, maybe a big one. He didn't want to go anywhere because of his ethnicity. He didn't want to be the *two percent Latino officers*, which meant he didn't want to be on the Diversity Council, he didn't want to be the voice of the Hispanic Action Coalition, and he didn't want to be interviewed when this or that gang member looked to be Hispanic. So he had weighed his options and chosen what was, per capita, already the most diverse state in the nation: he had joined the Cold Case Unit of the Alaska Bureau of Investigation.

In Seattle, he had been a rookie peripherally involved in the complex Green River Killer investigation, and had worked in their Cold Case Unit for two years after making detective and a stint in the Troopers. He had come to be Alaska to partner Annie Brewster, a middle-aged, pithy, brilliant detective who had actively recruited him as she put together the "squad." The two of them and an intern, at this point, ably assisted by some great forensics people. Notably, Eli Carson, an Alaska Native--Dena Athabaskan, he needed to remember--who was head of their forensics lab: smart, organized, and terminally funny. Arturo was already more comfortable here than he had been in Seattle. The pace of life was different, to begin with, but he felt really good about his new boss, his partner, and his support system. Most days, he hummed.

There was a lot to learn. Though Anchorage was, relatively speaking, a big city, its population was only about 350,000. Most crimes were somewhere else in the huge state, especially the cold cases. \Arturo was learning, but Alaska was actually a mishmash of cultures, and he was trying to get up to speed as fast as he could.

Annie was in Oregon observing the only suspect they had for the chronologically youngest of their top cold cases, Commissioner Richard Grossman's death n 1998. They had trailed a woman for whom they had strong circumstantial evidence, afraid all of the time that she would be too sympathetic to be prosecutable. Arturo figured that this case would not be closed. Solved, yes. There was no doubt in his mind that Sue Parkinson did kill Grossman, but there were some cases you just couldn't take to court. He would be surprised if Annie came back with a confession. He was more interested in the case before him.

Of course, they didn't know what had happened to the village girls. Maybe they would never know. Like many other crimes (was it a crime?) that took place in the villages that dotted the Alaskan bush, it wasn't just evidence, suspects, witnesses, it was getting anyone to report the crime to begin with. And then there was the magistrate system, which he was learning was the court system in the villages, and the local magistrates were loathe to prosecute in their own community. Some towns could not empanel juries, because everyone just said they were related to the defendant, and, in some cases, this would be true. And forget evidence collection out there. If the cold didn't preserve it, it would likely be gone before anyone could investigate.

Rumors of missing and abused girls were common in the bigger towns, but there were also some complex cultural kinship rules that may mean some of the girls simply went to be someone else's daughter or back with their biological parents. For some of the girls, there were names; for some there weren't. Once he found the original villages and sorted similarly aged missing persons cases from that time period into piles, he began to put names and ages in the space under each village where they had originally appeared in the first grade records. What had actually happened that began the investigation? Since there were no bodies, how did anyone decide a crime had happened?

He found the original investigation notes. Someone who reported something fishy, back in the 90's.

From what Arturo understood, the fact that any girls were missing had been discovered by accident. A guy had been sent out to do some special ed evaluations by a resource lab that served that district. Once a certified person did those, the required "appropriate educational experience" might actually be carried out by other staff, but you still had to monitor whether the IEP was in place, and whether there was really anything special being attempted. Federal law. It was beyond difficult to deliver special education in Alaska's villages. Staffing was a perennial problem, as these were the rarest of staff in the whole nation, let alone the state. Small villages took what they could get, and delivered what they could.

So this Special Ed resource guy, whose name was John Dubrow, had looked through things, made corrections and recommendations, worked briefly with the children in two villages to see how they were doing. Like that. Then it began to blow and snow. No planes were going to come in for at least a week. Dubrow had been an ethical guy. They were paying him. What could he do for them in the down time? The superintendent said, "Why don't you look at our last standardized test results and see what progress kids are making on the state test? I can get you files from the last five years."

Dubrow had done that. He finished the elementary school and saw it immediately. After first grade, there were no girls in what he had been told was a complete roster of district students, by school. He had gone forward and found there were no junior high or high school-aged girls either. He went back and wrote down numbers: Second grade and third grade, no girls. Fourth grade, two teachers' girls. Fifth grade, same. Sixth and seventh grades, a teacher's girl. Eighth grade went to the high school. No more girls except the teacher's. None in any high school class. Even the teacher's girl was gone, though with the high staff turnover in bush districts, that was probably just the teacher's family leaving.

Dubrow had *slogged* through the snow to the high school (his words, with quotes). He commented that it was a big school for 43 children, grades eight through twelve. All of the village schools were huge, Annie had told Arturo, because the state had built them following a famous court case that dismantled the regional high school concept. Children shouldn't have to leave home to go to school, which was an especially sensitive issue with Alaska Natives. There was a school in every historically occupied village, and they were all impressive.

In the principal's office, which also contained an office for the superintendent, Dubrow had asked for and received enrollment in all grades, copies of the annuals for the previous five years. The "area principal", as those with responsibility for more than one school were termed all over the state, was over in the next village with a new teacher. The secretary had said she didn't care if Dubrow sat there and looked at the files, but she couldn't let him take them. He only wanted copies. They had called the superintendent.

He had *slogged* back with an armload of files to copy and return. Checking back and forth, he had become suspicious and alarmed, his notes said. He had asked the superintendent what happened to all of the girls. The superintendent was new. He really didn't know, but he hadn't heard anything. Dubrow had put his copies and some notes in his briefcase and left on the first plane. He gave his notes to the state troopers, and there had been a cursory exploration, probably predominantly phone calls, to see if there was anything to it. These were the only notes as old as the file.

This intriguing set of notes was the source of girls who were suddenly "missing" from the first grade on. Was this still happening? At what point did detectives stop calling the village to see if any of the girls were found? The box was empty after 1995. What if there was another box down there, mislabeled? Like Annie, Arturo had constant, low-grade fear that something germane to a cold case was misfiled; like a misfiled library book, misplaced evidence was a ghost, sometimes irretrievably gone. If you were Ohio, and had 120 cases in your cold case room, you didn't have the same fear as Alaska, where the two evidence rooms contained over 1200.

Arturo made a chart and began inserting names, birthdates and last known in the village dates. Seven missing and reported, but over the years, 18 girls had simply disappeared in elementary school, with sibling boys still there. And that was only between Dubrow's visit and

1995, as far as he knew. What was happening out there now?

More importantly, he thought, looking at the display in front of him, what did they know then that wasn't written?

His phone rang. He stretched and reached for it.

"Arturo?" a breathless voice whispered.

"Annie?"

"Yeah. You aren't going to believe this. Are you sitting down? Do you have Maalox handy?"

"Are you okay?"

"Fine. F'd up, Insecure...you know. Sue's here and she's so pregnant. And all I can think of is the old adage, *don't try to remove a rug you're standing on.*"

"Huh. I think you need to withdraw carefully without spooking them and back off. We need to regroup. You remember what Janet said."

"I said it too...JOHN, WILL YOU PLEASE TELL JASON TO GO INTO THE LAB AND GET ELI? THEY HAVE SOME NEAT MACHINES HERE THAT HE MIGHT WANT TO TALK WITH VANDERBERG ABOUT."

"Okay, I get that you can't talk. Do I really go get Eli?"

"Safe now. Yeah. Tell him to call Vanderberg later in the day like it's the normal follow-up. I'm going to get out of here before someone decides to lynch me."

"What? Are they acting like they know why you're there?"

"Big Daddy does. Talk to you later."

The phone went dead. Arturo trotted down to the lab and saw Eli. who waved him in.

"Can't leave this, it's almost finished. Whadup?"

"Annie just called, coded conversation like some CIA thing, called me John and gave me a message for you. Oh, and Sue is knocked up bigger than a house."

"No...wait. We can't do anything with this til she gives birth, right?"

"Well, it would be my bet that we don't want her on the stand holding a nursling any more than we want her there pregnant."

"So, why the *CIA thing*?"

"Annie was talking, and then her voice went into this strange zone about you calling Vanderberg. Her explanation, after whomever might overhear her was apparently gone, was that you could help to normalize the visit by calling Vanderberg about some machine, because Vanderberg seemed to know why she was there? I don't exactly know. You know Annie better than I do."

"Well enough to know that she's megacareful about being in dangerous situations, and she doesn't do surprises so good. She's never said or done anything that indicated she is afraid. She's always armed. She watches everything--you couldn't sneak up on her unless she was unconscious. Generally speaking, she's cool all the time.

"So if she was going dark, there was a reason. She's what, 5'4"? The Vanderbergs are the WWE amateur champs for the Pacific League. Anyway, I'll work up something to call Vanderberg about right away, like she thought it was a big deal, and let me know if she calls in after she's outathere."

Arturo walked back to his office. He went past Jason's desk to Annie's office door, which was open, and walked in to look at the murder board. Grossman to Sue Parkinson Vanderberg was now a red, fuzzy line. He walked over and wrote, "Parkinson pregnant, 5/2003." Then, just for fun, he drew a jury box, a witness stand and a judge, all shaking their fingers at a dark-haired man and a blonde woman at the Prosecution table.

Made in the USA
Columbia, SC
13 January 2022

53571868R00346